DUE DATE

THE RAVEN

THE RAVEN

A NOVEL BY

Peter Landesman

Baskerville Publishers, Inc.
7616 LBJ Freeway, Suite 220, Dallas, TX 75251-1008

Library of Congress Cataloging-in-Publication Data

Landesman, Peter, 1965-
   The raven : a novel / by Peter Landesman.
         p. cm.
   ISBN 1-880909-37-5 (alk. paper)
   I. Title
PS3562.A4762R38   1995
813'.54--dc20   95-35301
                                                    CIP

This, everything I write, for Liana.

CONTENTS

1941

FOG BALKS HUNT FOR 30 ON PICNIC CRAFT

June 30. Low hanging fog which blanketed Casco Bay today balked a grim search for the pleasure cruiser *Raven* which has been unheard of since putting out yesterday...

FEAR ALL 35 MEMBERS OF PARTY HAVE PERISHED

July 2. Tragedy stalked the rock strewn beaches of Harpswell as the sea gave up two members of the ill-fated deep sea fishing cruise which left Sunday. Sealed lips held the secret of one of the state's worst tragedies. No life preservers were found with the bodies...

FEAR ALL HAVE PERISHED

July 3. The Coast Guard's Portland Port Captain tonight attributed to a very powerful explosion the loss of the cabin cruiser *Raven* in fog-choked Casco Bay. Lieut. Thomas J. Sampson said that the *Raven* "reeked with gasoline fumes," and that "there was no question but that there was fire and an explosion aboard the 44-foot cruiser." Authorities point to the burned clothing and charred wreckage that has been found...

MEDICAL EXAMINER FINDS NO BURNS ON BODIES OF VICTIMS

July 4. Isolated patches of redness which appeared on the bodies, which curious onlookers believed were caused by burns, were probably of a circulatory nature induced by the cold water, sunburn or bodily contact with hard objects...

WHY NOT SEEN?

July 5. The weather in the area of the ill-fated *Raven*'s disappearance was clear, authorities state. The fog that shrouded the islands for three successive days, hampering efforts of searching parties, came in from the sea at 1:48 a.m., Monday, according to official records. Authorities are wondering, therefore, why, if the weather was clear, someone on shore did not see the smoke that must have been given off by a fire or heard the explosion if such took place. Seven miles at sea is not too far for the naked eye to see a craft the size of the *Raven*...

TOWN DEVASTATED BY DISASTER

July 6. "They were only going for the day," the distressed wife of one of the missing said. "They left in the morning, and then the afternoon came, and then night, and they hadn't returned. No one came back to pick up their cars. Rehoboth has just stopped. There's no one left to open the shops, the bank. And now they're washing up to shore, but just the girls. Twelve of them, thirteen, I don't remember. They're washing up all together, like a flock. I don't understand it. Why just the women? Someone told me they were holding hands. And then one more, the captain, the only man and he has nothing on. They're dressed and he's naked. And I have a feeling there'll be no one else. That's it. The others are just gone, disappeared, without a trace."

BEAUCHAMPS

The Rehoboth Paper Mill was an island city at the confluence of the Androscoggin and Swift Rivers. An intricate monument to man's making of things, complete with main streets and side streets and alleyways; a ragged skyline of bellowing towers which were the digesters, and various heights of stacks which emitted particles too minute and numerous to note. Dunes of wood chips and mountains of logs rose even with the hillsides that hedged in the valley.

In the morning the mill cast a dark shadow over the brick rowhouses of Sutherland Park, the valley bottom where once only the millworkers and the Pollack butchers and Italian stonecutters and Chinese laundrymen and their families lived, which now was home to the general poor. The mill's management and the teachers and shop people still occupied the hillside. At the top were the lawns and grand columned homes built by the Sutherlands, who had also built the mill. The other homes fanned out below them in concentric rings, the depth of green and measure of lawn between them steadily diminishing as they descended the hill. The homes farthest down, though not as far down as Sutherland Park, were identical in height and shape and the number and placement of windows; and the color: they were one of three, never two in a row of the same, pale yellow, pale brown, pale green, the paint bleaching and scaling off. The hillside got the first of the sun and stayed lit all day, except for the shadows of the stacks which swept over both the hillside and Sutherland Park like successive hour hands telling and retelling the time. On summer afternoons the sky was not blue but a blanched milk, and all of Rehoboth burned together in the acid sunlight.

It used to be that the Androscoggin drained the entire Umbagog watershed, Upper and Lower Richardson, Kennegabo,

Sawyer, Mooselookmeguntic and Parmachenee. That was before the third dam, when the water was peat black, tireless, peaked, and the river fanned out of the White Mountains and shallowed. Fish leapt out of those rapids. In winter the edges were blue with ice and the sunlight was wide and it cut through the surface to the thick stands of reeds tilting downriver. Then the river turned a certain bend and there began the steady drizzle of fly ash, the first stack over Berlin and then the second, the welders' blaze flaring through the foundry smoke like mute lightning. The water was abandoned by the birds, and there it entered the mill. On the lee side it came out subdued and sweating a yellow vapor. The reeds and ice were gone. Chunks of sludge as large as refrigerators turned slowmotion pirouettes in the current. Then the Androscoggin passed through the Rehoboth mill, and the mill down at Jay, carrying off all the bilge and the tailings and the acids from the tanneries and the entrails and feathers from the poultry plants and the raw sewage from all the river towns, so much rubble riding the river that by the time it poured into Merrymeeting Bay, north of Bailey Island, if the light was right, ice floes as big as cars and small trucks could have been passing, coursing through the arctic, accumulating glacial debris.

Before the third dam, the boy had never eaten his breakfast nor swung at a baseball nor done his arithmetic nor looked at the stars out of earshot of the mill. By then the unceasing and unvarying tempo of the racket was indistinguishable to him from the wind, and the boom and splash of ten million trees spinning day and night over Rehoboth Falls indistinguishable from the properties of water itself, whether a swift current or a puddle in a tub: whenever he heard water run, he saw the limbless, denuded trees. For ten years every day of life was divided four ways by the shriek of a steam whistle more authoritative (and cruel, he would have thought, if he'd grown old enough to think it) than anything else in the valley—in the universe. He and his parents and all their friends and relations, and all the natural world, knew only one sort of attention to pay that whistle, and that was homage, and obedience was the only kind of response.

At the height of the Maine summer, when dawn came early,

the town did not see the daylight. The whistle postponed it, held it back until announcing the morning shift at six. When he heard it, the boy knew that every logger having his coffee in all the camps from here to Umbagog Lake was hearing the progress of the trees he'd cut and hauled the day before. The whistle was lord; they were all vassals. Then heat turned solid and the air putrid, the tin roofs of the millworkers' tenements started knocking and groaning, the dark green and black slopes of the valley went brown, and the mill whistle proclaimed morning over and afternoon begun. Eventually it called the haze evening, even with the summer sun still pouring fire onto Congress Street. Even with light enough for a full nine innings or a complete battle with branch-swords against the Sokokis Indians in the remaining treestands around town. Under the cover of woods rejected for paper or beams (or for one reason or another just spared) little girls, recruited sisters—Mavis and her friends down the hill—would die with stray bullets in their necks and lie happily in the shadows, watching their older brothers spring overhead like deer; circling, whooping, taking arrows mid-leap—crumpling in the sun-dappled leaves.

But then the whistle blew and the children got reeled in and suppers got put before them; the shops closed and the dust settled; the fireflies took flight; and the relative silence of night came on quickly, all of it long before dark.

After supper, the boy, Ivan Beauchamp, lay down beneath the twilight that the whistle had named darkness. He could still see. He watched on the ceiling the camp he and Gordy and Walter McAlister nearly had done; he watched it finish itself; he watched Gordy and Walter and himself sitting on the porch in the deep wicker chairs, blinking through the shadows of beams hewn by their own hands. Then, despite the light, the whistle coerced itself into his dreams. At midnight it blew. Outside his window, up and down the streets of Sutherland Park, screen doors creaked open and slammed shut, and some fathers and sons sank into some beds while others rose from other beds and filed down the hill to the graveyard shift.

In his dreams, his family was gone, had never existed, and there was only the molten roar of the digester and the chatter of the press stretching the watery pulp into rolls of paper as big as houses. Again and again he tripped and fell head first into the chip loft, through the chute, into the boiling fumes of number one digester, then exited as a dark blotch in a bleach tank of pulp. Then the whistle opened his eyes, and he lay there under the weight of knowing that if he wanted a job in the mill he'd only have to get through high school, take off his cap and gown, pick up his dinner pail and go on off down the hill.

But now it was April, 1941, and he hadn't heard the whistle since yesterday afternoon when it blew three hours before it should have, and not once but five times. His family had been sitting around the kitchen table waiting for it: "That's it," his father, Gordon Beauchamp, said, "Five feet above high-water. It's the heat. It's April but it may as well be August. All that snow in New Hampshire is running for the river. The mill has to shut now."

This morning the boy had woken and looked out his window and watched a barn drifting unhurriedly downriver. At lunchtime came a whole parade of barns, and shiny brass chamber pots, chandeliers, books, pages and pages of paper twirling on the surface like confetti, and a grand piano, its lid opening and closing like a great fish. Glassy-eyed and stiffened farm animals rolled like barrels, piled up behind treestands, then battered their way free with the sheer force of what heaped behind them.

Then, at afternoon snack, Walter had run into their kitchen and the news of it came out of him as though a code word, as though Ivan hadn't already seen it with his own eyes. Walter flew out the door, leaving Gordy and Ivan chewing their lips and wringing their hands. He'd been gone ten minutes when Gordy finally stood, then Ivan. Mavis stood, too, though she didn't know what for. Gordy commanded her to sit back down then bolted out the door. Ivan, only ten years old, repeated the order and went after his brother. Mavis, nine, sat. Seated alone at the table, she started to cry.

Now Ivan was running. He could hear only his own wheezing, and feel only the thumping in his chest. The ground slid under his feet; a dozen times already he'd been thrown face down into it. But without any hesitation he wiped the sting out of his eyes, and the mud, and stood and ran on, as though the falling was as much a part of the running as the panting and the thumping heart. Behind him the mill was silenced, or at least overpowered. When he stopped at the roaring and looked back down behind him, it wasn't the mill he heard, or the whistle, or the booming logs. It was only the river. All week the boy had heard his parents talk of a flood as a blessing. It would wash the river down and clean it. But the river was past cleaning. It was past splashing and foaming. Like a widening conveyer belt it scraped away more and more of the hillsides and carried off the debris.

The boy knew the state of things without having to see. The dams at Rangeley and Aziscohos were swatted down, the locks and levees at Lewiston and Auburn drowned—all the summer camps at South Arm, including his father's, were gone. There would be no more high water. Now it was where the Androscoggin was low that his eye went, where a rooftop and a stand of trees waded in it like tufts of grass in a muddy field, and where the mill stacks poked out like the masts of sunken ships. He knew everything was gone but the Scout Camp. Two years ago, on the advice of their father, Ivan and Gordy and the rest of the boys started building on high ground. On Saturdays and Sundays for two years they dragged the logs and planks up into the hills. Now it sat clear of everything. How dry it must be now, Ivan thought, running, panting; how maybe they'll all go live there. With the homesteads and the animals passing him downriver, it all seemed a dream.

And now, in this late afternoon, slipping after his brother along the ridge, Ivan stopped to gawk at the dream's culmination: an orange tide spanned the whole width of the flooded river, turning the bend and herding past the mill.

"God, Gordy, look!" he cried ahead to his brother, already fifty yards farther up the ridge. "Gordy! The freshet's got all the way to Lufkin's farm. All them pumpkins broke loose! Look at 'em!"

Gordy stopped and turned his father's face. It *was* his father's face, Ivan thought, almost exactly, pinched and lined. Ivan saw Gordy's chest heaving, saw him turn and look just over his shoulder. When Ivan saw his brother stop breathing altogether he drew a kind of satisfaction from it and turned to look again himself. He felt that at this moment when whole barns could float nonchalantly downriver and water could swat down bridges and bury entire towns a child had the power to liberate the harvests and livestock; and he felt sure that these pumpkins stampeding downriver with the dead animals were his idea.

In the corner of his eye he saw Gordy's head snap back up the hill and, arms and legs windmilling, vanish into the trees. His eyes stinging with sweat, he turned his back on Rehoboth and ran on, and the flatrock shouldering through the hillside came up to meet him.

Then it hit them at once: the gritty mist and the trees snapping. The trail took a turn and Ivan thought it was a snake that crossed at their feet, but it was already the foamy edge of the river. They stood at an opening through the trees where there wasn't one before. Both looked out across the river's breadth, chewing at the grit in their teeth. Ivan knew the mill whistle was gone. He felt not free but abandoned. His own presence here had become a sort of truancy. He was wrong. The orange tide hadn't been his idea at all.

They went down the slope. Ivan lagged behind. Gordy took his brother's hand and led him on.

The pine needles were soft underfoot. They could not see the trees, only feel them as they passed, hot and damp and silent. Beyond the trees which Gordy knew, and knew that Ivan knew, lay the ruined, bridgeless town. Through the last of the woods they could see fires lit over the hillsides, candles and torches wavering as distant as stars. Town seemed far away and smaller than ever. They could tell the trail by the mud under their feet. Then the heat of the forest was behind them and they stood in the swampy wind. No roads downtown were left, only canals; and no doorways or first floors, only the top halves of the second. The current eddied among and between the shops and the bank and the Hotel Rehoboth as black and thick as oil. Candles roamed aimlessly up and down Congress Street. Canoes rode low and heavy in the water, laden with people, splitting the scum of wood chips. Everything was silent except the gurgling of paddles and the muffled shouts from the far end of town. And above that the music, a small brass orchestra playing something fast and upbeat. It was his father's orchestra.

Gordy squeezed Ivan's hand.

Ivan looked up and Gordy saw in his eyes the brief astonishment, the numbness. There was something distinct in the way they looked at each other, not as two brothers, one young man just shy of eighteen and one young boy just shy of the capacity to understand what eighteen might entail. Both looked at each other out of innocence itself, the older boy out of his misuse of it, and the younger out of a hushed melancholy surprise at its loss, out of something already beyond regret.

All the boats seemed headed for the music and the din. Gordy could see it all now at the far end of Canal Street, an aura of light where the road once crossed the bridge. He could see canoes and rowboats tethered to the lamp posts, a crowd clinging to the high ground, torches held aloft and lanterns aimed over the edge. He wanted to see the road ending at the froth, he wanted to see what that was like, for the bridge he'd walked twice every day of his life to have been swept away like an arts and crafts toothpick construction. He and Ivan couldn't wade there, or even swim, though he was an expert swimmer and Ivan a very good one. He was certain that below the surface ran undercurrents that, if pierced with a fluttering ankle or downstroking elbow, would clutch and drown them without a fight.

Rehoboth looked to him as he imagined Venice did. He chuckled to himself. Feeling the weight of Ivan's glance, he chuckled harder. He laughed without humor, out of the realization that among other things ruined this night, the windowless house that Rehoboth was, and had to be for one to live in it without going mad, had just been punched through. The mill whistle had been silenced and this was his second day of fluid time. He had seen out, the world—or heard what it sounded like—and it was whistleless. He thought the surrounding towns must lie in ruins now, too. Paris, Carthage, Rome, Vienna, Athens—not merely the names of towns. The words were the great cities themselves, the great civilizations. He couldn't help thinking that giving them to towns here was no honor, nor even the kernel of a dream, but an affliction. Rehoboth, he knew, had once been called China. But the man who built the mill had saved the town by renaming it. Now it was the best of what was left of the local Great Civilizations.

In Gordy's mind the misnaming had been the town's big mistake: it made failure all the more devastating, and dreaming all the more delusory; it made people who had dreams all the smaller, and their floundering all the more inevitable. He thought the misnaming turned possibility against itself, turned it into meanness.

A rowboat knocked against the ground they stood on. "Your mama thinks you're drowned," a man said out of the dark.

Gordy led Ivan into the bow of the rowboat. Uncle Alban started rowing down Congress Street. His back was toward them. The wood chips parted against the bow. Gordy put his hand in the water and grabbed a handful of it. Brackish, a thin pudding. So the boat trip to Monhegan Island his father had been planning for the bank and mill managers and their wives and some of the children would be unnecessary. Gordy had begged until his father had agreed for the first time to his coming, and Ivan's too. But not Mavis's. She was nine and Ivan only ten, but Gordy saw to it that she would not come. And just this week he'd convinced Anne Stisulis, his lifelong friend and crush to come along. Don't worry, he'd said, he'd be there too. Then they'd laughed, nervously, both of them aware of the unmentionable and long-sought opportunities. But now they'd all have had enough of boats. Gordy threw the water back.

"Home's the other way," he said, almost as a point of information. He'd heard the music. He knew where they were going.

"I'm taking you to help your daddy," Uncle Alban said. "He called the orchestra together, what he could find of it, and he can use all the hands he can get."

"What're they playing for?"

"To calm folks," Uncle Alban said. "Your daddy always said music was to lift the spirits when you really need it, even if it's not what you think you want. He told me when I was over there before that it was the first time he felt useful."

Gordy dragged his eyes over the desolation.

"Tom Houston's drowned," Alban said, "trying to save his feed. Sally Gammon's hanging onto a branch of a cherry tree. The water's at her neck. That's where we're going now."

"Sally Gammon the old lady?"

"Wouldn't get out of her house. The water rose faster than anyone thought it could. Everybody told her to get on to high ground but she wasn't going. Then Robinson Gammon went out to milk and the water swept away the barn and him and the cow with it. He got hung up where the bridge is laying now, barely alive but they got him. Mrs Gammon stayed to lock the doors and the next thing you know her house with her in it is floating down the river. Some river-drivers got to her and carried her part way to the bank but couldn't get farther. They had to save themselves so they left her on a cherry tree. That was two hours ago."

"Two hours ago," Gordy said. "You seen all this? You seen her getting left on the cherry tree?"

"—A big log got lodged crosswise against the tree and is protecting her from the drift stuff. We got all the lanterns on her, and your daddy is playing for her, and everyone's calling out to her, cheering her up. But if the water rises another six inches she's going to get thumped to death if she don't go under first. Scott Richardson's already drowned trying to get her off it."

"Scott Richardson," Gordy repeated.

Ivan might have been speaking to either one of them, or neither: "We seen pumpkins," he said.

"Where's Mavis?" Gordy said.

"She's with your momma."

"Where's she?"

"With your pa and everybody else. She's worried sick. She thinks—"

"You said it already."

"Don't hurt to hear it again."

Alban rowed the boys through the streets, taking the alleys as any of them would have done on foot, the exact route the boys had on any summer afternoon after emerging from the woods and heading over the bridge for home.

The bridge was gone. A crowd looked down from the edge of a small island of muddy roadway. The torches smoked and flared above them and the yellow light on the brims of their hats and the hems of their dresses fluttered behind them in the mist-wind. All their eyes were little marbles of torch light. The boys' father, Gordon Beauchamp, was waving his arms at a cluster of brass trumpets and drumsticks, the big bass drum with *The Beauchamps* in bold letters stretched across the skin of it. The instruments glinting like glass. Everyone wet and muddy, hair matted and hats drooped. And the mangy, muddy dogs pulling themselves up on the island, charging it all at once like a fleet of amphibious rats, darting between spread feet, panting and shaking out and tossing their heads, the shadows slipping along their flanks and throats, stretching out into the water one moment then vanishing the next.

The other side of the river shone hot white as midday in the light of the lanterns, then evaporated into mist and shadow. But you knew all the time the other side was there because when the light couldn't reach, the screaming stretched back across the river, as regular and evenly tempoed as the notes from the band. And the band struck up louder, either by design or by unconscious syncopation, its cadence matching Sally Gammon's screaming. Gordy wasn't sure whether it was to soothe the old lady, or to spare the crowd evidence of its own impotence. When the light reached again, the women at the edge called out and waved their hands as though at children playing in the garden, and the screams gave way to a steady whimper. The conductor Beauchamp went on madly waving the baton, glancing over his shoulder into the river, changing tempi and calling out different tunes to match what he saw, no different from the conductor of a pit orchestra blundering through to the end of a badly planned extravaganza.

Alban drifted the rowboat between two others and tethered it; he and the two boys disembarked. A canoe paddled up with two of the men from the mill. The passenger kneeling low between them was old Robinson Gammon.

A man in spectacles and office suspenders emerged from the crowd. His cufflinks glinted in the torch light. He rushed at the canoe with his jaw jutted out, as though he intended to ram the old man with it. "McCabe," he barked, "I thought I told you to keep him in my home, keep him anywhere, anywhere but here."

"Couldn't keep him, Mr McAlister. He kept heading for the door—"

"I wouldn't begrudge five dollars to know where my wife is," Gammon muttered to one of the attendants. "Though I'd give ten to know where the old sow is." The old man took a step out of the canoe and fell face-first into the water. McAlister stood on the embankment with his arms crossed, letting the two attendants rush in waist-deep and straighten the old man and drag him up.

"Now Robinson, you listen to me," McAlister said, wiping mud off the old man's forehead, "she'll be just fine. We got her in the lights over there. I thank you for your help but we won't be needing it. That cherry tree she's on is as steady as stone, and she's got a good strong hold of it."

Gordy heard this and craned his neck and saw the cherry tree in the lantern light. It was almost parallel with the current. The end of the upper branches scratched the surface like phonograph needles. The old lady wasn't even holding on; she was snared in the branches like a rag doll, her arms pinned down behind her. The water was up to her throat. There wasn't any log laid crossways steering debris clear of her like Alban said there was. A steady stream of planks and tarpaper and logs was thumping the tree, pushing it farther over.

Gordy took Ivan by the shoulders and pointed him back toward the rowboat. "You stay in that boat, Ivan. I don't want to see you up here. This isn't any place for you."

"—Mrs Gammon's a fine woman, Robinson," McAlister said to the old man. "And I assure you she will hold on. The best thing you can do for her is go on back with these gentlemen and get a fire and a pot of coffee going. When she gets on home she'll need to get warm. She won't be long now. Robinson, you hear me?"

The old man hadn't heard a thing. His eyes were vacant, his moving lips mute. He'd been struggling silently against the attendants' restraint since they got him out of the water.

The crowd was crammed shoulder to shoulder and back to front on the shrinking piece of roadway. The talk was of the water's falling—as though the river had not been rising steadily for two days, and rising still before their eyes—that if it went down another few inches Junior Carey, the state of Maine high school champion in the Australian Crawl, might even be able to reach her if he got off to a good start. Gordy got a glimpse of Junior through the crowd. His mother had him wrapped in a blanket at the advancing edge of the river. His feathery hair and his throat above the knot of the blanket was as slender as a bird's. He stepped from one bare foot to the other on two skinny and pole-straight legs, swaying like a boxer not listening to the referee's instructions, refusing to listen, staring trance-like into the river, afraid to hear anything else or look anywhere but straight into the brown, foamy water. Junior standing ready in a glowing shroud of mist.

Gordy liked Junior Carey all right. He thought matter-of-factly that his loss would be kind of tragic. Though in looking at the frail, soggy boy standing over the river he couldn't come up with a particular reason why. He thought, then, that there were those whose lives were tragic, sometimes for no good reason at all, and their loss was too. And then there were those whose lives weren't, and their loss wouldn't be either—no one else's life would alter around their absence even a little bit. Like a pebble thrown into the sea, he thought. But Junior would be missed. For instance—here was a reason, he thought—he was supposed to come along to Monhegan Island in June with him and Anne Stisulis and Aubrey Arsenault and Earl Decker and everyone. Gordy liked Junior. He had a carry about himself. He could swim arm over arm farther and faster than anyone in Maine. That seemed to say something about him. But he thought the old lady snagged in the cherry tree one of the pebbles.

He looked over his shoulder: Ivan hadn't moved from the spot Gordy turned him around in. "Ivan!" He walked up and shoved his brother toward the boats again then turned back. Ivan stumbled a step then stood inert. He watched the backs of more dogs closing in on the little island from the darkness.

Gordy pushed through to his father. "Poppy," he said. His

father looked ready to dissemble, his hair matted, lips quivering, the bump in his throat leaping, his eyes wrenched far to the right to keep watch on old Sally Gammon. He was a short, round, harmless-looking man; everyone in and out of the Mill said they liked him and everyone did, and he looked it: he wore his popularity like a friendly, even clownish, suit of clothes. Now he waved at the three men and one woman and one little girl blowing into a flute, his own two arms barely in sync with each other, conducting some part of a beat faster than the players were playing.

"Poppy," Gordy said again. Gordon Beauchamp didn't even falter. He released one hand mid-stroke and sent it down and pulled it back up with the neck of a wet, twisted trumpet in its fingers. He flung the trumpet toward his son, though he'd taught him every instrument but this one. Gordy took it and began to blow anyway. The brown gritty mist had whirled up again and separated Sally Gammon from the crowd and the old lady started shrieking again. Gordy started blowing on the trumpet in rhythm with her cries. Steady, noteless honking. Soon the entire band did too, unmelodic, untuned, the older Beauchamp waving his hands as though egging Mrs Gammon on. Then the mist died and the old lady merely whimpered, and the band stopped honking and played *Stardust* in a minor key, which they knew well.

Over the bell of the trumpet Gordy saw his mother looking at him through the crowd. The lines in her forehead were gone; relief was drawn across her brow. Gordy nodded and winked and Frances Beauchamp clasped her hands over her nose and mouth in an attitude of prayer. Mavis pressed against her mother's leg and circled her arms around her waist. She peered at her brother from her mother's hip not with relief or even welcome, but with a kind of blank concentration. Gordy never understood what went on in his sister's head. He had stopped guessing a long time ago, and he decided not to start again now.

Out of the darker, stiller waters of town came another canoe. A man leapt out and ran toward McAlister, who had finally gotten Mr Gammon back into the other boat. "The water's surging," the man panted.

McAlister pushed the canoe with Mr Gammon and the two

men in it toward town. But Mr Gammon heard and looked back. He raised his arm and looked back and opened his mouth but nothing came out. McAlister turned his back on him.

"Bethel just radioed over," the messenger said. He was out of breath though he'd been standing still for a few seconds. "They're saying it's the last of it. They're saying it's actually down two inches in Gilead. But it went up four inches more real quick before it come down to that. It's torn up the graveyard up there and everything's afloat. They're saying to stay out of the way till it all passes cause it's a bad, bad mess."

McAlister turned and pushed his way forward through the crowd.

Upriver came a rumble and boom like the dynamite explosions that broke up the log jams. But this one didn't stop. The river started to bellow. Gordy aimed his trumpet across the river and blew. Old lady Gammon spit a jet of water out of her mouth.

Mavis saw someone whispering in her father's ear. He dropped his arms and the band stopped playing. Mrs Gammon's whimpering stopped. There was only the river bellowing.

A mouth whispered in Mavis's mother's ear, then all the mouths above Mavis were moving. Her mother pressed Mavis's face hard into her hip like she was crumpling the piece of paper that brought the bad news, but Mavis saw through her mother's fingers everyone looking into the river. The old lady was a white stain on the brown water, her turkey neck twisted and stretched toward them. She looked like some sort of ragged bird that had overgrown its nest and gotten stuck in it.

Then everyone around her tilted and stumbled a little and her mother almost fell. "Mr Caruso!" her mother called to the panting figure pushing past. Mavis recognized him instantly: the little man who every once in a while came to the door with a box of imported olives in his arms. Who now pushed his way through to the front. "Scuse," he said, "Scuse scuse."

"Mr Caruso!"

Caruso reached the front and stood next to Junior Carey and looked across the river.

"You cannot let her just drown like a pig!" he cried in stilted English to no one in particular.

Mrs Carey rubbed Junior's neck. Another woman, short with black hair, pushed by Mavis's mother.

"Scusemi, scusemi," She stumbled after Caruso, crying out at his back, "Balthasar, Balthasar!" Two long thick braids like ropes swung off her head to the bottom of her back. Mavis fingered the ends of her own braids.

Father Lefebvre got handed through to the front at the same time. Six hands held him out over the edge of the river next to Caruso, as though torturing him. Caruso stood on his own between the priest and Junior Carey, whose mother kept rubbing his neck. The three of them stood shoulder to shoulder, their faces ashen, their lips quivering, looking in different directions: the priest down at his bible, Mr Caruso at the old white bird in the tree, and Junior down at the surging water, though Junior's eyes didn't look like they saw anything. Branches and ears of corn and foam ran by their toes.

"Go ahead, Father," McAlister said. The priest fumbled with his bible.

Then it was her father who pushed through. "Arthur!" he said, "Arthur, you can't do that."

They had to yell into each other's ears to be heard above the river now.

"Say it!" McAlister yelled at the priest.

"You can't do it," Beauchamp said. He reached over the priest and Caruso and yanked the blanket off Junior Carey's shoulders, almost punching Mrs Carey. "Let Junior try for her."

Mavis thought her father was right. But she didn't say anything. Her mother told her never to say anything. If she was quiet and good and didn't interrupt her brothers or father or anyone then she'd be allowed to grow up and be anything she wanted. But her father always heard her anyway. She was sure he heard her now, so he knew she thought he was right.

"It's too late," McAlister said to Beauchamp. "He won't get ten feet." He shoved Junior Carey back from the edge. The boy's knobby elbows and knees crumpled into the crowd. Then there was only the priest and Caruso. The little Italian woman was behind him, slapping the back of Caruso's head, an unbroken string of strange sounds rolling off her tongue.

Caruso hadn't taken his eyes off Sally Gammon. His lips moved privately. Then Mavis watched Gordy clamp his mouth shut and crane his neck toward the back of the crowd. Mavis followed his gaze with her eyes and found her Uncle Alban. Uncle Alban faced the river with his hands in his pockets. He might have been standing on a street corner on a Saturday afternoon. But he faced forward anyway and Mavis followed his gaze and found herself looking at the back of Caruso's head again. Some man leaned out of the crowd and talked loudly into Caruso's ear.

"Go on, Caruso, show us what you dagos can do. All that honor. Big, big men you are. Go on, Caruso, save her."

The man turned around and came toward Mavis and her mother. He nodded and tipped the brim of his hat at Mrs Beauchamp. "Harry," her mother said. It was Uncle Alban's friend Mr Eustis. Eustis pinched Mavis's chin. "I told that little dago to go on and get her," Mr Eustis told her mother. Mavis looked up. Harry Eustis winked at her. Mavis looked at her mother. She was watching Gordy. It was a circle: everyone looked at someone else, but no one looked at each other.

Caruso leaned forward a little bit and the small, dark woman with the braids tugged at his hair and pounded on his shoulder. Her mouth opened wider, and longer and louder words fell out of it.

McAlister stepped up beside Father Lefebvre and Caruso and faced the cherry tree in the river. Its branches clawed at the water. No one listened to the small foreign woman behind Caruso. McAlister's chin jutted, his back straightened, his hands braced on his hips. Caruso leaned forward then stepped back, then forward again. Both kept their eyes on Sally Gammon. The priest looked down at the bible. "Do it now, Father," McAlister said, "Go ahead."

Father Lefebvre spoke quickly, as though reading off a recipe: *"The Lord is my shepherd; I shall not want—"*

Across the river the whimpering began, then gradually crescendoed to a shout, then a cry, then a single, continuous howl. The priest stammered, "—*leadeth me in the paths of righteousness*—" Then he stopped. The full force of the river's bellow arrived and there was only Sally Gammon's small empty mouth gaped far across the river in the sinking tree like an unfed chick's. The water frothed at her chin.

"Father!" McAlister cried.

"*Yea, though I walk through the valley of the shadow of death*—!" Then the priest stopped again. A cry did reach through, not Sally Gammon's but a deeper one. The priest turned his head toward Caruso. Then everyone did. The Italian shuddered. His mouth opened like he was singing. His trembling hands reached out toward the old woman, his eyes distended, enraged. Everyone watched Caruso now. Shards of Sally Gammon's screaming met his over the river.

"Quiet, man!" McAlister cried. "Father Lefebvre, get on with it!"

But it was too late. McAlister saw the first of it upriver. "Shut this man up!" he cried, "and put out those lanterns." The men and women holding the lanterns looked blank. Mavis looked from Mr McAlister to Mr Caruso. The woman behind Caruso had shut her eyes and her two hands had made a big fist in front of her face. Her lips started moving.

A wave of muddy foam and white sticks and the corners of wooden boxes rolled toward the cherry tree. "Put them out, put them out!" McAlister cried, then faced Caruso. Caruso wailed like a baby. "Get yourself together, man!"

Mr Caruso shut up. McAlister looked worriedly upriver. Caruso wriggled out of his jacket, brought his knees together, leaned forward and dove four feet off the bank in the general direction of Sally Gammon and the cherry tree. The water didn't part. Logs and branches swept by. The little man just disappeared. Mavis couldn't even find the spot where he went in. She looked downriver but there was only more logs and branches and then darkness after that.

There was a space now in front of the small woman with the long braids. She stood with her eyes closed as though she didn't know the space was there, as though she were in the middle of a crowd, not at the edge of one, a step from a frothing river. She might have seen it if she opened her eyes.

Mr McAlister pushed Father Lefebvre aside and snatched a lantern out of the crowd and heaved it into the river. The light swept by just below the surface then went out. A long black box passed at their feet. Mavis looked upriver. Louder, bigger water came toward them crowded with junk. Then the river went dark, except the little of it running red by their island in the torch light. Then that water leapt a little and a thin wash ran under everyone's feet.

Mrs Gammon's howl had not ceased. Then the crack of splitting wood, and the silence across the river shot out of the dark. Beauchamp took off his glasses and pinched his eyes.

DOVE

Spring had gone false and a clear sky green and cold. A soft, dense mist had closed in then turned on its side and whirled horizontally like a frothy river, a nor'easter sneaking up on the Massachusetts coast. The sea leapt like flames, boats were piling up in the marinas. The beach at Winthrop was lined by dozens, maybe hundreds of people, even the beggar woman who shuffled from garden gate to garden gate. All to see the surf commit suicide at their feet, where they could taunt it, mock it, call out at it and still skip back in time to keep their shoes and hems dry and go home laughing as though they'd beaten the foamy water in a contest they hadn't known was begun until it was over. Everyone in his rain slicker, in his own little cell of endurance and imagination, whistling again and again at the next biggest breaker they ever saw, imagining they were out there on the water. But they weren't on the water. That was the victory.

Somewhere across the harbor, somewhere in and out of sight, Boston was a swinging string of lights, a ship's rigging tumbling across the crests of the waves, threatening to dissolve or vanish; then doing it, vanishing, it was gone.

"Plenty widows made tonight," said a man to no one in particular standing down at the beach.

"Those fishing boats going to be stuck out there," another said. "Won't get in tonight, maybe not tomorrow, maybe not for good. They're saying those who're trying to get in are breaking up already like sticks."

"Best chance praying to god and running it out, I say," said the first, "It'd be snowing blind right out there, and they're dying in it. I'd head out for Newfoundland."

"But slow, slow as you can without it being too slow," said

the second, "You can't reach there before the storm's wore itself out, or else you just pile up on them rocks instead of these."

"You got that right. Hey now, watch it there. Somebody's poking something at me from behind. Hey—"

"You boys. Where you going with that canoe there? You want to throw that thing away just give it here and I can use it for kindling."

"They're not tossing it away in there. They got their swimming trunks on. Them crazy Doves is crazy." He meant no insult. It was a fact, like other facts.

"They was bound to die sooner or later," said the second, "They'll have good company tonight. Look at 'em running. Leslie even got that white rag on his arm. By god if it aint to find him better after he drowned. Them boys know it, they know they're killing themselves. Look at 'em run at it!"

The two brothers, fourteen and sixteen, pushed out of the crowd in swimming togs and ran the canoe at the surf like a battering ram. Leslie, the older one, had tied a white canvas sack around his shoulder. The crowd behind hooted and waved, only half-seriously calling them back, the other half wondering at the possibility of the walls of water crushing the life out of a human body before their very eyes.

The young men did hesitate, not for the calls of the crowd, but for a glimpse of whatever sky they could hope for to open between the towering breakers. A mound of water more than twice their height collapsed at their feet and surged up the beach behind them. And they were off in unrehearsed grace, laughing, running not out of courage or even impudence, or even camaraderie, but out of an unconscious agreement that they were high-stepping through the seawater out of the most human and irrational sense of humility. They had looked out of their parents' window and simply decided that to take a picture of the surf the other way around was the only thing to do on a day like this, with water like that.

They leapt head-first into the canoe, the older Leslie at the stern and the younger Adam at the bow, scrambling to post themselves before they and the canoe were thrown back into the sand. They shouldered their paddles and again laughed, though this time the laughter was muted, gagged by the just-offshore wind. They dug into the water as though into the ground and pulled it back, piling it up behind them like dirt. And again they laughed, already too far to turn back and stay conscious, or even alive, yanking at the flow of the ocean river at precisely, or less than, the pace at which it came at them. They no longer knew anything of their neighbors behind them, or even of home. Before them was the sea.

Though for Leslie there was something else. The wrecks piling up on shore, the wrecks being made of ships in open water. Leslie knew dying was going on out there this minute. He'd made a boyhood of knowing it. Of knowing right now that one mispaddle, one rebellious wave out of rhythm would turn them perpendicular, and later an empty canoe would appear yards down the beach, spinning on its side in the undertow like a top, and two bodies, both once young, would surface days or weeks after, limbs unhinged, eyes bulbous, rigored jaws like baskets full of writhing crabs.

The wind, tasteless and airless, was silent like a pillow over the face. They couldn't even open their mouths to breath it; just through the nose was almost enough to suffocate them. They paddled methodically, the water churning by as though they powered the current themselves. Swell after swell rose beneath and let them down in a trough out of the way, like a ditch they'd dug. Then the slight pause, the half-second of calm and false progress. The next wave broke directly over them and they were looking into the wind again. They couldn't see it, only what it did: the rubble of waves and seafoam tossed in the air like handfuls of sand.

Two-hundred yards out they turned a corner and entered the pass. The shore had vanished from sight. The water was quieter, but in the way a barren mountain top is, poised and sudden beneath a hiker's feet; or the rear hide of a bull patient beneath a single fly, the tail hovering within range.

Leslie stopped paddling and watched his little brother dangling over peak after peak, the muscles in his young back stretching and retracting, the arms windmilling: Adam flailed at the foam as though a spurned boy blood-red with fury trying to catch a vanished crowd. Then Leslie looked up and lost the sky: above now only the dark bile like the slick walls of a well. Only the wind coming straight for them told them where they were. Then Leslie suddenly remembered the reason for all this, and, reaching for the sack hanging beneath his right arm, he looked back over his shoulder and saw only more green mountains. He opened his mouth to shout but the pillow of wind stuffed his throat. Choking, he turned his face to the lee side for air, then lifted his paddle and tapped his brother. Adam turned, his eyes clenched, his teeth bared. He had seen nothing. "Far enough!" Leslie bellowed. "Good shots here! Back!" Leslie's brother nodded at something, but not the shouts, because the wind shoved the words back down Leslie's throat.

They waited for a particular valley, a calm one and with high walls to turn out of the wind. No opportunity for hesitation either, Leslie thought, and in a deep trough now, already feeling the swell whipping them back to the top, he shrieked: "Now!" His brother, eyes shut, cried out and hit the water wildly while Leslie in the stern pushed at it, peeled it off. At the top they had spun far enough. The wind shoved the canoe off the peak and sent it scurrying. The water clenched them, raked their chests, then rejected them and spat them out; and the canoe resurfaced, water pouring over the sides and out of the brothers' mouths.

Atop one peak the line of the shore appeared. The breakers were as high as the houses, shattering against the sea wall and onto the beach. Leslie pulled the camera out of the sack and took nine shots, a panorama of the curling hunchbacks of the waves, and stuffed the camera away again and took up the paddle. Together now they jabbed and chipped at the water, shouting, laughing, hearing nothing of themselves. Then the familiar rumble of the surf against the land; hands waving; Leslie's arms flew up, the paddle above his head: home.

The first copper light of morning was creeping up Great Head bluff and spilling over the harbor. Below, the water shuddered in the sunlight like foil. The harbor islands poked through the scattered neighborhoods of hunched backs. Across the harbor Boston town was a complicated dark mass, a brown, jagged skyline, the melancholy ruins of a monastery.

A hundred people lined the bluff's edge, all leaning over it at a precise angle, as though bowing to the ruins across the way.

"A widow almost made yesterday, and now today too," said one to no one else in particular.

"Them is boys," said a second. "No one down there is old enough to widow somebody."

"And at the rate they're going, they never will be, either," said a man with a bulky camera around his neck. The photographer was between them. A space had been cleared for him. He straddled a rope that had been tied to an iron stake then thrown over the edge of the bluff. The photographer raised the camera and pointed it down the bluff toward the water. At the bottom, two figures were urging a third toward the rope, gesturing at all the people atop the bluff.

"By god did you see him do it," said the first man.

"I did not," said the second. "And neither did you. That's why we're all standing here like we got nothing better to do today, so we can see him do it."

"But that was yesterday," said the first, scratching his head. "It don't need to be done today. It already been done. That Hurley boy already been saved. Can't see why that Hurley boy would want to risk his neck all over again."

"Because Dove paid him to do it," said the photographer, lifting his camera and aiming it down at the figures below the bluff then putting it down again, without taking the picture again. "He wouldn't do it again unless he was paid."

"Can't see why he would try to come up again even if someone pays him," said the first man to the second, as though the photographer were saying nothing, just silently prompting him. "Dove was lucky yesterday. Luck is luck, it's not something countable. You can't count it. It aint two after one, or three after two. It's two, and then maybe three. Or maybe it'll be one again. But that'll do you no good and you're done for."

The photographer toed at the rope. "But he's already good at it. It was him who sent in those pictures of that surf from the back side, wasn't it?"

At the bottom, one of the figures had gone away. The other two were waiting, standing still. Something had been agreed upon. The wind picked up, the dust swirled. Everyone backed away from the edge, straightened up, then the wind died and the dust settled, and everyone resumed their positions.

"Best chance praying to god, I say," said the first, "It wasn't blowing like this yesterday. Yesterday was luck. Today it's blowing. It aint three after two. It's never always like that. Today aint lucky."

"You got that right," said the second, "Today's as real as it was yesterday. The Hurley boy going to need to be rescued today just like yesterday."

"Them crazy Doves was always crazy," said the first.

"They was bound to die sooner or later," said the second, "But now they're not going by themselves. They're taking that little Hurley boy with them. Look at that Dove down there holding onto that Hurley boy. That boy don't want to risk his neck again today. But Adam's going to throw him up onto the bluff. He's going to make him do it. And them Doves know it, they know they're killing that boy. Look at Leslie Dove running up here."

Dove arrived at the photographer's side panting, hands on hips, bent at the waist. The photographer's smile was cruel, shameless, self-congratulatory. He raised his camera and pointed it at Dove, but still he didn't take the picture. A dry run.

"I suppose you want me to go down just like I did yesterday," Dove said.

"I suppose I do," the photographer said, still looking at Dove through the camera, still grinning to himself cruelly. "But you called the paper," he said, "I'm just here to take the picture. This here show is all yours. You do what you did yesterday. But it doesn't matter. You could do what you want today and everybody'll think it's what you did yesterday."

"Well, yesterday there were more of them," Dove said panting, "But it was only the Hurley boy who spooked. He just froze, couldn't move. The rest were able to make it down. There were four or five of them."

The photographer took out a pad and started writing down what Dove said. Dove kept an eye on the pad and saw the photographer was stuck, so he said it again: "There were four or five. The one just froze."

"So you want to rescue four or five boys today then go ahead and do it," the photographer said. "I'll stand here and take four or five pictures. Or how about a group shot. How about that." The photographer raised his eyes, and Dove did not see that they were no longer laughing, just fixed firmly in the photographer's head, watching out of competent and professional courtesy.

Dove leaned over the edge and waved. The photographer leaned over and looked. Everybody leaned over and looked. At the bottom a struggle commenced. From the top it looked like an elaborate dance, four arms entwined, four legs shuffling around and between each other. Finally the two bodies separated, and Adam Dove had the Hurley boy shimmying up the rope.

"How far up was the boy?" the photographer asked.

"Not half way," said the first onlooker.

"You wasn't here," said the second.

"But now I am," said the first. "I say the boy goes half way and then we go down and get 'im."

"It aint dangerous enough there," said the second. "You got to let him come higher, just this side of that ledge down there."

"Which ledge?"

"It don't matter. Any ledge'll do. Pick the worst one. Then we'll go down and get 'im." He rooted in his pockets to show he had no intention of going himself of course.

The hands below waved. The boy had reached his destination. He stood now flush against the side of the bluff on a narrow ledge, his hands over his face. His shoulders trembled. The wind carried up pieces of his sobbing.

"Just like yesterday," said the first, shaking his head, clucking his tongue.

Dove lowered himself over the edge with the rope. He splayed into the air, over the water, one arm flung back over his head like a trapeze artist. The onlookers leaned over a degree more.

29

And they were all in jeopardy. They grabbed one another, held one another back.

Dove slid down the rope, his feet skipping over the craggy face of the bluff toward the boy. The people along the edge shook their heads. The photographer peered down through his camera. From across the water Boston looked on out of its ruinous past. The boy sobbed. The photographer imagined tomorrow's front page and unsuccessfully hid his pleasure.

"Just like yesterday," said an onlooker, almost a whisper, to herself. Her husband shook his head and whistled.

Dove neared the boy. The boy sobbed on. The day seemed to brighten one notch more. Below them all the water crept up to the very bottom of the bluff. Dove's younger brother had fled. Dove sprang away from the cliff-face with one last triumphant shove. One could not know his measureless glory: the unending string of faces peering over the edge.

He reached and enclosed the boy in his great hammock of an arm, and with the other arm began to yank. The glory in his eyes fled, replaced by the weight of the boy, of himself and the forces pulling at his feet. Below, the water foamed and whispered. But up he came, inch by inch, up the bluff with the boy hooked in his arm.

"Just like yesterday," said a man.

The faces above Dove did not move. The camera eye steadied. Dove neared the top. No one breathed. The boy sobbed. Dove grimaced, sweating, his fingers throbbing. The camera shutter winked and the photographer looked up from it, up and away, across the harbor, triumphant. Dove rose beside him with the sobbing boy clutched in his arms. The string of faces folded and snapped and the onlookers converged hesitantly, apprehensively, as though upon an apparition, or a wild animal finally cut down.

The boy's face went a shade paler, totally bloodless; his eyes bulged in horror. Shrieking and flailing his arms, he bit and scratched his way out of Dove's grasp and hurled himself down the street, his footsteps measured and loud in the noon silence. He reached a gate and turned from the road. His wailing faded, a door slammed shut.

Everyone stumbled away, Dove and the onlookers. There was nothing left to do but wait for the paper. Dove had already given the reporter the headline:

With A Stout Heart and a Stout Rope: Young Man Rescues Boy Trapped On Great Head at Winthrop.

EZRA

The boy and his mother sat at table, heads bowed, about to say grace, when the door to the kitchen swung open. Sea spray and rain dampened them instantly, the lantern flames knelt and the table cloth fluttered. Clayt stepped out of the raven-blackness and lifted the door shut and peeled off his all-weather gear. He hung it and sat, his beard dripping into the empty plate.

"It'll clear by tomorrow," he announced. As though at the General Store meeting he'd just returned from, it was decided among the island men that they'd had enough of the storm and it would end that night. But Ezra could still hear the thundering of the rain against the mud. There was no sign of abatement, not even then; in fact the rain was harder, the air colder, the night darker. He hadn't been able to see the sea all this time though it was all around him. But it would clear because his father said it would, and he closed his eyes then opened them, and read the rain's relentlessness as a sign: his father had hinted that he might ride out with him the next day. Ezra turned his head to the window. He was going out into that weather at last.

Hattie rose and dished stew into each plate. Clayt tore the loaf of bread in half.

"The bay's all jammed up, all sorts of garbage floating around out there."

Ezra stopped eating. "It's the flood from upland," he said. "I heard it on the radio."

"I know it's the flood from upland," Clayt said. He lifted his bread, as though threatening his boy with it. "But what you don't know is what happens when those levees bust up there. Houses splinter and dam it up. Those damn mills spill out all that bleach and pulp. Cemeteries get churned up. Bodies and skeletons tangle in our traps—"

"Clayt—"

Clayt looked at his wife. "We're always at the wrong end of their damn trouble, like we don't have enough of our own. Anyway,"—dunking his bread into his stew—"tomorrow it's clear for sure. We'll finish that Lehman business tomorrow and we'll all get on with our lives. You coming with me, boy?" Not a question but a decree.

Hattie Johnson cast an unthinking look at Ezra, her nine-year-old boy. More than a mother's look, more like a lover's when she hears of something her man has done that will echo off her and make them both as big and fine as she'd dreamt they could be. Then something else echoed, and her eyes fled her son's face, and her smile turned obligated and stoic.

"You're sure Mr Lehman is dead," she said.

"He's dead. His skiff's been tied up out there for the three days of this storm and that's how long he's been dead. Say what you want about Lehman he aint never been no fool. Jesse said he took no food or water out there with him, and there's nothing out on that island but that shed. Aint no treasure, either," Clayt said, declaring it at his boy.

"He found coins, Pa," Ezra said.

"He found coins. He found coins," Clayt said. "That was five years ago, and they could have been anybody's. They could have fallen out of the pocket of the last fool before him. It could have been any kind of trash that flooded out to us the last time those levees upland fell apart."

"But he wasn't no fool. You just said so," Ezra said. He wasn't challenging his father, only defending something just spoken. Everything his father said was the truth. And besides, he'd seen with his own eyes Mr Lehman row out of Mackerel Cove to Pond Island every morning. Four years of summers and winters, and then this first part of this spring, as though he was in a rush to get started. He'd never known Mr Lehman to do anything but look for treasure, though Lehman had: he'd lobstered with Ezra's father and Jesse Johnson for thirty years, and the two men never forgot it. When most of the island turned their backs and laughed Lehman out of their minds, Jesse Johnson and Clayt Johnson would not. The others chided him and hu-

33

miliated him in their homes, but Jesse and Clayt forbade talk of Lehman's treasure hunting with the same breath they forbade talk of ghost ships. They went on treating Lehman like the lobsterman he'd been, and to his face asked after his endeavor gently, even sympathetically, like something they themselves might have done in another life.

Then six months ago Ezra noticed something growing on Mr Lehman's back, but like everything else about the man, talk of his hump was forbidden at home, and Ezra asked nothing. The bulge grew. Mr Lehman turned ashen and thin. The fishermen stopped laughing at him, just stood on the wharf and watched in silence as he rowed out of Mackerel cove earlier and earlier, and returned later and later. Then, at some point, not knowing why, Ezra started feeling that every morning Lehman rowed out there was going to be his last. Though no one dared say it, he thought then that he understood what Mr Lehman was doing, and why he'd begun to rush: he wanted all those gold sovereigns because each one would give him back another day of his life.

A month ago, he'd overheard Mr Lehman tell his father that if he didn't come back by nightfall he wasn't going to. That night Ezra envisioned the treasure for himself; then the next night, then the next. But he told no one. He could hardly bear to tell it to himself, he was so ashamed, stealing a dead man's only wish. Still, come nightfall, he dug at the bed and struck the top of the chest hidden by Spanish pirates, and opened it to all that gold, only at night, only in bed, and only after swearing an oath never to seek it again under his father's roof. Though he knew he would; as a boy might each time he sought out the most profane of his pleasures, then, after, rolled over on his shame.

Clayt's glare dimmed. He looked on his boy, then looked through him. "Lehman wasn't no fool but for this one thing," he said, then bore down on the boy as though to put the matter to rest: "Besides, he knew better than to challenge a storm like this one to outlast him, unless he knew it wouldn't have to try."

There was a woman this time too. The bored idiot's whine, the ghost's wail, the storm at the windows. The Ghost Ship of Harpswell had been coming to Ezra for years, coming full sail through dreams down Harpswell Strait, through all stages of wakefulness. But for nine years he'd been nothing more than a schoolboy, and barely that; for nine years he'd heard his father leave the house before daybreak and return after dusk, and the is-it-or-isn't-it ship which had corrupted the dreams of every Bailey Island fisherman when he was a child was kept at bay, a deception, nothing more than that. Though, by prohibiting talk of the legend in his presence, the boy's father put wind in the ghost ship's sails: "No use worrying about what you can't see on the water, boy. There's enough to worry about that you can. It's that which'll coax you and coax you until it gets a mistake out of you. And on the water you bury your mistakes—" It was what his father said at every sign of the boy's imperfection, as though fault were not a sign of weakness but a vice. Of a mathematics examination on which the boy scored in the ninetieth percentile, Clayt said: "It don't matter the ninety percent. It's the other ten that sends you down. Can't be mostly right. On the water you got to be all right. And the only time you're all right that I know of is when you're home already and you can look back. Looking back it's all hundred percent, hundred percent, hundred percent."

But Ezra couldn't deny the shudder in the middle of the night when he woke. The house sent creaks through the walls, as though the house could get away with it only because it was his solitary littleness awake; as if he was the only person in the world awake at night. But still, even listening to the walls, Ezra knew the difference between actual breathing life and a fairy tale, a mere corruption of his spirit. Not that he could do anything to prove it. Not until the day when he would stop living on land and get on the water himself and come face to face with the things he'd reckoned with only in his dreams.

And sitting upright in bed, he knew that that day had come.

But this time there was the woman's voice calling out from the Ghost Ship: "Billy, Billy!" It was Ezra's friend Billy Morrill she called to, who last Christmas morning went with his father to shoot sea ducks on a low-tide ledge ten miles out. Boxing Day the boat came back bucking high in the water, spinning unmanned in the boil in Merrymeeting Bay with the spite and elusiveness of a horse that had thrown its rider. Last month, Clayt was working the sinkhole outside the Teeth. The first four traps came easily and full, a good harvest after the waters had most of the winter to recoup. But then the winch began to groan, and Clayt slowed it down and peered over the side while John his sternman quit baiting the skewers and fished his pockets for a cigarette and leaned back against the house. But the *Hattie B* jolted and John flicked his cigarette over the side and leaned beside Clayt and looked into the water: threads of hair and flesh and a yellow sou'wester, billowing just under the surface, draped over the trap, six or seven lobster pinching at it through the wood slats. There was nothing to tell him by, but Clayt knew who it was. He knew the tides and he just knew it. He towed Ed Morrill in, letting him ride in on the trap, then left him on his own dock for his wife to see that her husband at least had finally come home.

Again Ezra was awake. It was near daybreak Saturday, April something, and Billy Morrill and his cousin still weren't back. The window flamed then darkened, then flamed again: The lighthouse can reach here, he thought. Pa was right about the weather. And though more firmly awake, Ezra was certain the captain of the Ghost Ship had brought Billy back in the storm, his rigored body laid across the bow like a wood offering, the woman wailing, announcing his reentry. If he just ran down to the Morrill dock—he was certain of what he'd find there.

Ezra slid off the high bed and into his britches. Below his window, the new spring water softly lapped against the rocks. So it would clear and it did. Ezra saw between the curtains that the wind had gone. The water was endless again, shivering like foil. Through the break in the window curtains the horizon outside Mackerel Cove was a red band, like a bolt of bright cloth stretched across the water to keep the boats from leaving. All was silent. It was the silence after a long battle, after which any noises less than thunderous were inaudible. He was awake and there was nothing. Except—Ezra remembered—the Harpswell

ship. He did see it in the storm's last hours. He did. He heard it
and he had sat upright. He was not sure his eyes were open, the
darkness was that total. But there, through his curtains: he could
not describe it. No one had been able to, not completely. No one
had to. There had been those who denied talk of it, but no one
of sound mind had ever had the courage—or recklessness—to
deny the thing itself.

He heard his father's panting breaths down in the kitchen.
He reached for his door and passed it and took the stairs down
to the kitchen one at a time, slowly, almost irritably, as though
this was not the first time he'd been up and around before daybreak, but merely one more day in a lifetime of days begun just
like this, at daybreak, to get to the water.

There was the line of light below the kitchen door. The lantern was kept burning through the night. He reached for that
door in the same mechanical, unafraid way and threw it open.
Without looking, though he'd never seen it himself, he padded
across the kitchen to where his father was, his grogginess expert, his nonchalance already unselfconscious, as though the
spectacle of his father at this hour was just one more spectacle:
Clayt Johnson asleep on his feet, lashed with ropes to the kitchen
wall where it met the chimney, his head jammed into the corner.
Untying him, Ezra was sure he should remember exactly why,
why the spectacle before him. But he didn't look. He would not
give his ignorance the pleasure.

"Pa, it's morning. It's a clear morning. Just like you said, Pa."

Freed, his father frowned at first at the sight of his son rather
than his wife, but then placed his outsized hand flat on the top
of Ezra's head, as though crowning him with it. Ezra raised his
eyes but quickly glanced away, anywhere, at the kerosene lamp
on the stoop of the window, then away from that, against the
shut door leading out to the dock. He'd seen his father and he
could not have done that, seen his father with tears in his eyes.
He could stomach the obscenity of him lashed to the chimney
stones of his own home like a petty criminal, but he could not
endure the tears in his eyes. It was not even a question of blas-
phemy: it was that the tears would never be for happiness, they
would never be for him.

That was not all he knew. Ezra knew there was once some-one else in this house, in his bed, and that if he were here Ezra would have been his brother. But if he were here he would not only have held the position of brother, he might well have held the position Ezra himself did, the heir, the Only Son. Ezra didn't dare to dismiss the possibility that if the departed one were here, he, Ezra, might not be, might not have been at all.

He never understood how he knew, who told him or why. Maybe he'd overheard it, or maybe his mother had told him late at night, after his father had gone to sleep. Or maybe it was knowledge he'd merely inherited from the dead boy himself, a gene of remembrance. Maybe he'd learned it in a dream:

It was a Christmas more than ten years ago. Christmas, 1930. Jeb, this boy, this man, this once son and nearly brother, was a new fisherman who left on Clayt's boat before daybreak to pull in the nearest lobster trap he and his father had laid down the day before, not three miles out from shore, to get his mother their Christmas dinner. By mid-morning a squall had surprised everyone, not least of all him. He was the only one from the island out. By noon the motor could be heard roaring full throttle off the north side of the island, where the boy was trying to get his father's boat clear of the rocks. But the snow was horizontal, no one could see him. Still, Clayt hopped in Ed Morrill's boat in Mackerel Cove on the island's south side. By the time he'd reached around to the north the snow had calmed, the sea flattened and the roaring of the motor ceased. But there was no boat, and no wreckage. Everyone assumed the boy had gotten clear and headed into the safety of open water, then made port somewhere else. Hattie Johnson stood on the rocks, wrapped in shawls, watch-ing Clayt riding the swells back and forth, finding nothing. He circled the Teeth, thinking his son had gotten caught on the ledges there. Night made the search treacherous, the water deceitful, but he would not come in. The temperature fell. Ice floes blocked the entrance to the cove. Clayt was forced to drop anchor in open water. All that night he beat back with a shovel the ice cakes that rode up his anchor chain and pulled the bow of the boat toward the sea, threatening to fill it with water. All that night, across the slushy water hardening over the shoals, the clanking of metal and the panting, the shouts, "Jeb, Jeb!" and Hattie answering from shore: "Clayton, Clayton!" No one knew what strains Clayt bore to his heart beating back the advance of the ice until dawn, but he would not sleep horizontally after that. He could not. In the ten years since then, after eating, or merely talking, or after making love, soon after nightfall his wife led him to the kitchen and tied him up, as though it were not merely his affliction but his penalty, and went upstairs alone. The kerosene lamp that the dawn had negated, that Ezra headed for after liberating his father and blew out, was not for his father on this side of the window to suffer the indignity of his own shackling, but for his parents' son on that side to know that they—and Ezra too now—were still waiting for him.

In Mackerel Cove, it was too early for sun. The water was down, the gangway steep, and everything stank of tide and mud and rotting wood. Empty dories scuffled around the raft with their oars crossed. Eighteen boats unmoored, motors idling, facing the horizon outside the cove. Half were singly manned, half carried full families, all in their Church clothes, their black dresses and black hats and pressed black trousers and ties. Their hair was everywhere in the gusts: a solemn mercenary navy imported by a poor place. But the hands on the throttles and wheels were expert, huge, pillowy fingers and broad, shovel-like palms; and the movements of even the children, the little shifts to keep upright while the boat rocked beneath, were simple. Everything was aimed at the open water. The silent fish-houses looked on.

A slim, clean-shaven man in black suit and tie came down the gangway, untied a dory at the bottom, pushed away from the wharf and rowed through the chop to Clayt Johnson's boat at the head of the flotilla. His strokes were even, unhurried, the blades twisting out of the water in perfect parallel to the surface; he made almost no noise. He pulled alongside Johnson's boat and tied the skiff to the mooring and stepped aboard. He took off his hat to Hattie Johnson, who stood beside her husband, shielding her eyes and looking over at him as though he were far off.

"Clayt Johnson?" the man asked.

"Who you be?" Clayt Johnson grunted, "A salesman?"

"Yes," the man answered.

"This is the wrong time for you—we got to go. You sit," and Clayt turned away, back to the wheel, and pulled on the throttle. The motor growled beneath their feet.

"What's your line?" Hattie Johnson asked.

"Religion. I'm your new pastor, Jim Sinnett."

Clayt Johnson whirled around: "I'll be damned." He squinted and looked the man up and down, and grunted on pitch with the motor.

"Where is Mr Lehman?" Sinnett asked.

"Pond Island," Johnson answered, raising his arm toward the cove's entrance. There was nothing there but open water. "Where you learn to row that way, a preacher feathering his oars like that?"

Sinnett only nodded at what he hoped was a kind of proposition of acceptance, but Clayt Johnson turned his back on him, and Hattie and Ezra reached for something to hold. Reverend Sinnett sat on the gunwale, gripping his slim thighs. The boat moved off below them. Behind, seventeen boats converged and snaked behind Johnson's toward the mouth of the cove.

Sinnett leaned on his knees to Ezra's level: "You've lived here all your life, young man?"

"Nope," Ezra said.

"And where else have you lived?"

"Nowhere," Ezra said.

"You've lived in no other place?"

"Nope," Ezra said.

"But you said you haven't lived on Bailey Island your whole life."

"I aint dead yet," the boy said.

Sinnett opened his mouth to laugh but, looking at the little boy, he saw it was no joke.

A thin strand of smoke swept back over Ezra and vanished in the wind. As though the exhalation were a signal, Ezra stood from the gunwale to take his place at the front, to the left of his father—his place, though it was the first time he took it. He had no wheel before him, but on his face materialized the solemnity of a lead pilot, as though it were his lot, this predestined place: his back stiffened board-straight, his feet slid slightly apart, his knees flexing like pistons, countering the pitch of the boat. He held onto nothing as they left the cove, but rooted his hands deep in his pockets, pitting his own slight weight against the accelerating wind of the open water: the father and miniature replica of a father, the real cigarette and the conjured one, the already nearly perfected echo of Clayt Johnson's silent and stone-faced melancholy jubilation.

Ezra saw no Ghost Ship of Harpswell. He knew he never would. It was just like Pa said: there aint no evil out here, just consequences.

In clear water Clayt Johnson opened up the throttle and headed the flotilla north, straight at the Sisters: Bull, Saddleback, Bald Dick, the tops of a string of granite ledges. Pond Island was another one just beyond that. The day was clear, everything had prominence, the land against the water, the water against the sky. But the storm's vibrations had not gone: the boats were not always visible to each other over the peaks. "You've got to watch these swells, boy," Clayt said to Ezra. He didn't turn to talk to him. He just looked ahead knowing the boy was listening: "A rebel one will turn you, and it won't ever come at you when you expect. You got to always expect it."

Clayt did not turn to talk to Sinnett either, but his voice was not muffled. He knew exactly how the wind would let him be heard and how it wouldn't: "I don't know you, preacher, don't know where you been, but just looking at you, seems to me you haven't lived long enough to sin enough to teach us folks anything about living and dying."

"We teach each other," Sinnett said. "It's the way it was intended." He tried on a newly cultivated smile and looked across the boat at Hattie Johnson with it. But she'd already begun staring at him with something else, something that had nothing to do with him. The boat passed on from that spot in the water. Sinnett left his smile behind like the survivor of a wreck.

His father was taking a wide berth around the Sisters, wider than Ezra decided he might have done. To the left it looked a clear, straight shot along Bailey Island to Dyer's Cove, to the right clean open water. On the horizon flashed a wink of light. "Halfway Rock," Clayt Johnson said, and Ezra nodded, again not fighting the man's intrusions into his thoughts. Something once between them had fallen away, some wall, some empty space filled up. "That's halfway across Casco Bay from Small Point to Portland. Billy and his uncle went shooting just this side of there. That's still bad water. The good water's beyond it. But Ed knew what he was doing. You always got to know what you're doing. Just sometimes it doesn't matter. Now look over port. What do you see there?"

Sinnett rose on his haunches and craned his neck from the other side. Hattie Johnson didn't have to: she and Clayt looked dead ahead at Pond Island hunched low on the water. Sinnett sat back and looked up at Clayt. He hadn't seen anything.

"Nothing," Ezra said.

"Look again."

Ezra looked again. "Nothing."

"Again."

Ezra squinted: a narrow channel of white film strung out along this side of the Sisters and vanished in open water, a mile or so from Dyer's Cove. Ezra followed it with his eyes, assuming it was only a tidal wash—he'd seen that from shore. But he obeyed and looked again, and again saw nothing to the left and right, nothing he was looking directly at. But something was there in the corners of his eyes—he gripped the side of the boat—something that ran below the wash past the Sisters, but only when he looked away, lurking below him, beneath his feet, barely visible. Then a wave broke over, a thin, wide wash, and as it passed it peeled off the water behind it like a sheet: a craggy spine jutted through, a knife's edge of rock. Then the water collapsed.

"The water's up now, see," Clayt said, "But that's the Teeth, nothing but a chain of high-tide ledges going straight across."

He turned to the water and spat. "High tide ledges," he went on, "all the way up straight to Cundy's Harbor starting at Pond Island. There's no way—they're channels. Just channels. That's all out at low water, and they look just like what they're called. You get hung up on there and—it's a bad spot is all. A bad spot."

Ezra leaned forward and followed the Teeth with his eyes. But there was something else now, something between them and Saddleback.

"Ma," Ezra said. But Hattie Johnson was looking off, ahead at Pond Island. Ezra looked back at the priest. "Mr Sinnett."

"Yes, boy."

But Ezra had already whirled back around, leaning unsteadily over the side, looking down into the water. Something dark and long suspending just beside the ledges.

"Ezra, pull in here!" Clayt snapped.

"Pa, a whale, I think," Ezra said.

"Shadows," Clayt said, "The sun casting off."

"Clayt." Hattie had turned and stood beside her son. "Clayt, for god's sake something's there."

Something was breaking the surface, something long though not as long as the Teeth. It was wider. The water in that spot went from green to black and began to sweat, then boil. Ezra stood up and back, not in reconsideration of his certainty about the Ghost Ship, but in realization of what he'd left out of his dreams altogether, what he'd never considered. None of this had anything to do with a mistake or ten percent or even things you cannot see, because he saw it now: the only way to keep a thing from happening is to not begin it. The mistake is always the waking, the opening one eye then the other, the going down to the jetty at dawn and putting a barrel full of chum and fish heads on the dock, then turning over the motor. He understood— as though he'd always known it, as though it was in his blood like the instantaneous replication of his father was—that from this day on he would never have trouble on the water when the weather was good. And that someday he'd have a fire in the engine when the weather was lousy. And then the boat would fill. It would be an accident borne only of carelessness, of not stepping off the tracks out of the path of an oncoming train hooting from a thousand yards away, a hundred, ten—of calling fate's bluff.

Ezra did not back away when the water burst apart. His mother screamed, his father barked a command, and the preacher Sinnett prayed. But Ezra took another step forward. If there were a gang-plank he'd have walked it: a long dark pole split the surface, a steel ladder after it, a rusted and barnacled conning tower after that—as though a wreck breaking free of the silt, filling suddenly with air and rising toward the light of day. None of it was magical: already Ezra wouldn't permit a solution so simple. Briefly, a vertical tube turned a blank glass eye on him and Ezra and the glass eye contemplated each other. Who's alive down there? he wondered. Who's dead? Who's neither?

The boat wrenched and banked severely to the right. The glass eye vanished, plunged, the ladder dropped, then the pole. The water sucked down like it was filling a hole and boiled again, and the long darkness swam beneath them toward open water as though not in it but riding the top of it, like the shadow of a plane.

Ezra squinted up at the pale, empty sky.

"They've started it here too now," his father said. "Russia won't be enough for them. All Europe won't. Goddamned Roosevelt won't declare war even though we're already in it."

The boats behind them were in disarray, banking to get away from the shadow passing beneath them, then banking again to avoid colliding.

"We've got to go back and report this, then organize into defense teams," Sinnett said.

Clayt Johnson looked back at the preacher. "There's nothing to do about that that can't wait another hour or two. Lehman's been out there long enough."

The boats hesitated, murmured and swarmed about like a confused crowd. Clayt Johnson pulled out his throttle and the *Hattie B* reared up and sped at Pond Island. The others converged in its wake and they proceeded.

Idling beyond the shoals of Pond Island they were still a hundred yards downwind of Lehman's shack but the air was already putrid. Jesse Johnson came alongside the *Hattie B* in his skiff and held to with his hands for Clayt Johnson and the preacher Sinnett to climb in. Ezra dropped alongside his father in the stern with neither his father's permission nor his protest. The boats behind them rode the chop, their bows headed into the foul wind coming off the island, the black-garbed fishermen and the fishermen's wives and children a silent and unmoving congregation waiting for the sermon to begin. The preacher Sinnett squirmed in the bow, sitting on the canvas sack meant for Lehman. Jesse's feathering strokes were long and propulsive.

"You know he's dead for sure?" Sinnett asked. "Who saw him?"

"Don't have to," Jesse said, "You can see him with your nose. He'd been dying for a year. Christ, he's been the walking dead for months."

Splinters and torn planks were strewn over the ledge. The shack itself was roofless, doorless, sunshot, more pen than shelter, braced together by ribbons of light. Inside huddled a form hurled against a corner like a rag doll, its arms outflung, its legs splayed.

Clayt strode toward the shack and put his head through. When he didn't pull out the others came up from behind and stood in the doorway looking in. Ezra headed them. No one touched the boy or held him or prodded him as they would another his age. He didn't want it. He'd known without thinking it that only after he served out this unguided and uninformed apprenticeship would he be permitted to speak. Though he'd seen all this before without dreaming it, though he'd experienced it all before without living it, it seemed to him that at nine years old he was witnessing his own birth; that the wood-eyed form rotting at his feet with its legs spread open was birthing him.

He glanced out through the wall of the shack. His mother stood upright in the boat, not even swaying as the chop pitched the boat side to side. Through the other wall he could see the dried up pond Lehman had quarried. A spade lay half-buried in mud. There's no treasure, Ezra said to himself. He faced the body they were calling Lehman. And Billy Morrill wasn't only dead, but irretrievable.

"We got to know what killed him," Clayt said.

"Don't you know what killed him?" the preacher asked through his hands.

"I want to see it," Clayt said, "Jesse, I want to see what killed him."

"You said it was a cancer," Sinnett said.

"I want to see it."

"Can't you wait until we get him on land and do this properly?"

"It isn't getting to land. Lehman always said just to fill him with rocks and take him out and let him go."

"But it's sacrilege to cut him here," Sinnett said, "I haven't given last rites, haven't said a thing. Besides, it isn't clean."

"Clean! After his lying here smelling this bad for three days filling up with crabs, any rites at all is sacrilege. What killed him is right there under the surface of his back. We been looking at it grow for six months, now I want to see it with my own eyes. I will if I have to cut him myself."

"At least send the boy out," Sinnett said.

"The boy stays. He'll be opening us up one day. He may as well know what he's going to find."

Sinnett clamped his hand over his mouth and ducked out.

Jesse toed at Lehman. Everything had gone bloated and stiff. Jesse and Clayt worked it with their feet, slipping in the mud and kicking and nudging to prop the corpse against the remaining planks of the wall. Then they kicked out the hardened leg and let it fall on its face. The middle of the shirt was pouched like a hunchback's. A fishknife materialized in Jesse's hand. It seemed a natural extension of his arm. The whole island knew how Jesse handled the fish on the wharf at Mackerel Cove.

Jesse straddled the body and pulled the cloth away from the back and slashed it and let it part. Underneath, the skin was sallow, spotted as a worm-eaten rotted pear, as formless and bloated; the rise of a boil spreading from armpit to armpit. Jesse laid the blade in the heart of it and ran it down once hard, as though opening up the belly of a fish. The skin ruptured at the seam, and there, splayed against the back like an octopus, was a black cancer with its branches fingering in every direction. Clayt stepped beside Jesse, his hands shaking, his eyes wet—not out of fear or sickening, but out of rage.

Jesse rested a hand on Clayt's shoulder and led him out. Outside, Clayt turned toward his wife standing alone in a boat named for her, facing her across the water as he did the same ten years earlier, though this time from land, and this time in warmth and daylight.

Ezra was alone with it. He stepped at it and without smelling, without breathing, straddled the ruptured corpse. The black liquor oozed out of the seam onto the dirt. His brow furrowed, his lips pinched, he looked down on the cancer sprawling like a root as though at an equation in a textbook. Then slowly, unpanicked, he lifted one leg and then the other, and made his way out of the shack. Outside, the glare blinded him. He stumbled for a moment on the rocks, a small boy, envisioning the dark bobbing shapes of a funeral waiting for him to begin.

Later that day, Lehman was foundering on the ocean floor. But the funeral clothes were still on the island men. None of their eyes met, as though the one bench in the General Store wasn't flush against a wall of tinned vegetables and the other didn't lean against a wall of tinned soup, and they didn't face each other from across the narrow aisle but looked out in random directions over a flower garden, or at the horizon off a boardwalk; as though everyone in hearing distance was there only by accident, and what was said was not for anyone in particular to hear but for the wind to carry in case someone should want to hear it.

"Terrible that sub of ours," the preacher Sinnett said.

Jesse Johnson nodded.

"I remember that other one," Sinnett said into his coffee cup, "Two something years ago—"

"Those boys are still down there," Jesse said, shaking his head. "Must have met up with the U-boat we seen this morning."

"I remember when they raised the hull," Sinnett said, "and they towed it to Portsmouth." He spoke mechanically, bullishly, as though he had a fixed agenda that he aimed to get over with as quickly as possible so he could have contributed and earned his right to sit in the General Store with the others. As though he always had sat there with them.

Jesse looked queerly at him: "They haven't raised her yet, preacher. She just went down—"

"—and the remains of those poor fellows kept tumbling out of the hull."

"I tell you she just went down just the other day. They're still down there."

"Every hundred feet or so they'd lose another body. A skeleton, really—"

Clayt Johnson hadn't uttered a sound yet. He'd said nothing to anyone since he lashed the rocks around the canvas sack with Lehman in it and he and Jesse Johnson hauled it over the side of the *Hattie B.*

"Forgive me, preacher," Jesse said, "but those boys are still down there in seventy fathom of water. There's got to be nothing but mash down there now, nothing left. I don't know about a raising. The Navy doesn't have anything that goes seventy fathom as far as I know."

"—and yesterday they got the *Robin Moore*," Sinnett rattled on, still into his coffee cup.

"The *Robin Moore*?" Jesse asked. "Now what's the *Robin Moore*?"

"It was off Africa and a U-boat commander radioed the captain that he was going to blow her up with everyone on board. Women and children. American women and chil—"

"—hell of a way to fight a war," Jesse said, "Telling someone you're going to kill them, then going ahead and doing it."

"The Germans set the passengers adrift in lifeboats," Sinnett said, "I believe there were women and children among them."

"What do you mean you believe it?" Jesse said, "You already said there was."

"The German was unmoved by the captain's pleas. They all watched from their lifeboats while their ship blew up. Then the U-boat just left them on the open seas. Three days they were adrift, exposed—"

"Those Krauts are all over the Atlantic," Jesse Johnson said, "Down there in Africa, sitting right out here, and we can't even get one of our subs out of the goddamn harbor." He glared at Sinnett: "And we can't raise them neither."

Clayt muttered under his breath.

"What's that, Clayt?" Jesse asked. "What're you saying?"

"The Squalus," Clayt said. "Preacher's talking about the Squalus. You're talking about the O-9. They're two subs. Two different goddamn subs."

"You mean we lost *two* subs in that harbor, Clayt?" Jesse puckered his lips to whistle, then didn't.

"What's the boy doing here?" Earl Varney said. He'd blocked off the aisle entrance. His hands were blacked with grease and he wore oil-stained coveralls.

"Oh say, it's Earl," Jesse said. "Didn't see you standing there, Earl. Fact, didn't see you out there this morning neither. Must be having eye trouble. I thought you and Lehman worked together." He rubbed his eyes and squinted above Jim Sinnett's head at the canned corn.

"He went crazy on me five years ago," Varney said, "I buried him back then to my mind. But I'm asking about that boy."

"That's Ezra Johnson," Jesse said.

"I know who it is," Varney said, "But what's he doing sitting on that bench?"

"He went out there with Clayt, stood right beside him. So now he's sitting with us all in the General Store. You want a seat? Here, I'll give you mine. The boy's earned his today." Jesse nodded across the aisle: "This here's Jim Sinnett, our new preacher."

Sinnett began to rise, his arm unfolding, his fingers extended. But Varney didn't take his eyes off Ezra who was sitting beside his father with a coffee resting on his knee like everyone else. Sinnett halted halfway up and fell back to the bench. His hands knotted in his lap.

"I was helping Floyd get the *Raven* ready for next month," Varney said, still staring at the boy. "He's got a charter, a pile of people coming from Rehoboth wanting to go out to Monhegan."

"I imagine there's a bit to do on that boat," Jesse said.

Floyd Johnson stepped out from behind Varney, in the same coveralls and with the same grease-blackened hands.

"You got a lot to do on the *Raven* there, Floyd?" Jesse asked.

Floyd Johnson cleared his throat, started to answer, then got caught and cleared his throat again. "No more'n you got on yours," he got out, and clamped his blacked hand over his mouth and muffled a cough.

"Just thought that maybe because you had to raise her twice out of the ice this winter, and she was looking a little tired last time I saw her, which was yesterday I think. I heard you got them people coming down and all, and I saw yesterday morning she was listed just a smidgin to port. But don't mind me. I was just thinking to myself is all, just thinking I'd want to get her out and around, maybe wind up that engine a bit before I put a whole lot of women and children and office-men aboard her. But that's just my thinking, just the way I'd do it. Don't you mind me."

Floyd Johnson began to speak but Varney interrupted him: "Well, don't overload yourself with all that thinking now, Jesse."

"Ha, well, maybe so," Jesse said, slapping his knee. "Ha ha. Maybe so. I can see your point there, Earl." His brow crumpled as though the point really did materialize in the air: "Yep. But by my figuring it's kept me and all my boats afloat so far. In fact, by my figuring"—he opened his hand to count and pulled back one thumb with the other—"I've only needed the one boat my whole life so far, and that one was my daddy's last one. So, let's see, that makes one boat in ... in ... let me see ... that's right, one every thirty years, I reckon."

He looked up at Varney and Floyd Johnson with fake expectancy. Then his face darkened: "But I'd think twice about taking those people out. I don't know about that *Raven*, but we saw a U-boat out there today. We been staying out of Hitler's business all this time, but it seems it don't matter anymore because he's made us part of it. We're in this thing one way or the other now. I don't know why they'd waste their time on the *Raven*. Christ, ha ha, I'd run the other way. No offense, Floyd. But they buzzed us pretty good today. You think twice is all I'm saying."

"I don't know what you saw," Varney said, "But it wasn't no U-boat. They got that submarine cable stretched all across the bay, and they didn't hear nothing come over it."

"You don't have to tell me about that cable," Jesse said, "I helped lay it down out here. But maybe the Navy boys in Portland are keeping it to themselves, or they're falling asleep. We know what we saw. Ezra got the closest look at it. Ask the boy."

Varney turned his eyes on the boy. Ezra turned his head slowly to meet them. His gaze neither fled nor warded off Varney's, but merely transformed, filled half with curiosity, half with contempt.

"What'd you see, boy?" Varney demanded, "You see a U-boat? You know what a U-boat looks like, boy? You know enough about that to know the difference between a whale and a U-boat? Or maybe it was just some old wreck. Maybe there were ghosts, a captain holding his own head? You sure it wasn't any Ghost Ship of Harpswell?"

Ezra didn't so much as think of anything to answer. He just looked at Varney as at an animal snarling at him through the bars of its cage, watching from the safety of the free air; maybe imagining what might happen should the bars vanish, but nothing more than that.

"There was a conning tower," Jesse said, "and a periscope."

"Is that what you seen, boy? You sure it wasn't some piece of trash flooding out of those mills upland?"

A trace of Ezra's contempt, the squinted beginnings of derision, appeared at the corners of his face. Varney's sneer vanished; his shoulders stiffened and his hands clenched as though he was about to pounce.

Finally Clayt opened his mouth: "Yesterday I read in the paper—"

"You reading the paper, Clayt?" Varney said, pushing out a single airy belch of laughter. He wagged his finger: "Boy, you and Jesse really are straining yourselves. You be careful you two. Soon you'll be seeing U-boats in your dreams. Soon Floyd and I are going to have to take the two of you out there like Lehman if you keep up all this thinking and reading."

Jesse slapped his knee again and shook his head. "Ha ha, Earl. Ha ha. Want to know what *I* read? Hey, didn't know the old man could read, did you? And guess what: I got me a college education. Didn't know that either I bet. Well, don't mind me. It wouldn't mean nothing to you. But Clayt's got one, too. We were classmates at Bowdoin College. But don't mind that neither. Just listen here: I read that the Federal Government—that means *American* government, Earl—is starting to squeeze on the Germans in this country. They're keeping them from leaving, and keeping them from staying. They're rounding them up and filtering the spies out of them, Earl, and the real spies are sure to try to find a way out. They'll be looking for any way to get out of America now. And you know what else that news said, Earl? They're saying it's the Maine coast—that's us, Earl—it's the Maine coast that's the easiest way out. With all these little islands of ours, it takes just a small boat to hopscotch a fair ways out, and not even a boat in any kind of shape. One pulled three times out of the ice in a single winter would do. A body can meet another body out there at night and nobody'd know. Or maybe a lot of bodies. They already seen U-boats off Nova Scotia. So we're sure to be tested first, they say. Now, isn't that an interesting notion, a test? You just might want to think about anyone wanting to charter any boat of yours, son. You know what a patriot is? That's pay-tree-ott. You don't want to meet up with any old U-boat yourself now. That is, if you got any boat left to meet it in. You wouldn't see nothing out there until it was atop you."

The grin changed on Varney's face: forgotten but not released, it hardened to a mask: "I don't know what you're saying there, Jesse old boy. A charter's a charter. Besides, I already told you there aint no U-boats—"

Clayt came to slow, scrupulous life. He raised his chin a notch and swiveled his head at Earl Varney and Floyd Johnson standing half behind him. He faced them but didn't look at them: "Yesterday I read in the paper about that British Commander again. Nugent. A.F. Nugent. He already lost two vessels against the Germans, one to a U-boat at Dunkerque, and the other to a mine somewhere else, I forget. He went back to the Admiral and asked for a third. And he got it, a frigate, the Jersey. Then last week that one hit a mine, too, and it went down. Three times he seen his men drown. Three times he watched his first mate get blown to bits. Three times he watched his boat burn and slip under, and this last time he watched his dead men just bobbing there with all the debris where his boat used to be. They was just more debris. But it was his, Nugent's, his boat, his men, his debris."

Clayt Johnson's eyes didn't move, but his pupils hardened and came into focus on Earl Varney and Floyd Johnson standing at the end of the aisle: "It's a hell of a thing. I seen people drown with my own eyes, and I seen people lose boats. And I tell you I don't know what's worse, or if they're any different. I saw Bud Brown after his dragger sunk from under him just out here. Just out here, Floyd, Earl, in that spot where you lost the Rainbow. This is two, three years already now, I suppose. Jesse and I were a short ways from it on the *Hattie B*, and by the time we got to him Bud was so crazy we had to chase him down off the top deck like a cat then get him then hold him then tie him. I told him I knew what this was all about, but he wasn't hearing nothing. He was hell bent on going down to the bottom with that tug. By the time we got him home he was just crazy as hell. And he didn't lose any bodies, just the boat. I've almost lost the *Hattie B* two or three times, and the only reason I didn't was because I stayed with her, because I would have gone with her if she went down."

Clayt still didn't move. No one so much as breathed. Floyd Johnson and Earl Varney were stone-still, as though Clayt's voice had them clamped by their shoulders:

"And now I'm going to tell you two boys something you don't know. There's an eighty-foot sardine carrier lying right next to Bud's dragger out here. I saw her going down, this was last year. I pulled alongside and lifted off the skipper. We put a buoy on her, a tuna buoy, a twelve-footer. The next week down came the skipper from Portland, dressed up all slick like no skipper I'd ever seen. He had two divers with him. Down he came and he wants me to take him and his divers out. Out we go. Buoy's still there. The boat's in ten fathom of water. His catch was still running up to the surface out of the hold. It looked like a slaughter out there. The divers followed the buoy down to where the boat lay and when they come up they said there's no boat there, not the one they're looking for anyway, just two others, a dragger and something else. I knew that was the spot where Bud lost his boat, and where you two lost the Rainbow. It's a bad spot. To tell you the truth I was nervous going out there myself, too close to them ledges. But jesus christ that boat of theirs was loaded with pogies and heron and those fish were still floating up out of that fish-hole all around us! But the skipper looked me straight in the eye, skipper to skipper, and said I might as well take in the buoy, it wasn't attached to anything, there wasn't anything there, anything that's his anyway. Then he put a hundred dollar bill in my hand and winked. I handed him back that hundred dollars and turned my back and took him in. I told him the next time he was in trouble off Bailey Island he'd have to swim ashore. But one of the divers told me something else when we got back to the cove. He told me that that other boat lying beside that dragger, not the boat they were looking for but another one, was punctured as hell, full of ax holes. He said it looked like crooked business down there."

Clayt drew up his shoulders and stared into the middle distance, as though he were finished. But no one thought he was. No one moved. He went on.

"You lose your boat, you got nothing as far as I'm concerned. You lose a second one, you got even less than nothing. After you two boys lost the *Rainbow* out there, and then when you lost your second, when your *Princess* burned, none of us on this island asked any questions. Nobody said nothing to nobody. We all kept to our business. We got enough to do. Christ, I've said nothing about it until this minute, not even to Hattie. But as far as I'm concerned there's only one kind of person who still has something to lose after that. That's the kind that's dead on their feet. Here's a war and here's skippers losing boats and men to bombs and fire and going back to ask for more because here's something bigger than them going on. I don't know how they hold onto their minds. Christ, maybe they don't, maybe that's the only way. And then there's people who're fighting nothing, spending their lives bellying up, just like their boats. As far as I'm concerned that kind's already dead. Can't even see them."

Clayt touched Ezra's knee and they both stood and walked one behind the other up the aisle at Earl Varney and Floyd Johnson and through them. Varney and Johnson pushed aside mechanically, as though that was their function, like a swing-gate.

DOVE

Strange word had been filtering through the papers and the radio of a particular small city in Poland, in which half the population had been herded off by the Germans and sent to a camp in the countryside and never heard from again. Inhabitants of the same city's northwest suburbs had been raising certain objections to the officers of the new local militia. Arms and legs, some of which still moved, were sticking out of the mass graves. The ground above the graves, they complained, continued to heave for several hours after the executions.

Every day, the newspapers carried photos of tracer bullets criss-crossing the skies above ancient cities. Breaths of flame and puffs of smoke leaping from the surrounding hillsides. A child's arm hanging limp from the window of a bombed orphanage. A bread-line reduced to scattered limbs and pools of blood. The carcass of an English plane bringing relief to besieged citizens smoldering on the airport tarmac.

Leslie Everett Dove had watched and listened closely. Word also came saying it was only a matter of time before America was pulled into the conflict. But he'd have gone now if he could. If the British had taken him. He wanted to go to see if these most unbelievable things could be true.

But he was sixteen, and Leslie Everett Dove went to walk out his resentment along the quay. He was too young to join anybody's Navy. It was nine at night. A light fog was in, the water calm. He stood watching the *Moxy* pull away from the pier, its stern and bow crowded with fathers and their uniformed Boy Scout sons headed for one or another of the islands in Boston Harbor. The plaid neckerchiefs and caps and pale badges faded into the fog, but the boys' excited voices lingered a long time, as did the silence of their fathers, who were too old to disguise their nervousness and distrust as idle, squealing chatter. Then that faded too, and Leslie was alone on the quay with his footsteps and a war he would not fight.

To the end of the quay and back. Halfway home he heard the shrieks again offshore, but this time the fathers had taken it up, too. Leslie stopped and peered into the night-fog, and it all died out. The water slipped and rolled beneath the sea wall.

He stood on the quay and looked out on the water, thinking the shouting was the fathers finally answering their sons in a reversed rite of manhood. As though Leslie had been mistaken: the trip's purpose not for the fathers to take out their little sons but for the sons to take out their fathers and teach them to be boys again. And then it was clear to him: in the night, on one or another harbor island, a great transmutation was taking place. The return of the fathers of Winthrop to their lost boyhoods, a mass purge of distrust and skepticism, of the authority that condemned all willing boys to remain out of the War. Dove sulkily walked on.

Then the waves started dropping them on the beach, plunking them down on the hard sand like dud artillery. Fingers already strewn with seaweed, badges shining through the fog like dull coins, their necks lynched by their Boy Scout neckerchiefs. Every mouth was a little round pool of sea water. The pairs of glassy eyes no longer corresponded, in death they broke ranks, each distended eye gone its own way. The trip, the transmutation, was not as advertised, but disguised instead as the already minutes-old war. The ship had not gone out to transport Scouts but to be sunk.

Though there were no rocks between shore and the nearest of the islands, no wind that night, no heavy surf, no one in the next days and weeks could bring themselves to really blame the Germans. No one ever did find the *Moxy* itself. There was no wreckage. It was as though the boat had been picked up and shaken out and emptied and then buried. Only drowned boys and their drowned fathers; as though the wreck were a great experiment carried out to prove to Winthrop that innocence had gone too far. That anything could be bought off by catastrophe. That innocence was not the natural state, bedlam was.

Dove saw all of history before him in the water: old collusions dusted off with a single puff of breath, and peace merely time stood still.

And the next morning, this tedious town, all its doors thrown open to the water, all its cats converging on the body-strewn beach below the quay.

RAVEN

No one knew better than those who lived in the Mountain and came down off it for food and dry goods that to be native to the islands, you had to start your life on them, knock up an island girl and marry her, or drown not farther than a mile or two away from shore. Only then would you receive respect while you were atop the islands, and then could expect to lay in them after you were dead. A highlander dying on island land wasn't good enough. Any fool could throw himself in front of a car, or fall off a roof. It had to be in the water because at the very least you had to get in a boat, which took something beyond getting out of bed and running into the street.

Though the Mountain was geographically a part of Great Island, anatomically the rump of it, the people who lived on it were not island people but Mountain trash, cat and dog-eating cannibals. Give them their own boat to lobster from and they'll sink it. Give them a job on your boat and they'll sink yours. Though it was Earl Varney who'd come down from the Mountain when he was thirteen, who'd built a house on Orr's Island and started a new life in it, it would be Floyd Johnson, and not Varney, found around Round Rock naked and bloated and presumably drowned; and so it would be Floyd Johnson, and not Varney, who would be promoted posthumously to island native. All his life Varney had been without a place he could point to and say that's where he was going; instead, he had only the Mountain to point to and say that's where he ran from. Part of him would envy Johnson dead, because it was Johnson who would lie in Bailey Island dirt, beneath a headstone put up at island expense: *Floyd Johnson, skipper of the Raven, June 29, 1941.* Varney would fight even the details of the inscription, certain as he was that Johnson had stayed alive at least until

June 30, or even the first of July.

Neither of them had thought seriously of fog before June 28. They merely mentioned it once or twice as a divine possibility. But by the time they drove to the General Store for their coffee late afternoon that Saturday, the white smoke was rolling in. Driving through it from Great Island to Orr's, then from Orr's to Bailey, the unseen road pitching beneath them, they didn't dare mention the fog, no less revise their plan around it. They merely watched it in silence, spiralling at the windows and parting at the headlights, holding their breath in fear they'd blow it away. Finally, stepping down from the truck, it was Varney who laid an arm on Floyd's shoulder: "It's the cream on the pie," Varney whispered to Floyd. "Sure fire now. It's straight, easy. Now there'll be no one out on the water to see a thing. You won't mind getting a little wet for two thousand dollars, will you Floyd?"

"Just a little wet," Floyd said.

"Just a little."

"And scared maybe too, hey Earl?"

"Scared too maybe. But them highlanders will live with it. It'll be their great goddamn adventure. And then we're done, you and me done, free as birds. We'll put up that little camp in them greeny mountains and get off the goddamn water, get away from these goddamn islands."

"And Beatrice," Floyd said.

"What's that?"

"And Beatrice. You and me and Beatrice. And then somebody for you maybe."

Varney's knuckles went white. "That's right Floyd. And somebody for me." Then, poking Johnson's ribs: "Or maybe somebody for you, eh?"

Floyd laughed. "You know, Earl, I never laid no claim for Beatrice. You know how she's always looked out for herself. But last night she told me she thought she should get a piece of the *Raven*'s policy when it comes in since she put down her own money for it."

Varney didn't say anything.

"She said she's earned it and I have to say I think that's about right," Floyd said.

"Seems right," Varney said cautiously.

"And she is my wife."

"Seems right to me, too," Varney said.

"And what she knows could put us in jail."

Again Varney's knuckles went white and he didn't say anything.

"I mean, she is my wife," Floyd said.

"Surely."

"So you know Beatrice. She's her own woman when it comes to money."

"I always liked that about Beatrice," Varney said.

"So what do you think?"

"About what?"

"About Beatrice getting a cut. A third, a third, a third," Floyd said.

"You mean two thirds for you and a third for me, don't you?"

"It's not the way I mean it, Earl!"

Varney gripped Johnson's shoulder. "Hush. Thirds seems about right."

"It does?"

"I just said so, didn't I?"

While they waited at the counter inside for their coffee, Varney was careful not to look at Floyd, but Floyd was eyeing Varney, his expression closer to surprise than disbelief.

Then Jesse Johnson stepped between them. "Howdy, boys," he said, "Nice weather we're having, eh? How's the concrete business?"

"What're you talking about Johnson?" Varney said.

"Thought I heard something about you spending the afternoon pouring concrete down the *Raven*'s keel for ballast? Good time to do it, I'd say, now that you got thirty odd people coming down from Rehoboth tomorrow, and you got all that work done this morning. Good thing you got around to it, weighing her down and all that, getting her nice and heavy. Darned how things here get around so quick, isn't it boys?" Jesse scratched his head. "But then, Earl, I keep forgetting you wouldn't know much about

60

that. You're not of these islands, are you? Still wet behind the ears. A veritable stranger. That's ve-ri-ta-ble, Earl. Veritable. So educated am I," Jesse sang. "So you see, Earl, the way it works around here is that someone sees something and it's like everyone's seen it. Nice and cozy, friendly like. They say it helps keep people on the right side of things. But what're your thoughts, Earl?"— Jesse rested a hand on Varney's shoulder—"Personally, I think times are changing—"

"I think I'm sick of you Johnson," Varney said, swiping Jesse's hand away.

Jesse Johnson's hands went slack. He took a step back. His mouth was grinning, but his eyes were slow and obstinate.

Floyd Johnson tried to pull Varney back, but Varney shrugged him off and looked ready to lunge. Jesse Johnson still seemed preoccupied with what Varney's behavior was saying rather than what it was about to do. But then the fire in Varney's eyes was damped out. His shoulders dropped and his arms went dead. He didn't bother to return Clayt's slow nod over Jesse's shoulder, or watch Clayt sipping at his coffee. He just turned when he saw him and shoved Floyd Johnson ahead of him through the door.

"Drive safely now, Floyd," Jesse called after them. Clayt joined him at the doorway. They weren't listening for the reply. They were watching the red pinlights of Varney's truck vanish in the road.

"It's one thing to take an axe to your own boat when it's just you aboard," Clayt said, "But when there's thirty it's something else."

"I'm not worried about Floyd," Jesse said. "Floyd Johnson don't have that in him."

"It's not him, I guess," Clayt said.

Outside, Varney and Floyd Johnson hurtled down the road toward Dyer's Cove.

"You won't miss us out there, will you Earl?" Floyd Johnson said.

"Quit it, would you!" Varney said. "I won't miss nobody. I'll radio and you know Clayt'll have the whole goddamn cove full of boats bearing down on you out there in five minutes. They'll be coming so fast their wake'll drown you before the surf will. You just tie that keg fast to your waist and I'll see it's you bobbing on top of the water and pick you out. It's gonna be just a little wet."

"It's Beatrice I'm worried about," Floyd said, "You didn't put a keg on for her. I want her picked out first."

"You can share the one keg," Varney said, "It'll float both of you until I get there. Beside, she's a better swimmer than you. She'll take care of herself."

The cracks in the roadway came quickly and evenly spaced; the pitch of the tires rose a notch. Then the truck reared up and banked slightly to the right. Recrossing the bridge between Bailey Island and Orr's they didn't talk. They never did. The water boiled around the pylons below. Passage over the strait was sacred. Varney squeezed the steering wheel and released it, squeezed and released it. Floyd Johnson pressed his nose to the window and tried to see the water beneath them; he saw only a swirl of foam. Then the tires hit Orr's Island.

Johnson knocked his forehead against the glass. "They'll know," he said. "Jesse and Clayt're already thinking it."

"Goddamn it, Johnson, you don't listen. I spelled it out for you, didn't I. It don't matter what they *think*. They got to have proof. They think there're Krauts out there, so as long as we keep shut up about it they can say what they want but they'll never prove anything. They'll never think you could have put all those people in the water on purpose. Just get out there nice and easy and get hung in them Teeth. It happens all the time. Just be looking the other way for a minute, take a pull of booze or tea or whatever those people are drinking, and swing the bow round just to touch it. Nothing criminal in that, especially in this soup."

WALTER

In Rehoboth, it was already the summer of waiting, six days old and already everyone was running from the heat. The short shadows of the doorways were filled all day with people snapping their newspapers. Children were drowning in quarries and subcurrents all over New England. The elderly in Boston and New York were decomposing in their rooms. While the Germans closed in on Minsk and Moscow, the FBI was hunting down grocery stockers and pipefitters suspected of being Nazi spies. At Portland Harbor, civilians and Naval officers lined the wharves, no longer waiting for the O-9 to resurface from its training run—waiting for the Navy-issue hats and shoes to begin bubbling to the surface. Ready to wait grimly for the rest. On land, at the State of Maine Supreme Court, Judge Goodspeed's courtroom waited in the heat for word of Luverne Joss's disinterment, to know once and for all whether her husband had shot her up with morphine before breaking open her skull with the flat side of an axe. Then the Nazis overran Minsk and two men descended the Harbor in a diving bell and caught the O-9 in their lights: crushed like a cardboard tube, the submarine's guts spilling through the cracks: the arms and legs of bug-eyed sailors. And Luverne Joss did surface, in Alabama, though without her stomach and brain (it dawned on the coroner at graveside that he'd removed them, which made a determination impossible). But that hardly mattered any more, because all this time Elizabeth Mayo, a waitress at the Triple Spa Coffee Shop, had been laughing on Judge Goodspeed's witness stand, telling the jury how Joss rode her piggy back and talked love to her in the back of his car. All Rehoboth was outraged. The German consulate was given twenty-four hours to leave the country. Twenty-nine suspected German spies were placed in custody in Florida

63

and Maine. The Rehoboth Falls Times printed a photograph of a British soldier standing atop a pyramid of hollow Italian helmets. Rehoboth waited for more.

A few minutes before six, Saturday, Arthur McAlister opened the kitchen door and closed it quietly behind him and, seeing his wife and son seated at table, walked quickly to his place, his mouth a straight line and his eyes unblinking. He took the chair and drew it up under him and sat. He bore down on his plate quickly without loosening his tie and letting his neck out of the heat, without speaking and without looking up at his son. The steadiness of his eating was testament to his agitation, and there wasn't a word passed across the table so as not to disturb the uneasy peace.

At some point his son Walter raised his eyes and said thinly and gently, "You're not letting me go, are you."

The mill whistle blew. For a moment the birds in the trees outside stopped singing. There was no noise at all, no child's yelling, no passing car. McAlister looked up to the window, as if in search of these things. His wife got up and began shuttling plates to the sink. McAlister wiped his mouth and threw down his napkin and stood. The birds began again. From across the yard, a cry, "Walter!" The whistle declared the afternoon evening, and the day began to cool.

The boy looked up to the door and half rose, but his father's gaze pushed him down again.

He stood in his bank suit at the kitchen phone. He ran his fingers through his hair, gazing slantwise down where a piece of low sunlight smoldered on the floor. He'd have to replace those planks soon, he'd have to replace the whole damn floor. He could feel his wife and son's gaze on him, and turned his shoulder so that he could speak in peace but so that they could hear.

"Hello, Lilah? I'm sorry to disturb you dear, it's Arthur McAlister. Look, Lilah, if you still want my two places on the *Raven* tomorrow morning you can ... yes, you're welcome. But you have to give Gordon Beauchamp a call right away. There are a lot of people in town who'd like those spots."

McAlister smiled at what she said; it must have been something. He'd always been fond of his secretary—they all were, she was so sweet—and had complained to Beauchamp that more places on the *Raven* should have been made available to clerks and staff. But it wasn't that large a boat, and thirty-six was already beyond the agreed limit.

"You're welcome, dear. Now, Lilah," he said, his voice growing gruff and commanding, just playing around, he liked to do that with her, tease her and pinch her cheek, pat her on the head, play the demanding father since he couldn't play anything else. "Now listen, Lilah. You and your boyfriend have a wonderful time. But I'd never be able to find someone else as pretty as you, so don't get drowned." He smiled, gleaming, "You're welcome. Yes. Have a good time—" and put down the phone. He winced. He could feel his wife scowling at him. He could see, in the corner of his eye, Walter's head hanging above a wedge of pie.

"Now Walter—" he began.

"That wasn't very nice," his wife interrupted acidly, "letting him know like that."

"Now look. I was born and brought up on Prince Edward Island. I was a fisherman myself before I jumped that train and wound up here. Gordon showed me a picture of that boat and it's about as sea-worthy as a bathtub. It'll roll if someone so much as breathes wrong. Now what they do"—raising his arm behind him, through the window and across the yard to the back wall of the Beauchamp house and beyond it to the general population—"is their business. But they don't know the water like I do, and I wouldn't step on that top-heavy tub just to sit there having a picnic in the cove. I certainly wouldn't think to ride it out into open water. And if I wouldn't ride in it, how could I let my son?"

"But at the last minute, Arthur?" she said, unpeeling her apron from her waist and sitting beside Walter. She blew a stray hair from her eyes. "You knew what that boat looked like weeks ago, and you wait until the night before the picnic to give Walter's place away? He's been looking forward to it for months. All his friends—"

McAlister leaned back against he sink, his legs parted, arms folded. "I did some more checking," he said, his voice low, almost ashamed. "Just to be sure. I made some calls and looked into this Johnson fellow who charters the boat and didn't exactly like everything I heard."

"Who'd you call?"

Ignoring his wife, McAlister swung at the air in Walter's direction. "Hey? Walter? Look up here, son."

Walter raised his head part way, as if he'd heard a distant sound.

"How could I let my only boy on that top-heavy tub? Hey? Look, I promise we'll go hunting up at Moosehead next weekend. How's that, hey? We'll bring up a canoe, we'll sleep outside. The whole nine yards. How's that?"

A glimmer of a smile appeared on Walter's face, obliged more than felt.

"And tomorrow we'll listen to the ball game. What's DiMaggio's hitting streak up to now, forty games?"

Walter's smile quickly faded. "Forty-one."

"Forty-one games!" McAlister looked at his wife in wonderment. "Can you believe it?"

His wife, arms folded, mouth a straight line. She looked out the window, skimming the tops of the laundry, to the house next door. "You told Gordon what you heard?"

McAlister's face gleamed in the kitchen light, a lock of wet hair like a tendril falling across his brow. He shook his head, slightly, unconvinced even by his own arguments. "We've had a bad few months, with the flood, this damn heat. With this war thing bearing down on everybody. There's grumbling down at the mill, men starting to snipe at Sutherland. It's been a bad time. Everybody needs to blow off some steam. They could use a day away from here, out on the water. I wouldn't want to spoil their fun." He slouched and rolled an empty cup in his hand, staring at it as if it was of sudden interest to him.

She, bitterly: "So that boat's good enough for them, but not for you? You wouldn't go, but you'd let them?"

"It's not for me to let them go or—"

"Arthur, they'd listen to anything you said. You practically run this town and they know it, and they like it because they like what you say, and you're usually right. If you told them you didn't think that boat was safe they—"

"It's only a hunch—"

"But you were a fisherman, Arthur. You know boats."

Quietly: "They need to go. Hell, they would go. They'd go anyway. I can hear Gordon now, calling me a spoil sport. So what's the point? Or they'd go and they'd be thinking the whole time, 'I shouldn't be here, I should have listened to Arthur McAlister.' It'd ruin everything—"

"Arthur, if you know something—"

"I don't know anything," he snapped, rotating the cup faster. More quietly now, apologetic, "Not for sure. Like I said it's only a gut reaction. That's all there is to it. I wouldn't be able to explain it to them. They'd just laugh me off."

He raised his head to his wife, and without looking at his son, speaking exclusively to her—as though Walter wasn't there in that room, or in the house, almost as though they hadn't a son at all, a son only in the abstract, an idea of one disillusioned by a father's irrational resolutions—"He'll get over it. I'll take him up to Moosehead next weekend. Besides, there's more important things to be worrying about today."

Something about her husband's sudden sobriety, a different tone of voice—something bigger than a boat, something defeating. The bank? The mill in default?—as war approached, less paper was bought, too much made, too much sitting in the warehouses upriver. Whole shifts were being cancelled. Already there was talk of a four-day week so that no one would be let go outright. Or was it their mortgage? Surely things were in order. After all, she was married to a banker. So maybe a distant relative—

"What is it?" she asked, with nervous politeness.

"Minsk fell to Hitler yesterday."

She didn't move, though her son did. He looked up.

"Minsk fell," McAlister repeated. "The Russians aren't doing well. They can't hold. I called Bill White today in Washington. He said there's talk already in the Congress. He's getting more and more telegrams from his constituency every day. It's only a matter of time—sooner or later we're going to get into this thing."

Still, McAlister refused to so much as tick his head to the left to catch sight of his son. But his wife did. She looked directly across the table at sixteen-year-old Walter with a brand of fear in her eyes the boy never knew she possessed, or anybody possessed; the brand you can't know exists until the instant it draws the line behind you, and you understand that everything over it was one kind of life, and everything before it, everything ahead of you, will be another.

She looked at her husband with the same fear. "A war like this," she said. "If we get into it. Could it last more than two years?"

McAlister nodded his head, once. "It's bound to. It'll reach everywhere. It's here now. They're saying German U-boats are all over the Atlantic already."

Her eyes glistened. A strange expression—was it a smile?—of forgiveness crossed her face. "Is that why you don't want to go out on that boat, Arthur?"

McAlister reached for his fork and tapped out a rhythm, a signal, a Morse code.

S.O.S.? Walter's eyes glazed. His palms grew wet. His parents vanished. So did school and the mill and Rehoboth itself. He had begun the most earnest kind of hoping, the hoping for something not a scrap short of divine intervention: that he be not three months shy of seventeen but that he be eighteen, though not merely eighteen: eighteen already for some time. He would go down to Congress Street tomorrow and walk into the Armed Forces Recruitment Office not because he had been for one year and three months and six days boyishly, irritably, waiting for his war to arrive like a mail order buck knife, but because he seized it then and there before he had to, like something he thought might be a man.

Later that night, wafts of invisible mill-reek passed between the houses. The upper windows in the McAlister and Beauchamp houses were full. Bodies hanging out over the draped sheets, legless, decorative gargoyles of the town's proscenium. Their voice faintly echoing, filling the night above the grassy lot with distant noises, coughing, speech, as if the star-flecked dome of sky were the arched ceiling of a vast cave in which they all lived.

"You taking Anne Stisulis?" Walter asked.

Ivan and Mavis laughed. "Shut up," Gordy said. "Yeah, I'm taking her."

"Why can't you come, Walter?" Ivan asked.

"I got other stuff to do."

"Your daddy won't let you," Ivan said.

Mavis giggled.

"It's a lot of things."

"It's too bad you can't."

"Yeah."

"You going to listen for DiMaggio?" Gordy asked.

"Yeah."

"You'll tell us everything?"

"When you get back. Yeah."

"Where he hit it?"

"Yeah. Let me know when you get back," Walter said. "I'll tell you everything."

"It'll be after dark." Gordy said.

"Okay."

"Maybe after midnight."

"Okay. Throw a rock at my window or something. Let me know. Hey, Gordy?"

"Yeah."

"The war's coming," Walter said. "For real."

A car passed. Headlights swept across the side of the Beauchamp house, catching three pairs of eyes redly, like foxes blinking in the scrub. The car passed and they could hear the crickets sawing in the nearby woods.

"How do you know?" Gordy asked.

"My dad called his friend."

"Yeah, who's his friend?"

"Congressman White."

Mavis dropped giggles to the grass like pebbles into water, ever widening echoes of itself, deepening, fading. Outside, footsteps walking slowly, becoming gradually louder along the street, passed their houses and faded into silence. Down the street a gate creaked open then snapped shut. In the silence of their cave they listened to the crickets, and then another car passing below them, down the hill. Then that faded too.

"You gonna go?" Gordy asked.

"A year and a half maybe," Walter said. "On my birthday."

"Yeah, me too."

"Me too," said a quieter voice in the dark, contemplative, almost angelic.

"Shut up Ivan," Gordy said. "You're ten years old. You aren't going anywhere."

"Am too."

The creaking of stairs filled the yard, the footsteps of—whose mother?—walking slowly. In the Beauchamp house upstairs lights came on one at a time.

"Let me know how it was," Walter said quickly.

"Alright, we'll let you know," Gordy said.

"Have a good time," Walter said.

"We will."

"With Anne."

"I will," Gordy said. "Sorry you can't come."

"Me too. Have a good time," Walter said again. "And let me know."

"We will. We'll let you know."

There was no time to say goodnight. The windows shut in rapid succession, like gunshots, and the boys and Mavis returned to the heat of their beds and the universe of their silent rooms.

RAVEN

One step off looked to drop you not six feet into the oily water but an unknown distance through the clouds. The *Raven* hadn't had a chance to fade. It vanished not ten feet from the jetty while the chortling and heckling and nervous bellowing of the *Raven*'s passengers still leapt around the cove from treestand to treestand.

Earl Varney parked his truck in front of the first of the sedans from Rehoboth. He pulled on all the drivers' doors. Every one was locked. He peered in at the ignitions. No one had left the keys. "Soft little bunny rabbits," he muttered, and felt his way toward the fish house. He nearly walked into her. Beatrice stood on the jetty with her arms crossed, facing the laughter and the *Raven*'s gurgle. Empty gasoline containers lay scattered around her. She wore sunglasses, and that thin red gingham dress he liked on her. But it wasn't a boating dress, no way a boating dress. He thought she was careless about that.

She hadn't heard him, not that Varney had tip-toed toward her or in any other way tried to muffle his step; the gravel was loose and the jetty creaked. But she stood with her face to the clouds so preoccupied with what she could no longer see, and what she could only barely hear, that when Varney put his hand on the nape of her neck, she felt her lungs reflex and the scream leave her throat before she felt the clammy palm stroking her like wet sandpaper. She didn't have to turn to see it was Varney, but she turned to glare at him anyway, then recrossed her arms and faced the water again. The tail of her scream still hung on the fog, as though she'd cried out in the nave of a cathedral. A second voice, Floyd's, calling her name—"Beatrice!"—had rung out and met hers above the water and muddled it.

"It's all right!" she shouted, but there was no reply. There was nothing at all. The *Raven*'s motor faded quickly. The wake spread and lapped against the fish house piles, then smoothed clear and dark.

"Off," Beatrice said.

"What do you mean *off?*" Varney said.

"O-f-f."

"Goddamn it why's everyone spelling at me," Varney said.

"Because you're not very smart, Earl," she said.

"Smart enough," Varney felt his way under the bottom of her dress. "Look who's out on the water and look who's standing safe here on the wharf with the pretty lady. I see you put that dress I like on for me."

"The pretty lady don't belong to you," she said. "And I didn't put it on for you either."

"Shouldn't put it on at all. Floyd really expect you to go out with him wearing that?"

"He didn't say a thing about it," she said. "Get your hand out of there."

"You calm down. Don't get jumpy on me now, Beatrice. I'm warning you, not now. Nice and easy. Now, what you told Floyd."

"None of your business."

Varney tightened his grip on her neck.

"Get away," she said.

He dug his fingers. Her knees buckled. "What," he said.

"I told him I got my monthly," Beatrice said.

Varney released her. "Did he believe you?"

"Would you have?" Beatrice said.

Varney opened his mouth and let burst a volley of laughter, then he shut it and the laughter stopped and he looked as though he never laughed, not now or ever. "Not with you in that dress."

"Well there's the difference between him and you," Beatrice said, "He believed me."

"Soft bastard."

"I want you to change it around, Earl. I want you to get Floyd, too."

"Don't get soft on me," Varney said.

"We'd still get the money."

"Yeah, but three ways," Varney said. "You've gone soft,

haven't you?"

"But we'll have two thirds," Beatrice said. "And then there's me. You can get me, too." Beatrice pressed her back against Varney's front.

Varney squeezed her neck and her knees buckled again.

"Earl!"

He put his lips to her ear: "You said the pretty lady wasn't in the deal."

"I'll give you my third," Beatrice said. "I promise you."

"Promise!" He laughed. "That's good, Beatrice. I like that."

"I'm leaving Floyd anyways. Just pick him up is all I ask you. The poor fool."

"You have gone soft," Varney said, "Well, anyway it's too late."

"What do you mean it's too late? When you're out there just don't leave him. Just pick him out with the others."

"It's too late cause I already decided," Varney said, "I aint picking up nobody."

"That's a good one, Earl. Now don't you play with me. This isn't the time to joke."

"Who's playing? I just said I aint picking up nobody. We'll just let it ride out natural, like a real accident."

Beatrice twisted herself free and stepped back to look at Varney. Her jaw hung slack. She pressed her cheeks. "You're gonna let them all drown out there? You're gonna—?"

"Some of them'll probably make it all right," Varney said. "Them that can swim."

"But Floyd will hang on that barrel. He'll know you went rotten on him and he'll turn you in."

"Turn *me* in? So I'm alone in this now, am I," Varney said. "Anyway, I lied a little bit. I am going out there, but not to pick no one up. I got to make sure old Floyd's tuna keg don't float him too long—"

Beatrice gasped and took another step back and looked at Varney as though at satan himself. "You Earl. You can't do that. That's murder."

"Beatrice, you're a funny gal. You're thinking of that now, are you? Yesterday you were ready to let him squeal in that water like a stuck pig."

"Mass murder," Beatrice gasped. She was looking over Varney's shoulder, seeing it all on the fog. She took another step back.

"You be careful, Beatrice, or you're gonna fall back into the cove there."

"You can't do it," she said in a hoarse whisper, "It wasn't what we planned."

"The fog gave me an idea," Varney said. "Lookit, Beatrice, now it's just like we got nothing to do with it. We didn't know Floyd was going to be too drunk to steer that boat. See what I mean? No one's gonna see now. It'll run its course like a regular accident."

"You lied to me. That's not the plan."

"What are you going to do, go tell someone about it? Go on, Beatrice. Go on and tell them how I was going to let Floyd drown. But don't leave out the part about me and you and how you been wishing Floyd gone."

Beatrice opened her mouth to scream but out came only a little trickle.

"Jesus christ, Beatrice, don't you start the dramatics on me now."

Varney dropped Beatrice back home then drove down to Cundy's Harbor. He'd moved his boat out of Mackerel Cove the other day to be able to come and go without being seen. Now he idled out of the Harbor. He leaned forward, the bottle tilted, his free hand pulling and twitching on the wheel and tapping the throttle. The weedy water slid by between him and the shoals and ledges. Some words or other rose to his lips but he tilted the bottle before they passed. He wasn't long for this place, he knew that much. He'd have the money and he'd be gone with it, with or without Beatrice, he didn't care. It was funny enough that the place he'd always had picked out for a camp was outside Rehoboth, upriver from the mill. He thought it right somehow that it be Rehoboth people to clear the way for him.

Varney laughed; his mouth opened and out came the staccato machine-gun pants. He turned his head and laughed at the water, then flung the bottle from his lips without even righting it first, the bottle glinting once then vanishing long before the splash. Then seeing something else he shut his mouth and pulled harder on the throttle and put both hands to the wheel: he saw his father bent forward under the weight of a barrel of flour, staggering up the Mountain with a trail of fishermen behind, laughing, jeering at the tin houses and paltry log shacks in the woods on either side of the trail. The store man Alexander headed them, stepped toward the boy Earl Varney and mussed his hair. It was a wager. The store man bet the boy's father that he couldn't carry the barrel of flour the ten miles from the store to the Mountain without slowing or stopping. The wager was the same barrel of flour lying across the new divot in his father's back. Earl's father staggered on, the fishermen laughing and the store man winking, and a crowd behind them, lobstermen from the coves and Mountain girls in their soiled dresses and their mothers and their yellow mongrels. It was a circus trailing Varney by the time he arrived and dropped the barrel and collapsed against it, "Ha!" Alexander cried, "Varney, you old fool you didn't think I was really going to let you have that flour, did you? You old pack horse, you Mountain trash!"

All the fishermen roared their approval, then rolled the barrel of flour onto a wagon and back down the Mountain to the road and then to the store. Earl picked up his father and put him to bed, then a month later walked down the Mountain a little way with a pick and shovel and buried him into its side.

Varney tugged on the throttle. He had it out all the way. His bow was high over the water. The boat was bouncing and snapping and he was banking right then left where he knew there was something waiting to rip into him. He picked the crow bar off the deck and leaned it in front of him where he could get to it easily. Dyer's Cove was passing on the right. He wound through the shoals and made for Jacquish Island, the tip of rock broken off the end of Bailey's nose. He'd turn there for Round Rock. He wished there was wind and chops, but that was the swap, fog for bad seas. This water was oily and flat. If any of them could swim a lick they'd make it if they could figure out where they were. But the water was too cold for bad decisions. They'd have one chance to get the direction right.

75

When he heard the water against Jacquish Island he pulled hard to starboard. But there was a strange light behind him. His head snapped violently and twisted to follow it, as though it had tethered him, looped around his neck. He waited for it again. There wasn't any light, he thought, There's no lighthouse. Then he turned back toward open water. But the light again off land's end—he shoved the throttle closed and turned to face it squarely with the crow bar in both his hands, his sea legs pumping to keep him level. The fog flickered around him, streaking like lightning low to the ground, or mute cannon fire. Or just fire, he thought. But then the flashes died like lightning does and started all over again, exact, patterned. Varney didn't know how to read it, but he knew what it was. Code. It had to be.

Well I'll be, he thought, I'll goddamn christalmighty be.

He cut the motor. He heard nothing, just the water slapping gently against his boat. And the fog lighting up around him. He stopped breathing to muffle his heart banging on his ears, and squinted into the water, looking for signs, an oil slick, a trail of white wash, a goddamn periscope. He felt the giant whales criss-crossing beneath him through these canyons, whales with motor-driven fins and an underwater cannon. He let loose a volley of laughter, not out of happiness as much as the exhilaration that comes with the most perverse of surprises, a reprieve not even he could have prayed for. He turned over the motor, pulled back on the throttle and raced toward Round Rock, calling into the wind: "Semicek, thank you, you old Krautloving bastard."

When he neared Round Rock he slowed the boat to an idle. The crow bar raised over his head, he searched the water for the keg among other things. Shards of wood. A hand. But there was only the sea foam, the muted deadly gurgle of the ledges themselves. He made long sweeps at regular intervals in and around the Teeth, but there was nothing. Or was there already nothing left. Again he cut the motor and he bobbed, listening to the suck of the water collapsing over the ledge.

Goddamn it, goddamn—

He gunned the motor.

Where—where are they. Goddamn it, Floyd.

The boat trembled, careened on its side, nodded its mast

toward the water which tipped like a river running swiftly down hill. He thundered toward Pond Island, then around it, and around it, and around it again.

MAVIS

Across the grassy lot from the McAlister kitchen, Mavis Beauchamp woke in a dank bed with her gown wrung tight around her. The room was airless and putrid and stifling hot, the window lavender with either twilight or dawn. It was the mill whistle that woke her. She didn't know the time, or how she got where she got; only that the other minute she'd been waiting at the supper table, her mother shuttling from her own seat to the stove, glancing from the clock to the stove. Then, finally, sitting for good, she looked only at the clock. Three settings still unoccupied, one at the table's head, one next to Mavis, one across from her. She was hungry. The clock was too slow. She smelled the postponed Sunday dinner but saw none of it, only that it was seven or eight, though outside it was not close to dark. She lay her head on her arms in her plate. Her arms were wet. Then she woke. The bed was wet. She heard a different kind of silence and rose.

She entered the hallway groggily and walked toward the stairs, past Ivan's open door—eyes not merely forward but dead ahead now—toward Gordy's. Something in her made her half-break her vow to not be a busybody any more, a daddy's-girl and keep her long nose and greasy paws and little-girlness to herself. Almost past Gordy's door she glanced in then bolted for the stairs, then stopped at the landing and returned. Gordy's curtains were open, the bed fresh, drum-tight, like he and Ivan had been practicing. Their Scout regulations.

She backed up and peered inside Ivan's room. His bed had not been slept in either. The silence in the house was total. Everything waited, even the walls. It was the kind of silence that was so complete it had a sort of hum, the noise of expectancy.

The stairwell was brightening. She knew now that it was

78

dawn, Monday, and yesterday had been Sunday and they'd gone out there like her Poppy had been planning. Like everyone had been calling about and leaving messages for years and years. Could they go? Was there room for one more?

But she'd been forbidden. Gordy had seen to that. It must have been fun. It must have been grand. She knew the boys wouldn't tell her a thing. Poppy would have to, but he'd make her wait. He'd make her wait until one of the walks they took together in the evenings when it was cooler and she could actually catch whiffs of the flowers and not just the mill. When they'd head up Mount Zircon, and stand listening to the slithering creepcrawling in the grass around them and the footsteps of monsters in the forest. And he'd hold her up, atop his shoulders, from where Rehoboth looked to her like a big city. He'd hold her up and he'd tell her everything. About the water. And about the boat and also all the sea monsters he'd seen.

But it would have to wait until tonight. They must all be gone again already, she thought, Ivan and Gordy in Peru with Walter finishing up the camp, Poppy at the organ at church. She didn't know yet it was early for all of that.

She stooped at the turn of the stairs and saw her own corner of the supper table still laid, the silverware pushed askew by her own elbows the night before. The faint odor of cooled meat hung in the air. Another stair, another setting untouched, her poppy's; another, Ivan's; another, Gordy's. One last one. Hanging off the bottom stair, her right foot suspended above the floor.

Nothing had happened yet. She knew she could go back to what was there behind her. Instead she went forward.

Her mother's tight bun sprung, spidery, the bottom half of her face dripping sweat, puddling into an empty supper plate. Things in both her mother's hands, paper things, darkening around the pinched fingers. Mavis squinted: the family picture, taken the Christmas before, and the boys' Mother's Day cards.

"What are you doing?" Mavis whispered.

"I am waiting for your father," her mother said without turning.

"Where is he?"

The phone rang. Both raised their heads but neither moved

for it. Between rings the clock ticked. Total silence between the ticks and the rings. There was no breathing going on in this house and Mavis stepped down completely and looked expectantly at the clock. The phone stopped ringing and the clock ticked then the phone started again and the clock stopped. Neither moved for it. Mavis finally looked: it was six o'clock. The phone stopped and the clock ticked and the phone started a third time. Mavis looked at her mother, then dropped her gaze at her feet. The phone stopped, the clock ticked.

WALTER

Walter sat at the kitchen table eating a bowl of cereal. He was thinking he had to call Gordy, see what the hell they were going to do that day. Gordy hadn't come to wake him last night. First he wanted to hear about the trip, then maybe they'd go off to the camp to finish what had to be done. They almost had it ready. For instance, though barely summer, they'd decided to stock it with firewood. They had to cut that, then stack it. And there was the news. DiMaggio had another hit last night. Forty-two games. It was unbelievable.

His cereal halfway to his mouth, the telephone rang. His mother took the phone. He didn't know who it was but—it was the way his mother reacted to the call—only that something had happened. She put Walter on the line. It was his father. He told Walter not to worry, there are search planes out and one of them has seen something on an island. Walter's spoon froze midair, dripping into the bowl, splashing the table. Walter asked, he wanted to know, what kind of plane was it. Arthur McAlister knew his son loved planes, he knew his son wanted to fly in the military, that he would have done anything to fly for his country. But he wore glasses so he couldn't. So Walter asked his dad what kind of plane was it because he knew them all, and Mr McAlister shouted into the phone what difference does it make what kind of airplane it is! and hung up.

But Walter had wanted to know, Is this a Hydro Cub or a Taylor Cub, which are short range, or a Stimson Reliant, which has a longer range and can travel farther out to sea? But his father didn't like planes, so he hung up on him.

Walter felt his mother looking at him, waiting, and he nodded and said uh-huh uh-huh, as if his father were still on the line. And then Walter said into the phone with his most important voice, please keep them informed, and put down the receiver and told his mother in his father's important way something his father might have said. But all Walter wanted to know was, How far out have they gone? just how far gone are Gordy and Ivan?

EZRA

The shape of a faint yellow sou'wester and a boat beneath, silhouetted against the fog. A skiff idling up beside a Sea and Shore Department cutter. Just then a lifeboat pushes aside the fog, and in the strangest of rendezvous its two men stand, and, riding the soft swells, tell the cutter Captain in subdued tones about what Clayt Johnson is finding in the water over Round Rock. The others listen to the first evidence that the pleasure craft *Raven* is down and its missing can no longer be called the missing because they are dead. And that is another matter entirely. The skiff pushes off, and the lifeboat, no goodbyes or goodlucks, and the four men on them head back into the fog. The cutter's Captain lifts his two-way radio as agreed. A moment later the siren put atop the home of Helen Murray that very morning for the Germans begins to sound.

A string of whoops repeats across the water. Without blinking the uninvolved at crowded Mackerel Cove put down their traps and gaffs and look up guardedly at water they cannot see. A drill, they believe, the siren not yet a few hours old. They return to their business, filling the salt baths, washing, drinking their coffee.

A mile offshore, Clayt Johnson reached over the *Hattie B's* side with a gaffing hook.

"Ezra."

The boy was at the wheel where he'd told him to go and stay. Clayt called to him as though to tell him the time of day. It was six, Monday morning.

"Pa," Ezra said.

"Come here, boy."

83

"The wheel, Pa."

"Leave the wheel. We aren't going anywhere. Come here."

His father was leaning over the side like he was being sick. Ezra stepped back, eyeing the wheel which shifted just a little left and right, commanding it to be still. Finally Ezra stepped at Clayt and stood behind him.

"You've got to learn this now, boy," Clayt said.

"Yes, Pa." Ezra still peered behind him angrily, ordering the wheel not to spin and ruin everything.

"Come down beside me and take it from me," Clayt said.

"Yes, Pa." Ezra knelt still looking back, coming beside his father and blindly reaching for the worn handle of the gaff. His father straightened and stepped for the wheel. Alone on his knees, happy now that the wheel was again manned, Ezra took a look at the catch. His lips parted. The two gray metal eyes peered up at him from the water. The blanched nape of a neck, spiders of hair breaking free of the bun, twirling on the surface. He leaned closer, and saw now the arms and legs suspending limply, the hands faintly blue, bloated, one stocking foot shoeless, a glimpse of pruning cheek. The dress rode over the girl's narrow hips, the strange female V, pink thigh, a shredded corset.

He quickly reminded himself that he'd seen this before—not this, perhaps, a girl specifically; a girl and her mysteries—but that he'd been prepared for death. It was long ago already—weeks, a lifetime—that they'd gone and gotten Mr Lehman's body off Pond Island. And they'd sliced it apart first. What was inside had been no shock. He'd helped tie the bricks. He'd had the dead weight of Mr Lehman's head in his hands and he'd helped his father and Jesse lift him over the gunwale.

He felt the cold mist on his eyes. He blinked them, blinked them again, then turned them on his father.

Clayt peered ahead and to the left and right, leading a definite course, all of it without any sign of distress, as though he was making his daily run along the route of his traps and what they'd come upon instead was routine. All the time Ezra uttered nothing, not a sound. The leaden weight tugged at his hands. The sharp gaff had it in the arm-pit, snared through the flesh like a butcher's hook through a side of beef. Like any other weight, he told himself, like any other weight: a loose barrel, a crate of lobster.

When they entered the chop off Bailey Island Clayt kicked a coil of rope toward him. "Rope it," Clayt said, "or you'll lose it off that gaff before we get in."

"Yes, Pa."

Ezra began making the noose like his father had taught him. That was last month, too, when they were lashing the bricks onto Mr Lehman.

"But don't get your fingers on the body proper," Clayt said.

"Yes, Pa."

"Don't touch it."

"Yes, Pa."

"Can't touch them but with the gaffing hook."

"Yes, Pa."

"Understand me?"

"Yes, Pa."

"Just don't."

"Yes."

"And keep your head up. You tell me if you see that Kraut sub again. We're in this war for good now."

"Yes, Pa."

At Steamboat Wharf in Mackerel Cove, the *Hattie B* was heard long before she was seen, its puttering close then far. No one paid attention. The lobstermen were waiting for the man from the pound to weigh their catch and take out his fat roll of bills and peel them off a few. Some of the wives and the smaller children were doing smaller chores in the fish house. Then the *Hattie B*'s bow split the fog. Chores at the fish house slowed when the fishermen saw that the *Hattie B* had passed its mooring at the head of the cove and bore down on the wharf. Then business stopped altogether when Clayt kept coming. An offended look crossed their eyes. What's he coming in here for?

Clayt stood white-knuckled at the wheel, bearing down on the wharf, his mouth a straight line, his pale unblinking eyes like chips of glass. The boy Ezra was kneeling over the stern with the tow rope tangled in his hands. He was rolling the catch over, hanging arms and legs swinging straight up into the air now like the legs of a table. Water washed off her bloated face, eyes bulged, an aborted gasp, her nose and upper lip already gone. A letter-sweater pulling away from blistered shoulders.

As though on command, the men and women on the jetties and the fish house dock and the weighing raft, and the lobstermen in their coveralls spraying down the blood and chum off their boats and into the little harbor—all straightened and fell silent. Some hats were snatched off heads and pressed over their chests, as though to cover a wound there against contagion, and a few among them quickly made the three-stroke sign of the Cross.

Jesse appeared at the head of the wharf with his own gaffing hook in his hand, as though he'd heard, or been waiting, or half expected it.

"Who is she?"

"Don't know," Clayt said.

"Off the *Raven*." It wasn't a question as much as it was a decision.

"Don't know."

"She wasn't sailing alone," Jesse said.

"I know that," Clayt said grimly.

"She wasn't no sailor."

"Nope."

"And you seen nothing else. It'd be better if you'd seen something else. Wreckage."

"I know that. There wasn't anything."

Jesse leaned down and with a quick snap of his wrist embedded the business end of his gaff into the pit of the other arm. Ezra let go the rope. A clean exchange.

Ezra unloosed the rope and pulled it in, coiling it neatly around his shoulder and elbow. There was a silent crowd building behind Jesse. They all stood looking at her. They looked at her shoes, at her sweater. At her skin.

"Too fresh to have been in the water for long," Clayt said.

"She's off the *Raven*," Jesse said.

Clayt shook his head and looked off, out beyond the mouth of the cove. The fog wasn't as bad as yesterday—there wasn't the blinding glare, just the infinite gray smoke—but it was bad enough. "There's not a goddamn thing out there. No wood, no food, no slicks. Nothing, nothing afloat."

"There's going to be others," Jesse said.

"Put her over on the raft," Clayt said, turning away, tugging on the throttle. The boat drifted from the wharf. "And find Varney."

"You want help, Clayt?"

"Just find that sonofabitch and get his ass down here."

"What about police?" someone yelled.

"I could care a good goddamn. Too late for them anyways."

Within three hours, everyone had tightened against the fog, and the fog's sea. Pilots waited in the cockpits of their grounded planes. Two hundred craft pushed away from public and private docks. Captains and their twelve year old sons. Ten-year-old Herbert Platz walked by a shawl, three times mistaking it for more of the flea-swarmed seaweed and driftwood draped over the darkened rocks below the high tide mark. At that, the Boy Scouts set out for the shoreline.

But it was only Clayt Johnson and his nine-year-old boy who kept going out and finding human backs bobbing like barrels, coming on them in a straight line as though they'd been dropped over to mark them a trail. It was easy catching. Like the year before when Bailey Island needed the money for the bridge and they had the tournament for the sportsmen and the Governor and the State Assemblymen, and Clayt got the Governor, and the tuna practically threw themselves up on the deck. Each time they returned now, the boy was leaning back to counter the tug of the two or three ropes in his hands, as though it was the sea itself that he was tethered to, chained to it like a slave. His father picked the *Hattie B*'s way through the cove, craning his neck over three or four more piled on the bow, the corpses waving and kicking stiffly at the air, compromising their bodies as they wouldn't have been capable of doing even in the privacy of their tubs and before their own mirrors, before even their doctors. As they would have thought no one was capable of doing.

And the cars kept coming, filing across the little bridges from Great Island to Orr's, then the brand new one to Bailey, five hundred an hour from Portland, from Boston: reporters and politicians and photographers and two policemen from

Brunswick to keep everyone back off the wharf's edge. Though the only traffic out of Rehoboth was the steady parade of logs and sludge riding the Androscoggin River to the Kennebec. Just that and the single black ambulance.

Clayt kept coming back with his bow full, a third time, a fourth time muttering, nearly singing: "Goddamn, goddamn, it's enough." And the boy, Ezra, his hands holding on to the two or three tethers at once, his expression precisely like his father's, remote, lips sealed, eyes resolved. Unconsciously calculating and measuring with his eyes to match his posture with his father's, increasing in his own eyes the resolution of his father's excruciating exactness, the dimensions of his perfection, the vastness yet he had to travel.

Again Jesse Johnson and the new preacher Sinnett rowed up to the raft to meet Clayt. And stiff, frozen, bent at the waist, they piled up the new bodies in front of the big scale as if waiting to weigh them, not lining them up one one one one as you'd expect, just laying one atop the other like cord wood.

The urgency in the hunt diminished, though the perseverance grew. The numbers grew and the pace of activity became a thick and steady march. As though it was the certainty of death or life that everyone was after—whichever it was it would be a kind of relief.

A fifth time Clayt and Ezra Johnson went out. This time Clayt shimmied up the tower toward the crow's nest. The seas were three foot and better. Ezra swayed below on the rolling deck, looking at the small gray face peering at him from far above. Clayt beckoned to him. There was no hesitation. Each of the slick holds up the ladder was another small forfeiture of his control. The distance to the bottom grew longer, the rocking of the pole to which he clung more wild, the brown sea around him more and more vast. Halfway and there was no going back, up as good as down. Suspended over the water, swinging back and forth, it crossed Ezra's mind merely to open the one hand fastening him to the pole and leap, to flail mid-air and be snatched—he assured himself he would be caught—as his father one night had once caught him; hoisted him, the boy, from his bed, and wrapped him in a blanket to transport him across the impossible heights of the outside: night and cold and empty outside; a moon; and at once there was nothing below and only the moon widening and contracting like a pupil, his blanket unravelling about him; again rising and landing onto musky terra firma, the iron beams, the sandpaper chin, the pillowed lips pressing once on each eye, the blanket pouring off his back. The impossible laughter, the gargantuan, monstrous bellowing—

"Goddamn—!" his father, distracted, suddenly remembered his son: "Put your foot in there and swing out around!" His hand shot out of the crow's nest, waiting. The boat rolled to its side. Ezra's foot slid out of the hold and he dangled, bicycling his legs over the water. Clayt barked at him. Ezra kicked and reached and stepped exactly how his father had said and without hesitation swung himself out over the deck. Down came the familiar grip, the fingers closing painfully around his arm. Ezra rose jerkily, his arms flailing, his face turned aside, his own father half bold about it, half embarrassed.

Ezra followed his father's gaze: the barrel bobbing in the swells.

When they came back this time they had just the one, lashed not to the bow but to the afterdeck. Its left hand slipping out of the canvas that strapped him: clawed, blue, blistered from the cold, a man's body, the last and fifteenth recovered that day.

Clayt didn't throw off the canvas like Ezra expected. He bent as though making to untie it, but it already was untied; Ezra had pulled the knot at Clayt's command halfway down the throat of cove. His father's fingers struggled with something else, and only Ezra, with his back to the open water, could see what it was: a small keg two-foot long, stenciled: *Captain Floyd Johnson, Bailey Island, Maine.* It had been lashed to the body with a knot Ezra hadn't ever seen. Clayt muttered under his breath, and Ezra bent to listen. "Goddamn Johnson, goddamn his knot," his father hissed, then, sensing Ezra's eyes, froze and looked up, not at Ezra but just to the side of him—

"Shut up, boy," Clayt said.

Ezra backed off. "I didn't say nothing, Pa."

The knife glinted and the keg fell away cleanly. Clayt kicked it out of sight into the stern of the boat. Holding the canvas in his fingers, he turned to Ezra.

"This isn't what it looks like, boy. And if you can't say what something is, you can't say nothing. So say nothing about it. To anyone. Never."

Then he yanked off the canvas and Floyd Johnson lay stripped to his socks and underwear, and frozen in a piece, the whole thing—by then he was hardly man—shifting like a board beneath the canvas as the fog sea lifted the little boat and put it down again against the wharf.

Ezra saw Floyd's face was different from the others, unastonished but not acquiescent either; the eyes narrow, the blue lips straight, hardened by some unknown consent, some last affirmation. There was no judgment in them.

Though it was already quiet on the wharf the silence dropped another notch at the sight of one of theirs. Clayt pried Floyd Johnson's body off the afterdeck with a plank, and, in spite of the preacher's insistence, maybe provoked by it, rolled it in its socks and underwear right onto the pile of women, leaving it atop them, sprawled in a lewd pose, like a man resting against an unsprung hayrick. Then he shoved at the raft with the plank, pushing the *Hattie B* off, and announced: "There'll be no more today."

Before the boat swung around Ezra caught sight of the truck rolling down the hill to the wharf. In the driver's window Earl Varney's head turned and faced the raft. Varney caught the boy's gaze and held it. The boy remembered the venom in Varney's face yesterday at the general store, but now he saw nothing there, nothing he could call horror or surprise or even acknowledgement, as though Varney looking at a cove and a pile of people off a boat he half-owned, one of them his best friend and partner, was just a fact among other facts.

Then the *Hattie B* turned and Ezra and his father reentered the fog, idling away toward the mooring at the cove's mouth.

Rain popped against the empty canvas. Then there was only the water left, lapping softly against the wood and the boats in the cove. The utter silence fell like a loud explosion. The startled reporters looked up from their notebooks. All eyes pointed at the tangle of bodies. Heads and limbs twisted without loyalty to front or back. More exposure of female anatomy than many of the younger island men had ever seen, and some of the older ones, even some of the married. Then everyone lifted their eyes toward the open water they could not see. Then down at the raft. Then up into the fog again. Two or three called out from the wharf toward the *Hattie B* but the boat had already faded, and neither Clayt nor the boy were answering anyone, not the reporter who called out that he was from the *Boston Globe,* not the motherwife. The mob began to murmur to itself. Some looked down on the naked dead man reclining on the women. The others started mouthing the same four words: "fluke," "Germans," "kidnapping," "miracle." The murmuring crescendoed to a general uproar, arms lifting and fingers pointing out of the throng like sighted rifles, voices crying out to the daughters and wives lying on the raft, "My god my god," "Lord have mercy"—as though until that instant the tangle of corpses on the raft were but poses, a feigned slaughter. Now they were fourteen girls and women in immaculate white sweaters and camisoles, nearly cherubic, chaste and at the same time erotically half-nude—as though they'd all been at the same lawn party, and, upon hearing behind them the clamor of a drunk doing a striptease atop a table, glanced over their shoulders and, like Lot's new wives, turned to pillars of salt, then dissolved with the drunk, drunk themselves, in a heap. As though, perhaps, in some way they deserved it.

At that moment something got figured out by the crowd all at once. The bewilderment turned to rage. The women aimed all the children away. The photographers looked ready to stampede. Jesse Johnson hopped out of his dory and put himself between the pile of bodies and the wharf. He held off the photographers with his eyes while feeling in the dory for his gaffing hook. Then, in a single fluid motion, he whirled and snared Floyd Johnson's stiff corpse, the arms and legs hanging midair, and tugged it down off the pile of women to the raft's edge, facing it the other way. He stepped into the dory and he and Sinnett rowed off.

The reporters lunged for the telephone. Up and down the wharf, people had begun to cry. A woman, gone faint, fell to her knees. The photographers stormed the railing and took aim like a starved infantry picking off fish from a bridge.

McALISTER

By noon, the line outside the *Rehoboth Falls Times* had snaked around the corner. When the newsboys filed out and began glumly handing over the *Extra*'s, the townspeople fell silent and stepped uneasily from side to side, as though sensing rain. Then they scattered, stopping to read in the middle of Congress Street one name and then the other, *Ruth Hemingway, Bessie Strople*. The crowds dispersed and reconvened farther down Congress Street like flocks of birds, crossing and settling, moving along and settling again before Jack Kersey's Jewelry, then the adjoining Dorcas Shand Kersey Millinery Shoppe, whose curtains were closed and doors locked mid-morning on a weekday. Little speeches were given there about Jack and his wife Dorcas, whose story the newspaper had instantaneously made legend: Dorcas had decided against the outing, she'd thought the water had been fouled by the submarine disaster and the debris from the upland flood. But Beatrice Roach came in to try on a hat and to say she was going with Harry Hutchins and wanted to look nice, and Dorcas went next door to tell her husband that she wanted to go after all. Then Dorcas Kersey's two clerks, two girls, said they did too. And they went like a family, fussing for three days, what to wear, what to wear.

The people at the curb listened to the speeches and snapped their papers, studying their reflections in the darkened windows. It would have been them, they said, If there'd been more room it would have been them. Everyone said it, and everyone said they'd been invited to go. Everyone still alive, all of town, had intended to be on the *Raven*.

At the top of town, beside the Hotel Harris, appeared the illuminated headlights. The Hotel's ornate facade was such that one expected cars of all makes and colors to be turning in the avenue. But there was only the one narrow street and through it drifted only George Cummings' black ambulance. All of Congress Street fell silent as it passed with its curtains drawn. George Cummings refused to look anywhere but over his big knuckles, giving nothing away. The townspeople abandoned the doorways and the sidewalks and followed the ambulance up the hill. At the hospital George Cummings swung aside the ambulance door and pulled out a girl still in her white party dress. Her feet were bare. Her spectacles still hung from her neck. Her eyes were open and staring, her mouth open too, lips just parted, as though mid-breath. Her hair was threaded laurel-like with seaweed. In the corners of her eyes there were grains of sand. There was sand in her mouth. One ear had been nibbled away. Though marred, and a little blue, she looked more asleep than dead, caught in a daydream lying in a meadow, staring up at the sky.

The doorways along Congress Street refilled, the portico of the Rehoboth Falls Trust swarmed with the families of the missing. The Trust had shut because half its secretarial staff was being hauled out of the Atlantic by lobstermen, and its President, Arthur McAlister, was down at Bailey Island keeping count. He found out by chance that finally the lobstermen had found the corpse of a man. But it wasn't Rehoboth's. It was Bailey Island's, the *Raven*'s skipper, and no one from the island phoned Rehoboth to tell them. None of the lobstermen were talking about it. And McAlister wasn't asking. Back in town, he merely alluded to the fact of the captain's retrieval. To Rehoboth, the Bailey Island skipper hardly seemed to matter.

Tuesday, George Cummings made three more trips *(Elizabeth Howard, Edith Coburn, Mary Chapitas),* the pall hovering over the ambulance, trailing it into town like a flock of gulls, contaminating the stench from the mill, pulling it down about the town in thick clouds.

Wednesday morning at ten, again George gassed up the black ambulance for the long drive back and forth, back and forth. Tired already of people dogging him and waving for him to stop to get a look-see inside, he took the back way, by the mill, by St Athanasius Universalist. He passed Mrs Roach heading for the Church alone, her shoulders shuddering, her lips quivering, news of Beatrice, her only child, had finally come. George thought about stopping and offering her a ride, but he'd never had live passengers, and he'd just carried her daughter to the hospital that morning. It wouldn't be right. That was what he told himself, though in fact he wouldn't have been able to speak to her had he opened his mouth and tried. He couldn't talk to the town, to the living in it, he'd cut himself off. How else to look on and handle women he'd first seen as little girls skipping across the street, then as young ladies graduating high school, then as women beginning to make their way in the world, now green corpses hanging off fishermen's gaffs, bloating like fish on the wharf at Bailey Island?

Mrs Roach watched the ambulance follow the river then slip into the trees, then slipped herself through the seam between the big wooden doors. In her hands her daughter's postcard. It had beaten the news by minutes: *Feeling fine, not seasick, but there are still many miles to go.*

Two hours later, a crowd of men, some just beginning their mill shift and others just ending it, gathered outside the Church's doors. From the road the Church looked diseased, scaly, malnourished. It had been built with stones from the Androscoggin River, which were oblong and dark, but there hadn't been enough to make one big steeple so they made two little ones instead, small triangles like floppy ears. The Church stood between Sutherland Park and the mill, so all the millworkers heading to or returning from their shifts passed it; and on occasion, when a baby had been born or a parent died, someone made Father Lefebvre grateful and entered it. Now the millworkers craned their necks to read what was on the doors. Father Lefebvre had used a stepladder to tack Monday's Papal Declaration beyond the reach of even Napoleon Ouellette, the tallest man in town.

"Read it to me, Farnum," Harry Eustis said. A few others in the throng called out their approval.

"Read it yourselves," Farnum said, knowing they couldn't.

From the back of the crowd Napoleon Ouellette hollered it out word by word: *"To trust in God means that God can permit here and below the pre-pre-"*

"Predominance," Farnum muttered,

"*—of athee-...*"

Farnum: "*Atheism. Atheism and impiety.*"

"*La-lam—*"

"Lamentable!"

"*Lamentable ob-obscuring of the sense of justice, isolation of law, tormenting of the innocent, peaceful, undefended and helpless. God at times thus lets trials befall in-in-...*"

"Individuals."

"*—and peoples, trials of which the m-mal-...*"

Farnum couldn't stand it any longer. He got it over with in one breath: "*—trials of which the malice of men is the instrument in a design of justice directed toward the punishment of sin, toward purifying persons!* The biggest bunch of hooey I ever heard."

A rushed scrawl darkened the bottom of the Declaration. "What's that say?" someone said.

"It says: 'He who blames another will never know his own guilt. Bear down, friends. This too shall pass.'"

"Bear down my ass," Harry Eustis said. "Easy for Lefebvre to say. He aint lost at sea."

"We're all lost at sea," Father Lefebvre said. He'd come and stood by the side of the crowd. The men exchanged remarks.

"Now, Father," Eustis said, "I know Alban Beauchamp, and I know he can't swim a lick."

"But Junior Carey can swim from here to France," Father Lefebvre said, "and he isn't back either. So all that is left for us is to pray that the rest are safe and will be found soon."

"But the tides are bringing them in one after the other," Farnum said. "That fisherman in the paper said he don't think there's anyone alive."

"Yes," Father Lefebvre said, "And he also said he's been through hell, fire and brimstone, and he's stood it and can stand it a little longer. Fishing people face the sea every day of their lives. We must be as brave as they are."

"But fourteen bodies and only women, Father!" someone said. "It's too much!"

Father Lefebvre averted his eyes.

"And they were all blacked up, burnt to a crisp," someone

said.

"That boat tipped," another said.

"They was burnt. They exploded," said the first.

"They wasn't burnt," said the second, "I been on that boat and I tell you she just didn't feel right. She was a top-heavy tub."

"What boat? You told me you never even seen the ocean."

"I seen pictures."

"It's the damn Krauts!" Harry Eustis said. "They had a time with those poor gals, then burned them up like they was steaks and threw them in the ocean."

A frenzied look crossed all their eyes. They let off a battle cry. Fists shot up, some holding dinner pails in the air like flags. Then they caught each other's looks, turned away and shut up.

"Let me ask you boys something." It was Arthur McAlister. He was standing at the back. "Any of you heard of two boys named Mundt?"

No one said anything. "Okay, that's fine," McAlister said, "probably nothing," and turned to leave.

"What about them, Mr McAlister?"

"Yeah, McAlister, who were they?"

"We don't know," McAlister said. "Frances Beauchamp gave me Gordon's final passenger list and their names were on it. That's all we know."

"I know what they are!" Harry Eustis cried. "You're just not saying it, McAlister." He turned to the others: "The Feds been picking up Kraut spies heading like hell for Canada and Cuba and whatnot. That's who these so-called Mundts are— Krauts, spies! They hijacked that boat and met up with one of their Kraut subs and had their time with the women and threw them in the water and took the men and boys with them back to Germany!"

Arthur McAlister turned purple from the neck up. He faced off with Harry Eustis, but he was a head shorter, so he craned his neck. Aiming his arm like he was pointing out an airplane, he pressed his forefinger into Eustis's chest: "Goddamn it, Eustis, can you just for once in your empty-headed, godforsaken life shut yourself up! We don't know anything like that, anything at all. Those two boys could have been little Ivan Beauchamp's friends. They could have been the captain's sons. Goddamn it they could have been Franklin Roosevelt's nephews! Those fishermen down there know more about what they're doing and saying than anybody I've ever seen. And one thing they know is how to keep their mouths shut when they don't know something for sure. Don't you have anything better to do than get everybody worked up over your trash?"

Harry Eustis reddened, his chest swelled. But Arthur McAlister's finger pressed harder. Eustis's chest caved, his eyes went dark.

McAlister turned to the others and punctuated what he said with his finger: "You all keep that to yourselves now, you hear? I order it. You'll do nothing but torment the families who have people on that boat. And anyone who does open his mouth about this will just have to take his money and his loan applications to Lewiston."

No one said a thing. Sobs came from behind the Church doors.

McAlister shot a look at Father Lefebvre. "Mrs Roach," the priest said.

"But did they reach Monhegan?" Gus Farnum asked, quietly. "They were heading for Monhegan."

McAlister kept his eyes on Father Lefebvre.

"Arthur—you're a good man, Arthur. Just tell us did they reach Monhegan Island?" Farnum asked.

McAlister dropped his gaze. "I don't know. No one does. No one on Monhegan says they saw them, but a man sardining says he saw it headed there, or at least some boat with people atop it. But it's the ocean. There's bound to be boats on it."

"But it was foggy!" someone called out.

"Yes, they say it was foggy," McAlister said.

"How many boats would have been out there in a fog? Had to be them."

"There was storms!" another called out.

"I didn't hear about—" McAlister said.

"Lightning on the water," said the first.

"I heard it was clear sunshine," said the second.

"It was a weathery day all right," said the first. "They had no business being on the water."

"What was it, McAlister?" someone called out.

"It's not clear what the weather was," McAlister said. "It depends where the boat was at the time of the—" he shook his head.

"Fog would be good cover for a sub, wouldn't it," someone whispered to another. But there'd been a lull. Everyone heard it. McAlister searched the crowd for the culprit. Just then a young man with wild eyes breathlessly flailed toward him. He was the same one who'd canoed over to the crowd watching Sally Gammon hanging from the cherry tree two months before, and he spurted this news the same way he spurted the news of big water bringing the Gilead cemetery downriver: "They found the *Raven* with five bodies in it!"

"What bodies?" McAlister said.

"The radio didn't give up no names," the messenger said, "Just five's all I know. They said they were men!"

The throng turned on their heels and stampeded into town. McAlister headed with them but quickly fell behind, limping along in his shiny shoes, the tail of his suit jacket flapping.

Stopping to pick his hat off the road, he looked up at the retreating men. He looked down the street. On the sidewalks were a half-dozen clumps of people, their faces turned his way. Up and down the street, dust whirlpooled into narrow cyclones, weaving drunkenly between the buildings. A child cried out, then was hushed. He looked up the hill toward the hospital and took a step then stopped. He took another step and found himself stopped again.

He felt his way backward with his hand, as though suddenly blind, and lowered into a park bench and he sat, throwing a worried glance over his shoulder, afraid the crowds might rush him. His head in his hands, he peered through his fingers at the grass; a line of ants passed under his shoe, in one side and out the other, impaling it. He felt a sob rise in his throat and subdued it with the back of his hand. What did he do with the picture, the picture of the boat? He patted his pockets, felt it there in his jacket, and stood. He walked more slowly now, not quite right, as though he'd just woken, or he shouldn't have woken at all.

MAVIS

Walter and Mavis had heard it all from behind the legs of Napoleon Ouellette. Standing together now before the Church, they stared blankly at the big wooden doors, listening to Mrs Roach sobbing Beatrice's name over and over. Mavis had heard that kind of news on the radio three different times already, three separate sightings of boats called the *Raven*. One sighting was off the coast of North Carolina, eight men with one woman, all nude, all suicides. One sighting had no bodies but it had sardines. And one other sighting with nine women and one man who'd had his way with every one of them. But it turned out to be from a boy watching traffic on the Mississippi off the bank of a small town in Missouri.

They walked up to the Papal Declaration and Mavis reread it to Walter. What sin? she wondered, What have Poppy and Gordy and Ivan done now? "Walter, Ivan doesn't have any friends named Mud," she said.

"Mundt," Walter said.

"Them."

"They'll find your father," Walter said.

Mavis didn't even blink. "No they won't."

The black ambulance passed behind them, its curtains drawn. They followed it with their eyes as it slowly climbed toward the hospital. Walter took Mavis's hand, and unemotionally, even neutrally, they plodded together up the hill.

Inside the hospital, the sour smell of the mill was gone, chased off by the reek of heat-drawn humansmell, and wafts of other things when someone churned up the air with a hand or turn of the head: disinfectant, and something else under it all, something not immediately identifiable.

The nurses and reporters and spectators stood motionless as

99

Mavis and Walter passed. The men tipped their hats. Mavis thought she saw one woman bob and curtsy. She'd been there only once before, two years ago when her father had had his appendix out. She'd been swept aside by doctors, chided by nurses when she ventured to the bathroom by herself. The hospital had smelled purely of antiseptic then. Now, though, the adults flattened against the sticky wall to give her and Arthur McAlister's son room. Her mouth turned up at the corners, Mavis walked down the aisle with Walter. They were a mismatched, ill-fated bride and groom. She had been jilted by his very showing up, condemned by her guests' silence to pass her remaining days burdened by a grief so insurmountable that she now walked before them enclosed by an incandescent shroud, crowned with a martyr's halo. The women among the crowds covered their mouths and looked upon the girl neither in pity nor in sorrow, but with a kind of homage. Walter, that young patriotic boy, was but her shadow.

"Mavis," Walter said.

She peered up at him, impossibly tall.

"I'm sorry," he said.

"Okay—" almost cheerfully.

"My father said the boat was bad."

Mavis gazed down the hall.

"I didn't go because my father said he knew the boat wasn't a good boat. My father saw the picture of it."

Mavis nodded and walked out from under his hand.

The musk thickened as they approached the end of the hall. The dimness against the far wall was broken by light pouring out through an open door. Mavis's mother was there, and Mrs Caruso. After the flood waters receded and her husband hadn't surfaced, the little Italian woman sliced off her long braids and gave away her wardrobe. In these last two months her new black dresses and black shawls and black shoes had made of her a Rehoboth landmark, a human beacon as visible as the yellow of a fire hydrant, emblematic of caution and punishment.

Thinking her mother Mrs Caruso's protégé, Mavis locked eyes with her in a kind of mutual rejection. The girl, past obedience, even deference, knew her mother had been holding against her this separation from her husband and sons for these three days. From Mr McAlister's first phone call early Monday morning she'd made it out to everyone that she almost did go on the *Raven*, that she would have gone if it weren't for Mavis, that she would have preferred it (Mavis overheard her saying) even now, after everything, she would prefer it. She'd sobbed and sobbed, but forbade Mavis to so much as utter a sound. Now, in the hospital hallway, the girl thought her mother wore her grief before the others like a banner.

Frances glared once at Walter for bringing Mavis here. Then she softened, fluttered her eyes, and lay her head on Mrs Caruso's shoulder. From four feet away, though, Lydia Carey, Junior's mother, began to sneer. Frances straightened and smiled stiffly.

"I'm sorry, Lydia," Frances Beauchamp said.

"So am I," Lydia Carey said. "My Junior's a good boy, I raised him good and polite, so he'd never say no to people. Your Gordy asked him to go, but he didn't want to. I tell him to say it, not to go if he don't want to, but he wouldn't insult Gordy or Mr Beauchamp." Lydia Carey's arm rose parallel to the floor and pointed into the room. "And now look," she said.

Mavis did: there lay Anne Stisulis in her pink dress, her pure metal eyes locked on the ceiling, her nostrils and fingertips green and frayed. Lydia Carey stabbed the air. "Just look at this, just look at this!" she shrieked. Mavis kept looking. A nurse ushered Mrs Carey away, her sobs faded down the hall.

"But they don't all have to be dead!" Frances Beauchamp called after her. "I have a husband and two boys out there, I have three!" Then she started to lay her head down on Mrs Caruso's shoulder. But Mrs Caruso was cradling her face as though she was about to scream. Trembling, her black dress shivering, she gawked at something down the hallway, over the children's heads, past the nurses and reporters, through the wall. Everyone fell silent and turned to look: nothing but damp, agitated people and the greasy cinderblock walls. But Mavis saw it: the empty two feet of muddy ground where Mr Caruso had stood, and before it the river that had swallowed him like a rain drop.

She walked up to Mrs Caruso and touched her hands, then

hugged her around the waist. Pressed against Mrs Caruso, she looked into the room at the corpse. A foul wind broke over her. She'd heard Gordy talk a lot about Anne Stisulis. She didn't think this was what he meant.

Joan Carrier, the head nurse, parted the onlookers, marched into the room and stood over the table. Sweeping her eyes over the full length of Anne Stisulis, she said, "I want her examined properly."

The news spread rapidly through the hallway. No one had yet said out loud what a few had considered in passing when Bessie Strople turned up third, what struck the whole town at once when the fourth body turned out to be a woman, too, and then a woman fifth, and then sixth. And now here lay young Anne Stisulis. Thirty-six had gone out on that boat, twenty-two of them men, and only the women were coming back. No one asked Arthur McAlister what he'd seen when he lifted the skirts and privately certified the undergarments whole save the punctures where the lobstermen had to hook on with their gaffs. Publicly, he'd merely said it would be best to expedite the bodies as quickly as possible. The women had drowned, or froze before they could, that was obvious. Get them in the ground, he'd ordered George Cummings. And intact, he'd insisted, the bodies should be buried intact. There hadn't been a murmur of dissent.

Frances Beauchamp filled the doorway and said defiantly, almost mockingly, "And just what are you saying, Joan? Anne was a *Christian* girl."

The nurse cut and peeled aside the top half of the sodden dress, and suddenly before Frances Beauchamp lay the young, partially nude girl Gordy had been after, her young breasts inflated gently atop her ribs. Her eyes fled toward the window, as though she'd not merely seen Anne Stisulis but walked in on the girl entwined with her son. She blinked at the sunlight, she'd actually envisioned them, first in her son's small bed in their house, and then in a death grip under the water. "What are you saying!" she cried, "That my boy is a monster? You want people to think something happened to those girls? She's just drowned, it's plain as day!"

"This is real terrible, Mrs Beauchamp," the nurse said, "But

I just want it finished properly."

Arthur McAlister arrived at the door panting like a man who'd just missed his train, the front of his shirt dark with sweat, his tie undone. He opened his mouth to speak, but saw the corpse stretched before him and shut it. Drool dripped from his chin to the floor.

A voice called out from the hallway: "Was it men they found out there, Arthur? Heard they found the boat with some men on it."

"No boat," McAlister said, grimly, "And no men yet. Just two more of the girls."

The reek poured unabated out of the operating room. Those in the hallway who had handkerchiefs put them to their faces. They began to rumble like a vigilante mob. Some filled the doorway to the operating room, jostling each other to get their turn at forcing from the dead girl a confession that what was happening to them was no pointless accident, no ordinary misfortune. No one, not even a nurse or doctor, asked McAlister who the last two bodies were, as though the women no longer numbered fourteen but had smeared into a single, faceless femaleness, each of the women merely one-fourteenth of a single reprehensible act, an ambush by female complicity made not in cooperation with the *Raven*'s men but against them, against all of malehood.

"It would be better to leave all's well alone," Frances Beauchamp said to McAlister, softly, smugly, as though she knew well enough she spoke for the silent mass standing behind her. McAlister patted his sweating forehead.

The nurse didn't even look up from the body: "All's not well, Mr McAlister. There are laws."

A doctor pushed by McAlister and removed scalpels and scissors from a drawer.

"All right," Frances Beauchamp said, and closed the door on the others. "If you must. But I'm staying right here." She stood beside McAlister, her feet splayed as though barring the door. Behind her back, though, her hands nervously fingered the greasy wall.

The doctor and Nurse Carrier finished undressing the corpse

and turned it on its side. Arthur McAlister kept his eyes on his shoes. But Frances Beauchamp watched cautiously, scientifically, the doctor part the legs, then heard from far away, as though over a great distance, his declaration of Anne Stisulis's virginity. The scalpel glinted mid-air. Frances Beauchamp heard the spill as though the girl had broken water. An undigested chowder of vegetables and clam slid over the table and spilled onto the floor. The doctor, nurse and McAlister all clasped their mouths and nose and squeezed their eyes. Around Frances Beauchamp the air took on weight, wetness. She smelled the rot and heard the murmur of the sea, perceived the dry heaves rising in her throat, gurgling traces of her own voice—but all of it from a hazy distance. The hard floor rose quickly and slammed her knees. She vaguely understood a dripping table and two sets of green toes. But before her materialized only her husband's cry, "Gordy! Ivan!"—a father's grope in the darkness for his sons; it was as though the sound of Gordon Beauchamp's band-leader's crooning and the flash of his baton through the air had taken on the properties of a young girl's rotting flesh. Before Frances Beauchamp stretched her lifetime of horror and emptiness. She vomited into her hands.

Arthur McAlister helped her up. Looking straight at the girl's innards, a vaguely gratified expression crossed her eyes, as though the sight appeased her: this could not have happened to her boys. "They are still alive," she declared, dabbing her cheeks with the back of her hands. "I'm sure of it."

There was a commotion in the hallway. A fist pounded the door. "Here I am, here I am," McAlister said.

The door cracked open. A boy pushed his head through the opening and craned his neck to see into the room. Arthur McAlister squeezed the door on him. The boy cried out, then backed off. "George Cummings is out front again!" the boy said, rubbing his head. "He says he's got a dead man in the back."

McAlister threw open the door and ran for the hospital entrance. Frances Beauchamp was right behind him, suddenly breathless, worried that she was wrong. She'd had her grand understanding and she didn't want it taken away. So much already taken away. She followed in McAlister's wake as he pushed his way through the crowd to the back of the ambulance and found herself beside Mrs Caruso. The little Italian woman took Frances Beauchamp's arm. "Strong," she said, and clasped tighter, as though demonstrating how to do it: "Strong!"

"I waited for you, Mr McAlister," George Cummings said.

"Yes yes, George, thank you."

"Just like you said, Mr McAlister."

"Who is it, George?"

"It's gonna surprise you. The lobstermen told me they had to sink a dory under it or it would have broken apart like a piece of soggy bread."

"George!"

George Cummings twisted the handle on the ambulance. He'd had his handkerchief ready and clasped it over his mouth and nose and stepped back with the door. The wind shot out of the darkness. Those that didn't scatter clasped both hands over their face and braced forward a little as though against a gale.

"Funny they found it floating around in the rivermouth when they were looking for them others," George Cummings said through his handkerchief, "On the phone that one fisherman, Clayt Johnson, said it was in the water a lot longer than three days, but he didn't know who it was. I asked if it could have been two months and he said it could have darn well been."

George Cummings pulled out the stretcher with an oblong puddle of flesh and hair and rib. The belt Balthasar Caruso had made himself lay kinked in the middle of it like a dead snake. Mrs Caruso crumpled to her knees. Frances Beauchamp heard from her own mouth a single breath of relieved air, as if: that one doesn't belong to me, mine are still alive.

The remaining crowd straggled away as George Cummings talked on. But he saw only what lay on the stretcher.

"They couldn't believe it when I said this was ours, too. They must think we're a bunch of crazy cannibals or something. A bunch of them came round me in a circle asked me what the hell we were doing up here. One of them said he was getting tired of watching Johnson having to pick our people out of the water. I said he doesn't have to, they've got a whole island full of fishermen and now the Coast Guard, too. Then one of them gives me a little shove and says to keep quiet about what I don't know nothing about. They say this Johnson's the only one doing it, they got a dozen boats out there looking but he's the only one coming on them."

When he finished it was only him and Mavis Beauchamp and a hospital orderly standing back by the ambulance. Arthur McAlister had led Mrs Caruso away. Frances Beauchamp was already halfway home.

EZRA

The only one eating was Clayt. Hattie hadn't even bothered to put a plate before her boy but Clayt made him sit there. In the night he could hear cars passing on the road. It hadn't stopped since yesterday morning.

"We should send him inland," Hattie said.

"I need him here."

"I can send him to his aunt's. You can get Jesse to go out with you."

"I need him here for him. Look at him," Clayt said, pointing at Ezra with his knife. "He wants to be here. Don't you boy."

Whether he did or he didn't Ezra didn't know. He was here now and he didn't think there was anywhere else to go. It hadn't struck him to think about leaving. Right now he was thinking only about getting back on the water with his father and picking up more bodies. Not because he wanted to but because he thought he should.

"Besides," Clayt said, "everyone in Maine's going to want to come down here to see this mess. It's a goddamn carnival down there already. You don't think people aren't listening to their radios all over the country over this? He's going to hear about it in Augusta the same as he'd hear about it here, only difference being what he'll hear up there'll be mostly stories and lies. He stays here and he sees it first hand. Beside, your aunt's just going to drag him back here in the back of her car so she can get a look herself."

At the knock on the door Hattie rose automatically, as if she'd expected it. It had been like that since yesterday, one continuous movement, one reaction after another, turning, standing, sitting, running, constant motion between home and the wharf and the store for coffee.

Arthur McAlister stood in the doorway with his hat in his hands.

"Didn't mean to interrupt your supper, Johnson," he said. His hat was shaking, he moved like a newly converted drunk, suit disheveled, shoes caked with mud; his hands moved airily before him, his lips quivering. As though a shell-shocked banker who'd just lost his fortune in the stock market were now making the rounds among neighbors for handouts, money, clothes.

"Come on in, Arthur," Clayt said. "Have dessert with us."

McAlister didn't move.

Clayt turned around. "What."

"Something's been found."

Clayt put down his fork.

"Who."

"Not who," McAlister said. He looked apologetically at Hattie, who took him by the elbow and led him in toward her seat at the table.

"A pickle bottle," McAlister said. "A note was stuffed in. It said *ON ISLAND—JACK.*"

"Jack," Clayt said.

"Jack Kersey," McAlister said. "We had a Jack aboard. And his wife, Dorcas, and their clerks. He was jeweller. Good girls his clerks. Could have been Jack Kersey."

"Sit down, Arthur," Clayt said, stabbing into his meal. "When's the last time you ate?"

McAlister lowered himself into the chair.

"Ezra, take Mr McAlister's hat," Hattie said.

Ezra walked around the table and took the hat and left it on the counter not a foot away and returned to his seat.

"They're rowing out there now," McAlister said.

"Who, Jesse?"

"And some police and that Priest—"

"Jim Sinnett."

"Reverend Sinnett. Yes."

"Now," Clayt said, his mouth full of food. "What was this note written on?"

"I don't know. It was dark when he brought it down. Looked like wrapping paper."

Clayt stopped chewing. He swallowed. "He."

McAlister raised his eyes.

"He who," Clayt said.

"He said his name was Earl Varney."

Clayt and Hattie exchanged looks.

"Earl Varney," Clayt said. "You sure."

"Yes, he said he found the bottle washed up to shore about an hour ago. I wanted to come out here and tell you right away, I thought maybe you'd want to come down and see—"

"Awfully lucky of Earl to have found that bottle."

"I suppose it was—" McAlister said.

"In the dark."

"In the dark, yes, I suppose—"

"Now where did Earl say he found this bottle?"

"Back of Great Island. Somebody's cottage—"

"Leslie Simmons," Clayt said.

"Yes, that's it," McAlister said. "He mentioned the name Leslie Simmons."

Clayt pressed his hands to the table and made as if to rise, but didn't. He watched Arthur McAlister from across the table. "Hattie, get Arthur a cup of coffee, please."

Hattie stepped toward the pot, then stopped and stood behind her husband. She took his shoulders in her hands, and Clayt blinked slowly, his chin dropping slightly, on the verge of peace or even sleep. She gazed for a moment out the window, past the lighted lantern, toward the water, and walked on, for the coffee.

"You know Earl Varney?" McAlister said.

"Which islands?" Clayt said.

McAlister looked confused.

"Where'd Jesse and them go to look?"

"He didn't say a particular one."

"There're ten islands out there, Arthur, fifteen if you count low-tide ledges. There're hundreds more a little farther out. Thousands beyond that."

"Somebody said they'd seen something."

"Somebody."

"Earl Varney, maybe, I don't know, said he thought he saw a light out on one of the islands."

"Earl said that, did he. He found the bottle and seen a light?" Clayt shook his head and made a face that began as a grin but slipped, as though he'd changed his mind. In the end he was grimacing. "Arthur, there's people living out on some of those islands."

"But he said it looked like a signal, some kind of code."

Clayt looked at Ezra.

"Go on down there and wait for them to come back and run back and tell us what they seen," he said.

"Clayt, it's so late," Hattie protested.

"Do you think he'd sleep tonight, Hattie? Go on, boy. I want you back here's soon as they get in."

Ezra stood and went for his coat. He waited by the door. His father pushed back his chair and stood and leaned back against the sink, looking into the middle distance. He didn't seem to mind that Ezra hadn't left; Ezra, coat in hand, waiting by the door.

"It's a hoax, Arthur," Clayt said.

McAlister didn't move, as though he'd half expected it.

"It washed up too quick. For it to land back of Great Island, the tides would have had to keep it a day or two more at least. And off those islands—" Clayt shook his head, "If he'd've tossed it off one of those islands, the chances it would have gotten past those currents is almost nothing. But in one day? That would have been some toss. I'd say old Jack should be playing with the Red Sox."

Without raising his head, McAlister nodded slowly.

"Maybe you should go out there anyway," Hattie gently prodded Clayt.

"We'll need our strength tomorrow," Clayt said to her. "Who knows what we're going to see in the morning. This bottle's part of Varney's little dream."

McAlister looked up.

Clayt held up his hand. "Don't ask, Arthur. Can't prove a damn thing."

"I can't tell you—" McAlister began, angrily, as though he'd seen something there in Clayt's face. "I saw a picture of that boat last week. I knew it was bad news. I could have told them."

"Floyd was a good pilot," Clayt said.

"But it was a terrible boat. You could see it in the picture."

"It was a terrible boat."

McAlister bent his head, as if in prayer, then wiped at his eyes with the back of his hand. "I sent my secretary in my place," he said. "And her boyfriend in my son's."

"Then be thankful you're alive," Clayt said. "From the looks of things, you wouldn't have done anybody any good out there."

"But I sent them," McAlister said. "It didn't have to happen. You don't know." He looked up, trembling.

"I do, Arthur," Clayt said. "I know."

At that moment Ezra saw them all, converged on their dinner table, his brother, those girls, the men they hadn't found, the others yet to come walking and breathing and the living standing behind them, their sponsors in disappearance, bunglers, murderers, mere miscreants; the stalkers and the stalked; those unseen we walk amidst. Not ghosts. Living, alive, the breathing dead.

Clayt looked up toward the door. "Go on, boy," he said.

Ezra opened the door and slipped through. The night on his skin, strands of it running between him and the water. He could hear but he saw only the dome of light hovering over Mackerel Cove, as though the wharf had been ignited. And above, the pinpricks of light wheeling on. It would be dawn soon, then sun-up, and he did not know what he would see. He started down the slope toward the hissing water, the murmuring engines, the mercurial muffled shouts, then lowered his head and ran.

MAVIS

All the rest of that summer, Frances Beauchamp, convinced by friends to take up something, work, anything to occupy her and get her away from Mavis, sat on an assembly line at the mill making gun barrels. At dawn, Mavis lay in bed, wide-eyed, her hands behind her head, staring at the ceiling, following with her eyes the riversystems of cracks, listening for the nothing from Ivan and Gordy on the other side of the wall. She heard only the roar from the mill.

Beneath her a porcelain cup rattled against the sink; the water ran through the walls. A door closed, the window panes shook. Her mother's slow, floating descent down the steps off the front porch. The mill whistle blew.

Mavis leapt from bed and roamed the house. She began at the livingroom window sill. She ran upstairs to sit on Ivan's bed—still made, the sheets changed weekly—then Gordy's; unconsciously reaching in her gown for the anticipated fullness of her new breasts. Tears rising, nostrils flaring, at the last moment she restrained herself, sucked everything down, removed her hand from her nightgown, forbade it, gathered herself and went on. The mill whistle shrieked. Noon. Lunch. Then two. Her mother was due back at quarter past three.

The air settled for sundown, the house again putrid and airless. Mavis at her father's piano propped the book on the music stand and leaned her elbows on the keys. She turned to the window to watch a small boat cross the measly fenced-in yard and disappear into the milky white vapor of the summer day, never to return again. She concentrated on the whiteness, the negation of shape—she saw nothing—of fact. She turned down to the piano and began to play. She sang. The tears rolling off her chin onto her fingers, she sang louder, drowning out her other noises.

One song after another, any song that reminded her of anything, thinking always, It's not me crying, it's not me. It's the music. Her tears beading on the piano keys, her fingers slipping, the more she tried not to think the more she saw. "He's gone!" she cried, "Gone!" And the water opened to receive the little boat, and death in the form of a white figure rose out of the chasm—

Her mother's footfalls on the porch. Mavis's eyes on the clock. Quarter after. She didn't run. She pounded on her father's piano. At the doorway her mother's face drained. Mavis played a bar from her father's repertoire. Her mother collapsed in the chair, staring at the family picture with a stricken expression. But not horror, Mavis thought. Confusion.

Evening fell. She peeked into her mother's room. There on the floor, beside her mother's slippers, were her father's, dusted, aligned, waiting with heels against the wall as though the band leader Gordon Beauchamp were about to step from the shower.

So he was alive.

Now she knew where she was headed, where she'd never been alone and was told never to go without her father, or certainly not without her brothers. But Mavis had known it and seen it. Because it had been forbidden to her so often she'd gone to live there in her dreams. Nothing was left of it, she knew, but the corner piles and the chimney and a flight of stone steps once leading up to a porch and now leading only to a point in space four feet above the ground. The Mount Zircon Hotel's charred beams had been just criss-crossing rows of ashen dirt as long as she'd been alive; even longer.

Once, the Hotel had sat just at the foot of the summit to Mount Zircon, its perch there over Rehoboth and the Androscoggin River a kind of perfection. It was Kate Donner's good luck that the view she owned over the fastest growing paper mill in the world and the valley that fed it its trees was enough to draw people up the logging road for a room. Then the Hotel's perfection became more than just good luck; it became perfect by design, a sister to the Balsams, a grand hotel on the Canadian side of the border with a basement big enough to drive in a small convoy of cars and close the big iron doors behind it; big enough to load the cars in secret and set them off in darkness back across the border.

All the Beauchamp children had known well how those men could drive the notches and almost climb a mountain around a road block, as though they'd done it themselves. Which they had, for two-dozen Saturday afternoons; Ivan and Gordy and Mavis and Walter McAlister had lived out the final run of liquor in a stand of trees, the convoy fishtailing the logging road up Mount Zircon at night, the sheriff down below cutting the Hotel's phone lines, then crawling his way up with fifteen deputized Italian stonecutters. The surprise was absolute, the appearance in the rumrunners' eyes of a sheriff leading a band of short, dark men, not one of whom could speak a word of English; and in the sheriff's eyes how much beyond his imagination the liquor operation had grown on his watch.

Gordy, as sheriff, once took out three of the rumrunners before they'd been able to turn their backs and run, then stuck his head into a clump of thistle, opening the cellar door on four hundred gallons of rum and two tons of mash. Mavis, as Kate Donner, died early on with a stray bullet in her neck and happily lay in the sun-warmed leaves listening to the bees. Then Mavis giggled—the boys would never forgive her—as the dead Italian leapt to life as still another of the dwindling rumrunners. It was near dawn when the shots stopped ringing through the forest. The puddles of blood skinning now, the bodies sprawled, distended, flies piling in and around the filmed, yellow eyes and bullet holes. Holding on as the last Italian alive, little Ivan tied the wrists of the sole surviving rumrunner (whose French-Canadian accent got draped around Walter's neck every Saturday) and marched him down Mount Zircon into town, ending the fight, settling the dust, sending the children their separate ways.

But it wasn't until now that Mavis understood the greater magnitude of her inheritance. From the hallway outside her mother's bedroom, she could hear gunshots ringing out on Mount Zircon again. And she didn't for a second think it was over liquor. The rumrunning had stopped long ago. But something in her awoke at once, something bigger than her brother's empty bedrooms, and her father's empty slippers. Even at nine—maybe especially at nine—she accepted it without struggle or even surprise. As though she'd carried it her whole life without knowing it. As though whatever it was—her brothers and father and uncle rolling dead in the waves—had been merely lent her as all of a woman's past is, recollections that might have been hers or might not have been. Pictures and noises of people who perhaps had never existed at all anywhere, their tales just fluttering down her like layers of leaves, this-year's clear and distinct, and the year's-before worm-eaten and the year's-before-that pure mulch, fertilizer, plain dirt. Tales of dead brothers and dead fathers. Empty slippers against the wall. Had they existed at all?

Her mother was in the shower. Mavis sat up. Anchored to the bed, she watched herself rise and dress and go quietly downstairs and out to the dark. A ground fog hovered just over the lawns of the neighborhood. Down the street the deep woods began. There was a steady and thrashing sound of water. There was a report of gunfire.

Sheets hugged to her chest, from the window she watched herself race the trees across the slope to Mount Zircon. She didn't ask how she knew the name Parmachenee, or why she couldn't come up with one good story explaining how she suddenly recalled it. It was another story, older, earlier, that they could have played, for they all, somehow, knew it: why Gordy did not play Parmachenee himself; why Ivan did not proxy for Benjamin Lufkin; or Mavis for Lufkin's wife Sarah; or why it was not the slave Plato who was forced on Walter. Something was known but avoided, like one of those tales you think is useless right up until the moment it walks up to you and exits your imagination and steps before you real and breathing life.

Running uphill, the trees flew by. The river fell out of earshot. The mud was running beneath her. The trail had turned to a clear creek. Her pant legs were soaked to her knees. The Moon Tide Spring had been stopped up; that much she thought she knew. It once flowed at forty gallons of cold clear water per minute. On full moons the spring ran at sixty, and the Sokokis came down from Aziscohos Lake to drink from the rushing water. They filed up the hill in the moonlight and danced solemnly around it, then kneeled and drank to their eternal health. Then the Massachusetts Commonwealth called the land around the spring New Pennacook and granted a deed to Jonathan Keyes. Keyes gave $400 and one acre to Nathaniel Knapp to build and keep in good repair one good saw mill and one good grist mill, then returned to Boston and printed a thousand papers that read:

Trees as tall as ships' masts! Dam on Azischohos Lake in advanced planning stages, will give 54,000 horse power to Androscoggin River. Three canals planned; heads, 30, 50 and 100 feet. 125 miles of lake storage. Grist mill sites. Farm opportunities. Residence lots 1,200 acres. Abundance of hard and soft wood for manufacture. No low water, no back water, no anchor ice.

What followed was more an Indian retreat than a white advance. The Sokokis went north and stayed there, except Parmachenee and occasionally a few others who returned to drink at the spring with each full moon.

During a November night in 1781, Jonathan Keyes heard from his homestead in the valley a single musket shot from the direction of Mount Zircon. At daylight, he and Nathaniel Knapp trudged up the hill to investigate and found bears pawing at the bodies of Parmachenee, who'd taken the musket round in his chest, Benjamin Lufkin, his wife Sarah, and Plato, all stabbed in the throat with a knife, sprawled in the mud around the spring. Keyes refused to speculate on either the provocations or the order of the deaths. He buried the bodies in one grave with a single wooden cross as a marker, then notified the Commonwealth. Squire Rangeley came up from Boston and had three African slaves fill in the spring's mouth. With their hands they packed the spaces with bricks and mortar, taming the mystery, the demands of information, of romantic Saturday afternoons, of childhoods not begun for another hundred and sixty years.

Mavis neared the ruins. The gunshots were no longer dull thuds echoing off the hill but crisp reports, punctuated by the snapping of triggers. Just below the summit clearing she sprawled in the mud. A bullet whistled through some leaves and thunked into a nearby trunk. Cold clear water ran over the grass of the clearing and under her down the hill. In the clearing up ahead two men stood ankle deep in the flooded grass, firing .22's into the ruins of the Hotel. A third man, a short dark man, had dropped his pistol at his feet and was gesturing at the others, imploring them drunkenly in Italian. It was her Momma's friend, Balthasar J. Caruso; she'd seen his body herself, melted, worm-eaten.

Out of the middle of the ruins blew a geyser the height of a man, spouting steady and blue in the twilight. Sheets of clear water brimmed over the foundation. Three or four black bears prowled back and forth between the men and the geyser, waving their paws and gnashing their teeth at the bullets. Already the bodies of two or three other bears lay in the water, their paws in the air, staring at the sky. Each of the men had a molasses jug at his feet. The Italian's lay on its side, empty.

"Shut the Dago up!" It was her uncle, Alban. Not dead too? He hadn't been found. So he was here. They were all here. Uncle Alban looked at the Italian: "Dago!" he said.

"No Dago," Caruso said, waving at the bears. "No. No Dago."

"Can't shoot him." It was Mr Decker. He was on the boat too.

"Why not?" Uncle Alban said.

"Not the bears. Caruso."

"Why not? He's nothing but a Dago." He closed one eye and squeezed off three quick shots into the ruins. The stone steps sparked twice. After the third shot one of the standing bears staggered and waved its paw. Its teeth were bloody.

"Just give him some more to drink," Mr Decker said.

"Be a good Dago," Uncle Alban said, holding his jug out to Caruso, then the gun. He briefly aimed at the Italian, then turned back to the bears and squeezed off another shot. The leaves behind the ruins snapped. Caruso stopped talking. His arms hung at his sides. His eyes were averted toward the forest. Uncle Alban turned toward him and screamed at him to shut up, then put his jug to his lips.

"He already did," Mr Decker said.

"What?"

"Caruso. He's shut up."

"I tell you these bears is all Parmachaw's ghosts," Uncle Alban said. "Italians don't know nothing about Indians." He sighted

117

the barrel of his pistol at Caruso again. Caruso's eyes shifted toward him but didn't change expression. Then Uncle Alban laughed and whirled and stooped and fired like a cowboy at the bears. He laughed again, once, dryly. "Parmachickasaw. I tell you they're all damned Indian ghosts, every one of them."

"They're not ghosts, just bears," Mr Decker said, taking a last, reluctant shot. The bullet hit far into the forest.

Then Uncle Alban fired and the bullet thunked into the belly of one of the downed bears. "These guns're too light for them," he said.

"That one's already dead, Alban."

"Can't be sure," Alban said. "Ghosts don't die easy."

Now it was just Alban firing at the bears. He emptied his chamber into one of the bears. The bear fell over and lay still in the water.

Alban shook the empty shells out of his pistol and rooted in his pocket for more, his lips stumbling: "Parmasickanee." He held his pistol shakily toward the ruins and fired. The bullets snapped into the trees. He turned toward the others but forgot to lower the gun. Mr Decker dove for the ground. Caruso didn't move. The gun barrel swept over their heads as though anointing them.

"Christsake, Alban," Mr Decker said.

It was hard to see from where Mavis lay. Up ahead the two live bears moved easily in the dusk. The sky was fluid, dark above, then gold touching the trees, then brass between and through them. The three men were shadows set in relief against the clearing. The column of water stood behind them in the shadows of the ruins, and then the greater darkness of the woods behind that. One of the bears stepped out over the rim of the ruins and waved its paws. Uncle Alban turned and a breath of flame leapt out of his pistol, then the report, a mere pop against the rustling of the forest. The bear kept coming and Uncle Alban emptied the whole chamber into the bear, flames and sparks panting out of the barrel. Uncle Alban looked drunk and crazy. Then the flames stopped and there was only the trigger and hammer snapping. They all heard the bear fall over before they saw it, then they could make it out lying motionless on its side, its eyes glinting once, rolling up, then going dark. Behind it the last bear splashed through the water.

The moonshadows of the three men swinging their jugs stretched before them. The musty liquor breath lingered in the trees. When they'd gone, Mavis stood and peered into the clearing. The humps of the dead bears rose out of the water like shoals. The last one stood still ankle deep surrounded by the black humps, snout in the air, arms at its side, shoulders and head bathed in the cool moonlight. Mavis took a step forward but someone held her by the shoulder and pulled her back. Then Mavis turned back down the trail. She stopped and someone gave her a little shove onward. She stopped and she got shoved again.

"Don't even look at it. And don't tell nobody." It was Gordy's voice. She could hear it as sure as she was standing there. "If you tell it, it won't stay true."

1952

DOVE

A small, spectacled man, his collar and cuffs unbuttoned, an overcoat thrown over his shoulders, sat behind the wheel of his car at the end of the jetty, peering over his knuckles toward the beach as though hiding from what was there. Through a break in the granite sea-wall, he was watching a crowd, large, dense, overcoated, drawn in a semi-circle at the water's edge. How does he do it? he wondered, This early in the morning pulling hard-working people from their beds? Getting me out of bed.

His little eyes struggled in the early sunlight, his pudgy, over-burdened legs pumping on the sand, craving asphalt. He worked his way unsteadily down.

There was strangely little of anything in the air: shouting, even a murmur. The tide was down, the water percolated softly against the sea wall. There was a mood of quiet solemnity about the crowd, as though a congregation circled around its pastor, last rites given there to some stranger or friend.

The editor made an end-around at the prong of the crowd, and there—how could he possibly be surprised?—was Leslie Everett Dove, sweating and breathing hard standing still, twitching his head in this and that direction as though he wanted to bolt, looking for a way out. But that wasn't what Dove was looking for, and when Dove saw heads turning he wheeled around and grabbed the editor's arm and smiled maniacally, then pulled him closer.

At the crowd's feet lay the partially decomposed remains of an enormous creature, a massive, elongated skull, high tubular ribs blooming out of the sand like the half-completed infrastructure of a large boat. Sea-weed and patches of dark, leathery skin clung here and there to the bleached bone. The space inside gave the impression of a creature of huge volume. Hash marks had been drawn in the sand along its length and width, big numbers traced by foot, forty feet by ten. Arrows pointed up the beach and down it, a crude map of some archipelago with more arrows showing, apparently, the direction of currents or tides, or were those migratory patterns? Apparently Dove had just completed his morning lecture on where this creature had come from. Maybe Atlantis. Or someplace as yet unknown.

"It's a sea serpent, Mike," Dove said in a whisper. "This little boy found it this morning when he came out to skip stones before school." Dove reached out with his enormous arms and produced some feverishly grinning child, then pushed him away. Dove spoke quickly: "Forty feet long, ten feet in diameter, it once had fins six feet and longer, you can tell that by the expansion of these bones here that look like wings." Pointing with his foot, he looked up: "Where's Sammy. You brought Sammy with you."

The editor thrust his hands deep in his pockets, as though suddenly cold.

"You didn't bring anyone to take photographs?" Dove complained.

"Look, Leslie, it's six thirty in the morning. You just got up. Give me a chance to open my eyes. I'll call Sammy if we need him."

"What do you mean if we need him? Look at this thing. You don't think we need photographs of this? Look there, the fins have talons, and there's fur between each one. It's a sea serpent, Mike."

The editor raised his head to the crowd. Various nods of assent. Patient and neutral stares at worst.

Dove grabbed him high up on the arm and pulled him closer. "I'm telling you, this'll be big news, Mike. You're going to want to get in on this. Don't make me call the *Globe*. This is just right for the *Ledger*, something to finally get this city to take you seriously over there. *New York Times*, wire services, I could have called them but I called you. I'm setting up a live radio broadcast later this afternoon from this very spot. *Quincy Ledger* exclusive, I'll say. You'd sell as many papers as you can print."

The editor swept his eyes once over the length of the remains, as though making sure it was dead. He wriggled his fingers in his pockets, kicked at the sand.

Dove leaned into his ear: "Do you know how many fisherman have told me in confidence that they'd seen one just like it? Their descriptions fit this monster exactly. I don't know if we could use their names, but I'm sure we could get quotes and portraits drawn up from the information they give us, you know they don't forget a thing, those people, and we could set up a comparison, portraits detailing these fishermen's sightings and the remains of this monster here."

The editor cocked an incredulous eye.

"Look, I've told you I've had Captain Kidd's skull in my possession for years but no one seems to take that seriously either."

"And where did you say you acquired this skull, Leslie?"

"Redbank, New Jersey."

"Redbank, New Jersey."

"Yes sir. Unfortunately, I can't reveal much about that—"

"Of course not—"

"—except that it was given to me by a fraternity at the University of Virginia. Charlottesville, Virginia. The brothers made the recruits drink wine from it. I would happily document the genuineness of both artifacts if I were free to do it, Mike. But I'm not free. You see, you can't just reveal the details of pirate skulls until everybody connected to them is dead, or else expose them to terrible fates. That's a well-known fact. I'm just protecting you, you and your family."

The editor showed no signs of hearing him. Dove sighed, and went on: "You see, this particular skull has a string of bad luck tied to it, and unfortunately I've inherited it. After I was given it bad things started to happen. My car was stolen, my house got robbed, my wife almost got run over standing on a corner on a rainy night. It's for your own good that I not tell you much about that, Mike. But this is different—"

"So you can show me the skull but you can't tell me how you know it's real," the editor said.

"That's right."

The editor sighed and stared at a random spot on the skeletal remains, deeply distracted, seeing nothing.

"Look, Leslie," he muttered out of the side of his mouth. "You know as well as I do that this thing's a basking shark."

A well-rehearsed expression of disgust and surprise came to Dove's face. "Basking shark!" he exclaimed.

The crowd began to murmur.

"Sea monster," some shouted. Other assenting shouts.

The editor levelled his gaze at Dove. "Come on now, Leslie."

"Come on? You're covering it up just so you don't scare anybody." Turning to the general crowd: "Anybody here scared?" Heads shaking. "Or do you just want what's rightfully yours? This monster up on your beach, would put this whole town"— Dove spread his arms—"on the map. You'd have tourists and newspapermen and TV broadcasts. Isn't that your right? After all, your sea-monster—?"

The crowd looked on the verge of stampeding.

The editor was shaking his head at the sand.

Dove said loudly enough for everyone to hear: "This is not fantasy, my friend. This here is the real thing, and you and skeptics just like you will never believe there are things in the sea that we do not nor ever will understand. You don't like surprise. You don't like wrinkles in your expectations of your life. They throw off your vision, make you uncomfortable. You'll use some term like 'basking shark' to label anything you don't understand."

Was that a smirk on the editor's face? "Leslie, then why don't you call the zoo?"

"What happened?" Marie Dove asked as Leslie bolted by her, talking to himself, waving his hands. "Did they come to take the pictures?"

Pushing past, Dove took the steps two at a time, then three, accelerating past the families of conches lining the stairwell to his attic office, a wind-shot cupola atop their house across the street from the quay. Here, as from a boat's wheelhouse, his universe lay before him, the murky water of Boston Harbor, the ships coming and going. Out of sight behind and below him each street was the same bleached canyon raked by tumbling wrappers and tin cans, walled in by high cliffs of faded clapboard and closed anonymous doorways. One-way and stop signs shuddering in the harbor wind.

A plane approached out of the nearby airport. Its shadow passed through the little office, taking the warm sunlight, then, rattling the windowpanes, growled off. Dove turned his eyes on his windows, past the lobster-pots and ships' knots and coconut heads draped over the railing of his widow's walk, and set them on the line between the two halves of his sea, the one green and the other, today, an empty pale suspension.

Paper was strewn everywhere. A lithograph hanging askew on the wall: the Minot Light toppling into the surf, the waves licking at the feet of the plunging keepers. Scrapbooks and bottles of paste and cutout articles of the young Dove braving gales in canoes, performing heroic acts. A slightly older, heavier Dove straddling a treasure chest, brandishing a pirate's sword, holding a human skull.

Maritime memorabilia littered the walls, engravings of ships, lighthouses and storms; movie posters of Clark Gable and Charles Laughton, John Wayne in flyer's leather, Douglas Fairbanks, Jr in desert fatigues, Errol Flynn beneath a three-cornered hat. On a drafting table against one wall lay a pile of ships' blueprints: cross-sectioned schooners, submarines, slave galleys.

The coconut heads swung off the widow's walk like the shrunken heads of monkeys.

One couldn't discount the possibility that Dove had picked it all up himself during voyages to distant islands, shrunken heads and all. Yet Dove was the sort of man who sent for things, who owned one well-worn chair, who picked up his evidence, his atoms of truth, in the sand below the quay at low tide after storms. A caricature of himself.

Dove stumbled around the office, leafing through stacks of paper, digging into a pile of envelopes. He pulled file after file out of a tin cabinet, glancing in and tossing them aside.

Breathing hard, his face flushed: "You want a real sea monster, I'll go get you a real sea monster."

He turned and looked at the letter he had clutched in his

hand, already well thumbed up, the stilted scrawl:

Bailey Island, March 19, 1952

Dear Mr Dove,

I happened to see a copy of your new book, which of course I have been looking for. And I must say I was surprised to see your chapter on the Raven. I asked myself, Did my first letter mean nothing to him? I am most unpleasantly surprised that you would have not come up here and spoken to me as I thought the Flying Santa was the one a woman like me should confide in.

Anyways, since I sent that letter, I have taken in possession some new information of an even more frightening nature, that I am positive will give you cause to reopen this investigation and get to the bottom of this mystery. You found the Portland. We can make a name just by finding this boat. Just think of all those poor people in Rehoboth.

Yours, Beatrice Varney

Talking to himself, Dove ransacked every folder and cabinet he had, but couldn't find the woman's spindly handwriting on anything else.

EZRA

On an early April dawn, the tide poured down the throat of Mackerel Cove. All the boats aimed at open water, the pale horizon. Above and below was still a kind of luminous dark. There was no wind, the air was warmer, bearable. The last ice was slipping off the rocks.

Halfway around the cove Ezra Johnson pulled his pickup truck alongside a low tin hangar, more shelter than home, a bunker shouldering through the snow. Tufts of yellowed crabgrass pushing through ladders and traps and buoys and a skiff thrown in the mud; an American flag wrapped like a dishcloth around an old mast for a pole; an aluminum canoe listing in a sooty drift.

Ezra set his coffee on his knee. Drizzle popped against the roof of his truck and fell around the boats in the cove like bits of broken glass. He could hear the tin fish house clattering and scratching, and in the lit window down there below the overhang a lone figure in a rubber hood was bayonetting the salt baths with a pitchfork. Squinting up into a sky sealed like a trap door, now out beyond the mouth of the cove, the horizon erased, he fooled with the radio dial for the weather out of Portland, couldn't get anything but staticky float, clicked it off and left his truck with the motor running, the door open. He knelt before the canoe.

By twenty, Ezra had not grown much taller than the boy he was in 1941. He stood at just over five and a half feet. But thick-armed, thick-waisted, his hair closely cropped and his boyish face already permanently ruddy, he was a raw young man who gave the impression of having too much strength. His quiet, steady face was broken through by fiercely blue eyes that already spoke of unnameable experience and cruelty; as though his youth were a mask, a ploy, and what lived beneath his skin was already old. He was more citizen of these particular islands, of the water around them, and especially of his boat—an anarchic, warring country of minor mutinies—than a citizen of Maine or any stretch of dry land that lay beyond it.

He brushed through a patch of snow to get a look at the green-painted wood. His sweatshirt hood, steeply pitched overhead: a lone monk kneeling at prayer at a partially disinterred altar. There was no one about. Not even the grass stirred. Only the steady, monotonous dripping of the flag and the soft hiss of the rain on the snow and shreds of fog slinking past.

"Can I help you?" The voice came from the shop.

"Just me, Bernard," Ezra called. "Just looking at the canoe."

A figure appeared in the doorway, the light behind him outlining his girth, the cap on his head, his elbows working, spinning unseen nut and bolt. "Careful today. Looks like a scale."

Ezra made a single, loath stroke across the canoe like a boy reaching out at a prize horse in a stable.

"Make me an offer."

"Don't want to buy it."

"Buy it, Ezra. You want to."

Ezra eyed it up and down. "Maybe."

"What for?"

"The cabin out at Rangeley."

"I didn't think your father went out on the water up there," the dark figure said.

"He doesn't. Can't stand it." He stood and brushed the snow from his knee. "What do you think?"

"I think you want it."

"What do you want for it?"

"Make me an offer."

Ezra raised ardent eyes, cobalt, translucent, as though they had false bottoms, like crystal chips held up to a light. "Just tell me what you want for it."

A hand waved in abdication and the figure disappeared. "Just take it."

"For what?"

"For nothing. Whatever I'd ask it'd be less than I owe your

father anyways."

Ezra fished a damp roll of bills out of his coveralls and left a twenty on the canoe under a rock. "I'll come for it."

The rain was not as heavy as it sounded or looked on the water and it was not as cold. At the fish house, the snow had retreated to the ditches and the shrunken drifts of shoveled debris. Ezra's breath hung heavily before him. Everything was wet. Everything dripped and poured with rain and meltoff.

Inside, his father Clayt was forking salted fish into barrels from the baths. At fifty-six he was already an old man. As one of the oldest lobstermen still working Bailey Island, he was unmindful of any distinction between outside world and inside, water and land, air and soul—the coalescence had happened long ago. He, like his boat, was just a shell of movement housing sometimes one, sometimes the other, and sometimes all at once. Past having delights, he worked the pitchfork steadily, in no hurry but neither would he stop until the barrel was full.

Ezra joined him wordlessly and stepped up to the opposite end of a full barrel and dragged it to the gangway. Together they guided the barrel down and dragged it to the edge of the raft. Clayt put his foot in a dory and bent to undo its tether, already down in his seat, kicking off and turning to take up the oars. He looked up, surprised, at Ezra.

"What, what are you staying or coming."

Ezra strode hard over the growing space between dory and raft and tumbled in.

The rain came straight down in little explosions, suddenly cooler, as if someone somewhere had opened a window to the true outdoors.

Clayt guided them without seeing, first letting up on one oar then the other, tugging them backward around the moorings and rafts. The fog coalesced into shadowy lumps, then darkened—antennae and tuna tower—a boat: *Alexander P, Tonka, Dragonfish,* then *Snook.* They patrolled the crowded neighborhood of ghostly masses, the low fog parting then closing like the water below; the two layers of water, one they could breathe. Clayt raised an oar and grabbed a fistful of water, looked at it in his palm then threw it back. As if not liking what he'd seen. As if water had the power of counsel, of giving allowance or giving notice against its own exploitation.

His back spread, his hands came together, the oars took flight. A single massive stroke and the dory lurched toward the last anchorage, a boat like all the rest, spare, clapping steadily in the water. He tied the dory to the mooring and boarded. They stepped into yellow coveralls, hosed the boat. The outboard ripped into the dawn quiet and Clayt guided the boat back along the way they'd come, swinging to at the raft.

Dawn was general all over now. Men were at the fish house, the cherries of their cigarettes idling down about their knees. Pickup trucks were rolling down the hill to the cove from up- land. Clayt and Ezra loaded the barrel and Ezra reached in and started pulling out handfuls of skinned fish and running skewers through their eyes. Clayt tugged at the throttle and the water in back boiled and the boat moved off below them. Land pulled away.

Swells passed through them, shoals surfaced without warn- ing. Somewhere to the left water gurgled onto shore, only some- where there, and there. Sound as well as light was sourceless and confused. The wind bit. The black water kept coming. The fog was right on Ezra's eyes, but he knew his father knew his speed and the direction and that his hands were leading him. Clayt twitched on the wheel then pulled hard at an invisible corner and the boat awoke, bucking against the swells, the bow high over the water. The boat was bouncing and snapping and Clayt was banking right then left while behind him Ezra worked his hands steadily around the skewers and fishheads, his bib bloodied, his knees pumping to keep him level with the pitch of the boat. At some distance to the right Clayt heard the water smack against rock like steady gunfire and he pulled hard again and shoved at the throttle. The bow dropped and the boat gurgled in idle and coasted to a stop at a nameless address. A cluster of flagged antennae bobbing and leaning in the swells off the star- board. The open water oily, swollen. A fog sea.

The skewers were racked up in front of Ezra. Clayt slipped on insulated gloves and leaned over and grabbed a blue flag and looped its rope to a winch. The winch groaned, the boat tipped a little to that side, then the weedy traps came up out of the water one at a time. Clayt opened the trap door to a fight. He rattled the lobster in the cage and fought them out, ducking below and around the snapping claws like a boxer, going about his boat business while sliding his head in and out of the lobsters' jabs. Then he crossed their claws and the lobster were defeated. He eyed them and tossed the small ones over his shoulder into the water with a plop. He handed the big vanquished lobster over to Ezra who banded them and dropped them into a wood banquette. Then he hung the rack of bloody young fish in the trap by their eyes. Ezra grabbed the trap and half-squatted and leaned back and sprung and heaved the trap onto two running boards behind him. At the wheel Clayt looked very little and ashen with his big young son heaving the traps through the air. But everything went very smoothly. Ezra went back to the skewering while Clayt tossed the buoy overboard and washed down the blood and chum with a hose, then aimed the boat another way. The stern sank, the water passed, and the empty traps flew off the running boards after the buoy and then after each other and disappeared.

Two hours later they'd hit all their addresses but the banquette was only half full of writhing lobster. Clayt squinted upward. The brilliant fog had given way to a gray, constant light and the rain had turned cold and feathery.

"Want to do some drag hauling?" he asked.

Ezra looked up into the rain.

Clayt lifted the mouthpiece to the radio. He rolled the volume knob in his fingers.

"Jesse."

"Go."

"How about some dragging."

After a pause, "Where."

"Round Rock."

There was no answer for a time and Clayt said nothing. He hung the mouthpiece and peered into the banquette.

Jesse's voice finally came through: "You feel lucky?"

Clayt lifted the mouthpiece. "I feel poor."

"Ten minutes."

Clayt rehung the mouthpiece. He didn't look at Ezra. "Set out the nets."

He slipped the boat into neutral then climbed up on the bow and shimmied up the tower toward the crow's nest at the top. Up top he grabbed the duplicate controls, smaller levers and a miniature wheel, and swung the *Hattie B* into the white wash before him. Paler water boiling. Then a swell knelt and unravelled, taking the lee-side water with it, peeling back and baring a rocky spine. The ledges gleamed in the air briefly in the gray light then plummeted as the water gargled and spat all around them.

Ezra could hear the waves murmuring against the rocks now, the rebel waves breaking with the sound of cannonfire. He straightened and looked into the water, then up to his father.

"Don't worry so much, boy," Clayt called. "Tide's up."

Ezra's face twitched, his pale eyes hardened as his father took the boat closer. Three low mounds unfolded out of the general sea, one behind the other, then simply dropped away and drew back below the ledges.

Jesse drew up beside them. "Ezra, why don't you haul those nets across," he called over.

Ezra squinted into the boil then donned gloves and fed the nets across from rear starboard to Jesse's rear port.

The boats danced forward, Clayt and Jesse feeling in their fingers the pull of the current and the tug of the nets. Working water and haul against each other to settle in a kind of stalemate or truce between boat and the force of water and air.

"Just a quick shovel then we're out," Clayt said.

"Haul it!" Jesse called.

Ezra threw the lever. The boats leaned, a kind of bow to your partner. The tuna towers pinched together. Jesse and Clayt peered in, their knuckles whitening on the rail, then letting go as a patch of water rose and the nets surfaced empty but for a few strands of seaweed and the remaining corner posts of an old wood trap.

"Nothing," Clayt breathed, softly enough for his son to hear relief. Ezra lifted his head to see his father's back turn on the Teeth, and his father's fingers gingerly back the *Hattie B* off and swing her away.

Later, Ezra stepped through the door of The Sebasco, a low, long construction that had once been a motel and was now the only restaurant on Bailey Island. Showered, changed out of his togs into pants and shirt, he stood blinking in the dark as the noon-light pinched off behind him.

There had been only one other car parked in the Sebasco's lot, an old gray Chevy that belonged to Jeannie, the restaurant's owner, cook, hostess and waitress. A lone bicycle had been left leaning into the bushes. The long lot had been otherwise empty; it was too early in the season for the tourists up from Boston and New York, and too early in the day for the lobstermen up from the cove to come through the bar, and too late for the fishermen's wives.

Ezra's eyes adjusted to the dark and he stepped into the dining room, where a lone diner, an old man, sat in a booth, facing the sea. In both hands he held steady a glass tumbler drained to the ice. His face was deeply mapped, his forehead a craggy ledge, his lips a grim line, as though callused shut, no longer in use; a white beard cupped his chin. His pantleg was rolled up and clipped where it might have gotten caught in the crank of a bicycle's pedal or smeared with grease.

Ezra had known Nathan Morrill his whole life. It was Morrill's only son, Ed, and grandson, Billy, who had gone out to that ledge to shoot sea ducks on that Christmas day in 1940 and didn't come back alive. It was Ezra's father, Clayt, who had found Morrill's son caught on one of his traps and left him on the Morrill dock.

And after that day, Nathan Morrill had abandoned the cove where the women in his family had been bearing children and the men had been fishing, and all of them dying and getting buried in a continuous occupation of that very plot of land on Morrill Cove beginning with Morrill's great-great-great grandfather, Isaac Morrill, present at Timothy Bailey's and Clement Orr's purchase of Sebascodegan and Little Sebascodegan Islands for one pound of tobacco and one gallon of rum.

Isaac Morrill who, in 1782, had been sailing his family north from the Carolinas, waiting for something to urge him to build his family a home and a farm to tend. Drifting past Cape Elizabeth, he passed an unflagged schooner named Picaroon off some as yet uncharted island. He'd heard the name, he'd heard it, here and there associated with a skirmish in the waters off Cape Hatteras: and if this was the same Picaroon then the boat and crew were British. Morrill sailed for the nearest harbor, dropped his wife and children, summoned the fishermen there and led them to the schooner, and with him at the head the small fleet of skiffs and dories with two muskets for cannon, they surrounded the Picaroon and captured it. Reluctant to leave the battle grounds of his heroism, Morrill led his two terrified children knee deep into Sebascodegan harbor, then pushed their heads under the water, proclaiming himself a fisherman and baptizing his children a fisherman's family.

The string of Morrills fished, then they lobstered, until Nathan Morrill went to college at Bowdoin instead, up the road in Brunswick. He agreed at least to keep his family on the cove, and to punt across the water between the islands before they'd built the squat bridges, to be a Professor of English.

But after Christmas morning, 1940, Morrill's only son and grandson were dead. He would have no more children. The Morrill clan was to end with him.

It was Morrill who'd seen to it that Clayt Johnson and Jesse Johnson had gotten an education at Bowdoin. And it was Morrill who went to Clayt three years ago and asked that Ezra be allowed to matriculate. Clayt had said nothing, which Morrill had taken as assent, and nothing more was said about it.

Now Ezra slid into the bench opposite him. A stack of books sat at Morrill's elbow. Morrill still looked off, down the slope, where the wooden flakes stretched like acres of fat ribbon out over a clearing down to the cove, completely covered in a blanket of mackerel and bluefish. In the water, the boats rocked at their moorings, their tuna towers swaying. Beyond them, across the strait, the blue cylindrical waves rolled up against the shoreline where they were pinched high into the air in white geysers, spraying the white clapboard summer homes of Harpswell Neck which had begun to encroach on the water.

"Professor."

Morrill sniffed, wiped his nose with the back of his hand, and looked up. His eyes were dim, his fingers trembling.

"You want to tell me why you're quitting? Christ, boy, you have a month before you graduate. I was going to recommend you for honors."

Ezra turned his head to the window. "My father quit after just a year," Ezra said.

"I know he did. And when he did I called him and sat him down just as I'm sitting you down here with me now, and I tried to convince him otherwise."

"Did you?"

Morrill brought his spent drink to his lips and took a piece of ice in his teeth.

"I had about as much luck as I believe I will have with you today."

Footsteps behind them as Jeannie rounded some corner, and Morrill raised his glass and rattled the ice.

"What are you having, boy?"

Ezra raised his wrists off the table. "I got to help Pa down at the cove later."

Morrill leaned forward over the table, whispering. "Why don't you just stay with classes one more month and get that goddamn degree?"

Ezra examined his yellowstained fingertips, calloused and spread like paddles.

"Damn it, boy. Why go to the trouble of three years of hard study—and some damn good study, I might add—and let it go just before it'll mean something."

Ezra looked up, surprised. "But I did it. That means something."

"I'm talking about the degree, son. The degree. It's why people go to college in the first place. To get the degree."

Jeannie came around and exchanged a fresh glass for Morrill's, and Morrill immediately lifted it and drained off half. Ezra watched the amber liquid run from both corners of his mouth into his beard, where it darkened his gray bristles.

"I don't need a college degree to lobster," Ezra said quietly.

Morrill sat back hard against the back of the booth. He crossed his arms. "You going to lobster for the rest of your life?" he asked acidly.

"I will," Ezra answered quickly. "As long as I can."

Morrill came forward again, his hands open in supplication. "Then stay in for just the month more. You'd be the first lobsterman on these islands with a bachelor's degree. That's two hundred years of history you'd be changing."

"But I'm not out to change anybody's history," Ezra said.

"Not even your own?"

Ezra looked out the window. "It'd only be trouble," Ezra said. "It wouldn't sit right with the others."

"Oh bullshit," Morrill said, slapping the table with the palm of his hand. "That's just ignorant fisherman talk. Christ, boy, I'm not some uplander intellectual who looks down on this place. My family was lobstering these islands before your family could call itself a family. Every man in my family but me worked down at that cove doing what you and your father are doing. I know what I'm talking about. I made a choice. Just like you can make a choice—"

"I made a choice," Ezra said.

"But you'd be an educated man. There's nothing shameful about being an educated man."

For the first time Ezra looked up and returned Morrill's gaze. He cleared his throat.

"I'd never be as educated as them anyways, so what's the point of the paper? It's just a paper. It's got nothing to do with lobstering or the sea, or living here, or working down at the cove. I did my time up there. I learned with you. I learned with some others. I read some books. I was able to do my runs with Pa in the mornings before class, so it didn't bother me. I was glad to do it. But I was never doing it for the paper."

Morrill sat his full height, tall and lean, and seemed to peer down on Ezra from a high perch. "You going to sit there and tell me you didn't like reading those books? Melville? Conrad? You, a sea-man yourself and you're going to tell me those books didn't mean anything to you?"

Ezra's eyes glazed. After a time, he nodded. "They meant something," he said.

"They didn't just mean something. They *are* something. That great white whale. It's not just a whale. It's life. Getting that diploma, conquering it, reeling it in class by class, semester by semester—those books tell us about ourselves. They make our lives clear."

Ezra's brow wrinkled in confusion. "I liked those books—"

"You didn't just like those books," Morrill said, raising his voice. "I read those papers you wrote. Those weren't just any papers. That wasn't just *reading*. That was first-class thinking. You *understood* them. You felt what they were saying." Morrill raised his arm and extended a quivering finger in some general direction behind Ezra. "You could write circles around most of the students at that school. What those books were saying about our lives *moved* you, boy. I'm not sitting here telling you what to do with your life, what to do for a living. You could sweep floors for all I care. But you earned that diploma, more than most any student I ever had at that school, and that's over forty years worth of perfectly capable young men going through there, going on to good careers in government, education, up at Augusta, in Washington D.C. But what you did up there meant something to you. It meant more than it meant to most of them. And if you sit there and tell me otherwise I'll call you a liar to your face."

Ezra looked up. He opened his mouth to speak then shut it. He lifted one hand as if to say, Where would I begin?, then let it fall to the table. Once more he looked out the window to the water, and his eyes followed a boat, Jesse's, out of the little harbor toward open water, as if all the answers were written there in its wake.

"I read those books in the night, before I went to sleep," he said, quietly, as if to himself. Morrill had to lean forward to hear him.

"Sometimes I didn't sleep so I could get the reading done for class the next day. But in the morning I'd go out on the water with my father and we'd do our chores and our lobstering, and it was like the books just left my head. On the water they didn't mean anything. I liked those books, and they seemed real when I read them, but when I was on the water, they felt all wrong. I don't know how to explain it. In January, out here—those books weren't nothing next to the bite of lobstering out here in January. And sea monsters—I can't be thinking about that sort of thing when I'm out there. You got to be a hundred percent out there, or else you're dead. The water in those books and the water we were working on—it was like two different oceans, two different worlds. But one of them I had to go back to every morning. No matter what, I was always going out to lobster in the morning. Even when I started up there with you three years ago, I was always going back out."

"I see. Then you were always going to quit," Morrill said.

Ezra didn't answer. He shrugged a shoulder.

"Was it Clayt? Did your father say something to you?"

Ezra shook his head. "My father never said a thing to me about it in three years."

"Your ma?"

"As long as I did my runs and my chores, they didn't care what I did."

"They never read anything you wrote?"

Ezra laughed, to himself. "My father doesn't even bother with the newspapers anymore."

"Then what's the difference, boy? Why don't you just push through to the semester's end? After that, you lobster for the rest of your life. You don't even have to go to commencement. I'll send you the damn diploma if you're too embarrassed to come pick it up."

Ezra sagged back in his seat. He shook his head. "It's just done," he said resignedly.

Jeannie appeared from the back.

"What'll you eat, boy?" Morrill asked.

Ezra shook his head.

"We'll have two bowls of chowder," Morrill told her. "And I'll have another Beefeater. And bring the boy a beer."

Morrill peered across the table at Ezra, considering him, as if making up his mind.

"You think about that."

"I will."

"There's something else." Morrill rolled his drink in his hands.

Ezra sat up, settled his arms on the table, and listened to Morrill placidly, as if he were sitting in class.

Morrill slid the stack of books away from the wall and turned their spines toward Ezra. "Recognize any of these?"

Ezra's eyes skated over them. They all bore the name of the same author, *Leslie Everett Dove, Leslie Everett Dove* repeated in gold leaf. He read the titles: *The Vengeful Sea and Tales of Survival; Amazing and True Sea Stories Never Told Before; Catastrophes, Calamities, Castaways; Gory Gales and Dire Disasters; Voyages Uncharted, Voyages Unfinished.* Ezra was surprised. He thought the titles interesting, sort of dramatic: adventure tales written for children. He'd seen it before, those badly written, pumped up stories of heroics on the high seas in *Reader's Digest.* They'd made him laugh. If they only knew.

Ezra felt Morrill watching him, not with suspicion but with expectancy, as though he was waiting for a particular reaction. To console him, he picked up the book off the top, *Wrecks Along the Atlantic Coast,* and fanned the pages slowly. Inside were mostly photographs of the aftermaths of collisions and storms and bad decisions: beached freighters, the ghostly undersides of gargantuan liners, bellied up like harpooned whales. Artists' renditions of sailors' last moments, their eyes bulged and wild, the eyes of terrified horses: a zoo boat caught by a hurricane, elephant trunks and lion manes sinking into an icy sea. He flipped a page and scanned one towering wave after another pinning one schooner against one craggy ledge after another, page after page of futile rescues and toppled light houses, each loss more calamitous, each more terrifying than the previous. He stopped on a particular one, a photograph of a freighter with a strip of limp roadway draped over its bow, as though a father holding in his lap his dead child; above it a suspension bridge, a long span of its outbound lane missing, as though not yet built. Below the photo was a list of names. The caption said they'd driven over the edge. It had been night and for a long time no one knew that the bridge had collapsed. They'd gone over one after another into the water, plunging into the bay.

Ezra closed the book and looked up, smiling wanly. He couldn't understand why Morrill would have anything to do with these books. They were sensational, beneath him.

"They're not *Moby Dick*," he said.

"But it's him that people read, not Melville. Ever heard of him?" Morrill asked.

Ezra looked up.

"Leslie Everett Dove."

Ezra shrugged. He looked at the book's jacket. The name seemed vaguely familiar, though he couldn't recall how. "Don't know. Maybe."

"Clayt ever talk about him?"

"Don't recall."

"Maybe you heard his name on the radio. He has a radio program. He tells sea stories and ghost stories."

Again Ezra felt Morrill staring at him. He just shook his head. "Doesn't mean anything to me."

Morrill picked a book out of the middle of the stack, *New England Sea Tragedies,* and held it his both his hands, as though making to hit something with it.

"I didn't know much about Leslie Everett Dove either. He's the guy who started that Christmas gag last year, calls himself the Flying Santa."

Ezra nodded. "Okay."

"That mean something to you?"

"Maybe."

"Last week someone showed me this book," Morrill said. He put the book flat on the table and lay both hands atop it, as though forcing it down. "Inside it, there's a chapter about Ed and Billy."

Ezra narrowed his eyes.

"I remember a couple years ago someone from Boston had overheard me talking to someone else about it—I don't remember who. And he came over and asked me a few questions. I don't know what I thought. Maybe he was a reporter. Back then, reporters and police were coming to the house for weeks, until people started to forget. So I didn't give it another thought."

Morrill opened the book to a dog-eared page. "It was Leslie Everett Dove. He'd heard down in Boston about what happened to my boy. He read about it in the paper, or someone told him, I don't know who. I didn't tell much of anything to anybody before that. There just wasn't much to say. No one knew what really happened and I don't see how anybody could. People just assumed the boat somehow got untied and drifted away from them and they were caught on the ledge when the tides came in. They wouldn't have lasted thirty seconds. I accepted that as what happened and left it alone. Anyway, it didn't matter."

Jeannie came by with two steaming bowls, set them down at the table's edge, and went away. Ezra and Morrill lifted their wide spoons and sat there holding them up until the soup skinned over.

"I guess I must have told Dove a few things but I don't know what. After all, what did I know? What did anyone know? Then out of those few things, the little I'd told him, and the little he must have dug up out of the papers and read—out of just that little appears a whole chapter in this goddamn book."

Morrill lay his palm on the page, his fingers stretched as though pinned there.

"But he's twisted it all up, see. He says that Ed shot Billy with his shotgun. Now he'd asked me about that, whether it was possible he might have done that. Because they had shotguns with them, and they found a lot of duck carcasses floating out there when they went out there looking for them the next day. So they know there was shooting going on. But what I'd told him was not that Ed had done that, but that that's what *I* would have done. Me, if it was me and not him. So it wouldn't be the freezing or the drowning to get them. I would have shot the boy myself to save him, make it easier. Billy, and then, if there were any shells left, I would have shot myself."

Morrill threw back the rest of his drink. His hand was trembling. He brought the glass down hard, spilling some ice onto the table, which he quickly brushed off onto the floor.

"But Ed couldn't have done it," he said. "He was a good man, but he didn't have the courage, or the fear, or the rage or whatever it is that would let a man shoot his own son in the head and then turn the barrel on himself. And then there's the question of ammunition. Knowing him, and seeing all those birds on the water, there wouldn't have been any shells left, not even the two or three he would have needed, or the two or three more to make sure the boy was dead. And then there's the one for himself. Anyway. It doesn't matter. None of what anyone thinks about it matters because they're both dead. Your father found my son, and my grandson, god help him, is still drifting somewhere down there in those sinkholes. But Dove wrote that that's just what my son did, that he shot Billy in the head, and then shot himself. As if he'd seen the body, which he hadn't. Of course you could say that, you could say look at Ed's body. But everybody knows that by the time Clayt found him there wasn't much left, just some bones and some flesh held together by his rain slicker. But you see—"

Again he slapped his hand down on the book. His eyes widened in horror.

"—now everyone will know it like that, like it really happened that way. That my boy shot his own boy. Can you imagine? As if it wasn't something he might have done out of mercy, but as if it were a murder. As if it happened that way at all!"

Morrill glanced sideways at the cooling chowder and let it go. Ezra sat unmoving, his eyes on the water, listening carefully.

"I've been thinking about this Dove," Morrill said, wrapping himself in a false calm. "I'm a writer of stories myself so I have some experience in these matters. Why he would have done it. Why Dove would have twisted a sad, sad story like that, and made it sadder, more tragic than it had to have been. Do you know what I decided?"

Ezra turned his head and looked at Morrill.

"Because you can't make a goddamn legend out of some poor son-of-a-bitch who goes down to the corner store and buys a loaf of bread and some sausage."

Morrill's face reddened and he turned in on the empty tables of the restaurant, as if to beseech them. Though he wasn't seeing them. His stare locked somewhere in the middle distance, on something that wasn't there but that he was seeing as clearly as if it was.

"I think about why it happens," he said. "Why it happens like that. Someone will go out and you'll just say goodbye in your everyday way, as if you'll see them again in a couple of hours. And that's it. You never see them again. And you don't have a chance to say goodbye. It's like a punishment. I've been thinking about it since the very day my son and grandson disappeared. And I've decided that it's a sentence, indiscriminately laid down against random men and women by some unseen jury up there."

He turned and stared Ezra full in the face. "It's as if these things—like that thing that happened to your brother all those years ago, went out just like my son on Christmas day and didn't come back—it's as if all these terrible, terrible, *terrible* things are sentences meant to keep entire populations at bay. They're messages, Ezra, our notifications that innocence is not the law, it's only a temporary reprieve. As if innocence is the crime, the insanity. And these stupid, stupid things that happen—they're our penance."

Ezra looked away as Morrill wiped his eyes with the back of his hands. He thought then about this brother of his he never knew. There were no pictures, his father would never allow any. But he was always there in the house with him. He was there every night when his mother led his father to the chimney to tie him to sleep. Every night in that lantern they kept burning in the kitchen, and in a familiar smell on a draft through a crack in the kitchen door. And in the way the sun rose at dawn on Christmas morning, and the way his father would never let him out on the water all that day. It had become a ritual: Ezra would stay at home, and Clayt would go get their Christmas dinner himself, alone, snow or not. The way they sometimes looked at him, Ezra. The bed he slept on, the place he had on his father's boat, even the clothes he wore. None of it was his. Even his very existence; he'd inherited his own life like a hand-me-down suit.

Morrill opened the book on the table to the title page and slid it across to Ezra.

Ezra just looked at him.

"Don't look at me, boy," he said curtly. "Look at the book."

Obediently, Ezra looked at the paper.

"The table of contents," Morrill commanded. "Read it."

Ezra ran his finger down the list of chapter headings: 'Famine on the *Peggy*,' 'African Adventure,' 'The *Margaret* Meets Disaster,' 'Papa, Won't God Save Us?'

He reached the bottom and looked up.

"Turn the page," Morrill said.

Ezra turned the page and scanned the chapter titles down. Halfway to the bottom, his finger stopped.

"That's right, boy," Morrill said. "That's right. Look at that. Look at that."

'The *Raven* Mystery.' Ezra blinked. 'The *Raven* Mystery.'

"This Dove character really has our number," Morrill said.

Ezra looked up. "Why are you showing me this?"

"Go ahead. Open it up. Read what he says."

Ezra snapped the book shut.

"I'm not interested."

"But you were there."

"I was not."

"You were. I was down at the cove when you and your father were bringing all those bodies in. You were there the whole time. You were towing those bodies in. I was watching you. I was wondering what it would have been like if it was me down there with your father instead of you. I don't think I would have slept for a month."

"I didn't."

"I don't think I would have ever been able to forget it."

"Well I did." Ezra squirmed in his seat. "It's got nothing to do with me. Show it to my father." He slid the book back.

"I tried to. He wouldn't even look at it."

"He doesn't believe too highly in books."

"I think you're right about that. There was a time when he did, though. He loved reading *Moby Dick* in my class almost as much as you did."

Ezra threw Morrill a look of utter disbelief and shook his head. He went back to his bowl and pulled it toward him and started spooning the thick stew into his mouth.

"You don't want to remember it," Morrill said, smiling. "Now why would that be?"

The spoon stopped midair, dripping, his mouth open, Ezra squinted into his soup. His shoulders stooped a little, his eyes closed off to this day and he saw again the infernal black ambulance, heard its motor idling on the wharf waiting for him and his father to return. As if the driver knew they could be counted on to deliver. Ezra saw it racing down island, passing through the clusters of houses, passing through them again. The children and their mothers who had come up for air, for an ice cream at the wharf, seeing the headlights approach like match heads off in the distance. The humming tires, the brass eagle perched on the end of the hood, the big gray knuckles on the wheel. They'd chase back into the house, the mothers shutting the blinds, sullenly leaning a shoulder against the front door, the children past curiosity, frozen to silence. At home, over dinner, Ezra's mother asked Clayt why he didn't just tie bricks to the bodies and let them go like they did with Mr Lehman. The bodies weren't doing anybody any good. "We're not breathing, Clayt," she said, "Everybody's stopped breathing." His father spiked the food with his fork and tossed it in his mouth like coal into a furnace and said nothing while Ezra's dinner hardened on his plate.

"The fog didn't lift," Ezra said to Morrill, quietly. One eye squinted then the other. He shook his head. "Didn't lift really anytime, not the next day, not the day after. After that it did lift some. But we'd gotten them already. All those bodies."

Ezra Johnson blinked his eyes clear. He looked at old Morrill a long time.

"I guess I haven't thought about it for—I don't know how many years."

"Eleven years," Morrill said.

Ezra nodded. "Eleven years."

"Well, I think you should read this."

"Why?"

"Because it has to do with you. Because you were there and handled those bodies and were part of it, and it changed you whether you know it or not. You never come out of a thing like that unchanged. Just like I was in that story about my son, even if it was all lies. You're in this story, too, whether you like it or not."

"All right," Ezra said, and turned the book and opened it. He read with his finger, stopping to reread each paragraph more slowly still. The chapter began with a list of the dead and the missing. Their ages, their occupations. He stopped on each name. He couldn't see the faces. He saw the bloated flesh, but they were faceless, worm-eaten, chewed off. He never knew their names. He put his finger on them: *Gordon Beauchamp, 41, sons Gordy, 16, and Ivan, 10. His brother Alban Beauchamp, 38. Earl Decker, 52, sister Helen Decker, 46. Jim Carey, 16. Beatrice Roach, 28. Lilah Sanders, 26 ...*

Then the article related one idea about the boat exploding, and a second about the boat capsizing. There was nothing about why the women returned but the men didn't. *The years went by,* Leslie Everett Dove wrote—

In 1950 a report was filed that wreckage had been found which might prove to be that of the Raven. *I organized a search to attempt positive identification of the remains, but the results of our underwater endeavor did nothing to solve the mystery. I was informed that a Captain Earl Varney had been under water in an attempt to find the hull at Bald Dick Ledge a year or two after the disaster, but had not been successful.*

At the current writing, August 1951, the mystery as to what may have happened has not been solved. However, in my opinion, because of newly revealed information, the mystery is greater and more troubling than ever.

A letter currently in my possession states with certainty that unidentified parties might have decided to sink the Raven *for reasons which to me are still obscure, and that Captain Johnson was unaware of the plot.*

One of these letters suggests a strange theory, after which it concludes as follows: "It's just too fantastic to believe, but I know."

Another writer says with assurance that a German U-boat sank the Raven.

The diving which was conducted under my supervision earlier this year has added nothing to persuade me one way or another so far. I would be very pleased to show anyone my dossier of material on the Raven. *I do not dare print some of the letters I have received due to the almost unbelievable implications.*

At the time this book was going to press, I had not yet been able to undertake further investigations. But I will, at my earliest opportunity, pursue the dastardly suspicions raised by these most unexpected and perhaps revealing clues.

Ezra looked up.

"There hasn't been anybody diving off Bald Dick," he said resentfully. "Not in the last two years. Not anytime I remember."

"Earl Varney never went down there?"

"Earl? Who knows. Ten years ago? He could've. Haven't seen him in a long time. You'd have to ask him, though nothing goes on in this water here that we don't hear about eventually."

Morrill nodded. "Exactly."

"And why would Varney go diving in those ledges, anyway? Floyd Johnson never would have put that boat in there. It's bad water all around. Can't haul. Can't set traps in there without a lot of trouble. Going in there with a boat full of people would be suicide. Everybody said he was too good a skipper for that."

"He was a drunk," Morrill said.

"But he could skipper blindfolded."

"You were nine."

Ezra eyed Morrill. "Most people around here can probably skipper better drunk than sober. He was a good skipper." He laid a finger on the page. "Anyway, what's this? You know what he's talking about here, about these letters, these 'too fantastic' letters?"

Morrill shook his head.

Ezra looked off. "What does he mean he's going to pursue these suspicions?"

Morrill leaned forward on the table, elbows splayed, and eyed Ezra. "You haven't heard anyone talking about this?"

"Nothing that hasn't been told and retold a thousand times already. Nothing here gets said without it being repeated a dozen times a day."

"Maybe some things do," Morrill said. "Maybe someone better talk to Varney."

"Maybe someone better talk to this Dove," Ezra said.

Morrill nodded laconically, his mind already elsewhere. "Maybe somebody better."

In the General Store, eight men, all occupying a small range of old age and infirmity, sat hunched on opposite benches like rival teams of the old, sick and abandoned. Ezra bought a five-cent cup of coffee from a high-school girl, smiling at her, reddening when he said her name, Darla, and loitered down the aisle from the benches, feigning interest in the collection of canned vegetables and packages of instant cocoa. Those of the men whose eyes had filmed or gone opaque let loose nuggets of the weather, speaking past each other in the wrong directions, hoping to be overheard but not addressed. The other half looked unable to hear, their eyes overactive; they did not speak of the weather but bellowed.

Ezra slowly moved closer, knelt and picked out a can of green beans and examined the label absentmindedly, and stood. "Here's college boy!" one of them said.

Ezra stood, smiling foolishly.

"Why, hello there Ezra," Jesse said. "Where's your dad?"

"Down at the boat house, I guess."

"How're them books treatin' ya?" another shot out.

"Not too good. Not too good, Ray. I'm leaving books alone for a while."

"But you got to graduate soon, don't you?"—it wasn't a question as much as a probe.

Ezra kicked at the floor. "Don't think so," he said, as if it meant nothing in the world. "Can't see why I should or I shouldn't."

A hand clapped him on the shoulder. "You might be making more sense than you think. There's nothing important you can learn by sticking your nose in some book that you can't learn out on the water earning your living just like everyone else."

Pleased faces, sidelong glances seeking agreement.

Ezra suddenly turned serious, rubbing his chin—casually something coming to mind that had been bothering him.

"Anybody know where Earl Varney is these days? Haven't seen him down by the cove for—"

Ezra stopped as he noticed that the chatter between the benches had stopped cold and that silence had come down like a hammer.

"Gone back up to the Mountain," Jesse said, eyeing Ezra up and down.

"The Mountain," Ezra said.

The others were panting on the benches, their eyes locked in divergent directions.

"He's still up there, then," Ezra said.

"Didn't say that," Jesse said. "That's just where he went back to. He might be buried in it by now."

Ezra didn't move. He looked around, as though picking subjects abstractly out of the air. "I was just thinking lately about that boat—must have read something—about those people from up around Rehoboth. About the *Raven* and all that."

There was no pause among them, no need to conjure either the memory or the boat itself. Their conversation turned to the *Raven* as though that was what they'd been talking about all along:

"Where they found them bodies and everything!" one bellowed, "Had to have happened right here, where Clayt fished! Jesus christ Clayt never went any goddamn distance except right here off the bell buoy!"

And another: "Then Clayt found Floyd right out back among the shoals. I found the last one, a gal—"

And another: "They was all gals, Lyman—"

Then the one called Lyman: "But this one was right out in the tuna fish area—"

The other: "They was all mostly in the tuna fish area, Lyman—"

Lyman: "Oscar Gilliam really found her—"

"That's right, Lyman. Now you're getting it."

Lyman: "Fact, ran right over her. And Oscar come up to me and I had a dory that day. It was a weathery day, a fog sea, and

Oscar's outboard had chewed her up some. She was just a young pup. I didn't know how I was going to handle her without her breaking up in pieces like a piece of soggy bread. We sank the dory underneath her so she flowed right in. Then the father come down from Rehoboth and thanked me and all that, didn't even say nothing about the propeller chewing her up, and he took her back up there to be buried with the others."

And another: "That one you're talking about, Lyman, had that watch on her. Froze at ten something," Orrin said.

"Nine," Jesse said, "It said nine something."

"They took that in for evidence, but they never knew which it was, ten in the morning when that watch got wet—"

"Nine in the morning—"

"Or ten in the evening."

"Nine," Jesse said.

Lyman: "And when Clayt found Floyd, he had that keg tied to his body. Of course he perished in the cold water—"

Ezra made a fist, as though something had hit him, something he was supposed to have remembered, and he was readying to defend himself if it hit him again.

"It was a fog sea!" said another.

"What keg?" Ezra said, quietly, trying to see it: his father cursing under his breath at a knot; a glint of metal—

"—in order to go back to Middle Reef, Floyd wouldn't have retraced his steps. No. He swung out around and set his course for Dyer's Cove."

And another: "You don't know that, Jim. They aint found nothing out there."

Another bellowed: "Wasn't that a foggy day!"

And Lyman: "Didn't Earl have the other boat, looked just like it? A long, narrow son of a bitch."

"That day I was working on putting in a new engine," Jesse said, not with any interest, as though merely playing a role, passing the plateful of conversation along through the air. He kept his eyes on Ezra, surveying him. The others shook their heads, seeing more and more, their memories outrunning their knowledge now.

Another said: "Wasn't Clayt just about doing it all, going

out there again and again like he was possessed or something, picking them gals up and towing and hauling them in by the load and dumping them right off here"—his arm floated up, he looked at Ezra—"off here in Mackerel Cove, like he was the coroner himself."

And Lyman: "And all them cars lined up at Dyer's Cove for so long because all those people had the keys in their pockets. Took a month or so—"

"Took three months, Lyman—"

Lyman: "Three months it took, at least."

Ezra leaned in: "What about this keg tied to Floyd?"

The silence fell hard, like something off a shelf. Everyone went still and unfocused as though the electricity had gone out, except for Jesse Johnson, who focused on Ezra. The question settled like dust.

Then: "She had no bearing underneath her," one said, shaking his head, and everyone else came back to life.

"She was just like a file for christsakes. Floyd dumped two tons of concrete to ballast her, but she still had no business being on the water."

And another: "The one I brought in, she was blacked like she was burned. I still say there was fire. That U-boat snuck up on her, took the men and set her afire."

"There wasn't no fire. Anyway what would the Germans want with a whole bunch of businessmen and boys from Rehoboth? You talk about finding only the women. Wouldn't it be that if you got a situation like that, something happens and the boat's sinking, the men would get off first and leave the ladies on board in the hope that, you know—"

And another: "In a panic you do things you wouldn't ordinarily do. In a fire-panic—"

"I still say there wasn't no fire."

Ezra listlessly cast in his question once more like an apathetic last troll into a barren pool: "What about that keg tied to Floyd?"

Again the silence, but this time from impatience.

Jesse Johnson tipped back his empty coffee cup and flicked his tongue at the last drop. Then he looked at Ezra. He did not speak to confide in him, not even to dispel a rumor or replace it with a fact, but only to speak to him, whomever he was: "Why are you asking us now," he said, finally, no more passing the plate.

They all looked at Ezra, then, their eyes knowing, as though not one of them had forgotten for a moment the eyes of the young nine-year-old boy who'd brought every one of those bodies in.

"You were there, Ezra," Jesse said. "You were in the boat, too. You fished out those women yourself. You had Floyd roped around the neck."

"I've seen something in a book," Ezra said. "It's not my recollection. I just wanted to check."

"What," Jesse said.

"Leslie Everett Dove," Ezra said.

"Dove," Jesse said, "Yes, him. Dove. Fool."

At the southern tip of Great Island they turned their back on the shore and tilted up the hillside, ducking and shifting along Strawberry Creek like a convoy of boxers, arm over arm through stubby bunion-knuckled trees pointing listlessly into the air like crowds of old men. They were singing and shrieking, calling out to Ezra at the head of the line, branching off through the low forest, branching off again.

"Ezra!" one of them called, a boy Ezra's age, smartly dressed, glasses, soft in the hands and face. "Where are you taking us?"

Ezra could feel the breath of the girl behind him. He had not turned to see her. He only just knew her name. Rachel. She was someone's sister, maybe the sister of someone who was there. He didn't know. There were these girls, friends of his friend Bobby, from Mount Holyoke in Massachusetts up to Maine to taste the promised wilds outside Bowdoin's clipped green quads and old stone buildings, the spires, the clock tower. The infamous craggy shore. Take us, lobster-boy. Noon. They'd met at noon. There was Ezra's pickup. There was Bobby's daddy's car. There were fourteen of them, seven and seven. Screaming in the back of Ezra's pickup. The clinking of bottles. Up front it was quiet. Just him and—it was Rachel. Rachel. Remember: Rachel. He would not look at her. He could feel her glancing at his legs, his thighs, his arms, his chest, his thick neck. What did she look like? Dark hair. He hardly knew. He wouldn't look, and neither said a thing.

He'd promised Bobby he knew this swimming hole up on Great Island. Yes, Bobby, quiet. Yes, Bobby, secluded. Hardly anyone knew it was there. It was warm even in Spring. A peat and blueberry bog surrounded by wild berries, flowers, the smell of the sea but none of its cold and dark.

Bobby poked him in the ribs.

Bet you've worn out the grass up there, though, eh?

Ezra hadn't even smiled. It hadn't occurred to him what Bobby was driving at until the words—Wouldn't know what you're talking about—were halfway out of his mouth.

Bobby lost it. Mistaking Ezra's innocence for amateur dead-pan humor, he howled with knowing laughter, clapping Ezra on the shoulder, Atta boy, it'll be great, and I got just the girl for you.

"Perfect, old lobster-boy, sounds perfect!" followed by a sort of laugh. More snorts.

Now they were walking.

"Which way do you live?" she said from behind him.

"Not here. No one lives up here but the Mountain people."

"Mountain people. Sounds spooky. Like a horror movie."

"It's not a movie. They're just real people. They don't fish. They just live up here."

"What do they do."

Ezra shrugged. "Just live, I guess."

"Are you really a fisherman or was Bobby just making that up?"

"I really am."

"And your daddy?"

"He really is too."

She squealed. "A real fisherman," she said to herself. "My friends back home won't even believe it."

"It isn't anything to believe or not. Just is."

She was looking at him from behind, he knew it.

"You live with your parents around here somewhere?"

"Two islands over. This is Great Island. I live at the end of Bailey Island. I'm building my own house there."

"You mean you're going to stay here?"

Ezra glanced back at her. He guessed she was pretty, though he couldn't have said how. He'd never thought much about it.

"It's as good a place as any."

She was looking through the trees.

"You stay there now?"

"Where."

"The house you're building," she said.

"When it's not too bad. I don't have it insulated or anything yet. Just getting the roof on now."

"But on a nice night, if you wanted to, like if you had company, you'd be able to stay there?"

The sea and the eyeless fish houses and the briny chum dropped quickly away. The branches flashed in the low sun like sabers. The wind sailed down the Mountain: apples and woodfires and sugar and human excrement. Criss-crossed glimpses of the rooftops of tin privies. The trail banked, hard as asphalt past plywood and tarpaper and corrugated metal shouldering against the sweet-and-sour wind, the hot dark insides loud with children and yapping mongrels. Stove pipes blackened the branches above.

Far behind and getting farther, his Bowdoin friends and their Holyoke girls, singing and laughing, filled the woods with themselves.

They were pulling away. Ezra could hear her breathing.

At the mountain's top a slight depression, suddenly out of the wind and in another country. An overwhelming fragrant somnolence. One at a time as they turned the bend, Ezra watched their faces stretch.

A peat-black pond, still water, grounded version of sky. As if below them lay another world, twin to this one, headed the opposite way.

Berry bushes closed in on the water's edge like blue and red clouds rolling in, converging on this one point. As if this were an apex of this island, its source of gravitational pull.

Spring fed, a gurgling source somewhere under the thorns.

A clap on his back. A wink, a knowing nod. "Way to go, sport. You're a hero."

They were clapping his back. The girls touching his elbow, as if for good luck. As if he were a lucky statue perched outside the exam hall doors whose elbows and knees were worn by the grazing fingers of generations of superstitious students. He didn't even know their names. There was Bobby. And Rachel. But he wouldn't be able to pick her out of the bunch even now.

They moved down to the water line, a small glade for a beach, instantly littered with bottles and letter-sweaters and paper bags of cheese and bread and grapes. And now a blouse, a pair of pants, one shoe then the other, then a pile of shoes, as if gotten together for a collection for the poor. A hat, a shirt. A brassiere, fluttering weightlessly to the ground. As if these bodies had melted out from under their clothing.

They were screaming, not even in the water yet. The white and blue flesh bobbling in the sun. Geometric patches of hair.

Ezra stood back against the berries.

"Ever been to a Bacchanalia?" Bobby had asked him last week.

Ezra had looked at him.

"Why're you looking at me that way?"

"I don't know what you're getting at, I guess."

"A Bacchanalia. A great big party with girls and wine. To celebrate our graduation, our send-off into the world."

He never told them they were going off without him.

She was hanging back with him, pretending to be interested in some insect on a berry plant. She'd thrown down her sweater, taken off a shoe, then seen him and slipped it back on and stood there looking away.

The perfect water broke. White bodies against the black peat. They were pairing off. She was looking back at him over her shoulder.

"Come on lobster-boy!"

They cheered him. They cheered for him.

Ezra raised his head. His work pants, his unravelling sweater. His hands like shovels. The berries receded, leached of color, gray, gray fog roiling.

In the water a girl rose up and sprang, arching awkwardly back down, skimming just below the surface, arms circling and legs circling, her face compressed as if by a stiff gale. Her head rose like a weed-draped stone. And then the rest of her, slick and bluish in the sun. She went to her back and threw out her arms, opening her legs, her breasts afloat, her hair and the tips of her dark triangle coiling and unfurling at the surface, like algae. And she came to him, he saw her there in the pond: the points of her shoes and her gunmetal stare aimed vacantly at nothing, like a mannequin. Then the other women, spinning slowly in the center of the cove, arms outflung, legs sprawled. Their hair had come undone, puffing up and back, up and back with the white petticoats like the folds of jellyfish. Their faces were blue, and their stillness not a mass death but as though a momentary pause in group exercise. They converged, bumped apart and converged again, making transfiguring designs of the black water between their legs and each other like a string of snowflake cutouts across a night darkened window. They were faintly, delicately beautiful. They had only just begun to prune.

He was breathing hard, sweating, blinking his eyes clear. She—Rachel—mistook his agitation for desire. Maybe a game. He felt her hands in his hand and he looked down on her, and saw himself twinned in her eyes. In the water they were looking up at him.

Her head tapped against his shoulder then leaned. He took the weight of her head, heavier than he would have thought, and felt in his hands the weight of the first girl his father had found. Her nose and mouth already gone, as if shot away. Her eyes cataracted. Otherwise, she looked merely blind, vaguely alive.

In the water the others were coupling like ballroom cripples, leglessly, armlessly dancing, looking up to the sky and writhing in palsied shudders. Then she was on him. She gently prodded him to the ground and he looked up to her—Rachel, he reminded himself—her face eclipsing the sun, which spread around her hair like a fiery halo. A small soft pressure on his own face. He turned aside, grimacing not at her hand but at a fleshless palm, torn, pierced through by the end of a rusted gaff.

A soft giggle, the girl's throaty moan. She took him by the shoulders and drew herself atop him. Their underwear shackled their ankles. He touched one knee by accident and her legs fell open bonelessly and swam around him as she took him and guided him toward the dusky center of her straddle.

He opened one eye. Spread throughout the pond, seven pale piles of limbs, bared teeth, faces curtained off by their hair. The top of a girl's head, swinging up, a glimpse of open mouth, her eyes closed, chin tipping back and then whipping quickly forward and plunging down.

Rachel leaned back and Ezra looked down at where he disappeared into her, overgrown, glistening, chafing steadily against her at an unmediated tempo erratic and designed for no momentum he could think of. He fingered one of her buttons, and she undid them herself, ripping at the last one, and her breasts fell out, splotchy and pale. He cupped one in his palm and she fell forward and put her tongue in his mouth. From within he was given a vague signal that this was the time to stand up and away. But the slow-rising, the tightening everywhere both too soon and too late. Everywhere she was tight. She was like his rod itself and he forgot her. Pressing up, he clutched at a pair of feet, surprised to find them bare and perspiring. Rising, bracing her, he lifted, cradling her bare halves in his hands, suspending them both above the grass in a stationary jitterbug.

Oh, not yet, not—

His thighs tightened, and looking up directly into the sun twitch twitch twitched into her. Emptying. He made no noise. His legs gave and he fell back. He tasted warm wetness on his tongue and touched his lip and took away a bloodied finger. He felt the finger taken. She had it in her mouth, stropping her teeth as she still grinded against him, eyes shut, mouth parted, lips curled at the ends into an impish grin. Beads of sweat were catching in her bleached moustache. She let out a soft whelp as she closed her eyes then popped them open and stared mutely into the berries. Faintly like the drowned from the bottom of a pool. He shut his eyes. But there in the dark he saw the pile of women stacked on the raft, some eyeless, like a crop of tuberous vegetables.

She caved, draping over him, her arms circling his head. Her lips pressed into his neck, groping there like the end of a tentacle. Her dark hair in his mouth, in his eyes, in his nose, unsprung and everywhere.

"I can't tell you anything more," he said.

She sat still. "What?"

But his eyes were averted, seeing not the inky pond water below them but the horizon on a mid-July dawn nearly eleven years behind him. The last of the found—but for the ragged and eyeless one in Biddeford yet to come—had been gone already for weeks off the big raft, packed away in the black ambulance and into Rehoboth mud. His father beside him, and his father's father beside him, and Jesse Johnson and Jim Sinnett and the rest of the Bailey Island lobstermen standing not shoulder to shoulder but scattered over the wharf and in the fish house, digging into the salt baths for their chum—they froze in their places, as though they'd heard a shot; their gaffs hung the lengths of their legs. Even Earl Varney, who'd come down to negotiate himself a new partner among them, shaded his eyes east into the sun. It was Jesse who'd seen it first, digging in the fish house: "Well, I'll be," is all he said, and one by one the others heard it or saw someone who had: the dim skyline of a ships' convoy like a distant city passing along the horizon, headed south out of Casco Bay.

"That's the whole lot of them out of Hampden Yards," the preacher Sinnett said, "They've been getting ready for weeks. They're flushing them out all at once."

"Well, we're in it now," one said.

"Not yet," another said, "This don't mean anything. Just maneuvers."

"That Kraut sub probably criss-crossing beneath them right now," the one said.

"Well we'll be safe then," the other said.

"They're not for us," Jesse said quietly. "No fleet that big is for us."

"Pearl," Sinnett said. "First the canal, then Pearl Harbor."

"Which way we going to fight?" one said.

"Looks like west to me," someone called out.

"East," said another.

"We're fighting in neither," said a third. "I'm telling you we're staying out of it."

"Look out there, Orrin, and tell me what you see," the one said.

Clayt scanned the wharf. "Where's Semicek? Semicek should see this."

The others took up the cry: "Semicek!"

The man had shrunk into the corner of the fish house and was wheezing in the dark.

"Semicek," Jesse said, "Go on and signal your friends now. Better hurry before that convoy gets out of range."

"He can't, Jesse," said the one, "It's daylight. He's got to wait till dark or he might get seen."

"Better hurry, Semicek," Jesse said, "You got till dark to prepare. Look it up: Con-voy. Dot dot dash dash."

"Quiet you old fool," Semicek said, "You don't know what you're talking about."

"Ha ha, Semicek," Jesse said, not laughing but panting out loud, "Ha ha. Hey now, Semicek. We seen the light. Didn't know you were so clever. Didn't know you were smart enough to know Morse Code. You fooled us. But don't worry, it's our little secret. Dot dot dash."

"You fools!" Semicek cried. "Seeing things. Which one of you was the one? Who saw it? Hah!"

"Dot dash dot dash, Semicek," Jesse said.

"Who, Johnson, who? That's right, nobody!"

"Don't matter," Jesse said. "Just a little secret between you, the Krauts and all of these men standing here on this wharf and their wives. Don't worry, we wouldn't let it out. Oh, and of course the poor bastards on the *Raven*."

"Fools! Who saw it?"

"Don't matter—" Jesse said.

"The boy, Semicek," Clayt said, pushing Ezra forward a little, "It was the boy who saw the light on the water."

"Him? Ha! Boys make things up," Semicek said, "Born liars—"

"On the water at land's end, Semicek. Once last week and once before that. On the water. Then he walked the rocks and saw the blinking from your window—"

"He's made it up," Semicek said, "for attention. He's always been a dreamer. There wasn't no light in my win—"

"Dot dot dot dash," Jesse said.

"A boy like that gets bored," Semicek said, "The island's not enough for a dreamer like that. He's got to make things up himself so he can grow—"

"So it was the boy, Semicek," Clayt said, "And when we catch you we're going to put an end to it. And if it turns out it was a Kraut sub that took out the *Raven*, and it was a signal of yours that guided it, we're not going to tell nobody about you. But by god you're going to wish we did."

Gargling now, Semicek burst out of the corner and pushed through the forest of lobstermen.

"Dash dash dash, Semicek," Jesse called after him.

Everyone watched as he hobbled quickly up the hill. Everyone but Ezra and Earl Varney. Ezra looked straight at Varney, Varney looked back and forth from Semicek to Ezra, as though comparing them, as though deciding which one was telling the truth. No one but the boy had seen Varney when Floyd Johnson came back under the piece of canvas. But the boy had seen Varney's face at the window of his truck. All the boy knew in that circumstance was grief and worry and surprise and rage. You could hide part of it, he knew, because his father let loose only the rage. But he thought there was no way to hide it all; until he saw Varney's eyes that day, as scientific as marbles. He had no words to describe them, he didn't think there were any. Then he and his father went back into the fog. But now, eleven years later, he was certain what he'd seen in Varney's face when Semicek ran away up the hill: still no grief, or surprise; and rage was gone. But worry had begun to show.

It was late afternoon. Ezra stood alone in the Mountain woods. The sun was low, coming up the hillside through the trees from below, surrounding each tree with a halo of orange fire.

Ezra stopped at the edge of the clearing. Earl Varney was squatting over the creek, dipping a stockinged foot into the water to wash his socks. He spotted Ezra and straightened taught and tall as a pole.

"Ezra Johnson," Ezra called out. "Ezra Johnson," he repeated, not the name now but a password. As soon as Varney looked settled Ezra moved. He approached the creek, looking furtively for signs of someone else. He saw no one. Varney sniffed, wiped his nose with his hand and backed his other foot into the water.

Somehow, Varney was a ragged shadow of what he was the last time Ezra had seen him. His eyes red-rimmed, his jaw spotted with patches of beard. His head was cropped, shorn unevenly, mere tufts in places, the scalp bared in others, like a sheep's. It left the impression that he had been hurried along an assembly line through some sort of institution during an epidemic for lice; that there were others just like him up and down the Mountain, shorn and freshly disinfected.

"Hey."

Varney squatted by the water. He didn't look up. He took a shirt from a pile and pushed it under the current. "What're you doing up here, boy."

He lifted one arm out of the water and raised it toward the trees. He might have been pointing the general way down, or he might have been indicating the greater distance to the horizon, banishing Ezra from these regions for eternity.

"I heard you," Varney said.

Ezra looked at him.

"You oughta learn to keep it down, boy. Sounded like a goddamn whorehouse up there. You oughta have more respect for a person's home."

Ezra stepped from one foot to another. He squinted off into the trees.

"I'm sorry about that, Earl. I didn't know—"

Varney snorted. He didn't even look up. "What would your daddy think of you if he heard you brought up a bevy of little girls for your schoolfriends to fuck in the woods. You know what those good people of yours down there think of fuckin', don't you? They'd throw your soft ass off the water, out of the cove."

Ezra turned to look the other way as if he was being followed. In the distance, down the hill, cooking fires played off the trees.

Varney laughed. "Don't worry, boy. There isn't nobody up here that can hear us. You just remember that you aint no better than anyone else. You get hard like every other man on these islands, and you want to put it in her just like every other man on these islands. Every other man. We're all the same. The rest is bullshit. Church talk. On the water, and in the bed, we're all the same—" Varney spat in the water.

Ezra swallowed. All his life Varney was wrong. He was the one everyone pointed to to say what was wrong with the world. When he was living in the fish house on Mackerel Cove, he had girls coming and going every night. Brunswick girls. Bowdoin girls. Locals under the cover of darkness. He had more girls than all the men who fish out of this cove put together. And the lobstermen knew some of their daughters were among them, had probably been among them that very morning, whatever morning they were sitting in the General Store mulling Varney over. A man didn't dare ask the others whether their daughters had slept in their beds because if those daughters had, his own might not. But Ezra never knew the full cause of the island's resentment against Earl Varney. And now, standing there, if his father knew what went on up here today, where would that resentment lie? It was as if everyone walked a thin line, walking toe to heel along some course, swaying in the wind; and the distance between good and evil was only as wide as your foot.

Ezra stepped from side to side in the dirt. Where was he standing now? Varney wasn't laughing. Maybe that told him where.

"Earl, a somebody named Leslie Everett Dove come see you or talk to you lately?" Ezra asked.

Varney's hands hesitated for a half moment under the water, then went on with their work.

"Don't you anger me with those nitpicky questions. Not after what I seen today."

"I was just asking."

"If he did what goddamn business'd be of yours?"

"None, Earl. I guess."

"You guess? You come up to a man's home and start interrogating him on his own property, especially after dirtying it with a bunch of high-class girl whores. And you just a punk who doesn't know nothing about what's life and what isn't except what some old men put down in some goddamn books at that college of yours? All those girls you go to college with? You getting soft on us fishermen, Ezra Johnson, I knew it all the time. Seen you growing up and knew you'd turn out to be a girl. I knew it."

Varney snorted to himself.

Ezra's breath didn't so much as quicken. "'Cause he wrote about you, Earl. In one of those books. He said you've been diving out by Round Rock."

At his full height, Varney was a head taller than Ezra. But his brawn was gone. His clothes hung at his armpits and crotch.

"Still that? People saying stuff about me and that goddamn *Raven*, still coming after me for that?"

"I didn't mention the *Raven*, Earl."

Varney's lip curled in a snarl. He stepped toward Ezra then stopped where he stood. He looked past Ezra into the burning woods. "Well, what else would someone write about me anyways. Goddamn *Raven*. I'll never live it down. What did he say."

"That you've been diving out at Round Rock."

"What else."

"Nothing."

Varney bared his teeth on something between a grimace and a leer. "Well. Then he knows, then, don't he? Nothin'. Aint a lot of fun but there it is. Nothin'."

Varney squatted and shoved a pair of trousers under the water, as though drowning them.

"What's out at Round Rock, Earl?" Ezra said.

Varney lifted his face. "You look out at the water and what do you see, boy?"

"Flat water at high tide, ledges at low."

"Well there you go. Aint you the genius."

Ezra looked at him. He gave nothing away. He had to give him credit. He'd never changed his story. No one had been able to prove a thing after bodies started coming in. There was only Earl's sudden silence, a kind of calm unusual for him. He didn't seem to care one way or the other. But that was no crime. Years passed and the talking stopped, and so did, Ezra assumed, the wondering; the island people had to get up before dawn and pull their living from the water. They had to eat, had to sleep. They went to church and died. They knew there'd be other accidents, other bodies, other lives; and there were. But never so many lives. Bodies that kept coming. And though the island went on with its working life, Ezra knew they were never forgotten. Yet no one had said a thing in years. The silence wasn't good, nor bad; it was a kind of efficiency of spirit.

"There're letters, Earl," Ezra said.

Varney pulled out a pair of socks, dripping from his hands like dead fish.

"People wrote things to Leslie Everett Dove," Ezra said.

Varney shook the socks as though trying to free his hands from them. "What things."

"He didn't say."

Varney snorted. "You just like your daddy. Trying to catch me out his whole goddamn life, like everything in the world's my fault. Like when he lost his first boy that was my goddamn fault too. He come stormin' over to my house askin' me what I seen. What I seen? What I seen? I seen the flat backside of some bitch's ass, that's what I seen. Goddamn day after Christmas and he asks if I seen his boy. Like I was hiding him under the bed."

Again Varney stood to full height. Ezra was losing him in the twilight. Just his face and his hands glowing dimly.

"I told everyone who asked I didn't know nothin' about the *Raven*. Goddamn Floyd. Go ask him. Go sit on his plot of dirt down there, sit on his big tombstone, and ask him what happened. I sure as hell don't know. And I don't care. It's eleven years already, and I'm sick of being asked. Somebody want to write that I know something, you send him up here to Earl Varney and I'll tell him in one word everything I know. Now get the hell down off my mountain before I—"

But the threat was cut off by a high-pitched mechanical scream, starting down on the water and flying up the Mountain, through the trees like an invisible flock of birds and by them.

"Goddamn Helen Murray tripped off that siren again," Varney said.

Ezra's first thought was that somebody was found, or raised. Who was lost? He didn't know, there was always something.

Then he looked down toward the water. A soft glow hung over Lowell Cove like a phosphorescent cloud. Then a flash, the sky lit briefly. A moment later the air percussed, a single clap of thunder, echoing through the trees like a rifleshot. The ground beneath them trembled, then stilled. The cloud had risen.

Ezra stepped then stopped, breathing hard. He turned back toward Varney, but Varney was already looking past him, clutching a sock in each hand, peering over the tree tops, toward Lowell Cove.

The last time the siren had been let loose was just two months before.

It had started off a clear February day. The coastal boats had done their runs and come in. A Bailey Island man, Leo Blackburn, a friend and one-time partner of Clayt's and most of the older lobstermen, was then skippering a large schooner that stayed out for days at a time. The *Angela*. The *Angela* was past lobstering; they went for pogies, tuna, swordfish. Whatever they could get they'd take.

This particular day had been the eighth out and the last. It had been an exceptional run, fine days, cool and calm, and crisp but clear nights. Blackburn had driven his men more than he ever had. A twelve hour day, a supper, then back out on the water for another eight. He knew the catch was going to be good, he'd told Clayt later. But it had been better than good, a record, ten-thousand pounds at least.

Below Blackburn his men huddled on the deck in a standing sleep, ripples against the black water and the black morning, steadying themselves for the last flying set of the trip. His brother, another friend and one-time partner of Clayt's, was down there somewhere among them. But Blackburn had thought about that: he'd made his brother part of the commissioned crew, then made good on his promise to treat him as but one oarsman among the sixteen boats he carried. He knew that all of them were ready to drop from fatigue, but he'd found them their fish. No captain on the east coast made his men more money, and they were all poor, all poor men.

A footstep broke the silence and approached to within ten paces of Blackburn and waited. Blackburn could hear Tom Hynes breathing, the water was that calm. He looked up and behind him, then ahead at the horizon, and again behind him. It was all silent, it had all been a string of good luck, but once you had the luck it becomes a fact and no longer just good fortune. He'd had seven facts of good days behind him, he told Clayt, and something else in front, not fact but not really fiction either: you can't predict it, it's going to happen, you can't make it up. But this sky he could read, he'd spent his life reading the sky, and he read that by midnight it would be the eighth fact, and that by the next morning they'd all be a little richer.

"Good morning, Tom," Blackburn said.

"It is," Hynes said.

Every morning on the water, it was what they said to each other. "How are they?" Blackburn said.

"Awake and steady."

"Set 'em off, then, Tom."

The men heard Blackburn's order, but they waited for Hynes to return to accept it. Blackburn could hear Hynes murmur, "Set 'em off." Still, the mass didn't move. Then another voice, the third that morning, Hynes's dory-mate Ben Harris: "Flying sets. Off we go now, boys." Only then did the huddle evaporate. They scattered in practiced and urgent motion, half to starboard, half to port, ringing two stacks of dories set one on top of the other. Eight pairs of hands hauled the top boat off, and four more swung in the three tubs of line, each fifteen-feet long, a thousand hooks per line gushing into the tubs; bucketsful of stars sparking through the red horizon light. Turning toward the water and collapsing like pallbearers, the eight shouldered the dory with all its gear and counted: "One"—swinging the boat over the side without commitment, then pulling it back: "Two"— threatening this time to let go, two men lingering off to the side leapt off barrels into the dory and scurried into the stern and bow by the time that—"Three"—the pallbearers heaved it all, dory, hooks and men, over the side, the oar-man rotating the blades before they hit.

Five minutes later the *Angela* had dropped the sixteen dories in a line as a fish will lay her eggs, and the men began to drift toward the same direction, filling the boat with fish to their knees. They hauled seine into nightfall and passed midnight. Sometime later, Leo Blackburn would locate the end of his dory line and the Angela would draw it back in, boat by boat, man by man.

The other nights had all been accounted for, every man, every hour. Not this one yet. The one thing Leo Blackburn could neither predict nor control, a nor'easter, blackened the horizon by noon. Cursing, his eyes wild, he swung the *Angela*'s bow at the nearest dory, two miles away, but reached only the eleventh of the sixteen by two in the afternoon. By then the sky overhead had gone green and come in low and the water had turned black. The air had gone brittle. A few flakes of snow floated past the deck and vanished in the water. Then a flurry. Then the world was cold and uncomplicated, white snow and black water, black water and white spray, living or drowning.

Blackburn could only guess at the line the dories took, knowing full well that the wind and swells had scattered them everywhere. But he drifted the *Angela* along the line anyway, stationing the returned men in all directions. The sea bucked but was not impossible. That would be another hour yet, not time enough to reach even halfway back to Bailey Island. But in the uncomplicated world an hour was a lifetime, and his brother, of course, was still out there. But he wiped that concern away. It could not be his first business, not even his business at all. There were nine others, ten in all, just ten men.

A half hour later the swells had eclipsed the boat and the snow had thickened. A man at port lifted his arm one way and a second at starboard lifted his another. Blackburn looked port and spotted his brother rowing strong and steady, his dory still full of fish. Off starboard he saw the small hunched forms of Hynes and Harris drifting away, Hynes's strokes already reduced to short jabs. There was nothing to decide. Blackburn turned starboard and pointed the bow dead at Hynes and Harris, but before he reached them they slipped out of sight. Again, there was nothing to decide. It was science, not desire. Blackburn turned his head, spun the wheel and ran the bow toward port, where he'd last seen his brother. But all he found was the impenetrable snow. Both boats were gone. The simple world: Blackburn turned the *Angela* at Bailey Island.

The temperature had fallen below zero. Hail plunked Hynes and Harris in their dory like stones. Frozen sea-spray cleaved at their faces. They chopped futilely at the ice massing in the boat and called to each other as though from miles away, warning each other not to close their eyes in fear of never opening them again. Harris stopped breathing and slumped over the stern before midnight. Hynes lost his mittens in the wind. Knowing his hands would be useless to him within minutes, he dipped them in the water and closed them around the oars and let them harden into claws around the wood and rowed his partner's body and his own into the driving snow.

Two days later, a search relay had been set up, up and down the coast, lobster boats and Coast Guard tracing ever-widening circles around the area where they were last seen to the Outer Banks. But Hynes had already rowed through all that. By the time the siren was blowing, he was rowing that skiff down the throat of Mackerel Cove. Heads were raised, and Hynes rowed right up to the wharf, his hands fused to the oars and he to his seat with Harris slumped dead in the bow.

That was two months ago.

Now Ezra pulled up to the wharf just as his father was running for his dory. Other dories were already launched, oars flying out in the cove toward the moorings like a panicked flock of birds. Motors gurgled in the water, warming up.

Clayt shoved off.

"Dad!"

Clayt whirled around, then pried the oars back and waited a leap away from the rafts.

"Get in here, boy, hurry up."

Ezra took the gangway three skids at a time and stepped hard into his father's dory, out of breath.

"Over by Lowell," Ezra panted. "I saw it from the Mountain."

Clayt rowed hard. The dory lurched beneath them.

"What were you doing on the Mountain?"

Ezra hesitated, then, shyly: "I passed by Earl Varney's."

"Varney! What're you talking to that piece of trash for?"

But Ezra didn't answer and the question was forgotten as Clayt rowed them to the *Hattie B.* Boats were already leaving the mouth of the cove, making land's end and turning back through the straight to Lowell's. Clayt and Ezra made no preparations. Clayt didn't even give the motor a chance to warm. Ezra dropped the mooring, the engine roared, the bow rose above the water and the land pulled away.

It was half tide. They hugged the shore, Clayt pulling hard on the wheel at unseen shoals, flying over low water. Ezra had never known him to take or even talk about such chances.

Then the air around them percussed, a mushroom cloud of vapor smoke rose behind the trees and towered roiling above them. Clayt yanked at the throttle, leaning forward as if to cantilever the weight of the stern, as if the few extra pounds would help their speed.

"What time is it," Clayt said.

"Don't know—"

"Goddamn it Ezra look at your watch."

Ezra held his wrist up to the bright cloud. "After seven."

"What after seven? Minutes, boy. How many minutes?"

"Six, seven."

Clayt bore down on the wheel. "It's been ten minutes then."

"Since—"

"Since the mayday. We were eating dinner. We were eating and he got on and started hollering mayday."

"Who?" Ezra asked.

Clayt said nothing.

At Dyer's Cove they rounded a finger of woods and headed straight for Lowell's Cove. The whole cove was lit as if it was day. Flames as high as a house poured out of the center, engulfing bow and mast as if a pyre had been ignited. The water around the fire was smooth as glass, black, like a standing pool of oil. A dozen boats idled in a wide circle around the flames. The rafts and the wharves were lined with standing bodies, and people were pushing down through the woods on either side. All their faces, and the faces of the pilots in the standing boats and the fishermen up in the tuna towers, were alight, themselves like dim lanterns held up to the brighter light.

When Ezra saw the boat he blinked to make sure he was right, then craned his neck to see into the water. There was no sign of life on the boat, and the water didn't so much as wrinkle for the wind. The cove was filled with the snapping and hissing of the fire and the silence around that.

Ezra hopped up on the bow and began climbing the tuna tower.

"That's all right, Ezra, I wouldn't bother."

Ezra came down.

"Just keep an eye on the water," Clayt said quietly. But it was automatic, a reflex. And they both knew it. There wouldn't be a thing to see.

Clayt shook his head. "He called his mayday and then he said he was going in."

"Going in? But he can't swim."

"I know that," Clayt said.

"Did he have his suit on?"

"You look at those flames and tell me if he'd have had time to get into his suit."

Clayt aimed the boat toward the burning wreck and they both stood—as every man in every boat stood—staring not into the water but into the flames.

"He done just what he was supposed to," Clayt said. "Send out a mayday, jump in and wait. Too damn long. Too damn cold."

"What was it, Pa?"

Clayt followed the vapor up into the sky, then back down

along the shaft of fire into the burning meat of the boat.

"Won't really know. Could have been a dozen things. My guess is that leaky gas line he kept saying he was going to plug."

A police skiff was pointed toward the *Hattie B* and motored across the clean water, breaking it up, peeling it back and passing wake through the wreck. It pulled up and cut its outboard.

"You Clayt Johnson?" called a voice.

Clayt stepped over, took a look at the man in uniform, a stranger, then stepped away.

"They said you're the one I should see."

"What for."

The policeman looked toward the flames, shielding his eyes. "About that."

"What about that."

"What happened?"

"It burned," Clayt said.

The policeman looked toward the boat as if this was news to him. "How?"

"You going to go in there and find out?"

"Nope."

"Then I won't neither."

On land, a pair of headlights stabbed through the dark and stopped at the wharf's edge and aimed out at the boat as if it needed to be spotlit. The motor was cut.

"Whose boat is it?" the policeman said.

"Jesse Johnson's."

"Where is he?"

For a while Clayt didn't answer. Then he looked at the policeman with utter contempt. "Where the hell do you think he is?"

"I don't know. Which one of you picked him up?"

"Could be just about any of us. We won't be seeing Jesse for a few days yet."

"He hurt somewheres?"

"He's drowned," Clayt said.

"What do you mean drowned?"

"I mean dead under the water, what the hell do you mean what do I mean?"

The policeman turned and took in the entire cove. He raised

his arm and pointed in no particular direction. Fish houses and rafts, various pylons and stray dories, the closest thirty yards away.

"He couldn't make it to one of those rafts floating over there?"

"Couldn't swim," Clayt said.

The policeman pinched his eyes as if overcome with a sudden stab of pain. He shook his head. "I'll never understand why you people won't learn to swim," he said.

"That's right," Clayt said. "You won't."

"Well, wasn't he wearing one of those rubber suits. You all are required to have those things on board, you know. They're supposed to save your life."

Clayt stepped over to the side and peered down into the skiff. He didn't say anything for a minute, as if wondering whether he should bother. Then he obviously thought he should, more for Jesse's sake than the sake of anyone still alive.

"You ever wear one of those suits yourself?" Clayt said.

"Can't say that I have."

"That's probably why you're still standing there breathing. You can't fish in the damn thing, can't move around in it. They say it takes but thirty seconds to get it on, but you try to put a rubber suit on in the winter, when the deck is covered in ice, and when you take the suit out of the case it's supposed to snap out. But it don't come out that way, it's frozen, it's stiff, the rubber's stiff and you got to pull it apart. We even took Matt Wardle— you know Matt Wardle?—up here to demonstrate getting into it. His boy and his son-in-law both drowned in the weather. Both had them suits on. Matt used to be a boxer and keep himself in perfect shape, but it took him five minutes to get into that suit, and on the water five minutes is a lifetime. It's ten lifetimes. When something happens you got thirty seconds tops to make a decision. Maybe you wouldn't know anything about that."

The policeman said nothing. He'd sat down in his skiff.

"So here's a man—Wardle—in excellent shape and he can't breathe he's so tired working to get into that suit. But let's just say for fun that you actually get it on. So you're up on deck and you jump overboard feet first like they tell you. Like we're

174

goddamn required. Nine times out of ten your head's going kerplunk right down into the suit, and then you're disoriented and you're going to drown anyway. We found two or three that way in the last year. And in a twenty mile an hour wind—which isn't much—you're in the water and suppose you do get over onto your back like they tell you to do. Then it's just a continuation of water going over your face and you can't breathe anyway. Find the body, yes, we'll find the body. We'll find Jesse sooner or later. Goddamn rubber suit. Nothing waits for you to put on that thing."

Clayt pointed at the flames, now dying. "Especially that."

After an hour, the *Hattie B* was one of two or three boats left on the water. Here and there, along the wharves, the cherries of lit cigarettes rose and fell and floated idling down about the level of the knees. Clayt stood leaning against the wheel staring, deeply abstracted, around him. The charred hull of Jesse's boat was listing, the stub of its burnt mast falling slowmotion toward the water. The writhing mass of the boat's contents—nets, wood banquettes, various equipment—began to fold upon itself, collapsing in a snapping hive. Sparks and minor eruptions scurried through like small red worms. Above, trails of burning ash spun on the heatcurrent, then released, eddying on the air, flying upward. A breeze, a small thing, had slid in from open water. The unseen pine trees at the cove's edge hissed softly, and the cove began to undulate, brushing aside the boat's debris, pulling piece after piece gently down.

The next morning, the lobstermen met at the General Store as they always did, though it was clear that some of them had been there through the night; they'd come through the neverlocked door and sat on the benches in the dark. Ezra's father was among them. No one had anything to say.

Ezra knew that on the water there was no such thing as luck, good or bad; that there were only consequences. It was something they all liked to say. It was something Clayt liked to say to him. But the island was going through a bad patch, starting with that morning Ezra and his father began hauling in upland women and laying them on the weighing raft. It had been a bad eleven or twelve years. But if this wasn't bad luck—and it wasn't—

then what was it? That was what Ezra at the General Store was thinking but not saying, wondering silently about these times, thinking about these consequences they were suffering. But consequences of what? To something said? done? What unknown crime? Was it not some visitation from the Book of Genesis, in which this small island was to bear the burden of some unknown original sin? Before June, 1941, it was no paradise, nor was it innocent; there were accidents—but it wasn't this. The sight of those half-naked women tangled on that weighing raft, uninjured, drowned, staring at the sky, and Floyd tossed on top there, was a vision of blasphemous hell.

Across the pond lights were coming on around the township of Rangeley. They wavered over the hillsides, as though a great city had lit its lamps. In the valley rose blue ropes of smoke, tightly braided and perfectly plumb, as though this depression were a hammock hung by cables from the blue dome of the sky.

A late spring frost had ambushed Maine the night before and was sunned off during the warmer day, leaving everything greener than it was. It had come again this night, glazing over the hills in the twilight.

Before Ezra knelt the old barn that had come with the cabin, listing heavily, ready to capsize under the weight of snows past and future. Each time he came here he remembered more deeply the nearby mountains, and the river running through them, a white froth, a flume beneath a snow crust, a deep black night without the stars or a moon. He remembered a hunting cabin that sat on the edge of a field, within hearing of a creek that slipped into the river. He remembered a winter moon that forded the currents of clouds. That he could see from his pallet where the snow ended, and where it began; and where it began it surged up against the fence and the old listing barn in giant drifts, breaking over the roof, twisting off in thick ropes like white smoke. It lay atop old upright things, worn and unused things, things that he had not noticed in spring: broken cars, abandoned commodes, tractors tipped on their sides that took shape out on the field as the snow set them in relief against the black forest. In summer, at night, the field was a still, pale water, the grass glimmering in the wind; the lights of the other hunting cabins wavering on the hillsides like distant ships. This was what he'd been told, lifted in the doorway by his father and told by him that when he grew up and started working on the water it would look like this, with the moon glancing off it and boats alight on the horizon.

Ezra arranged the sugarbeets and carrots and mangles and sifted over it the corn feed, then with two fingers made the small scrape in the slush.

His father had never believed in deer blinds. He'd derided the others, his friend Jesse Johnson for one, who would cadillac it with hot water bottles and portable heaters. He'd said that shining and scopes and shooting out car windows didn't need to be against the law. There were more important things they were against. Ezra had never seen his father hold a gun, or aim one. But Clayt had taught him to read the wind and the deer run and sit in a tree in the cold and get quieter as you waited until you could feel the blood moving in you and you were as still as the tree, or stiller. Turn your head so your face is in the lee of the wind and you breathe with the wind, you stir up nothing, like stroking a dory with a river current. Clayt took him into these woods and talked to him about that and left him, at first with Jesse, and later alone.

It was Jesse who'd taught Ezra how to hold a rifle, then aim it and fire it.

Ezra sat in a pool-deck chaise in the cabin doorway, a jacket over his knees and the rifle crossways over that. He had a cigarette in his hand. It had burned most of the way by itself. He'd taken up smoking this trip and wasn't sure it suited him. But he was willing to try. Something to relax him, and help him think through what he'd just seen, and was seeing, and figured he was about to see. He'd been in on that silent discourse at the General Store between the island men—he'd felt like a survivor, and for the first time in his life, though Clayt had never done anything but talk up the risks and the need to always be ready for something you cannot see until it's upon you, Ezra felt in danger. So he told himself he was relaxed now as he held his smoldering cigarette and watched the barn recede until it was a blacker shape against the black woods and the moon rose behind it, a peephole to another place, arctic, midday. He lay his head back and watched the darker half of the sky. The stars coming on. He heard the high buzz of a small plane. Faint news of the whistle from the nearby paper mill broadcast from the hillsides. But he wasn't relaxed. He felt the cabin empty and cold and dark behind him.

The morning after he and his father had pulled Jesse's charred remains up on one of their traps, he'd finally asked Clayt for a few days to himself and had had his request granted. Clayt didn't ask him why, and he didn't offer to come up here with him. They both knew it was less a vacation than a reprieve. He'd driven up here to his father's cabin in the foothills of the White Mountains to shoot deer, or shoot at them, or to merely load the gun and let it sit crossways across his knees, to eat something if he got hungry, and to think and to read. On the way through Brunswick, he'd stopped off at Bowdoin and taken out a few of Leslie Everett Dove's books for himself. They'd had four. One of them was this last one that Professor Morrill had shown him, the one with chapters about his son and about the *Raven*. Ezra had read it and was surprised by his resentment.

Somebody knew. Somebody knew something.

Ezra sat bolt upright. He shouldered his rifle and squeezed off a shot. The spit of flame lit the side of the barn like a flashbulb and he saw the deer flinch, as though it had been kicked, then arch and rise and make the woods in a single leap. He knew by the way she flinched it was a neck shot. He'd give it a half hour. That was something else Jesse had to teach him. If you went after it and made it a chase the meat would saturate with its own panic and would toughen and sour.

He sat back and listened to the report of his rifle fan out in the hills and broaden and wash over them, and he could almost see the sound of the cool emptiness it travelled.

Ezra went in and arranged the fire and the spit but didn't light it. He sat in one of his father's cedar chairs and lit another cigarette in the dark and sat with it burning at his knees with the wood arranged at his feet. He picked up one of Dove's books and fanned the pages and set it down again and watched it distrustfully. As if he knew he'd only just begun to understand its capabilities. As if everything suddenly were suspicious to him.

He didn't find blood right away and thought the wound had chilled and fattened. But then he did see it, three drops fingering out in the frost. He went arm over arm through the trees, swiping at the thickets with the rifle, head down, taking his time, letting the moon show him the tracks. His feet were wet and he knew they'd get colder before they warmed. He looked at the trees as he passed and here and there was a glistening black smear. Then the ground opened and the second growth trees were low and skinny and there was nothing but silvery grass between the trunks and the clear bloody tracks of the doe. The prints were getting closer together and deeper and he knew she was slowing. He took his time and lit another cigarette. It was full night now. The constellations unscrolled out from behind the horizon.

The tracks took him down a constant and slow descent then stopped at an old fence. They followed the fence then circled back around the other side of the pond. In an hour or so he found her in a clearing of stumpage wedged in the snow beneath a rotting log. Her eyes were closed but without feeling her nose he knew she was alive. They died eyes open and on the sky.

With one hand he placed the muzzle against her temple and when her eyes did open, his closed. He turned his head away. Then he opened his eyes and looked down at the doe panting in the leaves, her nostril and ear leaking black blood. He could feel in his finger the pressure of the trigger coiling. He released it. The rifle hung the length of his leg. He'd never had a hard time with this. It was a point of nature, his father had told him, a point of who they were. Man and deer. Man and man. It didn't matter. One died because the other lived, and one lived because the other died.

Ezra waited for the doe to open its eyes and look at him. Finally he kicked it and she did look up and Ezra gritted his teeth and swung his arm up, the rifle in line with it, the gun now merely an extension of his hand, and looking at her, forcing himself not to blink, he pulled the trigger. The shot leapt from treestand to treestand then growled in the woods like the lingering vapor trail of a fast car passing in the night. His arm shook and he tightened his grip on the stock of the rifle to still it. Then he exhaled and looked up at the sky and watched his breath leave him.

He dragged her by her hind legs to the edge of the pond and inserted the blade at the base and keeping a finger between the knife and the bowels he unzipped her to the breastbone. He curled his pinky around the breast muscle and snapped it. Steam rose around him and he reached in and lingered a minute to warm his hands. He rolled out the innards and reached behind the breast bone and snapped that. Then he lynched the doe in the trees. The guts lay in a smoking pile beneath the crossed feet. He made the slit at the neck and in three tugs ripped the coat down to the thighs, then propped a stick across the cavity to open it to the air.

The surface of the pond had begun to skin. He stopped and listened and when hearing no sound punched with the heel of his boot a hole at the edge. He put his hands in the dark pooling. Water rose around his wrists. His fingers hardened in the cold then burned then were gone from him altogether. The blood slid and clouded and turned in amongst the peat in tendrils like blacker ink. The deer hung smoking behind him as though cooking in the moonlight.

He went in and made the fire and opened his bedding to it. When the first coal fell he went out with a pot and a carving knife. Behind him lines of firelight scissored through the windshot planks and the roof of the cabin and into the trees. A dim square fell out the window and lay in the snow, a trap door to other, sunnier times.

The deer had cooled and now hung disrobed, its neck taught, snout averted as though having heard its name. Its limbs were delicately crossed at wrists and ankles. He'd always thought it hard the way they looked like dancers at the very end, interrupted in first position with their muscles wound just as tight and translucent with the cold. He lay the back of his hand against the flank. Then something about the way the deer looked made him turn his head toward the pond.

He saw the horseshoe cove, dammed off from the sea by

driftwood and ice. The steep and perfectly scoured walls had dropped, the floor heaved, catching only stagnant puddles of brine frozen at the edges. The underside of everything—everything covered over for good reason—stank like a drain. A sewage pipe dribbling muddy icicles dangled between the barnacles of the fish house posts. Scattered about below, abandoned lobster traps resurfacing out of the silt, and, like haystacks, tangled piles of women, no longer spinning slowly in the water, no longer faintly beautiful: half-buried elbows and knees, hair-snagged fingers not easily identified as this one's or that. Backs and bottoms chewed and nibbled at. Skin pulled aside as though cloth napkins off loaves of bread. Eyeless stares. Bared spines. Shredded corsets. Mounds of bloody buttocks.

Ezra whirled away and remembered the things he'd read in Dove's books. He remembered what his father had said to him about people who die on the water by profession, the captains who drown standing chained to the wheel; the sailors who, recognizing their end, lash themselves to a mast in the hope that at least their bodies might be retrieved and given a proper burial: those who in the calm afterward could be seen from shore caught high in the rigging, a blemish in the sky.

He cooked the filets and brought them outside. He leaned back in the chair and left the plate on his knee and eyed the pond while his food cooled. Eventually the meat skinned over and sat in a pool of jelly. The pond from this angle was merely a thin strip of water. He felt inside him the beginnings of a grudge, against what or whom exactly he did not know. Some unnamed person or thing in these woods or back on the water. The thought came to him for the first time that every fisherman carried a similar grudge; that he had to; and that it was a heavy thing, but also delicate, because you could not talk about it, you could not necessarily give it a name.

He thought that eventually, maybe tomorrow or maybe weeks or years from this night, the grudge would surprise him by surfacing again. And then it might take him back down. He thought that the water was filled with people like him who wouldn't know how to die, who wouldn't know what of themselves to save. He wondered if he might not find them all.

WALTER

Blackshirts pointed the graveyard shift with their billy clubs past the loading docks, past groves of paper rolls eight feet and higher. Camp cots laid in regimented rows across the concrete platforms, all shrouded in thin refugee blankets much the same material floursacks are made of. Duffle bags occupied the boxes of shadow beneath, split and pouring their contents onto the concrete floor, underwear, bluejeans, a photograph, a set of brass knuckles. Below the loading dock, four acres of nude and crosshatched rail. A line of empty boxcars, ready to deliver or receive their legions of sleepers. Other boxcars padlocked in the dimness beyond. In the cavernous opening where the rails braided into two lines, the outer dark was spotlit. Out there, just beyond the lightline, came the sounds of a town and its inhabitants, like the stagehands preparing the sets behind a curtain stretching from earth to sky. He stood holding his hardhat in his hands like some little boy looking grimly over the high school gymnasium after a flood had warped the first floors of half the houses in town and chased the occupants here.

They tracked light bulbs in grim and sightless formation, down flights of narrow stairs and channels of greasy banister into the flatulent warmth, the urine-colored haze. Through the grates Walter McAlister saw two flights down, then two more, then two more. Above, goggled faces rushed the railing. Through the air ducts leading outside came the steady rumble of the commotion at the gates. An occasional roar as if from a faraway stadium, the rhythmic chant, "Scab! Scab!" nearly an endearment, like the name of the home team's clutch hitter striding for the plate. He kept his eyes on the ground as he passed the ducts, and averted his face, as if they were cameras, as if the commotion itself would recognize him.

The familiar dark soured then stung with chlorine. The ceilings gave way to freeways of dangling steampipes and valves. The heat took on its spongy weight. A hot wind of eggrot and burnt cabbage. The silent men around him peeled off their shirts, their flexing arms and backs and chests sending peacock-colored tattoos swimming into the haze. He kept his on, suspicious as he was; the shirt masked his thin arms and caved chest. Though twenty-four, he was already old.

He turned to the actual old man shuffling next to him. He was short with one blue-black hand and the other arm half gone, ended cleanly just below the elbow. Dark hair sprouted off the stump as if off a swollen knuckle. His eyes wide and unblinking, his teeth bared, his nose a small triangle but his nostrils too wide and too dark—as though he had no nose at all but merely two holes for air; his face more the front of a skull wrapped with skin than the front of a live head.

"How old are you, pops?" Walter said.

The man didn't look up. "Too old for this shit."

"You ever operate a paper machine before?"

"Johnsonburg, PA."

"What year was that."

"1934."

Walter kept walking.

The man who called himself a foreman, but who Walter had never seen in Rehoboth before in his life raised a hand for them to halt. A Statue of Liberty bled blue-gray on his right bicep, an eagle flapped its wings between his sagging breasts. He sent two men to reconnoitre the approaching dark. The column shifted its feet. No one talked. The two scouts returned and nodded and the foreman led them on like he owned them, branching them off, branching them again as though eluding a posse.

"I got nothing against the union. And I got nothing against this company. I'm just here earning my money like everybody else," the old man said.

Walter said nothing.

"What's your name?"

Walter reflected. It struck him that maybe here he had a different name that he wasn't aware of, or if he didn't he should.

He repeated his name to himself. He thought if he gave it he would be lying, or making a mistake. He knew that in town he was in danger.

"Forget it," he said.

The old man waved his stump like a flipper. "Christ, this is bad business. The worst I ever seen it. Everybody circled up like wagon trains around the bleach vats and wood room and even the goddamn lunch table. I'm just earning a living like everyone else."

"Well, I don't know about Johnsonburg 1934, but these spools of paper here this year weigh three tons. You keep alert."

Sixteen digesters rose sixty feet like a bank of missile silos. The lime kiln belly rotated on giant cogs into the dark of the next chamber. The pipes and valves furred with woodchips as though by a half inch of sooty snow.

Walter paced the catwalk above the digesters. In the office upstairs he'd met the four men in blue suits who had arrived a week ago in a big Chrysler with Idaho plates. He'd told them he'd been third hand on number four paper machine for six years but they had him down for the digesters. At least make him millwright, he'd said, or put him on a maintenance crew so he could keep an eye on things. But they told him he would go down to the digesters, and he held his hardhat in his hands and said nothing and went. Now he stood above it all in the hottest of the chlorine reek, watching the wood chips pass along the conveyer belts and pour down the digesters' throats like curdled milk, and he waited to press a button to let the cooking acids loose.

At noon, in the sound-proofed wet-end booth, the foreman slouched beside him. The old man stumbled in, flapping his stump toward the outside. He would not sit. The others rose.

Outside, a small cluster of hardhats glinted in the darkness of the next chamber. Five in determined locked step dangling lead pipes the length of their legs. Their faces soot black, raccoon eyes grim, alert. One carried a rifle by its stock, a .30-.30, the muzzle bouncing off his toe. Inside the booth, the tattooed men pressed on the glass like children fingering at the snow.

The mob unravelled. Four made a phalanx before the booth,

tapping their lead truncheons, their feet splayed like a squad of riot police. The one with the rifle split off and made for the giant lime kiln poking into the light of this chamber from the dark of the next. He threw open the round vent, and the white light passed through him. His hair fled his scalp as if in flames. He shouldered the rifle, took two steps and leaned in. He squeezed off a shot at the calcium stone threatening to clog the core, then another, then another. You couldn't hear the shots, just see the man's shoulder leaping. Then the rifleman pulled out, shut the vent, clamped it down and returned with the stock of the rifle in the crook of his arm like a sharpshooter. He passed his crew as though through cursory inspection and led them out.

"Christ," the old man said. "Who're they protecting against. We're no better nor worse than them."

"They call themselves the North End Protection Committee," the scab foreman said. "Thing is they are the north end. They're their own committee. Never split up. Sleep apart from everyone in the lunch room. Go into town together. They don't trust nobody, not even other scabs like us."

"I'm no scab," the old man said.

"Even scabs like us," the foreman said again.

Walter blinked in the morning light. The shift was ended, the sun was not yet up, though it was daylight, full strength and gray. A cold wind came down the valley. Above the mill the sky darkened, the clouds' purple and black underbellies blooming out of the stacks as though weather for the valley was generated by the mill itself. The emission hung dripping over the river like mist and in the forest like ground fog. The valley walls were brown smears and then they were nothing. The nearby trees stood headless. The beacons at the top of the stacks pulsed in the synthetic thunderheads.

He stood far below the lower gate and waited for the others to go. He'd said he didn't need an escort, that he wasn't a replacement worker and that he lived here, that this was his hometown. But two blackshirts loitered behind him anyway. They couldn't have been more than nineteen or twenty. They'd just come on shift, their hair was still wet and they twirled their billy clubs like happy gunslingers at the O.K. Corral.

He watched the vans pass through the crowd. He'd ridden the van in once, last week, when the strike had started. He'd met the others at midnight in the darkened and silent bar of the Hotel Rehoboth. Stepping from side to side, looking away, up, anywhere like a horde of awkward adolescents, they filed outside into the van and sat and stared straight ahead with their dinner pails between their knees. No one flinched as the rocks and bottles and spittle clapped down on the roof. No one said a word, as if they'd all done this before, as if it were just habit. Out of the corner of his eye he'd seen in the windows men he'd known since he was a boy, boys he'd stood beside at Scouts, children who'd sat behind him in the seventh grade. They rocked the van; they strung out into a chorus line and in concert unbuckled their pants and bowed away and pried their hairy cheeks apart and showed him the pink cracks of their asses and then their pink tongues as they called things at him through the windows he'd spent every day since trying to forget.

He squinted toward the power plant. Four silhouettes with rifles, perched at each corner of the roof. At the gate a wedge of white helmets drove back the pickets. Bottles launched like mortars. The vans drove through slowly. The pickets closed their ranks. A group chased them across the bridge over the river, then changed direction like a flock of birds and converged on a logging truck and set upon it, climbing the grill, chopping at the tires, punching up at the windows. A convoy of other trucks had halted on the other side. Two broke ranks and backed into a turn and edged out and drove downriver the way they'd come. The set-upon truck retreated to the far side of the river; dropping a striker for every ten feet it retraced until it arrived at the opposite bank, idling before the stopped convoy, unobstructed and grinding its gears. The pickets roared. Fists shot into the air.

Walter turned and circled the filtration pond, a gelatinous yellow soup a hundred yards across goosed to a rolling boil by submerged aeration pipes. Witch's brew, to him and Gordy, when they were kids. Even then he never could take this part, where it all came down to the resuscitation of the mill's rancid pudding into livable water. Its foamy return downriver of the mill. His father always reminding him as he left for the bank that it smelled like money.

The blackshirts followed him to the footbridge.

"You keep your eyes open now," one of them said.

Walter stopped. Four men loitered on the other side, their backs to him.

"We'll walk you across if you want."

Walter turned. One regarded him from under his black hatbrim. The other smiled at him a pitying smile. But he saw nothing there to speak to, just two boy wonders with glints of adventure in their eyes who'd just as soon be strolling down the boardwalk with beers in both hands as patrolling his town with billy clubs and a packed ankle holster. Either way their leer was the same. A one way ticket through the zoo.

He squinted out across the bridge. The men there were smoking. One cradled a paper cup of coffee in both hands, stamping his feet as if it was cold. But the temperature had spiked. It wasn't less than sixty.

"You be careful."

When Walter started across he could feel the blackshirts wondering what he'd do when they jumped him on the other side. He wondered too. Halfway over he stopped and leaned on the railing. He saw the blackshirts stiffen and knew by the change in their expression that the group across the river had turned to watch him.

He could feel the river in his feet. He knew the water well, in other incarnations, and he hated it. He hated to be around it. He hated the way it moved, and the way it smelled.

Water reminded him that he had no friends, that he'd never been able to make another close friend since then.

Even through World War II, Normandy. In the infantry in particular one didn't make friends. Because it was easier to lose a mere acquaintance than someone you loved. Because the one friend he did make, Timothy Gallo, a boy from Abilene, Texas, peeked out of the foxhole he and Walter shared between Hill 192 and the Phillius Gap and gave the right half of his face to an incoming mortar shell, his hands minus a few fingers plunking down one then the other beside Walter's. Seven years later, everyone gone, and he felt on this bridge the intuitive refusal to know the warmth of friendship ever again out of fear that the friend will go off one clear late June morning on a picnic expedition to Monhegan Island and return only in the spirit of a few dead bodies bumping against the rocks like driftwood.

Walter felt the river in his feet. He straightened and spat over the bridge. "Fuck it," he said.

They fell silent among themselves when he approached. Though they were walking the pickets he did not know them. He would have, at least by sight. He thought that maybe they were some others delivered by the union from the Jay mill, where the strike was meaner and gunfire was ringing out at night and dogs were found shot and disemboweled all over town.

One of them smiled an unamused smile and put a hand on his arm. "McAlister."

"That isn't my name."

"Yes it is."

"You've got the wrong guy."

"Oh no. That's you. The banker's boy."

The one who talked offered a styrofoam cup of coffee; Walter took it wordlessly and wordlessly walked on. Last week someone had laced the coffee in the mill with arsenic. Two men from Maryland were taken to the hospital and had their stomachs pumped.

He peered into the cup. Below a slick of oil hovered clouds of undissolved creamer. He threw the coffee into the bushes, then crumpled the styrofoam cup and threw it after the coffee.

"Hey buddy."

He heard footsteps.

"Don't you know how to say thank you?"

"You fucking prick."

"Traitor."

"Fucking scab."

"Cocksucking scab."

"Taking food out of my boy's mouth. Taking my job."

"There's nothing we could do to you that's bad enough. It wouldn't bother us if someone got shot."

Walter didn't look back.

It was six in the morning. The mill whistle blew across town, and in other times it could have meant the old ritual: some men falling into beds all over Sutherland Park, others climbing out of them. Kitchen windows would be thrown open and children roused and the noise of morning radio programs and baconsmell would be out on the street. But when Walter fell in beside the fifty-yard stretch of crumbling sidewalk, no sign along it was alight, no door was ajar; no anticipation of coffee, bacon, or anything. The beds remained unmade. And no one had slept.

The houses were high and old. The criss-cross of wooden steps and wooden porches tumbled across the building fronts through the smokey haze. Walter paused in front of his, distinguished only by some number on the post and the angle at which the top floors leaned into the street. Scabby gray clapboards extended from block to block like a warped sunbleached fence.

He stared up at his third floor. The door was flung open. He listened and heard only the hiss of the mill behind him. He took the stairs two at a time. His door had been left leaning neatly against the back of a chair, colandered by a shotgun blast. Little blooms of pink wood popped up out of one stretch of panelled wall. A fresh hail of splinters and lead pellets lay evenly scattered across the livingroom floor. From the doorway he could smell the gasoline. The plants were already wilting. The African Violets had keeled over. A door opened and closed across the street and he stepped farther in and faced his spraypainted walls. They'd taken their time. There would have been no police sirens, no downstairs neighbor.

He sat on the edge of his bed, turned on the lamp then turned it off and lay back along the outside of the covers. After a few minutes he got up, stripped and slid in between the sheets. The bedding was saturated with chill, the lightness of the sheets upon him made him full of skittish nervousness. He felt along his back the slim and gnarled mattress and the fatigue of the springs. He touched the hard pillow with his lips as though he could defrost it, and remembered intercourse in this bed, her face turning to him, the clenched warmth of the float of her breasts, Maria, or Gwen or Lily, she had told him, a stranger in a bar in Lewiston;

189

she'd had enough of life as a secretary, and after years of night classes at Orono she would become a civil engineer and go to live in Greece.

Exhausted though he was, it was his anger as well as the chill that made it impossible for him to sleep, and as he tried for unconsciousness it hurt more and more to have to be awake. He dozed off and on but had no understanding of deeper sleep. At some point he heard the floor murmur with the television of his downstairs neighbor, a man known to have walked the picket lines but who now sat all day and night in front of his television waiting for a phone call, who would have heard a shotgun blast directly above him in the middle of the night. Then he opened his eyes to the wall shuddering with the commotion of the bed-springs jittering under the neighbor's cocked fists. The room was warm now and the window full of late morning light, and Walter couldn't distinguish between the room of the dream and the room itself. Then he looked into the livingroom and saw the empty hinges dangling from the doorjam.

In the mirror he saw the top of his own head and looked at it with a deep sorrow which seemed restored now like the ghost of a memory, living or dead.

Walter got out of bed and shivered and scraped the chill all over his body with the palms of his hands. He went into the bathroom and while he tried unsuccessfully to piss stood looking out the high window at the mill sitting on the other side of the river, then up the hill at his father's house, then farther up the slope toward the top where the Sutherland house perched over town, more fraternity house than private home since the Idaho paper men now running the mill had moved in to board.

MAVIS

The casket lay on a gurney along the far wall of Cummings' Funeral Parlor beneath a crucifix. The windows were thrown open. Outside, the wind had died, and the air was motionless. Inside it was almost visibly drenched with millreek and human sweat and the sickly-sweet combination of perfume and embalming fluid.

Mavis stood with her back against the rear wall, near the drinks bar, peering at the open casket. Powder blue, adorned with a bronze relief of the Last Supper, the benevolent Christ tilted forward for effect, his arms parted in a vague gesture— beckoning or beseeching?—to the roomful of neglectful mourners. No one had gone up to the casket itself to pay their respects. An old woman sat veiled in black in a corner, toward whom people nodded or quickly offered their hand. Mavis hadn't paid her respects either. She couldn't remember the name of the corpse, or what he'd died of; she hadn't asked. A boy sitting against the far left wall of her high school English class three years before was all she knew of him. His name escaped her. All she could see of him from where she stood was his nose, which she could tell even from here was bloated and blackened beneath a thick paste of white mortician's powder, rising defiantly over the casket's silk-lined edge, threatening the integrity of the casket-lid. Unless, Mavis thought, Mr Cummings had already thought to build into the lid a kind of annex, an extra box-like construction like a parapet to allow for the nose.

After the technicalities of boxing and burying unwieldy corpses, Mavis was most interested in the drinks bar, a table with glasses, a bottle of whiskey, half full, a soda siphon, a tin bucket of melting ice and an odd, mysterious looking bottle, mostly drained, of a dull red concoction like bad table wine, or

191

cough mixture. She'd seen it gulped and thrown back like shots of liquor at Company picnics, at Church functions, weddings, funerals and memorial services her whole life. It was what most of the men and women in Mr Cummings' funeral parlor were now drinking. She hadn't noticed it before her father and brothers and uncle went missing; bottles of it appeared at their memorial service, and the services—the non-burials—for the other men and the actual funerals with coffins and bodies and all for the drowned women. As though the strange red drink were a general antidote to some unmentioned malady, perhaps to one's proximity to the dead, or to particular sorts of dead, or to the mill, or both. A liquid talisman against a new brand of contagion.

The funeral parlor, she noticed, was split roughly into two, to her left and to her right. All of town was halved, the bars, the restaurants, the classroom in which she now taught French. All of it divvied up, who you talked to, where you walked, which letter box you posted your mail. For or against. Labor or management. The rights of Rehoboth or the health of the mill's new owner, the big-time company from Idaho. The death of family business, or the birth of a new industrial age.

Mavis had her eye on two older men, the Arsenault brothers, nearly identical in height and build—were they twins? Mavis never knew that either—who had drifted from opposite corners of the room and met at the casket's edge. They were big, brawny men, thick-shouldered from hauling paper broke their whole lives, their hair prematurely white, their fingers gnarled and puffed. Both were drinking the red concoction, though from the look of them it seemed not to do much good. Both were peering down at the body as though looking at what was in store.

Mavis shuffled forward to hear them talk. She knew they'd been on opposite sides of the strike. She and everyone else knew they'd almost come to blows themselves; just another family split down the middle by this thing; fathers against sons, brothers against brothers, wives against their husbands.

"You have balls," one, Ray, said. He tipped back his drink.

"Good to see you Ray," the other, Ike, said.

"Well it's not goddamn good to see you."

Ray rolled his empty glass between his hands. "I hear you got a shotgun by each door," he said.

"I only got one door, Ray. Besides, you ever know me to own a shotgun?"

Ray shrugged. "Guess I haven't."

"Then I want you to tell that to your friends."

"They're not my friends."

"Then whatever they are. Tell them to stop coming around to the house. They already killed the grass and that damn dog—"

"You hated that dog."

Ike nodded absentmindedly.

"They were just doing you a favor," Ray said.

"It was Mary's dog."

"Well, then, condolences to Mary."

"They're scaring the wits out of her, Ray."

Ray lifted his hands in a show of powerlessness. "You against the world, Ike. It's always been that way."

"No, Ray. Just me against you. And I heard what you done to the McAlister boy. I don't like it."

"Then you and that boy can come down the union hall and pick up a sign and walk that line where you belong."

Ike neither moved nor said a word.

"You going to tell me why you're doing this?" Ray said.

"Because I got nothing against this mill."

"It's not the mill anymore. It's the Company. Everything's the Company, and the Company don't give you shit."

"It gives me a job. It gives you one." Ike paused, looked down at the blackened corpse. "It gave him one, too."

Ray shook his head. "Don't you bring that poor sonofabitch kid into this thing now," he said. "They're a bunch of Mormon scum-suckers, Ike. They talk pretty but when you turn your back they stick it up your ass."

"So what else is new. Not this," he nodded at the boy. "You always said you either want a job, want to work, or you want to be a bum and a drifter. You have to make up your mind. Wasn't that you, Ray? Who doesn't stick it up our ass, tell me that. Sutherland wasn't no better. He just put a pretty face on it all, threw a picnic every year for us, let us have that fishing rodeo. Keeping the workers happy is all he was doing while he and his family laughed all the way to the bank. Nobody owes us a living, Ray. It's every man for himself."

"What the hell are you saying. When we started we took off our caps and gowns, picked up our pails and went to work, and Sutherland took care of us. And we took care of him." His knuckles came to rest on the casket edge. "Can't say that about these fuckers in there now. They couldn't care a goddamn. All they want is to break the union."

"And where's Sutherland now, then? You think he lost any sleep over selling the mill to those people?"

Ray Arsenault looked behind him. His eyes skated along the wall, and Mavis looked away when he saw her. She noticed that everyone seemed to have drifted a little closer, was talking a little less, watching their backs. Ray looked defiantly at the other side of room, the one his brother came from. Mavis saw his eyes narrow, and for a moment she wasn't just listening anymore. His glare pulled her in—and she wanted to interrupt—But wait, she wanted to explain. This is nothing to do with me. I have no men. Never have. I just teach French.

"Fuck 'em," Ray said, and looked away.

"Maybe what those Idaho boys want isn't so far off the mark," Ike said thoughtfully. "I watch Maintenance do a job on a paper machine, shut the whole thing down to change a secondary valve. They call in a millwright to change the pumps. Then they have to wait for an electrician to do the rewire. Then they wait for a piper, but the piper's always at another job. Then the piper comes, but it's already lunch. So there's another hour. Then they have to wait for the electrician again. Then the millwright. Then they finally get around to working on the valve, and all the valve would take if you did it yourself is half a fucking hour. All this time the machine is down. Hours. Days. That's big money, Ray. Big big money. The United Mine Workers wants a raise. Well, there's your raise. Floating down the river."

Ray said nothing.

"That union never did shit for us. They took dad's dues for the twenty years they been here and gave them to the national.

They took it happily. He'd been thirty years on one machine, fixing this and fixing that, taking shit from assholes like Walter Finnithy, and mom had to go down to the union hall and ask where his goddamn watch was."

"You done?" Ray said.

"No."

"Good, because I have something to say. Walter Finnithy is an asshole. But there's always assholes. I said that, too. None of that matters. Facts don't matter. And it don't matter if you agree with why we went out. Or if you believe in ghosts or whatever. We could have asked for fifty percent plus a profit share plus a three day week with five day's pay and it still wouldn't have mattered if you agreed or not. What does matter is your staying with your friends and your family. You can tell me stories till you're blue in the face. But are you loyal to this town?"

Ike waved his brother away. "You're living in the past. It's just not the same town. We're not talking about the same thing."

They felt the others in the room staring at them and turned simultaneously. Ike lowered his voice and tilted sideways toward his brother. "Tell me something, Ray. If family's so important, how is it that before the mill was family, and suddenly it's not?"

"Was. Was family. Used to be. That was before the Mormons came. But you're sticking too much to the facts, Ike. It's bigger than that. It's people. You always stay with your people. Maybe we called the mill family. Maybe we liked that. But they're not our people anymore, not us. Dad wouldn't have thought so. He would have been on that picket line."

Ike felt himself begin to laugh, then kept it down. "Bullshit."

"Then you didn't know him," Ray said.

Ike reddened. "What about me?" he said. "I'm your people. And your family. And you're all treating me like I died, like I don't exist. One day I'm here, the next I'm not. You talk about family like it's so damn important, more important than the truth, but here you are practically killing me off. I guess you'd rather have another brother dead than disagree. I don't remember it being so easy to lose a member of your own family, Ray."

The muscles in Ray's jaw worked like a mouthful of pebbles.

"It aint easy. People die on you all the time. People in this town are always dying. Okay. When Aubrey, and all those other people went down on that goddamn boat—well, we said we couldn't live without our brother. We didn't even have a chance to bury him, we complained. But look now—here we are living without him, doing just fine."

"Just fine, huh?"

"That's right."

Ike nodded down at the body. "Everybody always says they want to go where their friends go. I've heard that shit since we were growing up. We're going to hell, or we're going to heaven, but all together, right? But you think about this, Ray: did you ever wonder—who the hell are your friends? Because I don't think it's so easy to tell. You ask this boy lying here. You ask him what friends he had."

A sob erupted from the back of the now-silent room, and all turned in the direction of the boy's mother. But she had not moved from her seat, she moved not at all, as though asleep sitting up.

Mavis didn't bother looking. Without raising her head she'd located the familiar animal-like whelps of her own mother crying and tracked it to the far corner, where she had gone to stand alone in silent vigil for an empty moment to fill and turn things her way. Mavis heard the commotion. She heard her mother's screech:

"That boy was as old as little Ivan would have been."

An elderly woman strode to the head of the casket and faced off against the Arsenault brothers. "You should be ashamed mentioning that *Raven* business. Don't you know who all is standing in this room? You should have more respect."

Mavis watched her mother with fascination.

"We're fine. All's well. Gordon."

Her mother again. She was recounting the story of the telegram, which still sat folded in a box above the fireplace, untouched since it had been delivered two years after her father and brothers disappeared. She and her mother had been sitting on the porch. Walter was on the lawn, she didn't remember doing what, raking maybe. He was leaving for the war in a week. The Western Union boy in his pill-box cap approached the house warily—he looked worn out, the job of war-time telegrams falling solely to him, a tenth-grader picking up spare change, ruining his youth by doing the Reaper's work. Mavis heard he'd left town after the war. After all, he'd lost his friends, he'd lost his enemies; who, after all, would have anything to do with the bearer of so much news of death?

We're fine. All's well. Gordon.

They traced it to Europe. Wartime Europe. So they were alive. The talk returned to Germans throwing women overboard and kidnapping men. It seemed incredible; what would the Axis want with a bunch of small-town men and boys led by a band conductor? Yet there it was, unmistakable. And Mavis's mother—she'd seemed, almost, disappointed, her position of matriarch among lost men at risk. But after days and weeks and then months passed and eventually the war ended without another word, Frances Beauchamp began to brighten. Again, she fished her husband's slippers out of his closet and set them, heels together, like a fetish, outside the bathroom door, as if he were about to step from the shower. And to this day—nine years after the telegram, eleven after the disappearance itself—Mavis had seen those slippers set out beside her mother's bed, less bait than sentinel, standing guard over sacred ground too well seeded with grief to be trampled upon, even by the bare feet of the once-dead.

A crowd had gathered in the corner. Mavis could not see her mother but she knew the routine. The casket stood alone and unattended, a woman in black sitting beside it, robbed of her loss, whatever it was.

The emergency lights scissored though the trees. Red lights, ambulance lights. Mavis crossed the footbridge cautiously, listening in the dark for the river below. There wasn't a sound from the mill.

She turned down the block toward Walter's house. The street itself was deserted, the narrow plots of grass between the buildings an indescribable confusion of shadowy thorns and weeds. The trees were dusty and muscular, zealous visions of their former selves. The fetid smell of swamp seeped through the concrete. In the twilight the vegetation seemed resplendent, vengeful, beyond appeal, adamant now about its reclamation. Grass pushed up through cracks in the street. Vines slithered out of the brush. The crickets sawed in the dark. Mavis could easily imagine that by morning the streets would be a choking forest, and the scabs would gather before dawn with long knives to lead the first of the logging trucks into the mill. She hadn't been down this way in years. She hadn't realized how far things had gone. For the first time she saw the town as the arbitrary claim it was, the flowering of the remains of Hugo Sutherland who had come to build a mill over the falls, then gave up the life in which the natives were serving him well.

She took the stairs slowly and stood in Walter's doorway, looking right and left at the room, at the door peppered by shot leaning against the back of a chair, at the yellowed plants drooping over their pots, the table whose legs had been kneecapped. Walter himself sat on a disembowelled chair amidst the splinters and pellet shot, staring out a blackened window.

"Did it always look this way?" Mavis said. "I don't remember."

Walter looked around casually. "Most of it. The door's something new. And the plants."

Mavis eyed the daybed. "This still work?"

"Try it and see."

As Mavis lowered onto it, the daybed emitted a piano crash of chords. "I'm really sorry," she said.

Walter shrugged. "This apartment's not worth being sorry about."

"You going to move back up to your daddy's?"

Walter didn't answer and Mavis followed his line of sight. Though it was dark, she knew her directions pretty well and knew that it was his father's house that Walter had been looking at when night fell.

She cocked an eye at him. "Aren't you supposed to be working tonight?"

"What time is it?"

"Whistle blew an hour ago. Didn't you hear it?"

"I guess I didn't."

"Why are you doing this, Walter?"

"Doing what?"

"Working in there."

"I just work there."

"I don't see why you bother," Mavis said.

"Because I have for six years."

"I mean now, instead of staying out."

"The United Mine Workers're going to ruin this town."

Mavis looked out the door at the street below, at the lights coming on over the hillsides; at the red beacons atop the mill's stacks. "Well they're too late," she said. "Anyway you always said you wanted to be a journalist. This might be a convenient time to consider a career move."

Walter turned and looked at her as he often had. Mavis knew what he was seeing—knew the small, petite woman, good looking, hard, feisty. Walter himself looked drunk but there was no bottle nor glass in sight.

"Want to go over to the bar, Mavis?"

"I think you'd get shot."

Walter nodded abstractly.

"Trust me," she said.

He shrugged. "Then let's get married."

Mavis laughed.

"I mean it this time. We'll leave town, start all over somewhere else."

Mavis laughed harder. "And where might that be?"

"Anywhere."

"And what would you do?"

"I'd be that journalist."

Mavis clasped her hands in an attitude of prayer and sighted over her fingers into the middle distance. "If I leave town it won't be with anything from it. I wouldn't even take any clothes. I'd never get the stink out of them. I think I'd scrub my skin off before I got the stink out."

She looked at Walter. "You could've gone to college on the G.I. Bill. You still can."

"I'm working," he said absentmindedly.

"You're just getting old in there."

Outside, the cicadas ceased, and the rhythmic churning of

the mill swelled and passed over them, like the sound of a distant train that never got nearer, or farther.

"You really care about this thing?" she asked.

"I care about this place."

Mavis regarded him as though he was something strange and foreign, as though he were on exhibit. "Does it care about you? You've lost all your friends."

"I haven't lost you."

"You might," Mavis said. "I'm not staying here forever."

"You can't leave it," Walter said.

"You watch me."

"The only way to leave here is if you die. Like them."

"Cut it out," Mavis said.

"Gordy said he wanted to live here forever. We were going to work at the mill and he was going to marry Anne Stisulis."

"I said cut it out, Walter," Mavis snapped.

"—and I was going to marry you," he finished.

"I just bet you never said that to Gordy," Mavis shot out before she could stop herself. Then she pushed herself up and stood looking out of the doorway.

"I was at that wake today," she said.

"Who was it?"

"I don't even know," Mavis replied.

"How'd he die?"

Mavis shrugged.

Walter pressed himself to his feet.

"Let's go for a walk. I got something to show you."

Mavis snorted. "Likely story, Walter. I wouldn't walk ten feet with you in the dark."

"I mean it, Mavis. I've been wanting to show you this."

"What is it?"

Walter shook his head. He smiled crookedly. "It's too hard to explain."

Mavis didn't move.

"Mavis," he said grimly.

"It's too dangerous out there right now, Walter. I heard they're bringing in more of those blackshirts."

"You're going to want to see this."

Mavis watched him gather his jacket. Something heavy fell out of his pocket and clattered to the floor and lay hunched and dark.

Mavis looked at him. "You're going to get yourself killed, and that right there is going to do the job."

Walter slipped on his jacket and wedged the revolver in the back of his pants.

"Come on," he said, gently pushing Mavis out the doorway and stepping out, instinctively reaching behind him for the doorknob. Snatching only air, he did not turn around again.

When they reached the lower gate everyone was watching the mill, the strikers, the loggers, the blackshirts. All stood in morbid silence. The log pile cranes pierced the skin of light and vaulted into the night, their steel claws dangling from the heavens, still swinging. The chipper was shut down. Only the power plant hummed softly, the aeration ponds murmuring.

No one stood near the ambulance. No one needed to. The attendants wheeled the gurney across the lot without urgency.

"Wait here," Walter said, and went on and stood behind three men he knew, salaried superintendents who'd developed the habit of moving through the mill together, standing at tricornered attention.

The stranger spilled off the gurney, his head twisted in a hundred degree turn, his purple face elongated rubber-like, popeyed, mouthful of crushed teeth thrust forward like a rotting cadaver's. A halloween mask. Arms and legs twisted without loyalty to front or back. Legs rolled flat like dough. A hay scarecrow.

Mavis listened from a distance. Number five machine, they said. The guy had an air hose around him when he was blowing on the cylinders. He had the hose near his feet, and they don't know what happened, the hose popped, it may or may not have been him, anyway there was a little too much hose to control. It snapped and caught in the machine's nip and took him in with it and by the time they got the machine shut down he'd already passed through two of the rollers. When they slid him out he moved like a bag of crushed ice. They still didn't know where he was from. Still looking up his family in the records.

Mavis felt a hand on her shoulder. She whirled, panting, fists up.

"It's me," Walter whispered.

"Walter!"

"Follow me."

Mavis didn't move.

"Come on. It's all right."

"Who is he?"

"Replacement worker," Walter said.

"You mean scab."

"Cut that out."

"Well, he is what he is."

"And what am I?" Walter asked.

Mavis considered him. "I'm not sure. Not flat yet." She walked on.

"Could have been an accident," Walter said. "Come on."

They crossed out of the light and passed through the striped barriers. A temporary footbridge was strung over the river's elbow to the island construction.

"Walter, where are you taking me?"

"Quiet."

The pile drivers stood idle in the darkness, gray silhouettes like horses sleeping upright in a field. Four I-beams lay crisscrossed in the mud. The strike had stopped work for the new cogeneration plant. The contractor, a local, wouldn't cross the line. Everything was left as is.

Mavis heard the river all around her. Then she lost Walter and called his name.

"Here," he whispered. "Keep it down."

A flashlight popped on and stabbed at her eyes then went off and she could see only red spots do-si-doing around blue spots.

"Walter, what's going on?"

She felt him take her hand and pull her forward. Then his hands pressed down on both shoulders, and there they stood, embracing, or so it seemed, the air fluttering before her face. She came to about his chest. She could hear his heart beating as she wrapped her arms around his waist, hesitantly, as though around something that might float off, or explode. She felt his chin come to rest on her head. She smelled him, sweat, rotting eggs, like the mill. Wood chip slivers in his sweater. His hands hard and chaffed. His whole body was trembling slightly, quietly, like a dog out in the rain. Something in her lurched, something foreign and untested. She felt him pull back.

"Don't go," she whispered.

"What?"

"Are you cold," she said.

He shook his head in little flutters, like a child.

Her little hands found the cold metal of the pistol flush against his back, and she looked up at her old friend Walter and he smiled stupidly, and at that moment, cruelly perhaps, she knew he would never do anything, that he would die here, or near here, friendless. She released him and stepped back away from him in the dark. She had the pistol in her hands, and Walter said nothing and reached out not at all as Mavis raised it up and pitched it into the dark. A distant splash.

"Walter," she said.

He cleared his throat.

"Okay," he said. "Let's go."

She followed his footsteps, then ran up his back. The flashlight came on. The wand disappeared into the ground. "Peer on in there," he said.

Mavis stepped forward. She felt Walter's hand grabbing hold of the back of her shirt. She leaned in and let her eyes follow the beam. It glanced off something metallic, a silvery puddle at the bottom moving not like water but something thicker, a lunar soup. Mavis could feel her face harden into a plastic smile, like a plate of gravy skinning over.

She followed him to an identical pile-driven hole and peered in. Another and peered in. A fourth. They straightened and looked past each other in the dark.

"Why are you showing me this?" she said.

"Know what that is?"

"I think so."

"Mercury," Walter said. "They're laying those I-beams in

there soon as they can find a contractor willing to do it."

"They know what's down there?" she asked.

"It's one of them that told me about it," he said.

"So why are you showing me this?"

"You know what's under our feet?" he asked. He didn't wait for an answer. "A dump. We're standing on the mill's old dump before the Company bought it and started carting chemicals up to Fairington Mountain. We're talking ten years ago now. Twenty. Fifty. Back then Sutherland just drummed it up in leaky tin drums and stuck it in here."

Mavis said nothing.

"And you know what's under this dump?"

"More river?" Mavis guessed.

"Aquifers. The town's drinking water coming down from Rangeley."

Mavis looked over her shoulder. From this river island she had a clear shot of the lower gate. The ambulance was gone. The picket lines had resumed. The string of blackshirts was re-deployed, four spotlights had them caught in a box of gauzy light, their nightsticks fisted.

And below them all lay the veined dirt bearing along the tinctured water, dripping it through marbled rock and along the bottom of the river and into town to bead at the bottom of their kitchen sinks.

Mavis remembered LaSalle's restaurant closing last year be-cause the taps started running green and, no matter where they drilled, wouldn't stop. She hadn't thought anything of it. No one had. The jokes were just now slowing down. That's what happens when you sell to an Irishman, everyone said.

She looked toward Walter. "Why are you staying here, Walter? What do you really have here that's worth you putting up with this?" She could hear Walter kicking at the mud. "Why do you feel responsible for anything?"

"It's town."

"They're just using you, Walter," she said. "You don't see it? Company's using you to break the Union, Union's using you to break the Company. And Sutherland was just using all of us. Period."

Mavis stepped toward him and took his face in her hands.

"And you can't tell anyone about this. Because if you did the Company would go bankrupt and Rehoboth would be a ghost town in a year. What's going to happen is that this strike will be settled one way or another and the Company's going to stand these beams in these holes and men from this town are going to pour in the concrete and there won't be anything more to tell. And then mercury or no mercury, Walter, it'll be work or not. It'll be drink this water or not."

Mavis could feel the river moving around them. Lips of foam shone white out of the night like ice floes.

"The mill's been good to all of us," Walter said, pressing her palm to his cheek.

"Well, it's why we're here, I'll give you that," she said, stepping away—her hands fluttering at her sides. "But look down those holes and tell me if you still think you're right."

A match flared in front of her and she saw Walter's face.

"Give me one of those," she said.

"I thought you quit, what, two years ago now," he said.

"One year," Mavis said. "Now I'm starting again."

They both lit up and ashed into the mud and looked over at the mill.

Mavis looked into the night, into her past. She remembered her house when her father and brothers were there. She remembered the bare wood of the house and the cold boards under her bare feet, and the dampness of the air. The crack of light around her father's practice room door, the sound of his piano mingling and joining and then just becoming his sweet tenor voice wafting through the rooms, out the windows, filling the grassy lot between the houses. She remembered the smell of the carpets. An uncluttered house. Things neatly in place. The Hoover left upright in the corner as it always was. Her brothers wrestling on the floor. She saw the water pooling in the kitchen sink. She saw the cups of coffee on the table, the showers running, the toilets flushing, the windows opening. The house like the other houses, veined, a private fountain of clear liquid. She saw the mill, and she saw the whatever it was in the water settle to the bottom of her father's cup with the coffee grounds, and the lead dust in the air on the tips of her mother's feather duster. Then she saw her brothers' empty rooms and her father's empty slippers pinched together heel-to-wall. The bodies of those women, cut, bloated, which made her think that because her father and brothers hadn't been returned, they were much worse.

Mavis raised her eyes to the mill and understood instantly the trap they were all in. She saw the lights of the mill and the sulfuric clouds making yellow animal shapes against the black sky. And the dim, wavering lights of Rehoboth behind that. And she heard the mechanical pulse of all that was unseen that ran underneath. She saw Rehoboth and the Company bound together in mutual hatred and dependence, each the other's hostage. And both were slowly, methodically, being poisoned. And she saw that boat going out with the last of her good father, that good man and his boys, and then just the last of what was good, because everything had been too good too long.

And Sutherland knew it.

Mavis heard the river, she heard the mill stacks hissing in the night, the gurgle of the aeration ponds. She heard Walter breathing next to her.

He lit two cigarettes, gave one to Mavis and sucked his down in a half dozen long pulls. Mavis flicked hers unsmoked into the night.

"We get what we ask for," she said.

"What do you mean by that?"

"It means I'm leaving."

Walter said nothing.

"I applied for a scholarship to go to France. I heard last week I got it. Even after all that, everything, I didn't think I should go. I'm calling them back."

"But what're you going to do there?"

"Study French. Drink wine. Not be here."

Walter lit a match and lowered his face toward it. Mavis saw him peering over his knuckles over the river past the mill, into the hillsides, into the dark between the pinlights of town.

"What about your mother?" he asked.

She looked up, following the hills undulating up toward the Rangeley lakes, toward the sky. She almost laughed. "If I stay,

I'll teach school and that'll be that. It's kind of like being dead, Walter. You know, my mother refuses every man who comes her way because she's afraid my father's going to come home and see her. 'I'm Gordon Beauchamp's wife,' she's always saying. 'I'm Gordon Beauchamp's wife.' As if he were still alive. Then she'll collapse in tears, and everyone will run to her. And everyone'll start talking about the *Raven*. All those same stories over and over. All those stupid theories. And I'm part of her act. If she gives it up, she'll just be like everyone else, only less so. Without my father. Without my brothers. So should I stay here and die for them? Should I die for my mother, Walter?"

They said nothing for a time. Then she turned to Walter: "You have to be a certain thing if they're going to let you live. If you stay here, you have to be careful. If you're different you'll have to hide it. You're allowed to be different only if you're really the same."

EZRA

As Ezra drove into Rehoboth, he saw the pickets, thinned since he'd come through on his way to Rangeley; they seemed almost placid, their placards stacked against the gate. The strikers no longer looked toward the mill. They faced out or faced each other. Men loitering in town on a false spring afternoon. Blackshirts were riding the logging trucks in, their rifles standing on their thighs. There was construction next to the mill. I-beams standing foursquare and bare like the corner posts of a giant pen.

He stopped along what seemed the main street but was now mostly deserted. A lone man was walking by and Ezra lowered his window and leaned out and asked the way to the cemetery. The man eyed him coolly, saying nothing, as though the request was a mishandled password. His arm rose as if of its own accord and pointed south down Route 2 and hung there. Ezra nodded and drove off, glancing into the rear view mirror to see the man still standing on the walk, watching him go.

The cemetery was surrounded by a white picket fence, maybe seventy yards square. There were no trees. There was no church. No one in sight. Across an empty lot, on the other side, was an Ames supermarket. Route 2 ran past the front of it. Most of the markers were some sort of stone, but at the back end the graves were thinned out and the markers just planks bleached and cracked by the sun, their engravings almost faded. He thought these were the old riverdrivers and the older poor. The sun was behind the cemetery and shadows fell forward of all the tombstones toward the road and seemed to stand open as though at this time of the day they were all freshly dug and the remains disinterred for airing out.

To the side, near to the fence, in an empty stretch away from the thickly settled center, stood a pair of tombstones. Ezra looked hard at them. Chiseled into the first was the outline of a boat riding the crest of a wave. The boat did not look like Floyd Johnson's *Raven*; the boat drawn there would not float; merely some grave etcher's rendition of what a boat should look like. There was a date, June 29, 1941, and listed vertically below it were the names of nineteen men and boys. *Aubrey Arsenault, James Carey, Jr., Albert Cormier, Edmund Cormier...* Two cracked fluted vases full of plastic flowers tilted in the dust. The crumbled porcelain of a third lay embedded like fossilized prehistoric remains long entombed in silt and mud. Around the vases a half dozen metal stakes had been planted. At the top of each was welded a small frame of metal and glass, and behind the glass a yellowed, faded picture of one of the men or boys who did not lie beneath. An adolescent in Sunday pants and pullover sweater. A man, thirtyish, leaning cross-legged against a new tractor with studded tires. An older man squinting into the sun; someone's arm, frilly-sleeved, some woman's, was attached to him and could not be wholly cut out of the picture. Ezra peered at them, at the ones he and his father had missed. He felt the urge to apologize, then subdued it. The dirt beneath these pictures was level and the dead grass the same shag and density as the dead grass around it.

The second stone also had the outline of the same unfloatable boat, and the same date, and a list of names, fourteen women. *Marion Chapitis, Edith Coburn, Marie Rose Coulombe ...* Before it lay a stretch of disturbed earth just as dipped and pocked and slightly sunken as the other graves, with grass like theirs, almost imperceptibly distinct from the broken lawn around it, the difference not being the length or color as much as the density, the blades of grass per square inch. The once-turned earth before this tombstone, though, covered far more ground than any other in the cemetery, fifteen yards square by Ezra's measure. Here and there it was bubbled slightly in the shapes of inverted rowboats. Atop it lay no pictures, no plastic flowers, and no sign that any had ever been left. As far as Ezra could see, none had been left at any of the other gravesites either.

The Hotel Rehoboth faced the river's widening just below the mill, where it was difficult to tell whether the stench, which inside the bar was like rancid piss, came from the slack water or the billowing animal shapes of gas.

The valley downwind had cleared. It was not just a general fog.

A lumberjack peered down from the slate above the door, *Hotel Rehoboth, est. 1898, Joe Martin, esq., Proprietor.* The entrance was flanked by two mirrors the height and breadth of the first floor. Stenciled into them was a panorama of a lumberjack camp: thick-armed, barrel-chested lumberjacks going about their lumberjack business with the fires and with the forest and with each other. All their faces modelled on the same head, the one on the slate above the door, all leering with the same rueful leer of Joe Martin, Esq. To bisect the ax-bearing gang of identical, mute lumberjacks was to walk through the Martin family portrait gallery, all the ornery Martin ancestors bearing down at you with scorn and pessimism, with certainty that you will let fall to ruins in a single year all that they lived and worked to build over the course of hundreds.

Though the façade of the Hotel Rehoboth wasn't much more than the back side of Congress Street, its front windows marked out an irrefutable claim on the lowest common denominator of the American Dream: the cloud that makes the rain that makes the water that makes the steam that makes the engine go. The smell might be excessively bad, the forest full of Joe Martins seemed to be saying, it might even be inexcusable, but whatever you risked calling it, it was the smell of the money in your pocket, and the orange and yellow of the sky above you, the shade of your dollars before they were rolled, stamped and dyed green. Sooner or later, everyone had to pass into this place, through this entrance, and peer into these mirrors to find his place in the world according to Joe Martin.

Ezra stood on the sidewalk with the river and the mill over his shoulder. Three pickups appeared at one end of town like vigilantes out of the plains. Canal Street, empty, or not yet filled, seemed to have been deserted. Alone on the streets, Ezra turned his back. The pickups passed slowly to the other end of town, throwing distance, then turned a corner. Ezra stepped in.

A carpet of late afternoon daylight stretched under his feet, then pinched off. Inside, it was any time of the day or night. A man at the back leaned over a pool table, about to break; another stood half in half out of the light of the swing lamp. Three more sat on stools at the high wooden bar, their eyes raised toward the quiz show. On the television, quick bursts of canned applause. Well-spaced glass shelves were littered sparsely with shot glasses and American flags. Everything shelved was square to the edges and distinguished from corners and walls and from each other, everything symmetrical, as though perfect order made up for the lack. A string of colored Christmas lights flashed like jewels. The hand-lettered sign on the mirror said, *Scabs: America's Shame.*

Ezra stepped up to the bar. In the corner of his eye he saw the other men on their stools lift their heads. The pool players straightened, standing their cues on their thighs like rifles. Two balls clapped together then separated and stopped. No one moved and the easy quiet dropped another level to a bad silence. The TV murmured. The bartender appeared, the bloated forearms, the tattoos, the Marine Corps posture, then the young, muscular face, a youthful version of the one above the Hotel entrance, of all the lumberjack faces in the fake woods in the mirrors.

"Glass of water," Ezra said.

"That all?"

"I'll have a beer."

"Any particular kind?"

Ezra eyed the bar. "Whatever you have on that tap'll do fine."

The bartender left a glass of cloudy, yellowish water in front of him and stood back. Ezra let the glass sit but the water's color or its opacity didn't fade or settle. Though he was suddenly not thirsty for it, the consequences of leaving the water undrunk seemed traumatic. He picked it up, closed his eyes and threw it back. When the beer came he threw that down as a chaser.

"You mind if I ask you a question?" Ezra said to the bartender. In the corner of his eye he saw the other men at the bar lift their heads.

The metallic taste clung to his teeth. "Whew, that's some water," Ezra said.

"That what you wanted to say?"

"You ever hear of the *Raven*?"

"The bird."

"It's a boat," Ezra said.

The bartender straightened. "I heard of it. If that's what you really want to know about you might buy a round for the end of the bar and ask the gentleman sitting there that question of yours."

The end of the bar was just three stools away. His hair under the cap was white, but Ezra could see the man wasn't that old. From under the bill of the cap came the lopsided nose and scarred brow of a fighter, the lips and bottomless eyes pale with the TV light. The beer bottle played in his big hands like a thimble. Ezra sent the man a new beer, and the man pulled from it right away as if it was rightfully his. After a minute Ezra followed the bottle over.

"First they figured it hit a mine," the man said as soon as Ezra sat. "Then they said the Kraut subs were in there. But I always thought it was too messy for Krauts. They were good at that sort of thing. They would have done it better. What would the Krauts want with a puny boat like that? And why not take any of the girls? Sailors at sea as long as they must have been would have a certain need for girls; more than they would for men, if you get my meaning."

"You think they took the men?"

"Must have. None come back."

"Except the skipper," Ezra said. "They did find him."

"Yeah, maybe that's true. He wasn't from here."

Ezra rolled his beer glass in his hands. "You know anybody who was on that boat?"

The man tipped back his bottle then held it over his mouth and let it finish itself then pushed it to the edge of the bar. Ezra could see that he was holding the drunk off.

"Sure I did," the man said, "Sure I knew someone on that boat. My brother, Aubrey. It'll be twelve years this June. June twenty-ninth. I knew some of the other boys too. Those

Beauchamp kids, Jimmy Carey. A couple of them gals were real beauties. Some of Sutherland's big shots down at the mill. This is a small town, son. You all know each other in a place like this. A lot of them boys on there was building a Scout camp when they disappeared and it burned flat that same weekend they all went out on that boat. Never figured that one out, either. It's like it was a message from God or some horseshit like that."

The bartender put two more beers before them and they drank a while. The man picked his up and held it suspended over the bar.

"What's it to you anyways?" he said. He squinted at Ezra. "You're not from around here."

"No," Ezra said.

"Where you from, then?"

Ezra glanced up at the TV. "Over by Brunswick."

"You sure?"

Ezra looked at him. "What do you mean?"

"You just didn't look sure about that."

"I'm sure," Ezra said. "Over around Brunswick. There are some islands there. I'm from them."

"From some islands," the man said. He turned flush to Ezra and looked him up and down. Ezra could feel him staring at his hands on the bar. "You're a working man," he said.

"I work," Ezra said.

"You wouldn't be here to cross that picket line out there, would you now?"

Ezra could feel the eyes of every man in the bar on him.

"It's none of my concern."

"You sure about that too?"

"I'm sure."

"Okay then."

"Okay."

The pool game in the back went on.

"Then you ought to know that they started digging into that *Raven* business a little while ago," the man said. "They started it and all of a sudden they dropped it, and I thought that was a good idea."

"You telling me to drop it," Ezra said softly.

"What do you got to drop? You just come in here asking questions it doesn't sound to me like you know all that much."

Ezra nodded. "I'd say that's right."

"I don't know who or what you are, so I'm not telling you to do a thing. But what I am telling you is that you're going to have to start digging people up out of their graves to find out anything about all that now. You can tell this place is just a little distracted, so you might think of something better to do than poke around here asking about all that. For some people that business's still a little too raw. Besides, it's a little late. You're not saving anybody's life."

Ezra stood away and dropped two dollar bills on the bar.

"Thanks for the advice."

Ezra began to walk. The man turned his head. "Brunswick," he said. "Isn't that where they were going?"

Ezra kept walking.

It had begun to rain, a cold leaden drizzle. Ezra hopped into a phone booth beside the firehouse. The sky over town was yellow, as though beneath it burned a great fire. Below, at the mill, the rain had thinned the pickets. Beyond the receding streetlamps, the mist thundered with the ceaseless convoy of trucks unloading and piling skinned trees and pulling down the wood-chip mountains, and feeding them all into the digesters while the machines screamed out highways and highways of glossy high grade.

The shadows in the firehouse garage were moving, the cherries of three cigarettes arcing up, surging, then idling back down around the knees. A tin bucket had been set upright in the middle of a driveway. Bursts of sparks as the cigarettes hit the asphalt around it, then darkness. The cherries turned toward Ezra. One fired into the air and exploded on the ground halfway to the booth.

He turned his back and picked up a ragged telephone book and dialed Arthur McAlister, heard the busy signal and rested the receiver again on its cradle. The firemen called out to him, faintly lobbing over cries of "Scab!" Ezra pressed his back up against the glass. The booth no longer kept out the cold and rain. Next to the firehouse stood the civic building. Beside the stairs its directory lit by a single fluorescent bulb: Mayor, Sheriff, Town Court, Health Department, School Board, Historical Society. Historical Society. He shoved through the booth and ran through the smokey drizzle for the entrance.

Past traffic tickets and up the stairs to the third floor. Down a dim hallway, floorboards bowing underfoot, the narrow doors coming rapidly one after the other, unlabeled, windowless like rows of closets. At the end of the third was a door with a cardboard sign written out by hand: *Rehoboth Historical Society, hours two to three, Mondays only.* Today was Friday and it was after five. But there was a line of light at the bottom of the door, and inside the rustling of paper. Ezra turned the knob and walked into a high narrow space lit with a weak and twitchy light, more aisle in a library than room or office; a tunnel of books, *Maine— History of, Maine—Paper Industry, Paper Making—History of.* Shelf after shelf from floor to ceiling down both walls, bindings and ledgers and metal fileboxes and bundles of yellowed, flaky *Rehoboth Falls Times*. A plump, graying woman stood on her toes on a stool, sliding a filebox onto a high shelf. A second woman, shrunken, ashen, sat in a chair at a desk, her cataracted eyes fixed on the bookcase before her. Against the far wall, a wide back and a bald head ringed by a green visor leaned over a yellowing newspaper with piles more at both elbows like bookends.

"May we help you?" asked the woman teetering on the stool.

"Saw the light and thought I'd wander in," Ezra said.

"The hours are Mondays," said the man, neither turning nor lifting his eyes from the paper.

"I saw the sign. It's just—it's raining and —"

"You come looking for work?" the man demanded to know.

"Work?"

"If you come looking for work you're not welcome. Scabs aren't welcome."

"You come right in," said the woman, stepping down from the stool, "Don't you mind my husband."

"I didn't come to town looking for work," Ezra said.

"Well, that's fine," said the woman, her fingers playing nervously. Her eyes were fixed on the rows of gray fileboxes. Each was labelled with a year, beginning with *1898*.

Ezra called down to the other end of the room: "I wouldn't cross a picket line." The man showed no signs of hearing.

"That's nice," replied the woman, her eyes leaping from one filebox to another, her lips reciting the dates, all was in order, all in order. The man at the desk dragged his finger across the paper before him, mumbling to himself.

"I'm Rita," the woman said cheerfully. "Rita Perry. And that's my husband Joe, and this here's my mother, Theresa Masalsky."

The old woman didn't so much as blink.

Ezra scanned the row of fileboxes.

"It's just something I do," Rita Perry said, wringing her hands. "What's in them?"

She smiled stiffly: "Nothing important. Just things. Things having to do with particular years. Nothing important, really. Just little tokens people give us."

"I'm here looking for something," Ezra said. "I wanted to know what you had on the *Raven*."

Joe Perry's head snapped upright. But it was the old woman who came to life, who swiveled her head slowly toward Ezra: "There were some boys on there, and those boys were all very good swimmers, and they should have come back alive. That young Junior Carey, he was a very good swimmer, wasn't he, Joe?"

"Yes he was, Ma," Joe said. He still hadn't moved.

"He could swim all right," she nodded, her old woman's skeletal hand rising and snatching at the air: "Saved that poor old gal in that freshet, plucked her right out of that tree, god bless."

"Didn't they say it just exploded, a gasoline leak?" asked Rita. "Didn't someone out by Monhegan say they heard a blast? That's how I remember it being left. Poof," she flung her hand as though releasing confetti to the wind, "like a match."

"An explosion," Ezra said.

"That's what they said," Rita said.

"Who."

"Who?"

"Who said it," Ezra said.

"Oh, papers, you know, they're always speculating, coming up with theories." Rita looked away, shaking her head. "I knew quite a few good people on that boat, quite a few. Things never got back to being the same after all that. You'd walk into the bank and there were people missing, there still are. In those days if your friend was across the street you'd wave your hand and yell at him. After the *Raven* all that just stopped—"

"Rita," Joe said. His head was up as if he was looking out a window, down at the street.

"If you wouldn't mind someone poking around," Ezra said, "I've got some time to kill before I make a phone call."

"Poke, poke," Rita said, glad for the chance to smile. "That's what it's here for. You poke as much as you like."

"Why are you so interested in the *Raven*?" Joe asked, finally turning in his chair.

"Well," Ezra fumbled with his hands. "I was there."

"You were there," Joe said.

"Yes, sir, I was there."

Ezra could feel Rita staring at him.

Joe looked him up and down. "You would have been a boy."

"Nine," Ezra nodded.

"Then what would you have been doing there in that godforsaken place."

"I live there," Ezra said.

Rita raised her hand. "You're from Bailey Island?"

"Yes ma'am."

Rita turned to Joe. "I don't think we've ever had anyone up from Bailey Island before. Not even during the troubles."

Joe squinted at Ezra. "You saw that boat."

"No, sir. I didn't see the boat."

"Then what did you see?"

Ezra didn't answer. He looked around the room, not really seeing it. "I saw your people."

"You saw them," Joe said, agitated. "What'd you mean you saw them."

Ezra's eyes landed on a pile of newspapers. "I'm sorry. Maybe

I shouldn't've said anything."

Joe turned flush to Ezra, facing him off. "Tell me what you saw over there."

"I just saw bodies, sir. I helped fish them out of the water."

"But you were just a boy, you said," Rita exclaimed.

"Yes, ma'am, I know it," Ezra said. "It was my father more than it was me."

The high window flashed with mute lightning. The lights wavered, dimmed, then brightened.

Joe turned back slowly to his newspapers.

"Would you mind if I had a look at some of those?" Ezra asked.

Rita looked in Joe's direction then gave Ezra an uncertain nod.

At the far end of the room, to the side of Joe Perry's desk, he fingered through stacks of the *Rehoboth Falls Times* and *Boston Globe* until he found late June and early July, 1941. He leaned against a bookcase with the newspapers at his feet. He picked up a week's worth, starting with Monday, June 30. Entire pages were devoted to the *Raven*'s disappearance. Burnt clothing? Clear weather? Half of what was in these articles Ezra knew to be untrue. They'd never found anything but bodies. The possibilities had made no sense then, as they made no sense now. Anything would have left signs, wreckage, an oil slick, unless the boat was just snatched, taken away, or sunk in a single, solid piece. Even then, something should have floated up, a shoe, a handkerchief.

He glanced at the documents and scrap-books filling these old shelves. Diaries, town publications, published histories. He wondered about what they said. Why should he think he'd know what happened just by reading what they said?

He made a mental note of the byline above the *Globe* articles, Frank Dougherty, then sifted through the newspaper photographs.

They were mostly high school portraits of the dead and missing, a sequence of four pictures following the progress of a lobster boat out of a fog bank, nearer and nearer with each frame. A fisherman at the helm, a small boy seated in the stern, his eye on a canvas tarpaulin thrown over the afterdeck. Ezra put his finger on the photos. He knew that boat, he knew that very water, that very spot. That boy was him, and that man his father. The pictures seemed old, and they already dead and gone. He'd forgotten most of that. All he'd remembered were the bodies.

In the last frame his father's boat had been tethered to the wharf. Jesse was waiting, a long hook dangling from his hand. A policeman, a thin man in a dark suit. His father was facing dead ahead, as if still in open water out of sight of land. The boy—him, he had to remind himself—looked deep in thought. He thought he looked ruined. The canvas at his feet had wrinkled and kinked into the ghost contours of a human body.

Floyd.

Ezra casually strolled the length of the bookcases, running his finger over the spines of the books, noting the dates and the various descriptions of the contents. Rita Perry held a tiny diary in the palm of a hand as she would a baby bird. She noticed Ezra standing beside her and smiled weakly and said, apologetically, "I just like to know the weather on certain days. Silly little habit."

"No, no," Ezra insisted. He peered over her shoulder. July 10, in unimaginably neat and flourishing script, read, *Fine fine day. Corn knee-high already. Gustavus all day in fields.*

"What year is that?" he asked.

"1883."

"What's it say for January third?"

"Let's see," said Rita Perry, fingering the tiny pages carefully, "Here we are: *Sunny and cold. Six fresh inches last night. Baked three pies, Gustavus shovelled tunnel to barn.* Why?"

"My birthday," Ezra said, and chuckled together with Rita and walked on, fingering the old paper, lifting and peering at old grainy photographs of the mill and Congress Street at its various stages. He stopped at the fileboxes. His eyes snagged on some of them, the infamous dates—*1917, 1929*—and skated right over others. While Rita Perry purred over the weather of 1883, Joe Perry leaned over his desk, elbows splayed, nose to the paper, grunting at the hundred year old news, figuring all that out all over again. The old woman sat amidst her own thoughts.

Ezra reached up and pulled down *1941*. He fingered open the folder, *Pearl Harbor*. There amidst the photographs of the flaming ships was a list of names, four Cormiers, three Merciers, three Parises. He couldn't have known the sons and fathers who'd gone down to the recruiting office the very next day, nor could he have heard the town that night, that December 7, the shouts over dinner tables wafting through the windows and across the streets and lawns of Rehoboth, the phones ringing in old people's houses, the fists pounding, the silverware leaping, the mothers sobbing, the sisters breathing heavily, the sons' eyes blazing, the fathers' caught between torment and envy.

At the front of the filebox were the folders Ezra expected: *The* Raven *Mystery*. He lifted out a handful of clippings, but these, merely excerpts from the papers he'd just read, he slid back. Other sheets of paper, typed lists: the thirty-six who went out: the fifteen who were found: the twenty-one who weren't: a list of unrecovered effects below the names of the missing and the dead:

Beatrice Roach   April 12, 1921 - June 29, 1941

Patent leather shoe (left)   diamond brooch   purse brother Henry, parents Ellen and Dick

Harry Hutchins   December 24, 1921 - June 29, 1941

Leather flask   pair suede shoes   black wool trousers pair eyeglasses   wallet with $23   sisters Marie, Susan mother Louise

Lilah B. Sanders   March 21, 1916 - June 29, 1941

Pair tennis-type shoes   Opera glasses, pearl-inlaid, inscribed L.S.   boyfriend (missing), Charles

Ezra held these old lists in his wide, calloused fingers, holding them gently as if they were live things, the lost things themselves.

The old woman came to life at the other end of the room: "You're not the first person to come asking about that *Raven* business. Someone was here maybe just two years ago, poking around like you."

Ezra raised his head.

"But I don't know if he got a look-see like you did."

"He talked with you?"

"I suppose he did, but didn't ask nothing really good, just who was where and when, and who knew who and who knew what and such things as that."

"Do you remember his name?"

"Sure do. It's that writer fellow, I forget—"

"Leslie Everett Dove," Ezra said.

"That's him."

"He talk to other people?"

"Couldn't see how he could," she said. "He didn't know no more when he left than when he came."

Ezra slid the lists back and pulled out more photographs, folders of them, all the ones in the papers he'd just read, the high-school portraits and other shots of the missing, handed over for printing. He counted thirty-three different people, three short of the number of passengers who were aboard. Though even the papers hadn't gotten the count straight, thirty, thirty-nine, twenty-eight. Among the last of the photographs was the sequence of his father's boat coming out of the fog toward the jetty. Not four photographs, but five.

He held up the fifth to the dim light: the fisherman's hands—Jesse's—had retreated deep in their pockets, his face averted, his chin dropped to his chest, no longer looking into the boat but staring sullenly at the water. The boy had backed out of the stern. The pilot—"Pa," he whispered—had straddled the body on the afterdeck and had begun pulling at the canvas, the tarp now half on half off a body not clothed but naked save a shredded pair of white underwear. A dark hand, a frozen claw, a leg slightly raised, pole straight, the toes pointing into the afterdeck. Ezra brought the photograph closer, the better to see Floyd, assuming too that the picture was merely too—too *something*—to have been printed in the Rehoboth paper. He scanned the grainy faces he knew, the black water receding into the fog he remembered, the total absence of expression in his father straddling

Floyd's body. Then, there at his father's feet, something odd, something out of the sight of the men on the jetty, perhaps out of the sight of anyone but this photographer; something round and oblong, he couldn't be sure, a small wooden keg? He held up the previous pictures: the third and fourth clear and unhindered shots of the boat's interior: in them no keg, nothing remotely like it. He brought this fifth shot closer to his eye: around the keg the faint outline of a rope, the end of it cleanly cut.

Ezra raised his head. He saw that keg tumbling between his father's legs, the slit rope, like something that lay in his memory though it was until now part of his knowledge—

Shut up boy

Yes Pa

This isn't what it looks like and if you can't say what something is you can't say nothing   so say nothing about it   to anyone   never

"Excuse me?" Rita Perry was staring at him.

Ezra smiled politely. "Sorry, ma'am. Nothing."

She looked at him worriedly, then at the things in his rough fingers, then back at him.

Ezra returned the photos to the folder, the folder to the filebox. He could feel against his skin the cold, dead flesh where it touched him.

"You see everything you want?"

"Yes, ma'am, I think so."

"You see that letter in there?"

Ezra looked up. "Ma'am?"

"That letter that Mr Dove brought up to show us. He gave us something to look at, see if it meant anything. It didn't mean anything to me, or Joe, or my mother, but he said to hold onto it in case it—it—what'd he say, Joe?"

The old lady smiled a rotten smile. "Piqued our interest," she said.

"In case it piqued our interest," Rita repeated. "I just stuck it in there. Maybe it'd mean something to somebody someday. Some memento."

"No ma'am, I didn't see it." Ezra held out the filebox and Rita took it from him and fished out a sheet of paper, put it in

Ezra's palm.

Ezra's eyes went straight to the bottom and saw there the signature. He raised his head. No one was watching him. He waved a general goodbye, said his thanks, and left.

Outside, the rain had pulled up. A thick cloud of forest-mist and eggrot had come in.

Ezra hurried by the closed shops toward the river, back along Canal Street to the Hotel Rehoboth. He walked in. It was evening, it should have been full up with mill men after their shifts, but it was not, still mostly empty. The man he'd spoken to sat on his perch over the bar, as though he hadn't moved. He looked at Ezra when he sat on the neighboring stool then looked away, back toward the pool tables, down into his beer.

"You're from that place," he said.

Ezra put the letter and a picture of the *Raven* he'd taken from the scrap file on the bar. When he saw the man keeping his eyes off them Ezra slid them over. The photo was all pales and darks, over-exposed black-and-white. The letter was torn. The old man picked the picture between his thumb and forefinger and held it out over the counter with both hands as you would a trick dollar bill. In the picture a crowded boat idled down the throat of a small cove.

"What an ugly bitch," he said.

The boat was too high and too narrow, its bow tall and sharp like a meat cleaver, a vessel constructed for clumsy and reckless speed. It was so homely, when Ezra was young he'd almost thought it half beautiful. There was a crowd in the stern, some shading their eyes, looking off into a hopeless smokey glare. Others leaned over the gunwale watching their own reflections ripple over the black water. The rest were wrapped in coats and blankets, sprawled over the roof of the cabin with nothing to hold to, no railing or structure save the puny wheel. All of it, the boat, the passengers, was run through by the fog; everything translucent, already half gone.

The man turned the picture over. Scrawled across the top, *Last safe ride*. His fingers began to fumble. His eyes brimmed and his lids went red. The picture shook. There was a boy in it, tall, slim, slightly stooped in a white fisherman's sweater and dark trousers. His thumb pressed on the picture, on the boy, as though he could hold the hideous boat still, keep it from slipping out of the cove into open water; or, failing that, could sweep his young brother off the deck so that he could pick him out of the shallow cove himself.

"My mother knitted him that sweater for the trip," he said. "She knitted all the night before to get it done in time. And look how foggy it was. No one should have gone out in that. There couldn't have been no pleasure in it for Aubrey."

He raised his eyes and stared Ezra full in the face.

Ezra looked down at the letter. At the top he read the random, only vaguely meaningful, *Bailey Island, Maine Aug 27 1950*, scrawled in a stranger's fine, sloping hand. He looked the letter over once and filled with a strange and bitter buoyancy, a union between excitement and dread.

"Read me what it says," the man said, still fingering the picture.

Ezra looked at the man and decided he'd made a mistake by coming here, to this bar and to this town. The not knowing seemed to be the only thing keeping the lid on. He didn't know what would happen if he pried it off.

"I don't know what sense it makes," he said, "I'm not sure what it means."

"Try me. I'm not as dumb as I look."

"You said yourself I should leave it alone. They started digging and then they dropped it and you thought that was a good idea."

"Don't put words in my mouth."

Ezra looked at him placidly. "Okay, but I think you're going to want to read it yourself."

"Read it to me."

"What?"

"I can't read."

Ezra looked at him.

"Aubrey stayed in school all along. He was going to do something. Not us, though, me and my other brother. Ray." He laughed bitterly. "We got ourselves into the mill as soon as we could, like all the time we thought we were missing something."

Ezra picked up the letter and read it to him then stood away from the bar.

The old man called out after him: "You know what you're saying, Buster?"

"Not me. It's the letter."

"All this time we're thinking it's Krauts, and that's okay by me. Better leave it at that, I always said. And then you come dancing in here with this crap. Do you know what you're saying?"

Ezra backed away and headed for the door.

"You're from that place," the man called out after him. "That godforsaken island! Murder? Is that what they're saying it was now? You think some bastard just ate those boys and let them girls go?" The old man waved the picture. "What the hell happened to the goddamn boys?"

Ezra slipped out the door and ran around the corner for the phone booth. He slammed the door shut behind him and leaned panting against the glass. He gripped the phone to keep his hands from trembling. No one knew anything here. Not about the *Raven*. Not about anything. Everyone thought it was Germans or they didn't think. It might have been Germans, or it might not. But something had been kept from them, or they kept it from themselves. He saw in his mind that fifth photograph. A keg, its rope cut. He saw his father's face, his mouth moving, him talking. He was there but he hadn't remembered. He'd seen the keg but he didn't know what it meant.

Ezra picked up the letter and reread the first line. Written just a few summers ago, on one of those murky, briny twilights on the island. Already he saw her—he knew her—sitting with her hands between her knees in the strange room on Bailey Island with nothing on the walls but the unfaded ghosts of photographs, more pictures of the *Raven*, other crowds of people, more nervous, more fearful, pictures captioned: *1930, 1935, August 1940—last safe ride*. And the room inhabited by the woman who on August 27, 1951 went to the secretary and took out the last of the good paper, the ink well, the blotter, and from her pantry a bottle half full of liquor. Then pushing it to the table's far edge she put the quill to the paper, her stiff fingers rebelling against the confounded intricacies of writing *Dear.* Biting her lip she leaned in, next demanded from her hand a *Mr Dove,*

I may be talking out of turn, however I can't but think and have many times if my testimony could be right—God forbid—that one such as your Honor, should be informed.

It to me was a most tragic affair, the sinking of the Raven, as I was near being a victim myself.

But for these nine years I have wondered could it have been a planned affair?

In those days not many boats on the islands had insurance behind them but the Rainbow owned by Captain Earl R. Varney did. I know. Unknowingly I paid for the first and third installment on it, through Black Insurance Agency, Lewiston, Maine. I did not know the Rainbow was scuttled before burning in Quahog Bay but found it out on my own to my dismay. It seems the Rainbow which Earl Varney and Floyd Johnson owned and were operating together caught fire after coming in from dragging and it burned there on the water in plain sight. Mr Black paid them off on all the equipment which went down with it, but which I know <u>was not destroyed</u>. The next summer all that equipment began appearing. I understand the pump, diving suit, and etc., are still stored in a garage by Captain Varney's son Armand. Captain Varney then went to Florida and bought a boat, equipped it, and <u>it</u> burned, the Princess, also insured by the Black Agency. I know some equipment from the Princess is on land too, now under use with the diver at Cundy's Harbor, Great Island. I feel quite sure the Black Agency would not approve. That's why rates are so high.

As to the Raven her skipper Floyd Johnson was mixed up in many shifty deals with Captain Varney. No one knows this last part. The Rainbow and Princess are ones I only know about. And I know another thing no one else does, that Earl Varney was half owner in the Raven too. And he has been making out well since a couple years after the Raven went out and did not return, and it's not from working morning to night.

I've asked him where the cash comes from and he says work, but I know where he goes at sun-up and it isn't to any work at any cove I know of unless it's one named Sybil Fides.

I know of what I'm talking. Unfortunately at present time I'm Captain Earl R. Varney's wife—come October I hope not to be. I've had it.

On my part I know it's not a question of vengeance even if it can seem that way. I have only seen and known things that have happened, and I can't go on just seeing them and knowing them. I know I wouldn't gain out of my worst enemy that way.

I have wanted for a long time to confidentially tell what I know to the person I think I can trust. Knowing your goodness as Santa Claus and believing you want to do what's right prompted me to tell you what I know.

Believe me, this is not idle chatter.

Sincerely yours,

Beatrice Varney

DOVE

By the Spring of 1951, Beatrice Varney had taken up in one of Reverend Sinnett's summer cottages. Socks and rags filled the cracks under the doors and around the windows. Her daughter Pearl was with her, their turkey necks identical in shape and hang; their drained eyes. Two cold shut-ins, shoved in chairs against the wall by Leslie Everett Dove's sweater and wool pants and that white wind-blown hair. His deep radio voice inflated the little cottage. Dove asked Beatrice why she wrote she was nearly a victim herself.

"I was supposed to go on that boat."

"Why didn't you?"

"I just didn't is all. I stayed waiting at the Foster's all that day with Pearl. She was only eight or nine. But I'll tell you one thing. The day before was clear, but that morning started out foggy and only got foggier. And eleven o'clock that night it came in unbearable. A real dungeon fog. There was no sign of them so we stayed at the Foster's until dawn. We stayed up joking about how ugly that tub was, and how she was so ugly it was a wonder every time she did come back. She was so ugly I took a picture of her every chance I got. I even have a picture of her from that day. You can't see but the boat itself, the fog was so close. But it got to be light and they still didn't come in so I took Pearl home. Everybody said that Floyd Johnson probably dropped anchor somewhere to wait to the next day instead of coming in in the fog. But I knew that wasn't right. He wasn't smart about a lot of things, but water wasn't one of them. He could sail this water drunk and blindfolded. And he did, too, at least one time that I know of. That Earl Varney made him. I always felt something was wrong about this, something more than fog. They found Floyd, and then only women and girls after that. Now aint that strange? Where'd all those men go, I ask you. I'll tell you none of it adds up."

"Your letter alludes to sabotage, Mrs Varney," Dove said. "But I understand there is a perfectly good theory knocking about that Johnson kept extra gasoline aboard, and that it leaked out of the spare tank into the bilge and there was an explosion."

"There was no gas aboard that boat that wasn't running that engine."

"There are witnesses. I've already talked to the clerk who was at Small Point that day, Larry Hagan, and he's prepared to sign an affidavit that he smelled gas and saw the extra tanks and warned Johnson off about them."

Beatrice Varney shook her head. "Gas engines smell like gas because they run on it. But there was no extra gas on that boat."

"You mean you are today in knowledge—"

"—It's more than knowledge I have, Mr Dove. There couldn't have been no extra gas because the hose for the gas tank couldn't reach. They couldn't get near enough to it."

"Perhaps Captain Johnson found a way—"

"There's more than gas to it is all. Some sure did say those bodies looked as though they'd been burned. I can tell you a lot of people would like that, and I can think of at least one or two right off the bat. It would've ended things right there, tidied things up nice and quick. But you ever seen a body after it's been floating around in cold sea water? It can blacken and go crisp just like charbroiled chicken. It can look like a lot of things been done to it, but it's just cold sea water. I saw Floyd at the wharf that day. Now he wasn't black. I saw all them bodies. Their eyes were popped right out of their heads, the heads that still had them. Some of their feet and hands were blacked, but that's the cold I tell you. An explosion would have made a mess of them, and matchsticks of that tub. But they found no wood, nothing. It went out and nothing of it came back, nothing but some rich cows in petticoats."

"And Captain Johnson," Dove said.

Beatrice leaned back and examined her ragged fingernails with great interest. She mumbled something and Dove asked her to speak up. She mumbled something only a fraction more clearly, then looked at nothing through the window and let it leak out nonchalantly: "Just something else. You can check it yourself if you want. I do believe the Weather Bureau has logged down that that Sunday electrical storms were hit-and-running these parts. But I know the keeper at the Seguin light personally, and he swears the water around him was calm until 1:48 Monday morning."

"That was almost eleven years ago now—"

"He's got it wrote down," she said.

"I'll check it out," Dove said, "but now I have some things to ask of you."

"That means it wasn't the weather," Beatrice said.

"I know what it means, Mrs Varney," Dove said.

"It's just that some people said it was a weathery day. It was foggy but it wasn't weathery. It was a calm day, Mr Dove. A *calm* day."

"Yes," Dove said. "But I now have some things to ask that are of a personal nature."

"I'd rather it didn't go on record," she said, but to her fingernails, as though she'd rather it did. "I don't want it published around. But"—her eyes caught fire—"I do want to see justice done."

"Of course," Dove said, and turned off his tape recorder. "I understand the sanctity of privacy. In fact I have the utmost respect for it. I can't say the same of my colleagues. Honor and a man's word is lacking in the writing profession. Most writers abuse their power by exploiting their sources. But I assure you my intentions are honorable."

Beatrice Varney smiled gratefully, and so did her daughter. And so did Dove: he had another recorder, a smaller one, running in his briefcase.

"So," Dove said, "How did it happen that you were called the wife of Floyd Johnson at one time?"

Beatrice Varney reddened and glanced at her daughter, Pearl, who was sitting beside her, whose eyebrows raised and head turned just lightly to her mother.

"I don't know how that theory ever came about."

"Think back to 1941," Dove said.

"That was way back," Beatrice said.

"Only eleven years, Mrs Varney."

Beatrice reddened another shade deeper, as though she had more red in her and Dove could keep tugging it to the surface if he kept saying the right things. "At that time I wasn't interested in Earl," she said, barely a whisper, "I didn't know him too well."

"So you *were* married to Captain Johnson, then."

"Not exactly."

"In a manner of speaking, then."

"That was before anything—"

"Yes yes. And when was it that things between you and Johnson began to break apart?"

"Mr Dove, sir," Beatrice Varney said, "I don't think this is important. I thought you might be in the position to find out about this equipment I wrote you about."

"That is what I am here to find out."

"That's the only thing *I'm* interested in at this point," Beatrice Varney said, smoothing her lap. "It would have to be done very quietly and so forth and so on. It just seems to me that I have every reason to believe that equipment is still around."

"Yes you do," Dove said, "I've been up to these parts since I heard from you, and the people I spoke to, who shall remain nameless here, especially feel that it is as you indicated. There were certain things—" There Dove stopped. Neither mother nor daughter was hearing him now. He glanced back and forth between them.

"My daughter said I should just let it go," Beatrice Varney said. "My daughter sitting right beside me didn't think I'd gain anything from it. So that being that case, I just wonder how she thinks about it now. She knows I have nothing to gain. I told her I thought the Flying Santa would be in a position to find out anything if he had the right people giving him leads."

Pearl's young face had drained of color, her mouth stiffened to a thin line. She pointed her eyes at her mother and squinted.

"Fine, fine," Dove said, "But if any one of us here is in the possession of information which is of a criminal nature, then the statute of limitations enters in. Unless it is involved in manslaughter or murder, and it may be involved in manslaughter or murder, as you and I understand it. The statute does not run out on those charges. A dastardly act to secure the benefits of an insurance policy. That's what we're thinking of, isn't it?"

"It's tricky business," Beatrice Varney said.

"But it's what we're thinking of."

"Yes sir, yes it is."

"Then we have a certain duty," Dove said, addressing Pearl Varney. But she gave no sign of hearing. She hadn't taken her eyes off her mother.

Beatrice Varney sat up and stuck out her chin and her chest, and spoke for her: "Yes we do."

"Good," Dove said, sliding forward on his chair. "Now, as I am in a position to find out, there are three or four things I wish to clarify. Didn't you say that Earl Varney went diving around a certain area off Bailey Island after the *Raven* disappeared?"

"Yes, several times."

"Did he find anything?"

"Nothing as far as I know. One time he brought up a piece of wood, just some board that he found but it was never actually identified. But now that I think about it—yes, that's right—now it makes me think he knew something was down there. Otherwise, why would he keep going down in the same water even after having nothing to show for it?"

"Where was this spot?"

"Those ledges right out there."

Beatrice Varney's arm floated up and came parallel to the floor. Her outstretched finger pointed to the window behind Dove. Dove turned and saw the clean line of the horizon broken by dark flecks, which were the lobster boats, and above all of it a blank pale sky. The complications of the shore, the strings of islands that trailed off into the water and resurfaced abruptly farther out to sea, made it impossible to tell the true mainland with your eyes. Orderly ranks of waves broke one after the other up onto all the rocky beaches.

But Dove saw Beatrice Varney's arm still hanging in the air and knew he wasn't seeing what she meant him to. He dropped his gaze a little, squinted, and, while turning away having seen nothing, saw out of the corner of his eye a thin line of white water where there should have been nothing but gray. A broken narrow wash swept over something so close to the surface as to reach up and pull the breakers down, but far enough under to keep out of sight. Dove turned fully to the window.

"You know," Beatrice said, "Floyd couldn't swim."

"I see," Dove said, cold-bloodedly. His head didn't move an inch. His eyes watched the breakers wash over the invisible something where everything else told him there was only clean open water. "The Captain of a pleasure boat, a professional lobsterman, couldn't swim. You know quite a bit, Mrs Varney, for someone who claims not to have known very well either of these men at that time. But since you seem to know so much, how would you explain that only women were found besides Captain Johnson?"

"They figured the men were doing the cooking down below, and the women were up on top, so when whatever happened happened, the women went overboard and the men were caught down below."

Dove still didn't move. He spoke as though to the glass, his voice growing steadily more shrill, more insistent: "When whatever happened happened? Are you saying that it was a planned affair, Mrs John—I mean Mrs Varney? Do you possibly, or may I infer from your implication that what you mean is that the *Raven* might have been planned to be scuttled?"

"Floyd and I were never really—"

"—Are you saying that thirty-six men, women and children were sent to their deaths out there by an act of your husband's will, both of your husbands' wills? I just wonder, Mrs Varney, how you know so much about what Captain Varney did or did not find beneath the Teeth if you didn't know him that well. Or why you would have been in the position to put money toward insurance for the *Raven* if at that time you were finished romantically with Captain Johnson but not yet involved with Captain Varney. Or why you were going to go out with Johnson that day, or so you say, but decided not to go at all."

Dove would not move his eyes off the ridge of white wash. Beatrice would not speak, and Pearl was busy doing mathematics in her head. She was just eighteen and all her life her mother had told her that her natural father was a man from Portland, and that she'd been conceived during the one week of marriage they had together before he left for the Navy eight years before Pearl Harbor, where he died on December 7, which made it mean something that her name was Pearl.

But now Pearl had finished her calculating, and sure now that it wasn't the Navy her father hadn't returned from, and that if she only turned and looked where the writer Leslie Everett Dove looked she would see that she would have to cross no more water than what lay between her and the Teeth to see where her father took his last breath—sure about all that, she turned now and peered out through the window.

Meanwhile, her mother went on: "I know about the gas," Beatrice said, "because I'm the one that gassed that boat that day."

Dove snapped around and faced Beatrice Varney: "You?"

"Like I said the hose couldn't reach. I carried that gas down to the cove in five gallon drums."

"You gassed the boat? So, you and Johnson— Why haven't you said anything all this time?"

Beatrice stared silently into her lap.

Dove regained his composure, straightened himself in his chair, and sought now to regain the initiative, to keep Beatrice Varney off balance. "Why didn't you go out that day, Mrs Varney? There are pictures of the *Raven* going back quite a few years on these walls. You must have been fond of her."

She said nothing. Dove demanded to know: "Where is Captain Varney now?"

She ducked like a scolded child. "Back on the Mountain."

"He doesn't answer anything I write him."

"Well, he's right up there on the back of Great Island. If you take the path up, you can't miss it, just above Dyer's Cove, about a mile: Earl Varney, Captain, a picnic ground or whatnot at the top there. But you won't be welcome, I can tell you right now. When I was away one weekend, his son Armand moved into my home, which is why I'm hiring this cottage from Reverend Sinnett now. I went down to Captain Varney's and found them all there,

234

and I was told there was no place for me there, so I started divorce proceedings while Armand and his wife and five children all took up in my home. I hear Armand's wife and Captain Varney haven't been hitting it off too well. I was told just yesterday, this is just as I was told, that they got in a real argument the day before yesterday and she took a gun at him. So I guess that ended that episode for a while anyways. But I do know that all them Varneys have been very nasty to me and so forth and so on. And as a matter of fact that was my point in bringing all this out to you, because I just thought that as long as this stuff is going on, and they've been that dirty to me, there is no reason the rest shouldn't be exposed."

Pearl had sat straight in her chair, her hands overturned on her knees. Her forehead had creased, her eyes narrowed; she latched her stare onto her mother.

"I want you to know," Dove said to Beatrice Varney, "that the only reason I'm here is that I tried to find out something myself and found some funny stuff. I talked to a fireman who would have been involved with the search for the *Raven*. He'd been warned off, not to help me at all, by someone local he wouldn't name. He'd been told not to go into this too far, because he might find out something that might be an embarrassment to somebody else."

Beatrice Varney's eyes glittered, as though the entirety of her life, what it had meant up to now, had been legitimized by what Dove just said. She opened her mouth and out came another voice, a deeper one, full of the false graciousness only the already rich can afford: "And let me just say that Earl is a smart man. I believe in giving the devil his dues. He's been a very smart diver. And he has helped many fine parties."

Dove heard a noise and glanced at the girl. The left side of her face twisting into a snarl, her eyes pink with rage, she shot to her feet and threw open the door and ran out into the glare. The cottage inhaled the cold wind. Her figure retreated across the rocks toward the water, her coat flapping behind her. Dove was surprised she'd waited so long, one father, Johnson, dead; another one, Varney, indicted; and a mother meting out bile and condemnation at will. He went to the door and shut it.

"—But there have just been a lot of underhanded things going on that I can't go along with," Beatrice Varney said, making an indignant show of ignoring both the cold and her daughter's outburst. "And as I say Captain Varney has many fine abilities, and he's very capable. And it's unfortunate that we've had such a stormy marriage. If we haven't had so much interference I think I might have been able to straighten him out a little bit. We could have been happy. But everybody's got to accept their duty eventually."

"But why did only women come back, can you tell me that?" Dove said. "Women plus Floyd Johnson, of course."

"*They* didn't fix that," Beatrice said. "Floyd and Earl fixed one thing together, and Earl fixed one more thing without Floyd's knowing. I know that much. So that's one thing Floyd fixed, and two things Earl fixed. But there was something else and neither could have done it. Neither could have fixed what happened to the men and what didn't happen to the women. They didn't plan nothing about that. But those men separated clean like they were just carted off. And you'll never prove why because there's no one left that's going to help you. Everyone's under water or they're dirt or they will be before they're caught talking."

Jealousy, Dove thought, but not just a man's jealousy. The jealousy of a lover, a beast. Earl Varney may be satan, he thought, but how many things to fix does a devil like Beatrice Varney have?

EZRA

zra set up a stack of change on the phone booth and dialed the operator and asked for the *Boston Globe*. Outside, the firemen had shut the garage door, only a single window was lit now on the firehouse's second floor. But for him, Congress Street was shut down, the restaurants, the bars. The mill was a distant storm.

As the phone clicked through its connections, Ezra readied on his tongue something to say, then lost it. A female voice came on, asking for an extension, and Ezra asked for Frank Dougherty.

"Who should I say is calling?"

"He won't know me," Ezra said.

Frank Dougherty barked his name into the phone, rasping as though just running, or beginning to run, or wanting to. Ezra introduced himself.

"I'm from Bailey Island," he said.

"Bailey Island."

"You don't remember?"

"Remember."

In the background, Ezra could hear him typing and shuffling papers.

"1941. A boat that was lost. The *Raven*," Ezra said.

The typing stopped.

"I read what you wrote about it in the paper."

Through the phone wires a chair creaked, a cup of coffee was sipped.

"That was what ten, fifteen years ago."

"Eleven."

The chair creaked again, and Ezra could see Dougherty coming upright, elbows on his desk.

"That was an ugly mess," Dougherty said. "I guess if you're

from Bailey Island I couldn't presume to tell you much about that that you don't already know. What can I do for you, Mr Johnson?"

"I want to know about Leslie Everett Dove."

At first Dougherty said nothing. Then, "What makes you think I know anything about Leslie Everett Dove?"

"You both write about the water."

"So what do you want to know?" Dougherty's voice was wary, unsure who he was dealing with.

"I read some things of his," Ezra said.

"You and a million other people."

"I don't think they were true."

Ezra could hear Dougherty breathing.

"You think these things weren't true or you know that they weren't true."

"I guess I know," Ezra said. "He wrote something about some people from Bailey Island that he made up. And then he wrote something about the *Raven*."

"What did he write about the *Raven*."

"You know *New England Sea Tragedies*? It's the newest one."

"I've seen it. That and ten other books of his. He publishes his goddamn grocery lists."

"It's in there," Ezra said.

"And what he wrote about the *Raven*, is it true?"

Ezra wiped a hole in the phone booth glass and peered out. A dense ground fog flowed steadily down Congress Street to the end, like a river.

"I don't know if you could say anything about that boat that's true or not. But he wrote about it. He may still be writing about it. He's still poking around, I think."

"And you don't like it."

Ezra squinted outside. The fog ended at the end of Congress Street. As if beyond lay only darkness and empty space.

"Am I right?" Dougherty rasped.

"I guess I don't."

"Well I don't blame you. I wouldn't trust anything Dove wrote farther than I could carry him, that fat fraud."

More creaking through the phone lines, Dougherty sighing,

as if making himself comfortable, kicking back from his desk.

"Leslie Everett Dove," he said. "Oh boy he's as young—as young as me, but he's already a famous bastard, let me tell you. All this Flying Santa shit he's started. So just what *do* you know of Dove?"

Ezra hesitated, then stammered, "Just what I read on the back of the book."

Dougherty paused, as if not understanding who he was talking to.

"Well, then it's all on record, isn't it," he said. "All there. Yes, he's a fine gentleman. Every Christmas now he hires that little plane and drops all those boxes of gifts to the lighthouse keepers. Dozens, dozens of articles fall out of that guy. And all those books, ten of them already. By the time he dies, it'll probably be fifty and they'll have an exhibit. Yes sir." He trailed off, though not dreamily. "Da big time," he sang.

Dougherty's tone became suddenly dark, acidic. "What do you want with Leslie Everett Dove anyway? You aren't a writer are you? Because I won't talk to you if you're a writer. Never trust a writer I always say, not even me. *I* don't trust me. You read my crap? Fires and murders, fires and murders."

"I don't get to the paper much. And I don't really write. I mean, I can write, but I'm not a writer, like you, Mr Dougherty."

"So what do you do up there?"

"I trap lobster."

"You're a lobsterman."

"I guess I am."

Dougherty cleared his throat. "Well, Leslie Everett Dove. Now if you're going fishing, he be a whale. My father was master of a ship off Nantucket, so in all due respect I know a few things, Mr Johnson. I don't know what you fellas up there think of Leslie Everett Dove, but I'll tell you what the men on the water down here think of him. Dove goes to the wharf and those men look right through him as if he isn't even there. When he talks they ask their buddy if he heard something, a dog howling or something like that. Once he went up to Gloucester to interview Edward R. Snow, the master of the *Thomas W. Lawson*, the greatest schooner in Boston Harbor—seven masts she had, an acre of sail, forty-four thousand feet of sail, a real beauty—You know Edward R. Snow, Mr Johnson?"

"I believe my father knows Captain Snow."

"Then this'll mean something to you. Dove went up to get the *Lawson*'s story and Snow threw him out and told him never to come back. But Dove wrote that story anyway. He quoted Snow at length. Of course it won him some award or other. For christsakes Snow only said six words to the man, 'Get off my land, you blackguard!' My father said Snow was never the same after that. A man like Snow who worked his whole life with his hands, he couldn't understand how a man could continue to lie even when he was kicked off someone's land. Snow lost something.

"My father wrote the true story of the *Lawson* in *Yankee* magazine, as told to him by his friend Snow, who of course had the true story, which is the only story, which Dove couldn't know anything about. Only a shipmate would talk to another shipmate about these kinds of things, my friend, the way things really are on the water. And they won't put the gloss on, pretty it up, but you must know that, right lobsterman? You live by a fisherman's code up there, don't you?"

"I guess we do," Ezra said, seeing a burning hull, the cove bright as noon, fishermen standing in their boats.

"So you know that when Snow talked to my father he was talking straight dope," Dougherty went on. "See, that's the thing. Dove is just a bad actor. Too bad. He really has people going. But not the people who really matter, the people who really know. You may be one of those people, Mr Johnson. But all those pretty books with that name of his on them can get you going, can't they?"

"I don't know if I can say," Ezra said.

"Then what's this conversation about?"

"I thought it was about Leslie Everett Dove."

"It might be."

"What else could it be about?" Ezra said.

Dougherty didn't say anything for a while.

"Look, let me help you here," Dougherty said. "Let me tell you something about those books of his. My father was born in

1876. A very literate man he was. He kept a voluminous library. One day—this was about five years ago—I gave him one of Dove's books as a gag, and even though he didn't like the son of a bitch he sat down and read it, because that's the kind of man my father was. He knew Dove was a brigand and a liar, but he sat down and he read that piece of shit, every word of it. And when he finished he got up from his chair, walked over to his shelves and pulled down some book or other and blew the dust off it. He puts it flat on the table and opens the cover and shows me the copyright. It was 1880. Then he puts Dove's book beside it, opens both to the first page and reads to me the first line from each. I don't remember what it was, but word for word Dove's was the same, from the first word to the last. This fucking guy thinks he has an easy out, pulls the genies out of the bottle and then he signs them. He's discovered the secret of plagiarism. He's a master of it. These days it's easy, there isn't anyone checking behind you, no one gives a damn. Journalism is a new field, and along comes a guy like Dove who doesn't even bother to type. The fact of the matter is that when he was at the *Quincy Ledger* he hardly wrote a damn thing. He did paste-ups for christsake, cut up other people's articles and pasted them together. Maybe he'd scribble a sentence or two between the paragraphs to smooth it out. I know the editor who edited the stuff, and he couldn't believe it. The *Ledger* eventually let him go, then he did one or two like that for the *Globe,* then they got on to him and he was thrown out of here, too. But there always seems to be someone else who wants him, what with the name he's making for himself."

Ezra let his forehead come to rest against the phone box. "And this Flying Santa thing. Is that a gag too?"

"A gag? He's a jerk! Even the lighthouse people think he's a jerk. Last year, the first time he did it, it took some of these lighthouse people hours and days to find the packages Dove threw them. And a couple of those packages went right through the windshields of a few keepers' cars. So this year he'll do it again, and next year too, and when he comes, when they hear his plane coming, they'll run to their cars, and Dove will think they're waving to him, but they'll just be protecting their cars.

The whole thing's a stunt. You know the wives and kids in those places are lonely and bored, and their hopes are very high for something that interests them, something to take their minds off the water. So now every year, the keepers' families are going to look and look, and when they find those packages they'll end up finding mostly Dove's own books, books about sailors and lighthouses and lighthouse keepers. It's bad enough that Dove puts his name on books that he doesn't even write, but for a lighthouse keeper to be kept waiting all year, and to finally open the thing he's waited for and find himself reading some hyped up version of the past year, of his own life, about the treachery of the high seas and the loneliness and courage of the lighthouse keeper and all that hooey. What greater trick there must be to play on a lighthouse keeper and his family I'll never know. In ten, twenty years, there's going to be no one left in those lighthouses, they'll be disbanded and automated, and—mark my words—if Dove is still alive he'll still go and drop empty boxes on uninhabited islands. A stunt, I tell you. All for the publicity.

"Christ, I'll tell you how good this feels. I've been wanting to talk about Leslie Everett Dove for years. Ever since his first book. The man's a phoney. Let me tell you what really bothers me about that brigand more than his plagiarizing. Because not all writers are as bad as he is. What bothers me deeply—what hurt my father so deeply—and my father was an honest and hardworking man—is that Dove produces his writing as history. That's the bottom line. And he produces himself as a historian. He doesn't give a damn about facts. He murders them. This thing that made him famous, this story that he cashed in all his chips on a few years ago, that made people start listening to him for real, was the worst and biggest lie that's ever been told about the water and the men who work it. And it debunked and later destroyed the reputation of a great sea captain, a good friend of my father, Captain William Blanchard, master of the steamer *Portland*. Heard of it?"

Ezra took off his jacket and leaned back against the cold glass of the phone booth. He could hear Dougherty moving too, cloth shifting, his beard scratching against the receiver. Dougherty getting comfortable.

"—November 26, 1898, the great Portland gale, they call it. I remember my father saying that there was no such appalling calamity as this in all his days up and down the Atlantic coast. Nothing he's seen the likes of before or since. And he is to be believed, my friend.

"When the *Portland* left Long Wharf bound for Portland Harbor at seven in the evening, it had already begun to snow. It carried a hundred-fifty to two hundred. No one knows. There was bad glass that day, any decent ship's captain could see that. The barometer was down to twenty eight. Every other vessel between Gay Head and Cape Anne was looking for safety. They were coming in in crowds, piling up on the docks there. It was mayhem, a riot. And the *Portland* passed them all going the other way, slow, steady and proud. And so you're going to ask me why I'm defending Blanchard when all signs told him to stay at anchor. Because I tell you that ship was going with or without him. These companies live and die by passenger fares, money is their god. And once a ship like that was made, it had passed the point of no return, it couldn't just lie at dock. So the fares were collected, the ship was going come hurricane, cyclone, what-have-you. Blanchard said it was madness, and his boss told him to step up to the wheel or step aside, that there were plenty of other captains standing around the wharf who needed the money. But Blanchard knew his boat. He knew his course. He was trapped between the fact of his firing and his conscience. He had no choice. It was his personal protocol. You can't judge him like he was alive today, because Blanchard knew that no one could have brought those passengers into Portland Harbor if he couldn't. These were good men, honorable men. Blanchard stepped behind the wheel.

"The rest you can figure out. God help the poor bastards. No one could get through that night, and the *Portland* couldn't have lasted long. On the lee side of the Cape the winds were one hundred ten miles per hour and more. You can't anchor in that, you'd be pounded to pieces inside of a minute. The snow must have been as thick as fog. They must have been caught in a smother. Do you know what a smother is? That's the top ten to fifteen feet of each wave sheared off by the wind and ripping into your face. You can't see in it. You can't breathe in it. You can't navigate a ship in it. You know what kind of power I'm talking about, Mr Johnson?"

"Yes, Mr Dougherty, I do."

Dougherty started to speak, then he stopped. "Of course you do, Mr Johnson. I forgot who I was talking to for a minute. So then you know what Blanchard was facing that night. Maybe you've been in that sort of weather yourself."

He waited for Ezra to say something but he was busy listening. He was in the weather every day. Sometimes it was bad and sometimes good.

"But Blanchard was facing something else, too," Dougherty went on, "something he never saw or knew about. This is where the blackguard comes in, the brigand.

"It's forty-six years later now, 1946, and this soon-to-be Flying Santa has a reputation, but so far only a small one. In a column for the *Ledger* he puts the *Portland* down around Thatcher's Island, which would have put her on her usual northern course toward Portland. But if that were the case then Blanchard would have made the error of his life, and a man like that doesn't make that kind of error, because on the sea you don't live to make it again. He would have had to have panicked, turned her starboard against a westward storm. A huge, unforgivable error that would have been, trying to run her across a wind like that. Anyone who knows the sea and knows that night could tell you that would have been suicide. The wind would have rolled her inside a minute. Blanchard's only hope would have been to forget land and head due east, east I tell you! Keep her straight as a rope right into the goddamn wind!

"It would have been everything just to keep her steady, facing that way, just to stay afloat. And Blanchard was steady as stone, tireless. But the blackguard was just as tireless. That's one thing I'll give him. After that column came out he got two divers, two thugs, to go down outside of Thatcher's Island and bring up wreckage, and he claimed that it belonged to the *Portland*. Mind you, it might have been from a wreck, but there are hundreds along the Cape. It could have been driftwood found on some beach or in a garbage heap. But Dove published a whole book based on a few scraps of wood. And no one of any name claiming otherwise, the public had no choice but to believe him. Blanchard's family was in disgrace, one of his sons had his ship taken from him, another lost a job at the harbor. His widow was already old and weak, and she didn't last long after that book hit the stores. But worse, Blanchard's reputation was gone to hell, and reputation, my friend, is all you have left when you're dead, too dead to defend yourself. The *Portland*'s loss was in Dove's hands.

"But that's not all. In 1946, I was assistant at the *Post*, and I was there when this upstart led in his two lackeys. And let me tell you these were no divers, those fat, foul, liquoring ingrates, landlubbers, whores, they'd never seen the ocean but to piss in it. They carried in the *Portland* evidence on two two-by-fours. Evidence! A little bitty tin bell, two, maybe three feet high. A *dinner* bell! Now first of all there was no rust on it, no barnacles. Don't forget that by then it would have been under water for half a century. But second, the *Portland* was a sidewheeler, a real beauty, a giant of a vessel. The Fall River Line knew how to equip their ships. You couldn't lift the *Portland*'s bell without something a little more than two fat, slobbering goons—a truck might help, a crane would be better. Two tons of cast iron or more. And there's this little dinner bell sitting on the news editor's desk. But his hired guns put it down with a big thud. 'Extra extra!' Dove was saying, 'Proof that *Portland* went down near Thatcher's Island!' All the reporters and editors crowded around gawking and nodding their heads. I stood up and walked toward this evidence, this bell. I pushed my way through and looked at it and started laughing. Old Dove was getting redder and madder by the second and demanded to know what I was laughing about. 'That?' I said. I pointed at the bell. 'That? The bell from the *Portland*? Let me up!'

"But I was the only one laughing. And who was I? So publish the story we did. And the book was not far behind. In fact, so not far behind that he must have already written it and was just waiting to fill in the blanks. Then Blanchard's widow died. Six years ago I thought it was a conspiracy, but now I know it's just the way things are."

Ezra was looking at his reflection in the phone booth glass. "You didn't say nothing. Why don't you just say something?"

He thought he heard Dougherty laugh.

"You can't go up against that, my friend. My father wrote letters to the editor of every paper, but no matter how much he wrote he couldn't respond in kind, with a big book or anything. After all, what was my father? Just a ship's master, just a man who'd spent his whole life on the sea, sailed every kind of sea imaginable. And what am I? Any mariner worth anything would have tried to defend Blanchard if he could. You should know—people who work the water know what a reputation means, how you can tell everything by it, even things you can't see. But knowing isn't enough. I'm just another writer. I can't say a thing. Dove's a big hero now.

"But someday, somebody's going to find the *Portland* lying belly up on the ocean floor. She'll be far off course, exactly where she should have been if Blanchard had done what he should have, which was point her into the wind and pray. Which is just what he did. But anyway, it's too late. Everybody's dead, Blanchard, Blanchard's widow, his boys for all intents and purposes. And eventually Dove will be dead too. The bastard'll probably die believing his own lie."

Ezra cleared his throat. "But the book," he said. "The book says he was in the Navy for ten years, and that he'd sailed around the world, that he was in the war—"

Dougherty whispered hoarsely: "Find me the years he could have done all that in. He hasn't even lived that long. You know that Ph.D. his books say he has? He doesn't even have a Masters degree. Blackguard. And here's a sadder thing. It's not just someone passing off that bullshit as the truth, making stories and saying it's all fact. The sadder thing is that the sea is dramatic enough, it's deadly enough. I'll never understand how Dove lives with himself. You see, there's the difference between fact and fiction. Facts don't lie, they can't. Reputation is a fact, but Dove's is a fact built on fiction, and fiction's pure quicksand, there's no bottom to it. The truth is brutal enough, my friend, bitter enough. Wouldn't you say?"

Ezra glanced through the dark to the fire station. A single

cigarette surging then idling. Then it arched and vanished.

He cupped his hand around his mouth. He believed someone was listening. The firehouse was dark. He was standing in an exposed phone booth. He probed the glass door with his toe.

"How many people think like you do, Mr Dougherty?" whispering now.

"Damned few, practically none. He's fooled everybody for so long, repetition's pounding it in, book after book—"

"He must have a lot of people who like him."

"What? Eh? Yeah, he has a following. But hey, look at me, dumb little me. I got a following. They read my stuff in the paper and they write me. I got a whole drawer full of fan mail."

"So why don't you ever think about writing the truth about Dove yourself?"

"I think about it. I think about it plenty. Mostly it's because the people who really matter, people like my father, have Dove's number anyway. They laugh at him and let it go. The old sailors, there's only a handful of them that aren't dead or drowned, and they're just sitting by their fires, not caring to talk, just living out the couple years of rest they've spent all those years on the water earning. The days of that kind of sailor, no offense, are quickly coming to an end. And Dove knows it. He isn't writing for them.

"But it's bigger than that. He isn't stupid, that I can tell you. Someone who lies that well can't be stupid. He's got to keep his stories straight. You have to understand a bit of psychology. The fact is, my friend, is that people don't want to know. You take it from me. Dove's a big man around here. No one would believe the truth even if you put their nose right up to it. Truth is not entertainment, it's just the boring truth. That's why I can tell you all this—it'll never hurt me. Most people will say I made it all up, call me an old fart, sour grapes that I never made it like him, and let that be the end of it.

"Besides, talking to you is enough. I'm getting it all out of my system as I speak. Santa Claus, Historian of the Sea, all that crap. He's as much a historian as I am, and I'm just a two-bit beat reporter, a hired gun. I'm the city's whore. And that blackguard's too."

Dougherty fell silent. Ezra could hear typewriters clacking, telephones ringing, people yelling.

"Helpful?" Dougherty asked.

"I don't know," Ezra said.

"So what are you going to do about Dove?"

"I don't know."

"You going to look for this *Raven*?"

"I don't know. I think I'm going to try."

Dougherty grunted. "Good luck then. You're going to need it."

"I don't know. My father always says there's no such thing as luck, there's only consequences."

"Your father's a smart man. He work that water up there with you?"

"We work it together," Ezra said.

"You listen to him. He reminds me of the men who used to work with my father. They spent fifteen, twenty hours a day on the water. They did all their hauling by hand and filled their dories right up solid with fish, and by the time they rowed back to the mother ship it was half past two in the morning. They did not fuck around. They were brilliant, self-effacing men. They didn't have time for people like Dove, for such a fool as that. And they died broke, every last one of them."

Without qualification of any kind, and without the slightest belligerence—as much out of necessity as desire—Ezra Johnson and Frank Dougherty cut each other off.

Ezra pushed his way out of the booth, then felt he walked out not necessarily into this evening, a late spring Friday in 1952, but possibly 1941, and possibly both. And pulling away from the curb, his lights twin suns arcing slowly across the street, toward the Rehoboth Falls Trust, he thought he could faintly see a crowd between the bank's pillars, shifting their feet and grinning out of something halfway between eagerness and dread in the earliest moments you can still call morning. Moving toward them, he felt a chill of apprehension, and panic. And then following the course of the river toward the sea, hardly seeing it switchbacking below him, below him and to his left, Rehoboth fell quickly behind until all he could see in the mirror were the red beacons of the mill stacks pulsing in the night, the spotlights from the Company's security scissoring weakly through the ground fog. And then that was gone. The bends in the road came at the last moment. He caught something—a woman—in the headlights, standing at the roadside with a suitcase. A young woman, petite, good-looking in the brief instant, shielding her eyes and peering at his headlights through her fingers. He slowed, she seemed to recognize him, or what he was not, and turned the other way, toward the dark, and he drove on.

MAVIS

Why where—" Frances Beauchamp began, for there was no body in the kitchen. "Mavis?"

The clock tocked from the livingroom, its gears shifting as it rang three times—outside, the mill whistle was muted by the rain and mist, more foghorn than piercing wail—then rang three times more. She went to the stove, though she had nothing on. The skillet was empty in the corner, flecked with breakfast.

"Mavis?"

She leaned on the bannister, peering up the stairs. Mavis had shut the door but Frances could hear her opening and closing drawers. She traced her footsteps overhead as the ceiling bowed. A muffled drag of something heavy across her bedroom floor.

"Ma—"

Three quick raps on the kitchen door tugged her back. She trotted softly through the passageway letting out on the living room, and entered it and stood before the fireplace mantel. She filled the mirror, patting down the sides of her brittle hair. Her eyes only needed to shift slightly down to catch the sight of her family, Gordon and her and Gordy Jr., Ivan and Mavis seated on a couch before the fireplace. She touched the soft pouch under her chin. He'd be so displeased. She went back to the kitchen and reached for the doorknob, smiling pleasantly, and opening it to Walter McAlister standing sideways between streams of runoff from the roof.

Frances' smile fell. Walter removed his hat.

"Evening, Mrs Beauchamp."

"Walter." She didn't move. "What can I do for you? We were just sitting down to dinner."

But Walter had already given a sweep through the kitchen and seen and smelled nothing, and smiled patiently.

"Yes ma'am. I'm here to pick up Mavis."

"Pick up—?"

"Yes, ma'am."

"But Mavis isn't going anywhere," she said sternly, as though she'd just decided to ground her child, whose error she'd consider later.

"Yes, ma'am," Walter said, clutching his hat to his chest. "Can I see her?"

"No you cannot," she said, and closed the door.

Frances Beauchamp watched his shadow in the door's curtain, standing, then turning and walking off across the grassy lot.

She turned for the stairs, but Mavis was halfway down, jerkily dragging a suitcase a step at a time.

Her mother laughed.

"There's no dinner—"

"No."

"But I bought more eggs. I thought we'd have soufflé. Your favorite."

"Gordy's favorite, Mama," she said, as though for the thousandth time, stepping down, letting the suitcase's momentum pull her to the bottom where Frances moved her feet out of the way just in time before she turned her head to the tap-tap-tapping of a tree's gnarled fingers silhouetted in the street light, touching the window. Mavis stood beside her.

"But where—"

"France, Mama."

Frances laughed, "But you said you wouldn't take it."

"I changed my mind." Mavis shoved the suitcase against the wall with a kick.

"But—" raising her right hand, waving it through the air at all the things she could say. "They'll expect you at school."

"I told them today."

"I didn't know."

"I didn't tell you."

"Why not?"

"Because I didn't know either," Mavis said, sitting at the piano bench. She stropped her fingers lightly over the keys.

Frances raised her other hand, "Don't—"

Mavis spread her fingers, about to press, then lifted them quickly, as though off a hot stove. She smiled at her mother. Disaster averted.

"At least you won't have to hear it again." Mavis glared up at her. "I know how much it hurts."

Mavis stood, walking past her, brushing by her, almost sending her backward, into the kitchen where she pulled open the door to find the runoff falling in the doorway in four thick streaks like metal bars.

"Have you seen Walter?"

"I sent him away."

Mavis whirled. She gritted her teeth, then calmed. There would be no more of this after tonight. "My bus is at eight. He was going to help me with my bags."

"I didn't know."

"You didn't ask him in."

"He likes you," Frances said, turning back for the livingroom.

"So what if he does," Mavis called after her, following her calmly. "So what?"

"He going with you?"

"The scholarship was for one."

"He wants to marry you," Frances said matter-of-factly.

"He'll stay in Rehoboth forever."

"What's wrong with that? People do it all the time. I did. Your father—"

"He's dead."

Frances went on, ignoring Mavis, "Most everyone we know was born here and will die here."

"Yes, I know, Mama."

"And you will, too."

"I will not die here, Mama."

"You told those scholarship people you'd turned them down."

"I called them back."

"They wanted you that badly?"

"Yes, Mama," Mavis said. "Somebody wanted me that badly."

Frances opened her mouth, closed it, raised her hand and let it fall, silently, to her knee, where she motioned as if picking a piece of lint. She leaned back into the couch.

"Walter always wanted you that badly—"

"And now I have no one to help me with my bags."

"I remember him eyeing you when you were a little girl. When your father and brothers went away, he protected you like an older brother would. Like Gordy would have. After they went away, he thought he was all you had." She raised her eyes to the photograph. "You can't leave."

"Mama," Mavis said, going to the closet for her coat. "But they're not dead. They went away, remember?"

"Until they come back—"

"Until they come back," Mavis said. Slipping her arms through her coat, she went to the phone and asked the operator for the McAlisters.

"Walter," she said, "You can come back now."

"Have you cleaned your brothers' rooms this week?" Frances asked.

"No I have not," replacing the phone in its cradle.

"Before you go. Clean your brothers' room."

"They're dead, Mama."

"The linens need changing."

"No one's slept on them for eleven years."

"And dust—"

Mavis, striding for the fireplace, pointed up at the photograph. "They're out there, Mama. They died with all the others. Drowned, or whatever it was."

A look of utter serenity passed across Frances's face. "They're fine. All's well."

"All's not well, Mama," Mavis said, her voice rising, the rain suddenly louder as the back door opened and closed. Hearing Walter's footsteps in the kitchen, Mavis turned and walked out.

She reached for a glass and turned the faucet, and she stood, glass in hand, staring at the gush of water, remembering what Walter had shown her. She shut it off and left the glass in the sink.

She heard behind her a single note on the piano. A second.

The beginnings of some song she did not know what, but she feared it as she had feared nothing else these last eleven years, and pushed by Walter without saying a word and out into the feathery rain and the night, while the piano strung out to an echo of nothingness behind her. She began the song in her head, and heard her father's favorite melody; a child's voice, hers, sang it in her mind. She turned and went in.

Her mother's face was wet, her lips trembled. She raised her eyes. "You kept me and them apart," her voice quavered, rising a little in anger. "You were too young to go on a trip like that, so I had to stay home with you."

"You hate boats, Mama," Mavis said. "You always got sea-sick. You never would have gone."

The piano fell silent and Frances raised a hand off the keyboard, waving it in the air. "Thank God I wasn't along and you weren't orphaned like the Decker girl!" She looked to the picture on the mantle. "You kept me from them. You're keeping me from them now, keeping me from my boys. I would have gone, if it weren't for you."

The clock ticked. The rain was hissing on the roof. Mavis raised her head, "Goodbye, Mama" on her tongue, but the door closed, the kitchen light pinched off, leaving just the dim yellow shape of the window in the grass; the yard fell in darkness, and she said nothing. She could hear Walter's feet pressing in the mud. A pause—had he slipped?—she walked on.

She tried to remember when she had last walked in the open night—even the rain—at this hour. When she hadn't been cooking for her mother, sitting politely on the piano bench as they entertained some well-wisher, a widow of some man—her father's friend—on the *Raven*. Or Arthur McAlister, who had taken the responsibility of having their lawn mowed and keeping the house in good repair. How many times had she stood on the bridge over the river down by the mill, in better times leaning against the railing and listening to the water rushing below, literally praying for a chance to be grateful to be alive.

The gates of her neighbors were passing, the streetlights. Her footsteps echoed off the porches, up into the trees. She passed, here and there, through patches of warm ovensmell and the odor of cooked meat, like the mysterious columns of warmer water in a lake. Walter was catching up. Instinctively, she turned her head so that he would not see her face.

All's well stop. We're fine stop. Gordon stop.

The words had ruined a ruined life. She, like her mother, had waited for years. The words brought back that Christmas, when she had permitted her mother to convince her that Christmas morning they would walk through the door, their gift to us, and all we had to do was sit under the tree praying and singing and holding hands and waiting—

Her eyes filled with tears, her throat, her chest heaved in a deep sob which she kept down.

They had waited through the day, and through the night, sitting there in their vigil, the roast in the oven still raw by the next morning, the salad leaves wilted.

"Mavis?" Walter, keeping perfect pace, coming no closer. "Mavis, you have more than an hour."

"Leave me here," she said, hiding her eyes in the darkness.

There was movement in the trees, wind, or were those birds? Lightning bugs lifted out of the grass. Route 2 up and down was empty, vanishing southbound in blackness.

"You'll die of pneumonia before you reach Boston," he said.

"Let me be alone," she said.

"What if it doesn't come?"

"I'll wait for the next one," she said.

"It's not until the morning."

"I'm getting on the next bus, Walter," she said.

And watching him go—she'd given him hardly a peck goodbye as he stood, bent awkwardly over her, trying to give her an embrace without pressing her breasts; she'd patted his back. "Okay," she said.

"I—" he began.

But she looked at him scoldingly, and he seemed to nod, or cough, seemed anyway to accept the fact, and turned back up the hill.

He followed his shadow across a patch of streetlight then was gone, and everything blended into night; his footsteps drowned in the chugging and hissing of the mill, which lay spread

below her. She heard, briefly, the bitter rattling of little feet—
Ivan's—somewhere to her right, but she kept her eye on the mill,
its stacks sending gray plumes into the low overcast, as though
it was the measure of all things real, the most real of the real,
inescapable, scientific fact. She breathed deeply so that she would
remember the wet reek. For that, more than anything else, would
be all of this town she would remember: the smother of bilious
steam that filled the Androscoggin valley like a puddle of murky
water in the palm of your hands.

She turned and went on, seeing, suddenly, the invisible cloud
that had settled when the *Raven* was lost at sea and hung around
like the airless summer haze, trapped over Rehoboth after the
disappearance of the town's favorite sons and daughters. Friends
had stopped calling out to each other from across the street.
Small bands came and went but an orchestra like her father's
was never heard from again. The Sutherlands had sold off the
mill and its surrounding holdings to absentee landlords, multi-
national corporations, outsiders. Brothers split. The cinemas
packed off. It was as though the mourning cloud that had stopped
above Rehoboth had rained meanness and waiting.

The equidistant smell of the trees kept her on the road. She
dragged her suitcase behind. After a short time there was nothing to see, Rehoboth was well behind. She looked up and the
sky was descending upon her, and she wondered, briefly, if this
was what it was like to drown.

A light grew beyond a bend. Mavis slid carefully to what she
thought was the roadside as the bend brightened and headlamps
appeared and approached and slowed, then drove on.

She thought of her mother at the livingroom window, keeping watch over her street with a yellowing telegram in her hand—
All's well stop. We're fine stop. Gordon stop
—combing her hair and straightening her blouse at the ring
of any kind of bell. Every day seeing her husband and her boys
approach the front gate. She thought of her mother and she
thought of Rehoboth, the town, like her mother, a widow and
an orphan, condemned to wait forever. A town of ghosts. Ghosts
stood behind the tellers at the bank. They ran the shops. They
manned the desk of the city clerk and peopled a phantom or-

chestra. They came to spectate at weddings and funerals. They died thousands of silent deaths as cowboys and Indians and they bore themselves phantom children, who bore phantom children, who bore phantom children, who watched their mortal namesakes walk the streets and drink the poisoned water and demand wages that would never be offered and work machines that forgot them as soon as they were gone.

Rehoboth's parents were dead. And accustomed now to not knowing why, did not want to know it. To find them now, even their bones, would be to make them no longer ghosts and legends but merely missing people. It would be to kill them all over again and to give their loss a reason. And to give loss a reason is to take away hope. If their bones were found, they'd never return. Loss is better as is, without reasons, full of hope and longing and looking out. Rehoboth remained sealed, and the *Raven* was its one window. Not a way out—it could not have a way out—but its reason for looking out, and its way, over the mill, out toward the open sea. While inside the stories told echoed and echoed and echoed.

Breathing deeply, and though standing on solid ground, not on any bridge over a ruined river, she was finally grateful—

Again, light appeared down the road, brighter headlamps, higher. She stared straight into them as they grew sharper and harder to look at. The distant whine grew to a roar, the driver gunned the engine. Mavis held her ground. Tires flapping, axles creaking, the headlamps expanded to dual suns and then a starburst, and daylight overtook her, rubber tearing against the tarmac like ripping cloth, the air butted before the vehicle pushing into her, into and through her clothes.

The sound of a door opening. The throaty purr of an idling engine. A kind voice—her father's? a walk? a stroll through the woods?—she shielded her eyes: "Can I help stow that suitcase in the luggage compartment, Miss?"

EZRA

Pearl Varney did not seem much surprised to see him. She merely propped herself against the door to the cabin and patiently let Ezra conclude the formality of explaining why he was here. Her clothes were dark, though not necessarily black; merely brindled by the shapeless inattention of a lonely old woman—thickened and blanched by the cold and drink. Though she was near his age, not more than twenty—he wasn't sure exactly what.

"Where's your ma?"

She waved her hand out toward the greater dark behind them.

"I wanted to ask her something."

"I don't know when she'll be back. Sometimes she's not back till morning. Sometimes not even then."

She took a pose that at other times and on another woman might have been taken for an erotic appeal. On Pearl the stance was a sad attempt at some imagined provocation she'd once seen in a movie house.

Ezra stepped by her into the house. "I can wait a while," he said.

Her nod was indiscernible, with no appeal as to what and whom Ezra wanted to talk about. Just a slow blink and a shuffling step backward.

The small rooms were cold and drafty, but the livingroom smoldered in wood heat. The molten light from the stove mottled the ceiling, dark furniture hunched away from it along the walls. Still without a word Pearl brought Ezra to the tiny kitchen. She pointed him to a bridge table set up to face the sea. A plate of hardboiled eggs sat in the center, in lieu of flowers.

Outside, the moonlight had already capped the chops in white. It silhouetted the string of small islands that hung off the

opposite point, Bull, Saddleback, Bald Dick, and Pond Island at
the back. Beyond them the world was split cleanly in halves
between sea and sky.

At Pearl's elbow lay a pair of binoculars, a tumbler with a
brown iceless drink, an ashtray choked with cigarette butts and
a bulky transistor radio murmuring with the weather: three to
four-foot wave heights in Casco Bay, one to two feet in Portland
Harbor. Chance of rain inland, fog on the islands.

He sat opposite her and she smiled congenially then lifted
the binoculars. They clicked against her glasses. She scanned
just outside the cove then started over, scanning left to right, as
though reading a sea-born dispatch, as though on duty to notice
anything and everything. She replaced the binoculars on the table,
brought her drink to her mouth simply because it was there in
her hand. She did not drink at it. She set it down. Then she
turned her eyes on Ezra. He tilted his head toward the binoculars. "Help yourself," she said.

Ezra stood with them and put the water to his eyes. He went
straight for the ledges. The line of wash was pink in the moonlight.

"What do you want Ma for, anyways? You never have anything to do with her."

"Wanted to ask her about something."

"I can see that." She smoothed her lap. She took an egg from
the bowl and cracked it on the rim and began to peel it. "You
going to tell me what?"

"I don't know if I can say."

"Well, you might be not saying it for a while then," she said.
"I don't even know if she's ever coming back."

She pushed at the plate of eggs in Ezra's direction. "Help
yourself."

Ezra looked down at the eggs then at her.

"She went off someplace with Earl Varney."

Ezra put down the binoculars and sat. "Earl Varney."

"He was here in the afternoon and left in a hurry and my
mother went out after him. She took her coat so who knows
how long she'll be gone. He usually gets rid of her after a day or
so."

Pearl smiled drunkenly, turning her head and smoothing her hair with the the flats of her bloated palms.

"How's school?" she asked.

Ezra blinked. "I left it."

Nodding with neither approval nor understanding, just the fact of it, she poured herself another drink, lifting the dregs at the bottom of the bottle up to Ezra in a half-hearted offering. Ezra held up his hand. He turned his head toward the window and squinted out with his naked eye, though without the binoculars he could see nothing.

He settled in his chair. He eyed the eggs, then took one and peeled it. He made a pile of the peels on the table before him.

"Your mama ever talk to you about that business about the *Raven*?" he asked.

Pearl drained her glass, then tipped back the ice against her teeth, waving her lips at them. Then she set it down.

"That was my father's boat," she declared.

Ezra looked at Pearl. She was sitting erect and impassive.

"You don't know that for a fact."

She looked at him. "But I know it."

Ezra waited. Then she continued.

"I know everybody on this island thinks Earl Varney's my father, or they think it's somebody they don't even know, somebody my mother wouldn't even know but for that one night, or day, or whatever it was. Fifteen minutes."

Ezra looked down, following the scattered cracks in the vinyl cap of the bridge table.

"But Earl Varney never was."

"Floyd," Ezra said.

She looked at him as if she hadn't just told him that, as if he'd figured it out on his own. "That's right."

He picked out the last of the eggs and cracked and peeled it and bit down into it.

"What else do you know?" he asked casually, as if it wasn't anything to him one way or the other.

Across the table, Pearl rose and fell in her chair like she kept seeing something out on the water. Then she began to talk. Not a beginning but somewhere in the middle, as though Ezra had come in along a continuum of neverending speech, begun again when she was ready and put aside like a fat book when she was tired. The tumbler of ice shook in her hand. She smiled. Her teeth were brittle, yellow, ready to break.

Then she twisted away, squinted through the window and saw the black truck that she could see was Earl's in the drive instead of that writer Dove's; and Earl himself plugging the doorway to the cottage she and her mother had rented from Reverend Sinnett to get away from him. Earl hung from the cross-beam, swaying coyly over the threshold as though he wasn't blocking her mother from the outside but flirting with her. Pearl had been staring into the water for an hour, since the writer Dove had figured out for her in ten minutes everything she'd never understood for eleven years. Then it was Earl she saw in the doorway instead of the writer. She took a running start off the rocks, stumbling and tripping over the frozen moguls of marsh grass, out of breath by the time she lunged to deliver a feeble punch to the small of Varney's back. Varney had been chuckling about something, his shoulders shaking. He paused when Pearl delivered her blow, but that was all, just paused, and only momentarily: hardly glancing over his shoulder he stiff-armed Pearl down to the ground like an untrained and delirious puppy and went on chuckling while keeping the sweating, snarling girl at bay.

"You murdering animal. You killed my father, and you killed all those people."

Earl grabbed the girl, looked right then left down the row of shuttered summer cottages, and shoved the girl inside. He closed the door behind them and sat against it. "Now christalmighty, Beatrice, what garbage are you feeding this gal today?"

"Nothing she shouldn't finally know," Beatrice said.

"Floyd Johnson," Pearl snarled. "Remember him? And the *Raven*? And your going diving in a particular place?"

Varney slammed his fist on his knee. "Now look you."

"No, look *you!*" Pearl shrieked.

Beatrice was beaming, as though she was getting something for nothing, sicking her daughter on Varney, letting Pearl do her work. But then Pearl turned on her and leveled her eyes at Beatrice: "And what did you get? Just Earl, or did you settle for even even less?"

"Nothing," Beatrice said, "I got nothing."

"Wasn't her boat," Varney said.

"You, animal, shut up!" Pearl cried.

Varney rose slowly.

"You so much as look at me funny and I'll tell that writer I know for sure you killed them all," Pearl said. "I'll tell everyone. Unless you're going to kill me, too." Then she stood. She still had to look far up to see him. Varney went red. His hands shook with rage, but he sat, then Pearl sat. Beatrice, already sitting, sagged.

"Writer, Beatrice?" Varney said. "Writer? What is this crazy girl talking about?"

"Leslie Everett Dove," Pearl said, spitting out each word with venomous satisfaction, as though the name were an indictment: "You're done, Earl."

"I didn't do a goddamn thing," Varney said.

Pearl laughed.

"Not a goddamn thing, Earl?" Beatrice said. "I don't know what you did out on that water. You never told me what you saw. I don't know how you separated them men from them women. That was a neat trick all right. You always did say you didn't do nothing, you didn't do nothing, you didn't do nothing. Tell me another one, Earl."

"Christalmighty woman," Varney said. "You know Floyd was floating face down before we ever got the chance to do anything. I know what. You're still hot over that money, aintcha?"

Pearl's eyes burned with malevolence, purged of compassion or goodwill.

"Money, mother?" she said, eerily calm.

Beatrice's gaze fell into her lap.

"After they couldn't find nothing and the policy came in I wouldn't give her her half," Varney said. "Because she didn't do nothing. And neither did I. Probably was them Krauts, after all. The water was crawling with U-boats, Krauts looking to get a jump on us. They was taking out fishing boats all up and down the coast."

"Liar," Beatrice said.

"Lookit here, Beatrice, I keep telling you I saw that fool Semicek signalling them U-boats off land's end. Maybe I have to stand on my head to prove I mean it. But I keep telling you and telling you I seen him doing it myself that very morning." He looked at Pearl: "So your momma didn't get half that policy because she didn't earn it. It was something she didn't do that happened to a boat she didn't own. Christalmighty I wish you women would get that into your skulls."

"Okay, Earl," Beatrice said. Her eyes slowly rose to meet his: "Then tell Pearl here about the telegram. Tell her why you had that telegram sent to that poor man's widow in Rehoboth if you didn't do a thing?"

Varney shot up out of his chair, kicked it aside and stalked out the door.

Pearl Varney half sat again. She lay the binoculars on the table.

"So it was Earl who sent the telegram," Ezra said, looking out the window, hardly able to see the water behind his own reflection. He thought about all the isolated hours and whole days and the cumulative hundreds of years of life spent in Rehoboth wondering and hoping because of that telegram, all the nonliving because of it. And here it was, the great truth of it all, Earl Varney.

"But it came from Europe," he said.

Pearl laughed sadly. "Only thing Earl can do right is fool people. He has no friends left in this world, but back then he had one friend, after my father, in the post office in Brunswick. I guess it was him who fixed that. Earl probably told him it was a gag, a practical joke, and got him to go along."

"But why," Ezra said. "Why if Earl said he didn't do anything. Why send it?"

Pearl looked at him. "Why are you so interested in this, Ezra?"

Ezra braced his hands on the table, as though to keep himself from floating away.

"I was with my father out there picking up all them damn bodies. You don't forget a thing like that. And now somebody's looking into it all over again."

"That writer. Dove."

Ezra nodded slowly.

"He's been here. He's what set my mother and Earl off." She waved toward the empty rooms.

"Earl isn't even a man," she said. "I don't know what you'd call him, but he isn't even that. My father and all those poor people drowning like animals, and he only concerned with denying any part of it up and down. No matter what he was saying or not saying, word was that he doubled his share of that policy by doing something. But no one could figure out what. Only thing people knew for sure was that day was so foggy only thing it was good for was doing something that didn't involve seeing or being seen. In the morning my daddy went out with those Rehoboth people, and Earl was just another fisherman, a nobody, and then by evening no one's coming back and Earl's suddenly a rich man. And there wasn't a man or woman alive who could prove a thing. Something wasn't right about what Earl was saying but no one knew what. Maybe Earl didn't know himself. So he sent the telegram to give everyone, and maybe even himself, a reason to believe the Germans did it."

Ezra reddened.

"And all this time no one's said anything."

"Who."

"You. Earl. Your mother. Anybody."

Pearl shook her head. "Sorry, but this wasn't my secret. I just found out about it. Same as you now."

She grinned sadly, then lost the humor and frowned. "And anyway, say what? About the Germans?"

"About the telegram," Ezra said.

"Around here? Why would anyone care about that—"

Ezra gripped the table. "*Rehoboth*. To anyone in *Rehoboth*."

"Yes." Pearl knitted her brow. "But it could have been somebody else to say something and no one ever did. Could be you now. You know as much as me."

Ezra waited. After a while, he said, "I don't know what I know." He looked up sullenly. "What did you tell Dove?"

"Mr Dove? I didn't tell Mr Dove anything. I never had the

chance."

"You didn't—"

"It was because Earl left my mother for the third time, but this time for Sybil whatshername, that my mother wrote Mr Dove. Earl and Sybil aren't ever going to get married, but there're two children already. The first could have been some other man's, and I guess that's what my mother wanted to believe, because she waited for the second child to be born, the one that had to be Earl's. That's when she got it in her mind to get a writer up here to point the finger at Earl."

"About the *Raven*," Ezra said.

"About the *Raven*. And Mr Dove did come up and talk to us, just the other day, and he said he'd come around again after doing some investigating of his own. But he hasn't yet."

"Then Earl did it all," Ezra said, more to himself than her. "Everything."

Pearl stood and stepped up to the window. "At first I was sure he did," she said.

Outside, the sky over the ledges and the string of islands and beyond them was clear. And then below, in the black and shapeless water, the blackness was parting, two parallel troughs of white wash as though the little harbor here had sprung a leak. Ezra stood beside her.

"There he is. Come, come," Pearl was saying, lifting the binoculars, her hands trembling, the lenses tapping the window pane. The harbor, suddenly, was a coastal graveyard, one headstone overturning, and one plot coming undone. The enormous rounded oily back spouting up dirt and stones. And silently, almost clandestinely, the giant fluke made its appearance, ripping up through the water after the rest had gone under, flipping and waving as independent and recalcitrant as a kite's tail, then ceasing to climb, a vast and incomprehensibly perfect shape stalled up there flinging fistfuls of white dirt against the islands, against the moonlight, then plunging into the water.

"What are you saying, Pearl, it wasn't Earl?"

"Humpback," Pearl said, "He's been out there for six days, circling outside the cove at night. It's how I knew someone would come. I like to think that it's my father."

Ezra looked out the window and focused on the water but he saw no whale. There were no signs of anything, just the black water.

"So what do you think about that keg?"

"Keg? What keg?"

"The keg found tied to your father. What do you make of it?"

"I don't know about any keg. No one said anything about any keg."

The next afternoon, Ezra was sitting in the center of the empty frame of his unfinished house. He'd been there through the night, watching the boats tilting placidly, rising then falling as the cove drained into some vast sink beyond the horizon he knew not where. He heard the dawn before he could see it, the movement of some little red birds in the trees, like animated flowers, letting out their chirps *en masse*, like a chorus. Then he saw the dawn begin like a narrow secret, drawing gray swaths across the very bottom edge of sky and bleeding upward, against all common sense, until the tips of the boat towers began to glint moments before the sun itself came on like a spotlight and shot out across the water, and the chop flung out before him and ignited, and a truck came down the road. He watched the truck release his father and mother and they made their way to the fish house, where a light came on, dim, dirty, and they passed before it again and again filling barrels from the salt baths. Some boat—was it Bern Herrick's?—was sitting on Jesse's mooring. Others came, and the cove was swarming and he watched the boats leave, his father's first with his mother loading the skewers in the traps, one boat and then the other until the cove was empty save the naked rafts and the little dories left swinging in the moorings of the big boats like trained dogs leashed up to wait out their masters' return.

The day flattened and thin squads of seagulls stretched out their wings, hovering in one spot just beyond the wharf as though dangling from invisible wires, the cove before them vacant, unpunctuated and unclaimed, the water brackish. He watched as the man from the pound parked his truck and put on his hat and stepped into his dory counting his cash; how he looked right left and reached into his jacket for his narrow flask and raised it, but forgot midway what he proposed to do with it, whether it was something he'd wanted at all, or only to smell. He leaned forward and extended the flask, as if toasting the cove, or turning the movement into one of grave concern.

Ezra watched the first of the boats come in, then the rest, one by one idling beside the weighing raft and handing over the baskets of lobster and taking the cash in return. He saw the dories coming in and the men heading for the coffee shop underneath the fish house. At the end of the day he watched his father's boat, his mother in the stern, bloodied, propped up against the gunwale, her head hanging, she might have been asleep. He saw his father turn the hose on her, and she came at him, and they almost embraced, laughing; she slapped him playfully. He saw his father smile; it must have been a smile; he'd seen a flash; he couldn't remember the last time he'd seen his father smile.

He heard his father's truck idling behind him, its tires smoking with dust. Then his father himself, "Where you been?"

"Up at the cabin," Ezra said.

"You were setting here all day. I seen you when I went out this morning."

"I was at the cabin. I got back here last night."

Ezra reached into his jacket and pulled out his cigarettes. A hand reached before his face and grabbed the pack and flung it.

"Don't you start that business," Clayt said. "Not in front of me."

They still hadn't looked at each other. Ezra sat facing the cove and Clayt leaned against a corner post, facing the same way.

"You talk to Dove?" Ezra said.

"Not yet"—as if they'd had an appointment to talk it over.

"You going to?"

"That's my concern. Who I talk to."

Ezra could feel his father looking at him.

"I got a call from Arthur McAlister yesterday," Clayt said. "They're having their own troubles up there now, things I'd advise you to keep away from. That's nasty business. Someone might take you for something you're not and take a shot at you."

Now Ezra looked at him. "What about that keg, Pa?"

"What about your asking? Why're you asking me at all?"

Ezra looked at him.

"What difference would it make if I told you?" Clayt said.

"I don't know."

"You need to know or are you just wanting to know?"

"I don't know. Morrill showed me what he wrote. Dove."

"Morrill can barely read himself anymore."

"He showed me the book."

"He's a drunk."

"There was something about Billy in it," Ezra said.

"So what. Did it change his life? Did it change what happened? No. He's still a drunk."

"It doesn't have anything to do with Morrill," Ezra said.

He stood, peered up at the indigo sky, then squatted on his heels.

"What's it got to do with?" Clayt asked.

"I don't know what it's got to do with." Ezra looked up. "But what about that keg, Pa?"

Clayt went back to the truck and leaned as if to retrieve something, but came back emptyhanded. He stood in front of the sun, darkening the ground before him.

"I told you once to forget about that," he said.

Ezra stood.

"Get in my truck," Clayt said. He went to his truck and started the engine. The windshield was smeared with dirt and reflected back the perfect depth of the sky. Clayt and Ezra peered at each other through it, one hardly able to see the other, some contour of the vague life each knew, what had been, what was in store. As if they looked at each other out of a shallow pool of standing water, a pool into which time poured and moved across fluidly and without slowing. Like something you could pick up that would seep out between the fingers and leave you with individual grains of sand, which might be the entirety of your life. Though who was under water and who above Ezra did not know.

He sat beside his father and shut the door.

They passed the dirt road home. They passed the General Store. They passed The Sebasco Restaurant. They waved to no one who might have waved off the various porches or through the windshields of the passing trucks.

They took the short granite bridges out over the tidal pools, one, then two, the three bridges, Great, Orr's, Bailey. Clayt said nothing. Ezra felt his blood quicken. His eyes skipped from tree to tree. A low white church hovered on wood piles over a salt marsh off to the left. Scattered black pools of still water. *Dyer's Cove Road*. Clayt braked hard, pulled off and cut the engine. The horseshoe cove. They sat looking out. A bell buoy tolled from across the flat stretch of gray water beyond. Clayt looked over at his son as if waiting for a word, or just to see the expression of his face.

"You know what this is," Clayt said.

"Yes."

Clayt turned the engine over and felt for the accelerator with his toe and backed into the Harpswell Road. The trees sped by and Ezra's eyes let them pass. He was suddenly a stranger, an obedient tourist.

At Brunswick his father turned north onto Route 1. He slowed at the Bath Iron Works and Ezra watched the big ships beached in their dry docks, propellers as big as houses hanging mid-air, dripping rust, pecked at by tiny men in green helmets. Torrents of sparks cascaded behind them into the harbor. Empty and wind-swept piers. Warehouses yawning out over the barren yards and loading docks; rusted cranes fused to their platforms, punching at the air. The sun blocked the harbor mouth, a blood-red globe deflating into the floor of ocean.

"A few weeks ago when I went down to Boston I saw something I never thought I'd see," Clayt said. "I saw that giant drydock down at that harbor fenced in, barren. That fence was just put up, rattling there in the wind."

He said it was the largest dry dock on the east coast, built for the *Lusitania*, for the largest ships in the world. The *Queen Elizabeth*. And now it lay fallow. He guessed there hadn't been a ship in there for months. But it still worked. The cranes, they worked. But there wasn't anybody around to work them. Two-hundred-thousand men were working there last time he was down. You've got to understand, he said: a dry dock's more than just a place where ships get built.

"Now some fool's got plans to lay a tunnel on top of the harbor floor," Clayt said. "That's forever. The big ships'll be cut off for good. The end. We got upland politicians to thank for that, damn fools. Not one of those clowns is a maritime person. They don't know what they've got. The battleship *Massachusetts* was manufactured right in that place, everything built right here. You've got to understand there are no straight lines, no right angles on a ship. It takes six or seven thousand other businesses. A ship like that is a city itself. Now Boston gets offered the Massachusetts as an ornament. As an ornament. But they're not leaving enough water in the harbor to get her in there, so they had to turn her down."

Ezra looked at his father with surprise, though he wouldn't give it away. He didn't know Clayt thought about these things, or even knew about them.

Passing the iron works by, "We do it to ourselves," Clayt said. He said that the dry dock was the bellwether. That the geniuses wanted to turn it into an aquarium. That they were turning their backs on good things. On our waterfronts. "That's us," he said, "That's what we do. They'll spend millions to put the ocean in a fish bowl just so we can walk all around and underneath it and press our noses right up against it."

He said that Dove and his kind want to turn a working harbor into a theme park. Because that was something they could control. They could make sense of something like that. They couldn't make sense of real ships, or real shipmen's lives, because all that was hard work, and to understand it you have to do a bit yourself. "But they can make sense of plastic replicas and ships in bottles and rows of cotton candy carts and mobs of screaming kids."

Clayt looked over his shoulder, behind them, as though seeing something in the passing lane.

"You know why I'm telling you this?"

Ezra didn't answer.

They sped on.

At the sign for Pemaquid Point Clayt inched forward in his seat, his hands high on the wheel. Past the pillared old-money summer homes boarded up until summer. Then the black water. At the edge sat Pemaquid Light, a fat thumb of a tower held up to measure the measureless indigo sky. The keeper's windows were dark. Bolted planks criss-crossed the door. A virgin splay of grass traumatized by five months of snow sloped gently down to the water.

Clayt got out and walked the hill. Ezra followed him to the water's edge. They looked southeast. There was nothing but the horizon fading into the iron water. Every twenty seconds their elongated selves were flung before him, their shadows cast down by the lighthouse beam.

Ezra looked at his father but Clayt had his gaze trained on the water. In the corner of his eye Ezra saw the answer light, a blink in open water. Again the grass around them lit then went dark, then the light's echo passed the vanishing point.

"Are you looking, boy?"

"Yes, Pa."

"What do you see?"

Out in open water the swells were tripping up and collapsing.

"Nothing," Ezra said.

"Look again."

Ezra looked again. "Nothing."

"Again."

Then all at once the upper crust of the sun pulled under and shot along the water the horizontal last light of day, a fiery line drew across the middle of the horizon, the lip of Monhegan Island.

"That's Monhegan."

He looked at his father.

"That's where Floyd was headed. They paid him to take them that far, let them eat, then bring them back. They didn't make it."

Ezra peered at it as though at something he knew he could neither touch nor ever have. He blinked and looked, blinked and peered across the water, feeling like a sentinel posted at the

edge of the desert under orders to notice anything and everything, who had spotted and now watched the plume of dust of
the advancing enemy and thought about his mother and his girl
and the achievements of his boyhood.

"Where'd they go," he said.

"You keep looking, boy, you're going to find things you won't
want to know."

"There's a mass grave up there," Ezra said.

"I know it."

"They have one for the men and one for the women."

Clayt laughed, or exhaled—Ezra couldn't be sure. "I tried to
talk Arthur out of that but he wouldn't hear anything I said. I
guess they wanted it settled as soon as it could be done. You
can't put bodies in the same ground as ghosts. They didn't know
what else to do."

"And you never wondered about that."

"Wondered? What I understood was that it wasn't my town.
I figured they knew what was best for their own people and left
it at that."

"They," Ezra said.

"There're names on those graves up there?" Clayt asked.

"Fourteen women on one, the men on the other."

Clayt shook his head. "Mass graves're like the ocean. You
can't ever really know who's in them, and who's not."

He looked at his son with menace. "You understand what
I'm saying?"

"What reason—"

"There's reasons for no reasons," said Clayt, cutting him
off. "Just women coming back never made sense," he said. "It's
not chance. It's not bad luck. A man floats just as well, and
don't give me any bullshit about body fat and muscle. With something like this, that's just crap."

"You saying someone's still alive?"

"No, nobody's alive. And it's just as well. No survivor of
any shipwreck knows anything about the sea anyways."

His father turned to him and spoke softly, almost kindly,
anyway his voice was laced with his own brand of grudging
respect: "We did find one boy, though. A younger fellow, back

of Ragged Island. Jesse did. He and I knew what that boy done because he was the only one found that way. Everything else went between Pond Island ledge and the eastern gale buoy. But Ragged Island at the time had a family out there and they had gas lights in the house, and this boy must have seen the lights from the water. He must have been an expert swimmer, because it was cold. And the sea there's always rough, and by that time—christ, it's a good mile or more—he got tired, or just stiffened up in the cold and stopped feeling and just went down. Then he came up and we found him spinning in the breakers back of the island. But this was months after."

"There was a boy," Ezra said, squinting now toward Monhegan Island. He saw a young boy moving steadily toward the rocks, his discarded shirt undulating in the chops like a patch of blood. His pale arms spinning through the water like the oiled wings of a doomed bird. His naked back. Thin neck. The back of his legs appeared. His arms floated. A piece of debris in the chops, driftwood. Bobbing crucifix.

Ezra saw the pictures staked to the cemetery dirt, the flags, the old flowers. He saw the patch of grass, flat, unturned. "He's not in that grave," he said.

"No one would have wanted him," Clayt said. "It wasn't even as good as that gal we found down in Biddeford. Besides, they would have just made us keep hunting. We had enough. Jesse told me about it and we went down to his boat where he was keeping the body. We went out and tied bricks to him and put him down and we kept it to ourselves. I don't even think I told your mother. You and me and, well, Jesse would have made three of us that knew. Now there's only two."

Clayt turned to his son: "You got to understand, boy," he commanded. "They were not our people. It was getting to be like a plague. We never thought we'd get out from under all those bodies. And Arthur said just don't be plagued by them any more. And I thought that was fine. He and I had gotten kind of friendly after all that. I used to take him out fishing once in a while. Hell, he financed me in almost everything I've done since then. It's as simple as that. I wasn't protecting nobody. You and me, we were coming on everybody like we were meant to. A thing like that never goes away. There were months and years of bad dreams all the way around. Up there, too."

"So others could have been found," Ezra said.

"I wouldn't know."

Ezra turned and watched the lighthouse. He could just hear the hum and grind of the turret swinging the big beam around.

"But you would have been putting them down just like you put down that boy," he said.

"I would have. If it was me. If it was me to come on them. But I'm not the only one pulling traps out of this water. Some time or other everybody pulls up things they don't want to think about. Things missing for years. Even people missing for years. Kidnapped, Russians, aliens from outer space—most of them just get caught in the undertow and are swept out there and frozen and taken down by the tide like a piece of wood. A body aint no different than anything else."

He looked at Ezra. "So I don't know why you're looking," he said. "There won't be nothing to find. And even if there is—" he didn't finish, his voice not trailing off but pulling up short, not a thought but a sort of command.

"What did you tell McAlister about that keg?"

Clayt lowered his chin then looked up.

"That was a long time ago," he said slowly.

"I remember it."

"I told you to forget it," Clayt said. "I told you to forget about that keg."

Ezra peered across the water. The island was gone. The moonlight had dropped a straight trail from his feet to the horizon.

"Arthur McAlister told me what to do about his people," Clayt said. "I trusted him about that. But I didn't tell him about that keg because Floyd wasn't one of his people, and he didn't need to know about that. And it had nothing to do with Dove, either. And it shouldn't have had anything to do with us. Whatever happened to that boat, that keg was Floyd's affair. Nobody else's. But it was too late. When you saw it I told you it wasn't what you thought, if you thought anything. And that's what I'm still saying. You can't talk about a thing like that unless you know."

"But how'll you know unless you talk about it?"

Clayt said nothing and Ezra had his answer.

"I talked to Pearl, Pa," he said. "I know about Varney."

"What do you know about Varney," Clayt snapped. "What would you really know about that."

"I saw a letter."

Clayt turned. "Whose."

"Beatrice Varney's."

"The woman's barely literate."

"She wrote Dove."

"She isn't to be trusted."

"You mean she lied about Earl Varney."

"You can't lie about Earl Varney, boy. He's done it all, everything worth talking about and everything not. No matter what you say about him it's bound to be true."

"Then why can't you trust her?"

"Because she wouldn't know. She wasn't there."

"It was him, Pa, wasn't it."

Clayt turned his head and spat into the water without taking his eyes off Ezra.

"I don't know," he said softly.

"You knew him," Ezra said.

"No one knew him."

"You worked with him."

"There was no working with him."

"Why didn't you tell McAlister that Varney's the one who sent the telegram."

Clayt didn't so much as breathe.

"You don't even know," Ezra said.

Clayt turned and faced the water. "No, boy, I guess I don't. And I'd appreciate it if you didn't tell me."

Night had fallen. The wind began to bite. Ezra understood that he was not only looking for the dead but running with them, competing with them. And competing with Dove. Dove hadn't yet been able to tell the story of the *Raven* to the end. He'd started it in that book. He came up here and talked to Beatrice Varney. He went up to Rehoboth and repeated all the still unanswered questions. But he'd left with nothing. No one in Rehoboth knew anything. They knew what they thought (which would be good enough for Dove, Ezra thought, enough to speculate, enough anyway to keep writing), but nothing beyond that. Dove would say anything that made good listening. There was no one alive to fight him. Unless he just stopped. Unless there was something that ambushed him. Something that shut him up.

His father levelled his eyes at him: "Whatever did happen to that boat, wherever it happened, no matter what it was, it's going to surprise the hell out of you. I've been hearing about dying longer than you've been alive. Probably twice that long. Murder, kidnapping, drowning. Every one gets you, boy. If you really think about it, if you really get close to it, you'll want to scream for the rest of your life. It almost doesn't matter what happened to that boat, because a lot of people died, a lot of them children. And maybe there was something. Maybe there was a plot. Maybe I even know more than I'm going to say. Point is, it doesn't matter what you do, or what happens to you or what you find—I'm telling you you're going to end up putting yourself on that boat with those people and dying right alongside them. Know what I'm saying here? I'm saying I know. I'm saying it doesn't matter how it got done. A scuttling? Well, now that's a tidy explanation, though Floyd'd have to be a beast, a horny-toaded satan to have had the stomach to send down that many people. And I don't think he was. He was a weak, scared man. Just a scared little man. Earl Varney wasn't, but he wasn't pilot on that boat. Floyd was out there, Earl Varney wasn't. But scuttling's been done before and will be done again, because money makes you crazy. And it'd make a good story at that, wouldn't it?

"But whether the *Raven* got scuttled or not," he went on, "it won't be pretty because dying never is pretty. That's what that Dove does, pretties it up. That's how you know he doesn't know the water. He forgets that the water hurts like hell, and dying in it is no reward for living this life. Water's worse than anything, I don't care what anybody says. I've watched a person die every way a person can die. I've seen a fisherman burn like a marshmallow, a hunter's head get blown clean off by a shotgun, a little girl fall ten stories to the sidewalk, I saw an old lady who'd been sawed in half by a fallen window, I seen two or three people decapitated by their own windshields. I've seen drowning, all kinds of drowning, open water, cove drowning, swamp drowning, bathtubs, river drowning. It don't matter, water's worse, because if you're in it, and you're doggie-paddling away and losing steam, and you're looking up and all you're seeing around you is horizon, nothing, just more of what's underneath you, it's the worse sort of mocking humiliation to your ever taking a breath on this planet.

"People like Dove are dangerous sonofabitches. They can ruin men like Leo Blackburn. Dove destroyed him for what happened out there with those dories. All Leo's years on the water, sending out sixteen dories full of men most every day including Sunday for sixty years, a lot of them never came back with the others, and he knew that he was responsible because someone had to be. He hated it, all this, everything you see around you. I'd hate it. And sometimes I do hate it. Sometimes I just hate this life, boy. I don't do what Leo does because for every one of my men that I didn't send home to his wife I'd rather die twice. When your brother died—and he did die, I didn't see it, but I know it, I know he froze and it hurt like hell, and I know he lost his legs first and then his fingers and he died alone—when he died I remember feeling that I knew then what death looked like. It has two eyes, a nose and a mouth. It's the worst thing you ever saw, boy. Because it looks just like you."

Clayt and Ezra breathed quietly into the night, the water lapped at their feet.

"Twenty years from now," Clayt said, "You're still going to be living on Bailey Island. The politicians are going to be getting rid of us like they're getting rid of the rest of the maritime industry. Like they got rid of that dry dock down there. Bath Iron Works has fifteen, twenty years left. World's changing, boy. You have more than fifteen or twenty years left on the water, but not much more. Maybe you'll die a lobsterman, but you'll die a poor one. One day they're going to bring in big ships, as big as aircraft carriers, that'll do it all, and make you nothing, a spit in the ocean. I know you can't see it, you can't never see the life around you, only what's past—you can't see that we're alone, boy, but we are. What happens around us is nobody's business, because it's not their lives, it's ours. They can go back to Boston or New York or Rehoboth or wherever, but we got to stay right here. To everyone else we're like some curious thing, we're *interesting*, they'd say. Maybe we're *important*, who the hell knows, some historic piece of old America or some bullshit like that. Like we're in a goddamn display case. These tourists up from New York, most of them think we're grinning all the damn time, whistling while we work. But none of them aint never seen a wave bigger than a house rushing at you. If they did they'd know. If they'd known Jesse their whole lives, how hard he worked and how honest he was and what a good man—and seen how he died in that cold water, they'd just shut the hell up like the rest of us and get on with it. But they don't. We're the ones who're picking their bodies out of water when they drown, or when they kill each other. This is our lives, boy. It's going to be the last thing left to us. Unless you're going to leave it, you got to protect what we got left. Everything that's ours."

"Even Varney," Ezra said.

Clayt spat.

"Even Varney."

DOVE

In Gloucester, Dove left the car behind the rocks and began to scramble, all fours, toward the water. Above him any signs of true sky had gone, concealed by a steady sheath of black cloud unscrolling from the southwest. He stood panting on the highest of the rocks of Rafe's Chasm. Leaning forward into the gale, the surf boiling at his feet, Dove raised his face to the advance spits of rain plucking the sea. The swells off-shore were rearing up and advancing, sucking up the surrounding water, devouring it; they would crush him like a gnat, bury him. But before they could they hesitated, tripped and stumbled over Norman's Woe, a high-tide ledge one hundred yards from shore, which reduced the waves to benign froth, which gurgled harmlessly amongst the rocks at his feet.

Dove opened his mouth to the wind and shouted, mingling his voice with the roar of the surf so that he didn't compete with the sea but merely narrated it, told it its own story, quoting Longfellow: "*It was the schooner* Hesperus/*That sailed the wintry sea!/And the skipper had taken his little daughter/To bear him company!*"

Shouting, he conjured the *Hesperus*'s masts swaying isolated against the sky, the hull itself out of sight in the troughs of the waves.

He conjured again—as he did at these moments, in Gloucester, during storms, as though it was his defining vision—Nantasket Beach, when he himself, then twenty-three, had stood on the dry sand with the others in Joshua Jenkins' mercenary rescue party, watching the waves pound the *HC Higgonson*, waiting for a chance to launch their sole lifeboat into the breakers. They'd cleared the beach of the seventeen bodies so far lost off the wreck, among them the body of a young woman found lashed to the windlass. Again and again the lifeboat was thrown back by the surf. Seventy-five year old Jenkins paced the sand, his long white beard flapping over his shoulder, twisting to look, as though at a personal insult, at the corpse of the schooner's steward lashed to the foretop mast, outlined against the sky.

Dove stood by, ready to bolt for the lifeboat at the slightest glance from Jenkins. Then Jenkins gave it, moved his eyes from his men to the lifeboat, and the men bolted, Dove leading the way. But not more than twenty feet from shore the lifeboat filled and overturned and Dove and the others were crawling their way back up the beach. After an hour the *Higgonson*'s masts dipped and never righted themselves; the schooner was lost from sight for good. Dove looked to Jenkins but didn't see him immediately; then he did, a dark blotch at the far end of the beach. He and the others ran over and found him face down in the sand, the surf breaking around him. Exhausted, the old man raised his head and said nothing, then half closed his eyes and stopped breathing.

Then the tide did drop and the water flattened enough to get the lifeboat beyond the breakers. Dove took Jenkins's place at the bow, standing with his arms raised like a harpooner, directing the boat toward the dead steward suspended from the mast. (*"And fast through the midnight dark and drear/Through the whistling sleet and snow! Like a sheeted ghost, the vessel swept/ Toward the reef of Norman's Woe!"*) In his mind Dove saw the arms and legs swaying in the wind, the perfect circle of gaping mouth, the bugged eyes returning Dove's stare but seeing nothing. He remembered this face of drowning, the Boy Scout troop bumping like logs along the quay in Winthrop, their swollen tongues submerged like oysters in little round pools of brine. Splintered wood and shoes swirling round and round. He crossed himself, sat in the bow and ordered the men to row in. And standing now on the rocks at Gloucester, he watched the waves as though for the conductor's cue, the surf piling in, roaring at his feet. He opened his mouth and screamed into the spray: "*She struck where the white and fleecy waves/Looked soft as carded wool!/But the cruel rocks, they gored her side/Like the horns of an angry bull!*"

The rain fell in a solid sheet. The trees behind him were kneeling. The mud exploded. Dove did not move.

"The salt-sea was frozen on her breast," he cried, *"The salt tears in her eyes./And he saw her hair, like the brown sea-weed,/ on the billows fall and rise./Such was the wreck of the* Hesperus *in the midnight and the snow./Christ save us all from a death like this/On the reef of Norman's Woe."*

EZRA

At daybreak, Ezra walked up the Mountain to Earl Varney's clearing. He had to keep himself from running. There had been a frost in the night and when he got up to the top, he was panting, and everything hung with wet and was running off in large drops. The still trees were drawn down close on themselves and in the distance they looked tight and hard and the sea below carpeting the earth as far as he could see was blue as new iron.

Ezra saw no one. There was no smell of woodsmoke or of any human presence at all, except the garbage, which lay strewn everywhere, but was old, almost relics, almost evidence. He looked around the clearing and saw a cabin of planks and plywood shouldering through the far brush and went toward that.

A yellow dog with raked ears appeared padding back and forth at the doorway. Its snout close to the ground, its dry lips drawn back in an ineffectual snarl.

"Here boy," Ezra snapped his fingers.

The dog moved under the grim light, unable even to pant, then ran off into the woods.

Ezra stood outside the screen door and fingered the mesh. He couldn't see through it.

He heard nothing and stepped in, breathing hard.

A picture of some older woman framed in black ribbon sat atop a wood crate, and that was all. The rest was a patchwork of wood and cloth and old nails and some new ones. In the dark shadow of the corner Earl himself was draped over a daybed, an empty unmarked bottle at his feet, one hand over an empty tumbler as though to keep away the flies. His brow was slack, clawed at, ash gray. The arch of his brow said *What is this, suddenly?* Then Ezra stopped and peered and saw the twilight inside the shack was rose-mottled as though through chapel glass. A blood-splattered window, bubbling melon-sized in the middle; wisps of thin, light hair caught in the shards, tufts and other matter, gray, flecks of white bone, smeared on the plywood wall. Execution, Ezra thought: a black puddle frozen on the floor beneath Varney's head, the bottom half of his face broken off absolutely, a smashed melon, seeds and fruit dragging. A pistol dangling loosely, as though a harmless thing one might fall asleep holding in one's hand.

A crude bank of windows—more a narrow spyhole, for shooting out of, for keeping secret watch, as though the cabin were a fortress turret—had been cut into the back wall of the cabin and looked down on a long graceful slope which ended at a purple line of woods where there was still a hedgerow of snow. Beyond the trees, there was a clear shot down to the water, the straits between Bailey Island and Harpswell Neck, where Varney had watched the lobster boats coming and going.

Ezra stood at the windows looking down at the woods. He listened for a moment, but there was nothing. No noise. No neighbors. No witness.

Ezra looked at the picture of the old woman and without giving it another thought decided that it was Varney's mother.

"Earl," he said, as though he'd thought of something.

He held a shard of dirty glass to Varney's nose and mouth, then tossed the shard away.

He kicked around, walked from one end to the other. He sniffed the air and didn't think Earl had been dead long.

He stepped outside and stood in the center of the clearing, listening to the wind in the trees. He strode around the corner of Earl's shack to the slope giving out on the water. The Mountain leaned down on three sides, shrouded, its summit hidden. Somewhere a gunshot rang out. It passed along the treetops then lingered in the woods. Then it stopped. A bird took flight and circled, throwing down unfriendly cries. Then the cry was cut short, and he knew someone was looking at him. He peered into Varney's window. Varney still lay slumped over the daybed. In the corner of his eye he thought he saw something move and turned to look but there was nothing. Still, to that side, there

was something: dark shrouds of figures in the trees, mere sug-
gestions, tricks of light. Something. He whirled, whirled again,
but his scrutiny killed anything that might have been there.

He took a hesitant step toward the woods, but another gunshot rang out and he froze and waited for it to die. Then he
could not tell when he first started hearing it, not the gunshot
but something that must have started before it. The baby wailing. He couldn't tell, but he felt his lungs drain and his throat
close up as if he'd been hearing it a long time already. Then that
started to trail off too, but not as far as the sea, not that far, not
even outside him. And not completely. It lingered in the nearby
woods then fell at his feet like a shot bird and whimpered there.

Another gunshot rang out from the woods. The wailing grew
louder. He went to the shack and picked out a rusted shovel
from a pile of tools and began stabbing at the cold ground. The
crust gave easily, but the dirt beneath was cold and hard. He
dug through the muddy pudding until he had a shallow grave,
deep enough for a man but no more, no coffin, no shroud; just
the man itself.

He went in and hooked his arms under Varney, then thinking of those bodies thought better of it. He went around to the
feet and took Varney by his heels and dragged him out the door,
leaving a muddy trail of blood and hair. Varney was stiff, and
when Ezra slid him in the grave he had to stand on the one leg to
break it and get it to lie beside the other. He looked down, breathing steadily, his own breath slipping over him like smoke.

"I was coming here to tell you I didn't think you did it," he
said.

He shoveled quickly and in a half hour he was flattening the
rectangle of dark earth with the soles of his feet. Like a trap
door to the next world. He left, and left no marker but the turned
earth itself.

DOVE

The cigarette burned in the glass next to the saucer of red jam.
Dove wanted to get the scene straight in his head, the cigarette, the bloodiness of the jam, and the knocking about of
the lobstermen outside. He'd come by design. He'd told Pearl
Varney to expect him. But what he said to the old woman in the
pale housecoat behind the counter of the wharfside store was
that he was canoeing from Portland to Small Point and touching
every island in between, all sixty. Some with just his paddle, he
admitted, but most, the bigger ones, he'd actually stood on. The
old woman had looked over his shoulder. She saw his canoe
bobbing at the door. She looked at him, a bear of a man with a
barrel chest and a mane of hair. She looked back at the canoe.

It was no lie. He'd paddled here from Portland in a day and
a half. For twenty nautical miles, not counting the orbits around
the islands, his hair had flapped in the off-shore breeze, his arms
churning through the swells like some immense joke of a wind-
up toy gone amok. But he'd landed on Bailey Island to do more
than touch land. He was prepared to have another talk with the
Varney women. And after that, with Pearl and Beatrice Varney
at his side, to call together the media to announce his readiness
to launch an investigation into the loss of the pleasure boat *Raven*
eleven years after it was last seen. And all of it will have been a
happy, if not a storybook, coincidence: his having been canoeing in the very waters the *Raven* women had been found; his
having an inkling, an odd sensation; his coming ashore and running into Beatrice Varney. Then the new evidence she'd imparted
upon him, damning evidence that whatever did happen to the
Raven—still unclear, still unsaid—was the dastardly act of a single
man, still living in their midst, more than likely standing in their
midst that very moment. If he only had the courage he'd step

forward...

Now the cigarette burned beside the jam between the two fishermen sitting to Dove's right, and he wanted to get it down: the green plastic saucer, the half-darkness smelling of burnt grease and lavender and salted chum. The slap of the water at the floorboards beneath his feet. The skiffs and dories and the one canoe roped to the gangway outside the door like horses to a saloon post. There was a fair mix of young, dark and silent men and old, bleached and silent men. They all sat against the wall holding onto their tepid coffees, cupping them like fragile birds. Except for the two to his right. One mid-aged, settling into his bulk, the other young, built like a bull: his features somehow mimicked the man's, though the fact was that except for something about the eyes—something about their shape, their expression—the features corresponded only in a heavy, clumsy way. They leaned on the counter as though trying to tip it with their elbows. Dove wanted to get this right because they were a little bit too good, a little bit too opportune.

He let them go. He reached toward the old woman with a five dollar bill for a twenty cent cup of coffee, dangling it between his thumb and forefinger while he asked where the gentlemen who just left lived, threatened to release it, then finally did at the address, "Mackerel Cove Road." The woman watched the bill hit the puddle on the floor.

EZRA

Ezra stood on the porch of his parents' house and looked out through the mesh of the screen door at a man he thought he knew well, though they'd never met. Barrel-shaped, his face swollen and splotchy with permanent irritation, his hair coiffed into a helmet of unravelling curls, Leslie Everett Dove had clutched in his hand a tourist map of Bailey Island still sealed in the paper wrapper from the General Store. Ezra let the man in without a word and went and stood beside his father, who was seated at the window, facing the water. Clayt's attention was on the shortwave radio. The horizon was strung with boats. He slid the needle from frequency to frequency, listening to the squawks about tuna, then bluefish. Lobster was bad today, it had been bad all week. The ones who bothered to go out were having fun with the bluefish. The salt baths at the fish house were brimming with chum.

Dove sat across the table and waited. "Listening for the blues?"

Clayt didn't answer. He faced out but didn't see. He twisted the dial without hearing what he wanted. Then he turned the radio down to murmurs.

Dove held out his hand to Ezra. "Leslie Everett Dove."

Ezra took the hand joylessly. "I know," he said.

"I didn't know we'd met," Dove said.

"Didn't say we did."

Dove looked toward Clayt, who still hadn't turned. "Oh, you mean my books and the radio—"

"Nope," Clayt said, now turning. "Never read a single book of yours. And the only radio I own is a shortwave, and I keep it tuned to the water."

"Well," Dove said, folding his hands on the table and smiling. "Then you will."

"Will?"

"Read a book of mine. I'll have my secretary send you a copy of the latest."

"Have a seat, Mr Dove," Clayt said.

Dove looked about him, as though he hadn't realized he'd already sat down. "I apologize. You seemed preoccupied—"

Clayt held up his hand. Ezra wouldn't sit. He stood behind his father's right shoulder.

Dove ripped open the paper packet and spread the map on the table between them. "Look, Mr Johnson, I've been canoeing across Casco Bay and—"

"The whole bay?"

"The whole thing, yes," Dove said.

Ezra cocked his head slightly and pursed his mouth, like he'd just seen something he couldn't understand, something peculiar but harmless. He looked at his father.

"You're a lucky man today, Mr Dove," Clayt said. "In water like this you got no business being in a canoe in your own bath tub, no less a cove full of working boats."

"I like to think I can handle a canoe well enough."

"Do you now."

Dove opened his mouth to speak then shut it. He looked up at Ezra, smiled disconcertedly, as though he was missing something, and went on, "And I was resting down at Mackerel Cove just now," Dove went on, "having a cup of coffee—"

"I saw you in the store. Other side of my son here."

"That's right."

"You weren't drinking your coffee. You were just looking at it."

"Now I don't normally listen in on other people's conversations," Dove said, reddening. "But with all due respect, Mr Johnson, I happened to overhear you and your son talking about this and that. And I looked over and said to myself, 'Isn't that the lobsterman from those photographs?' And I realized that you were just the man I was looking for. Do you know that you were involved in something of grave importance to this island, not to mention an entire town of ten thousand seventy miles inland?"

Neither Clayt nor Ezra had a word to say.

Dove waited a moment, looking from one to the other, then spread his fingers over Bailey Island on the map and leaned forward conspiratorially. "I was talking to someone who told me that you might know something about a boat that disappeared eleven years ago."

"Did they now," Clayt said. "Eleven—how many years ago?"

"Eleven."

"Which one said I'd know, was it Jesse Johnson? Jesse would have sold you your own home if he thought it would make you happy."

Dove squinted as if trying to remember. "Yes, yes I believe he did say his name was Jesse Johnson. Yes, I'm quite sure."

"Really," Clayt said. "You must have travelled awfully far to ask Jesse about that, because Jesse was killed last week."

Dove reddened a shade deeper. He moved not an inch. He looked down at his map, then changed complexion and tone altogether, like an actor moving swiftly between moods. His voice low, thick with authority. "I wouldn't bother you about this business except that people seem to have a lot to remember about it around here."

"Then why ask me?" Clayt said.

"Because they didn't know much. One of them said you knew what really happened to it. The *Raven*."

Dove waited for reaction but got none.

"A charter of people from Rehoboth, thirty-six people. Mostly men, but only women were found from it, women plus one man, Floyd Johnson the captain."

Clayt would say nothing.

"I believe I might know where she lies," Dove nearly whispered. "The *Raven*."

"That's really something," Clayt said in full voice. "How would you come to know that?"

"Let's just say there's a little bird that's ready to tell."

"Who would he be?"

"Does the name Earl Varney mean anything to you?"

Ezra's eyes were boring into Dove.

"So you think you know," Clayt said. "Then what do you want from me and my boy?"

"What do you remember from that day, Mr Johnson?"

Clayt squirmed in his seat. He picked up a coffee cup and rolled it in his hands then put it down, his eyes abstracted as though looking over in his mind a list of possible strategies. His eyes skated over Dove's map, then he levelled them on Dove's face.

"My boy and I went out to haul the traps and then we just come on them."

Dove fished out a small notebook and set it on the table and wrote a line of notes. He looked up. Clayt watched the paper: "If I remember right some of them gals still had their specs on. Sometimes, as foggy as it was, we had three of them at once. They were all right there together, bunched together. We couldn't bring them aboard. The law of the ocean, you know, diphtheria. But then we did anyway."

Dove nodded, smiling, waiting for Clayt to go on. When Clayt didn't, he lifted his face to Ezra. "Do you remember anything, son?"

"I was nine," Ezra said.

"But surely you can't forget a thing like that," Dove said.

"The fog didn't lift," Ezra said. "Didn't lift really anytime, not the next day, but the day after that it did lift some. But we'd pulled them out already. I heard they were headed for Monhegan."

Dove nodded, gesturing vaguely in the air, egging him on. Ezra said nothing more.

"What about the skipper Floyd Johnson?"

Clayt considered. "What about him."

"What do you know about him?"

"Found him around noontime is all."

"Could he pilot a boat like you, in the fog?" Dove asked.

"I said I didn't know Floyd Johnson," Clayt said, turning his head and looking back toward the water.

"But you were there."

"I was there, yes. When my son hooked him out of the water I was there, and before that when I seen him here and there I was there too. I was on this island for forty years with him. But just seeing a man with your eyes isn't knowing him. To answer your question I suppose he was as good on the water as any other. Everyone who works this cove can navigate the water blind, drunk, in a dungeon fog like that one was. But it isn't just knowing the water that makes you a good pilot, and Floyd Johnson wasn't good enough, was he?"

"They never made it to Monhegan Island," Dove said.

Clayt swung his head around: "You asking or telling?"

Dove said nothing.

"That all, that all you want?" Clayt said.

"I want your help," Dove said. "You know these waters. It could be a collective effort. Certainly it would be in everybody's interest to raise her."

"Raise her."

"And solve the mystery."

"Solve it."

"That's right."

"And that would be in everybody's interest."

"Why yes. It could put Bailey Island on the map. You for one would certainly make a name for yourself."

Clayt looked down at the red outline of Bailey Island on the map. "It's already there. And I like my name the way it is."

Dove sat back. "If you—either of you—were today in knowledge of something about this one might say you'd be dutybound."

"To who."

"At the very least to those poor people in Rehoboth," Dove said. "But then there are matters of law to consider, for instance."

"Nobody from there or anywhere's come knocking on my door," Clayt said, "Until you, and you're not from Rehoboth. And you're no law."

"Maybe they can't see what door to knock on," Dove said.

"Maybe they're not looking. Maybe they don't want to know. Look, even if you knew where she was, how would you know how she got there?"

"You know Earl Varney."

Ezra turned where he stood and watched the water and listened.

Clayt sat back. "I know him."

"Do you know that he and Floyd Johnson were partners in the *Raven*?"

Clayt said nothing.

"Mr Johnson, we're busy men. Let's not beat around the bush. From what I understand I believe you do know what did happen to the *Raven* and perhaps even why. And something tells me you know exactly where she lies. I believe it's your duty, your obligation—"

"You said that already." Clayt saw something out the window and raised the volume on the radio. Jim Black was sitting in three solid acres of bluefish. On the vast water one gray blip was still, and all the other blips, a dozen or more, raced toward it.

Dove held out a pen. "I'll give you fifty dollars to draw an X over Round Rock. And I'll pay you fifty more to take me to it."

"You'll give me fifty dollars for marking a map. You could ask anybody down at the store to mark it for you for free but you want to give me fifty dollars to do it."

"I think you're an honorable man, Mr Johnson. I like to deal with honorable men."

"What's in it for you?"

Dove shrugged and pursed his lips and leaned his shoulders back to get out of the way of all the untold things that were in it for him.

Clayt Johnson looked out toward the swarm of boats, then up at his son. "The hundred's up front," he said, looking at Ezra.

Ezra swallowed and looked down at his father. All he'd heard about Dove, and here he sat, a barrel of a man, pushy in that City way, too slick to hold to, everything out of his mouth neither right nor wrong but somewhere between the two. All of it a means to something, never just the words themselves. Dove, sitting there with his bloated hands in his lap and his fake acquiescence hanging there on his thin-lipped smile—he was just what Ezra had been scared of, and everything he'd hoped. All he could do was think of him in his red Santa suit strapping himself into his hired plane, the snow swirling in the windows. And there was Bill Wincopah, the original Flying Santa, the stunt flyer who had the idea before Dove was old enough to drive, who made the mistake of asking the young Leslie Everett Dove with the growing reputation to take over last year so he could tend his sick father, who without knowing it had relieved himself of Santa duty in favor of (Dove said) a writer's burgeoning fame. Who since that day had merely steered the plane while Dove dropped books through skylights, cigarettes into water, and dolls into frozen breakers.

Dove lay two crisp fifty dollar bills on the map. Clayt pinched them up without looking at them, and stuffed them in his breast pocket. Then he folded the map without so much as looking at it.

"I don't like you," Clayt said, "But I'm going to help you. You won't need to see with a map. But it will cost you the hundred dollars to see with your own eyes."

"But for later," Dove protested. "When I raise the money I'll need to direct divers and such."

"You won't forget it."

Outside the cove the sky was a milky, monotonous overcast. The was air heavy, the water was a dull gray. The swells billowed harmlessly, the water slid around the rocks.

Dove pointed to a plaque Clayt had screwed into the control panel, as though a map, or emergency instructions. He'd written on it in his own practically illegible scrawl:

Nothing and no one dared oppose his wishes or delay the Persian tyrant Xerxes' plans. When a wind-raised sea destroyed a bridge of boats built at his order, he not only beheaded those in charge of the project, but punished the sea by having the surface of the water struck with three hundred lashes.

"That's an interesting plaque there your father has," Dove said to Ezra, "What does it mean?"

"It means," Clayt cut in, "I've rode out hurricanes, I've been under water in boats too many times to count. I've seen windows washed out of them, sails washed off them. And the only thing I've done to stay alive is to not do a goddamn thing. You start driving the boat and things are meant to happen. Did you know a boat will tell you when it's got too much water on it? It'll shake just a like a dog will shake its head. A boat going too deep will go down completely into a sea, come up and shake off. In the old days they just heaved to, let the jib up, and they survived all those hurricanes in vessels most people wouldn't take out of the harbor today. They went right side to it. Still, a boat, side to it, will withstand an awful lot. It means you'll be scared to death by water before you're killed by it."

Clayt led the boat through the blind channel at land's end, turned at the invisible corner and aimed for open water. The boat picked up speed and raised its bow and recoiled against each wave.

Ezra felt the line pass beneath them. The swells broadened, the wind sharpened, and fact was reduced to mere perception. They could still see the details of land, the windows in the house at land's end, the pole in the fisherman's hands. But on water this far, solidly beyond earshot, misfortune would look like a drill or a practical joke.

His father cut the throttle. The boat, bucking a little to the sides, swung into the wind. All around them the water went white, splashing, churning, folding over, as though it were a pool full of children.

Dove peered into the water. "Are these the ledges?"

"Ezra," Clayt ordered. "Get out the poles. Bluefish, Mr Dove. These are bluefish. Two acres at least."

Ezra handed Dove a pole and took one for his father. Clayt cast out. "Won't even need bait," he said. "Just let it run in the water. Then feel it, feel it." His line went stiff, twitched left then right. "There, come, come." The pole jolted. "Grab. Now! Take it up!" With the butt end clamped in his crotch Clayt yawned back against the pole's doubling over, face purpling, neck ballooning, the current tightening his arms. Out of a swell thirty yards off, the leap skyward, the blue-green crescent, the thrashing pirouette, then the flop back under. "Gaff!" he cried. Ezra grabbed the hook and ran to the side of the boat. Clayt reeled his catch through the mob below. Up it came, thigh-high, incensed. In one motion Clayt released his right grip on his pole, snatched the gaff from Ezra and swept it through the fish's cheek. The instant the fish hit the deck he pressed his heel to the base of its skull, the tail slapping at his calf, the razor teeth gnawing at the gaff. "Hammer!" Clayt cried. Ezra fetched that and Clayt snatched it from him and brained the fish, brained it again, and again. The skull caved, the tail shivered then flapped once. Then he heaved the fish into a wooden crate.

"Standing there, Mr Dove?" he cried. "Is that you just standing there?"

Dove cast in and at once stumbled forward.

Together they brought in fish after fish, six, then eight, then a dozen, the gaff glinting in the overcast. Ezra hammering the oily skulls to bloody sponge, half laughing, half panting, "Never so easy, never this good," Clayt said. Innards and scales splashed the walls of the boat. Pink sweat ran the length of their arms. Their faces were thumbed up with crimson smudges. After a half hour sixteen groggy and nearly-dead bluefish clamored in the wood crate.

"Enough," Clayt said. He leaned back with the gaff in one hand and the bloody hammer in the other. His forearms were a wash of blood and scale. "Christ, lobster are never this easy," he said, panting, "When you can get them like this, you take all you can. You like bluefish, Mr Dove?"

"Fileted and charbroiled with lemon."

"Can't stand it myself," Clayt said. "Too oily."

"But all this," Dove said, holding out his hands.

"Good fun. Just good fun. We'll cut it up, pass it around. Makes good chum." He turned the motor over. The white water fell away. There was just the occasional sputter out of the radio. It was the silence after a loud noise, bottomless, embarrassing.

Ezra scanned the horizon. There were no boats within four miles. Then the radio squawked his father's boat's name, then his father's.

"We saw them, Jim," Ezra said into the receiver. He looked over his shoulder at the distant cluster of boats. "Just been through them. Out."

After he rehung the receiver Clayt reached over and clicked the radio off.

Dove shifted uneasily.

"You should have waited for fog," Clayt said.

"Sorry?"

"It would be better in a dungeon fog just like they had."

"Yes, good idea, Johnson," Dove said, "A good effect for the occasion."

"I said I was going to help you," Clayt said.

"You're a good man, Johnson."

Clayt cut the motor, and, again, the boat drifted into a wobbly spin. All three men were acutely aware of their isolation, of all the sea between the boat and anyone else. And suddenly too of the blood streaking their clothes, racing down their necks. Finally, Dove leaned over the side and rinsed off his hands. Ezra eyed him while he picked the scales off his wrists with his thumbs. Pulp and bloody sweat ran through Ezra's fingers, down the gaffing hook, and dripped off the end of the barb onto the deck.

Dove looked up.

"How long can a man last in the water, Mr Johnson?"

Clayt looked up at the water, as though he needed to. "This water? I'd say about four minutes. A woman a little longer."

"What about a skeleton?"

Clayt's eyes darkened. "A skeleton can last a long, long time."

"Then there could still be something there," Dove said.

"There?"

"Where the *Raven* is."

"Where's there, Mr Dove? There might be something somewhere, if somewhere's where it happened. If they went down. But you got to know where there is first. It could be right out here, it could be way out there." His arm rose parallel to the water, pointing at the horizon. "It's bad water all the way to Halfway Rock. That's too big an area to find one particular place to start looking. And then I wouldn't look for nothing right there, where you decided it was. Everything gets washed downtide in some eddy someplace, then again, and again."

"But Round Rock. There could still be something near Round

Rock."

"There've been hundreds of wrecks all along this coast here," Clayt said. "There'll always be something."

Dove looked up at Ezra.

"What about particular things," he said. "Personal effects. Shoes, glasses. Or a watch?"

Clayt didn't answer right away. His face showed nothing, as though Dove hadn't said a thing. "Like I said, people are always bringing that stuff up. I brought up Jesse Johnson three days ago."

Ezra looked up quickly. Clayt hadn't said anything. There'd been no news of it in the cove, no sign of a funeral; his father had shown no grief. Ezra had driven by the island cemetery half a dozen times since he'd returned from Rehoboth and hadn't seen it broken through, no stand of shovels, no new headstones. He followed with his eyes the course of a patch of water swelling to a wave, its white lip curling back in a sneer, and, kneeling, unrolling over an invisible ledge, stretching into the infinite mass, and rising again, and again, the gray cylindrical waves rolling up onto the shore and pulling back again. A chill ran up him, he clenched his teeth. He knew that he would die here, in this water, in that wave, and he would be brought up, and sent back down again, a pile of bricks tied to his feet, eyeless, his face spared, hidden in a shroud. It was not a feeling but a premonition, a realization of fact.

"You think it was a German sub?" Dove asked.

"We had them out here," Clayt said. "No question about that. My boy here seen one himself before the war."

Dove looked over as if for confirmation, but Ezra was looking past him, toward land.

"The Navy knew they were here," Clay said. "They crossed that cable all through this bay. Each one had their own pattern, and we could tell them apart from the propellers after they'd been here a while. A destroyer came charging out of the sound here, seven or eight planes, maybe a dozen, and started dropping depth charges three miles and a half from the island. Next thing you know the surface is black with oil."

"Could it have been a U-boat?"

"They spooked fishing boats all up and down here. But they never took a shot at one, not as far as I know. The *Raven* would have been small fry. And there would have been wreckage. There was no wreckage. Just them females."

"A scuttling. Could it be that it was a scuttling?"

Clayt stiffened. His voice fell, turning gravelly and mean: "Here's what I'm going to do, Mr Dove," he said. "I'm going to drop you off the side of my boat now. Then I'm going to move off a ways. I'll give it about ten or fifteen minutes. I don't smoke but maybe I'll wait for my boy here to have a cigarette. He just started smoking. I'll listen in on the transmitter to Jim's haul, then I'll radio Larry Bailey and see what he's got. Then Ezra'll put out that cigarette and we'll come back and try to find you."

"That's very funny," Dove said.

"Now, seeing as it's the *Raven* we're talking about, because you're a man you're going to sink quick. If you were a woman you wouldn't sink, but you're a man so you will. But if I happen to find you before you sink then you won't know why, and you'll be out of luck. If I don't find you then you will know, and I suppose you can call that a sort of luck. You'll disappear just like those men did and you'll be able to ask them yourself what happened and how and why all those women floated. You writer fellas call that a scoop, don't you? But by then of course it probably won't matter to you much how those people drowned, or even if they did drown, or if it was planned, or if it was an accident, or if it was Germans or Earl Varney or the Pope. So I'll drop you in the water now if you're ready, Mr Dove. You can leave your shoes with me. I'll hold on to them in case you come back."

"I don't understand what you're—"

"The point is," Clayt said, "that the only people who'll really know what happened on that boat were on it. I know fourteen gals who can tell you anything you want to know, and any one of them knows better than me. So you can just get on in the water, Mr Dove. Or, I can take you back in right now and you can make up what happened in your head the way you make up everything else. And you can keep on doing whatever you want to all those other stories. There's plenty others out there and none of them are my business. But, you see, this one is my business, and you can't have it. And I'm not going to tell you why, because I don't have to, and that's my business too. But I know what you do, Mr Dove. And I can read. My boy here has him a college education, and I started on one but didn't take to it."

A bloody puddle spread under Ezra's feet.

"And if we ever read something you wrote about the *Raven* that you made up, or something we know you couldn't know, or shouldn't know, I'm coming to find you. Or my boy will. And when I do I won't write no letter to the editor. I've never hurt a man that I know of, Mr Dove, and as a general rule I'm not inclined toward that sort of thing, but I've always thought that I could do it if I had to. Looking at my son, I'm sure he could."

Dove pulled back his beefy shoulders in indignation. "Was that a threat, sir?"

"I'm just laying out your options for you. There are two. You have just two. Pick one."

"Then it was a threat."

Clayt said nothing.

"Johnson, if you know something you have to tell it. You may not have a choice."

"That a threat, too?"

Dove's face reddened. "Look here, Johnson, if it's murder we're talking about there's no statute of limitations. You could still be found in obstruction of justice, or worse. If you're innocent of the matter, then you have nothing to hide."

"Innocence," Clayt looked as though he might laugh. "It's got nothing to do with innocence."

"If you know the truth, then sooner or later you'll have to tell it."

"Well, that may be true. You certainly can act like you're defending the truth. But here's something that's also true. Two months after my boy and I picked them bodies from the *Raven* out of the water there was something else rose down outside Biddeford Pool. They called me because the whole damned coast knew what happened up here, and I went down there with Ezra to get it. They'd tethered that thing so it wouldn't get away, but they weren't letting it come inside the breakers. There wasn't no face left, no flesh on the fingers. The jaws were open like it was swallowing air, full of crabs and sea fleas. There wasn't nothing but the clothing to guess at her by. But the shirt had one of them pins from Rehoboth High School. And the tide was right—it just made sense is all. So according to them it was ours to do with as we saw right. What I'm telling you is that she'd been seen by some tourist down there so there could be no hiding it. We had to sink a dory under her. But if it was anyone from this island to first come on that body in September, after all that happened here, he would have more than likely tied something heavy around it and shoved it under. By God I would have too. An act like that isn't theater, Mr Dove. It's a kindness."

Ezra's eyes suddenly closed off from Dove and saw the unhinged jaw flapping in the water, the writhing nest in the gullet, the gnawed finger-bones wearing half gloves of blue flesh.

"But then you wouldn't know anything about that," Clayt said. "You want to bring the *Raven* up and make it all a show. You say you could put Bailey Island on the map. But this isn't no show, Mr Dove. So if you want to talk about the truth, first thing you got to understand is that when it comes to the truth of this thing here, you don't know the half of it. You make it look like you know where everything is and how to get there and everything else. Well, it's a load of bullshit, Mr Dove. You know too much, too many facts, too many details. No one knows that much about what happens on the water when something goes bad. You talk about good and evil on the high seas. You talk about fate and destiny and all that bullshit. Out here there isn't any such thing as good and evil, and fate and destiny. There's only consequences. But evil sells books, don't it? Consequences don't. So you're not going to know what happened to that boat until you get in the water."

"You don't think so, Mr Johnson."

"Nope, don't think. Know. Now, Mr Dove, what'll it be?"

MAVIS

Mavis Beauchamp had never seen the ocean. Her first time she meant to cross it. She was twenty, and she intended to stay on the other side of it for a year, on scholarship to read French. What she saw was not what she'd expected of an ocean, that which had taken her father and brothers and uncle, and had once swallowed a character in a book, and which now carried her away to France. Every night of the crossing she stood on ship's deck—impossible that such a thing could float when a little boat could simply vanish—to watch the viscous, cold oil rush the ship in the moonlight. She looked for periscopes and ghost ships and white leviathans but found only a black desert, vast, unnameable.

Then she waited, always smelling it first. The mildew, the rot, the white strands looping across the ship's bow, then up through the rail and around her feet. The inevitable fog, as if once each night the sea must grow old. She'd expected it. If she knew one thing about the ocean it was the fog. During those days of searching the newspapers had gone on and on and on about the impenetrable fog. When it came everyone else refilled the cabins. But she stood firm at the rail, dutifully seeing nothing, while with the back of her hand kept trying to wipe dry her cheek. Her clothes flattened wet against her legs and chest, she thought not of her brothers but the women who now lay together in the Rehoboth cemetery. It seemed no use to Mavis to wonder any longer about the men themselves. They had nothing more to do with what was left. Others already walked through town in their places, hiding the erasers at Rehoboth High School, sitting at their old desks at the bank, patrolling the counter at Kersey's Jewelry, drilling teeth at the dentistry, marrying and bearing the children and then dying off. It was the old ghosts of

Germans, murderers, spies and pirates that Mavis remembered, that had inhabited her brothers' rooms, that cleared the way for her to leave for France. They were much more engaging, and they had more to say. She was certain everyone felt that way, except perhaps her mother, who, still shut up in the house, seemed to have made a fair career of mourning. I'm sorry they're dead, I'm sorry they're dead, Mavis repeated to herself, on the deck of an ocean liner headed for Dieppe, still not quite believing herself.

She wondered if the rank stench would follow her beneath the hoofs of the marble horses of Paris, worried that she would see them on billboards everywhere she turned:

Beauchamp, Ivan   age 10   June 29, 1941
Converted rumrunning boat   Mavis Beauchamp
sister   remains unknown

(answering to no one except the whispering in her ear)

Beauchamp, Gordon   age 41   June 29, 1941
Converted rumrunning boat   Mavis Beauchamp
daughter   remains unknown

(then later that day the telegram from Rehoboth)

Beauchamp, Gordy   age 19   June 29 1941
Converted rumrunning boat   Mavis Beauchamp
sister   remains unknown

(as though she hadn't been told, as though to remind her. At the market, passing the brains shivering in a red puddle on the butcher's block)

remains unknown

(she'd nearly forgotten the baguettes and the wine, the good year}

June 29, 1941
Alban Beauchamp

(and she? and she?)

ex-niece

She knew what awaited her on the other side of the ocean, as she pulled farther and farther away from the stench, away from the permission to be different only if she was also the same. To be as her mother. To be widowed before she married. And Mavis sighed into the waves, nodding at the ocean for the first time, refusing it, refusing it all. She turned her back to the railing. There was no land left that she could see.

1985

MAVIS

avis De Vries sat in the livingroom of her Kansas home with a letter in her hand, before the picture window giving out onto her beloved rear gardens. She was not from these parts, hardly even *of* them—she'd had her husband, Henry, enclose the gardens with a high picket fence, as though to keep out native dust and spores. Though her friends—the wives of her husband's colleagues from the University—had mentioned to her that over the years she seemed to have taken on a certain character of the Midwest. A farmer's wife even, they dared to suggest. And why not? After all, she was short, stocky, small featured; she was severe, vulnerable only to hard-won humor, a little beaten, a little troubled beneath her placid watery eyes as though by not-so-distant financial worries.

Though Mavis was hardly a farmer's wife. Her husband, and the husbands of her friends, were Professors, Philosophers and Historians, and the house in which she lived was the vaulted, airy home they'd all dreamt of having when as graduate students they lived in their hot little bungalows and ate on slabs of planking and slept on Salvation Army beds.

There, out in the garden, amidst the fantastic blooms and the lush greens, as though to accommodate her desires, there was no life. Everything was ordered, everything in immaculately weeded plots squared to the fence and to each other, safely tiered, exquisitely domesticated. A neat gravel path zigzagged through the flower beds at right angles. A single wooden chaise longue and attending table perched on a wood platform, unused, unreferred to—drinks in the garden? sunset on the porch?—baking in the sun, alone, like—she had overheard more than once—ironic sculpture.

She was able, by her own design, to peer just over the spiked top of the fence. And it was there, after setting the letter in her lap, that she levelled her gaze. Beyond lay the plains, and the plains looked like the sea, and the street, she always noticed when they returned from their prescribed forays to the mall, looked like a jetty, ending where the plains began, easing down toward the wheat as if lying down at the water at half tide. And the wheat was still and pale, and the distance shimmered day and night, darkening and glittering under the unhindered sun, and then the moon that crossed and recrossed the swift current of clouds. Tails of dust slithered across the tableland and whirlpooled into funnels. Small cyclones jigged from fence to fence across the farms, atop the roofs of the barns, shattering against the walls of crossing winds. Ahead, a road black as a river, ending in a shimmer at the homesteads, themselves wavering on the horizon like distant ships.

She had been sitting, letter in hand, for some time, perhaps an hour. She was waiting, though not even she would have been able to say for what. Perhaps for the sun to drop. When she heard Henry's car pulling into the driveway at five thirty, as it did every evening, she decided that it hadn't been that. She tracked Henry's slow, measured footfalls to the front door. The door opened, and she could hear, briefly, before it shut, the bleached silence of their sparse neighborhood, the sunlight close to the ground, singing off the windows. Then Henry dropped his shoes, one and then the other, and she closed her eyes, bowing slightly. The delayed cross-breeze fingered the back of her hair long after the door had shut, opening her eyes at the sound of Henry's feet chafing along the tile floor in his slippers. Inside their home, one wore slippers, like surgeons, to keep the contamination at bay.

Henry, tall, ungainly and stooped, unloaded before Mavis a glass of orange juice and stood with his own in hand, joining his wife's abstracted gaze out the window, as if searching water for sinking boats. It was their well-oiled routine, seamless, crucial, portentous: how, after all these years, would it turn out? He rested a happily numb hand on her shoulder.

"What is that?" he asked, long after he'd seen the letter in Mavis's lap.

Mavis tipped her glass of juice up to her lips simply because it was there in her hand. She set it down and looked out at the flowers and vegetables penned in by the gray fence.

"It's from my cousin, Jackie," she said. She waved her hand, as if to reveal the mundane simplicity behind a seemingly inconceivable trick, then let it settle on her thigh. Henry lowered into a chair beside her and watched Mavis with usual things ready on his tongue, but he elected nothing and settled back.

She lifted the letter. The single page trembled a little in her hand. She laughed. "They always did say that Jackie looked like my father." She looked at Henry without seeing him. "I didn't see it," she said, "except that they were both short and round. Music played all over daddy's face, but Jackie was always a piece of stone. He was always nothing. He couldn't hold a job. He couldn't even hum a tune."

She set the letter on the floor and smoothed her lap, clasping her hands in her lap in an attitude of prayer. "Jackie just showed up in my mother's hospital room to pay his respects, probably before he went around the corner to his parents to ask for another loan. But he said he walked in and took my mother's hand and she opened her eyes and looked at him hard, like she was trying to memorize him. He said the wrinkles on her forehead went away. And she started saying my daddy's name. 'Gordon, Gordon, Gordon.' Then she began to cry. Jackie tried to pull his hand away. But he said it was just like getting your fingers stuck in a door. No one could convince my mother who was really standing there. She just kept smiling and saying over and over, 'Gordon, Gordon,' all that day and that night. And no one had the courage to tell her that it wasn't my daddy standing there, reappearing after forty-four years, and not aging a single day. And they let her think it, just like they always did."

Mavis's face stretched with wonder. She took off her glasses and lay them on her lap, her eyes misty, risen to the sky. Her hands fluttered, briefly, then settled again downturned on her thighs. "My father and the boys always doted on her," she said. "They always told her how wonderful she was, how beautiful she was. That year—the year they went away—they wrote her poems for Mother's Day, and when they gave them to her she turned to me and said, 'See what wonderful young men your brothers are!'"

Mavis cleared her throat. She levelled her gaze at the garden and blinked slowly, as if inspired by the order of her flowers to summon a more generous tone. "I knew from the beginning they'd never come home. I just decided that they were dead, all of them, as though I'd killed them myself"—shaking her head, laughing—"And there she was, keeping house, keeping their rooms as they were, pressing their clothes, cleaning their bedding, dusting their damn trophies. I even had nightmares of them reappearing, three skeletons in ragged clothes coming up the walk and lying down on their well-kept beds."

She turned to Henry. "So she's dead now."

Henry nodded, and Mavis lifted her eyes, sinking into her chair beneath the weight of the feeling she always had, left out, left out again, left alone, left behind, alive.

They rose, later, from their dinner of distinct and measured portions, and from this ill will, this uneasy feeling that also had something to do with the house. The night pressed in on the picture windows. The dust ticked at the glass, reminding them of the weather, some unseen squall. Mavis walked the hallway, along the scoured floors and bare walls, where there were no photographs, through their unsettled blankness, an absence of evidence that anyone really lived there, anyone in particular, anyone at all. Here and there, she crossed a sign that there had once been children, as though it would be just too much, too much in opposition to an old pattern to not leave any evidence at all. A bedroom still decorated in primary colors; an overlooked patch of wallpaper. But the instruments of childhood, the debris, the trophies, were gone. Everywhere the carpets were pulled, everywhere dust and dirt were frightened off. There was no odor, none at all. The hardwood floors were stripped and varnished into the floors of a museum. She had no time for any of it.

The only mirrors were long and thin, clamped to the back of bathroom doors. Mavis walked the uninterrupted floors through the entire, dustless house, no room for the children and adults in other incarnations who would not come back.

In bed, Mavis could smell him in the dark. Even after all

these years, she felt fatigued, drugged, robbed of spirit—certainly robbed of affection—as though the chief feature of her blank walls was their absorbency, to pull her in, under, down. She recalled the meat-cleaver bow of the long ship back from France thirty-two years before. The white hairs creeping along the deck around her ankles. Her arms draped over the railing and all the black desert below her. Nothing had changed over the years but the direction of the boat. And again, she found herself saying over and over, I am sorry, I am sorry they're dead. Still trying to convince herself.

But as the dark waves passed below, with each slow, vague pitch and roll, her year away began to disappear. Her routine, her schoolroom French that had become almost native, her baguettes and her wine seemed torn from the pages of the blue-jacketed travel guides. Because after everything, after all that, she was still leaning against the rail heading home, sinking with every minute that passed deeper into a chair in her mother's livingroom, beneath the photo of them all, posed behind her father's piano.

Until she found herself standing at the rail at midnight beside tall, thin Henry De Vries. That night, after hearing almost nothing of all that he had said, she'd taken him to her cabin. A life completely beyond arousal died as she led through her narrow ship's door a man the very same age—twenty-one—her drowned brother Ivan would have been. Mavis even imagined that Henry looked as Ivan might have looked, had he lived. Unbuttoning her blouse in the wan, sourceless mid-ocean light, atop the very waters in which they'd all drowned, she led Henry toward her narrow bunk and yanked off the raspy ship's blankets. After steering him to the bed she undressed, thinking how he even resembled her father: the same musky scruff and deep quavering voice she had known till she was nine. What Anne Stisulis would have done to Gordy, given the chance, Mavis did to Henry. She finally felt free to live the lives the boys had given up when the water froze them at ten and sixteen.

Her untested rhythm had been slow and exact. And not a wince. Henry had reached up to touch her face but—her gun-metal eyes open, glassed, staring through the wall, the straight line of her mouth blue—she leaned out of reach. He opened his mouth to speak but she closed it with her hand. Only her soft panting, the hum through the greasy wall and the bedsprings of the ship's engine three or four levels down, her thin papery blueness. Three beads of sweat appeared above her upper lip. Her mouth quivered and fell open and she caved, her hair dark and everywhere.

Mavis brought Henry with her to Maine. She told no one in Rehoboth she was coming. Frances Beauchamp had instructed that her remains be dispersed off Bailey Island where her sons and husband had last been seen. Mavis had known all her life that this was what her mother would want, to be returned to her men, though she never did say she wanted to be *with* them— only where they were last seen—because they were not dead, merely gone away. But she couldn't just be left there to rot. She would have to be spread about.

As Mavis and Henry drove into Rehoboth in their rented car, the snow caps behind them and the pine hills ahead were sharp against the sky. The river was glassy, clear not in a clean but in a sinister way. There were no birds. It was winter but there was no ice. When the Rehoboth stacks broke above the hills, the river jogged alongside the road, the water not even a clear broth, more like white liquor pouring down a gutter.

They stopped on Congress Street. Out in the air Mavis grew frightened. Her eyes began to water. Everywhere eggs were rotting and cabbage was burning. Together with the haze the stench had substance, as though she could stir it up by wriggling her finger in front of her face, or jar it and put it on a shelf. The town eluded her, the edges of its houses and storefronts not really sharp, the letters in its signs not quite discrete. The Hotel Harris, the Rehoboth House of Pizza, a Safeway, a boarded-up Woolworth's. The temperature had spiked. Gray patches of snow hid in the doorways. A dull, two-toned roar rose from somewhere beyond the around back of the shops; beneath them— steady and unceasing—the river rushed through the town. Everything was the same. Merely standing there on the walk was a kind of death. And Mavis was scared. But it was not Rehoboth; it was her mother, it was Mavis's obligations.

"In here, Henry," she said, pulling him by hand into a place that was new to her only by name. Ciccarelli's. The Ristorante was empty, the only movement a fan turning off the high ceiling and a woman in a pale green smock standing behind a long counter, wire-brushing a grill, as if expecting large crowds, as if the customers stood at the door waiting for a signal to come in. It was noon. The tin troughs in the salad bar for the tubs of cole slaw and macaroni salad were unfilled. Well-spaced glass shelves were littered sparsely with green cups and saucers and minia-ture American flags, a retouched baby photo, a box of donuts. Everything symmetrical, orderly in its scarce perfection. All of it seemed to her to give Ciccarelli's Ristorante the appearance of being dusty and cobwebbed though the whole cavernous space was spotless.

Outside, the pink and green neon sign—the only visible acknowledgement in town of urban commercial fashion besides the automatic teller machine—had said, *Italian Cuisine,* but on the menu was nothing remotely Italian except pizza, and this written in by hand, as though hypothetically speaking. At the counter Mavis and Henry feigned being last in line. They watched the clock, giant, luminous, the numbers nearly faded. It looked intended for something far away, the top of a court house or the far end of a bowling alley. The taps of the second hand echoed like water dripping into a sink.

They sat in a booth facing the rear and watched the entrance in the distended napkin dispenser. The outside blazed against the glass door. They were glad to be out of it. Their eyes had stopped watering. Mavis hoped no one else would come through the door, and when no one did, or even walked by it, she became more hungry.

The woman wordlessly left food before them then straight away took the wire brush to the grill. They could not hear the scraping.

The wholeness of the silence and the simplicity of spacing and angle, the barrenness of the salad bar, the failure of the fluo-rescent light to clarify—Mavis saw all of it and thought none of it despairing, but rather a kind of perfection, an achievement, a repudiation against the complications of food or customers and their mess and their history.

On his plot in Pleasant View Estates, encased in a blue velours recliner, Walter McAlister turned sixty years old. Emphysematic, wheezing, eyes distended. Rushing through sentences before running out of necessary breath, he began to cry. He leaned on the tin tray-table he had waiting, rasped, "Today's my..." he paused to breathe, "birthday," and diagrammed on a sheet of typing paper how their houses had once faced each other across a grassy lot—"Do you remember, Mavis?"—where their two mothers hung the laundry. He remembered how, in the summer months, he and Gordy and Ivan leaned out their windows and talked back and forth across the yard, over the draped sheets, into the night. How that night, June 28, 1941, he could never forget, DiMaggio's hitting streak had reached forty-one games.

They had played ball together... "Do you remember? We built that Scout camp on high ground that survived the flood. Never did find out how it burned. Like an act of God. We dreamt of working at the mill." Walter paused and raised his eyes: that Saturday night June 28, leaning out their windows over the grassy lot, they wanted the war, and after it ended a beautiful wife, and after that the mill was all they wanted—"Gordy wanted...only Anne S-stisulis. They found her... not him. You remember, course"—until one or the other mother's footsteps was heard and the upstairs lights came on one at a time, and they pulled inside midsentence without time to say goodnight, and the windows shut in rapid succession, like gun shots, for the last time. He never saw them again.

Beside Walter crying softly, retouched pictures of two overweight sons and an obese daughter stared Mavis down. A row of books all by a single author filled the shelf below, *Leslie Everett Dove, Leslie Everett Dove* repeated in gold leaf in the place of honor with Walter's children and the bible. As though staking a claim on the authorship of Walter's imagination, like a boy's first set of encyclopedias.

An American Legion cap, perched and primped alone on the shelf above, needed more primping, and putting her hands to the chair Mavis began rising to do it, as she might reach to pick the lint off the breast of a crying man, glad to put her hands to use. But Walter lifted off the floor and spread across his lap an album of heavy black paper whose edges had curled and faded: an over-exposed black-and-white photo of him and Gordy and Ivan sitting on wicker chairs on the porch of their newly completed Scout camp, on either side of them firewood piled high for a winter still six months away. Scribbled along the bottom: *June 1941.* Staring at the photo, Walter started the private complications of speech, the suction of air, the heaving chest, the prying mouth. The thought of getting up fell out of Mavis cleanly, as though it belonged to someone else.

Walter looked up, his face streaked with tears. "Do you rem-... your dad invited me to go along... Something you never forget...Thought the boat didn't look...seaworthy. But the little things that save your life. A photo."

Outside the window behind Walter's head, a backhoe roared out of a cloud of dust, making room for another trailer. ("Sorry ... Never-thought-I'd... live-in-one-of-these... *things,*" he'd said as he'd ushered Mavis in earlier.) His arm rose and pointed past the backhoe, past the road, past the trees. He twisted his mouth, motioned helplessly at his chest. He would never live in town again, the fumes, the emphysema. He dropped his hands and misfired a smile, then, resigned to what he had not yet said, a look of defenselessness crossed his eyes.

He shook his head. "Do you... know your town, Mavis? We've more men and women... WWII... per capita than any other town in the USA except Brooklyn, New York. Your family... Beauchamp. Beauchamp... grand old Rehoboth name. Royalty."

Mavis smiled wanly. Her eyes glittered. She touched her nose with the back of her hand and inhaled deeply. She leaned forward and smiled and touched Walter on the knee. "Mavis De Vries, now, Walter," she said. "Mavis De Vries."

A man from the crematorium followed Mavis and Henry to the edge of Dyer's Cove, at Bailey Island. Mavis clutched the heavy metal box against her lap. But the water there was frozen over. There was no outlet, and driftwood and old traps were hardened into the ice. Not wanting to leave her mother's ashes for the gulls, Mavis directed them further down across the bridge to Bailey Island. Over the water Mavis saw an area that seemed to be accessible to the public, a small bay opposite a lobster pound. They parked at the foot of a hill, and Henry and the man from the crematorium waited as Mavis walked out as far as she could on the rocks. Standing on the last rock it suddenly crossed her mind, being where she was, that her mother had meant for her to spread her ashes offshore, in the open water. But she was not prepared to go out on the water there. She thought it too much, too repetitious, too dramatic, too much of something that had always been too big.

She took the metal box out of the big paper bag Henry had carried. She lifted it and held it as far out over the water as she could, thinking that this place, this random moment in this overcast, would do. This, she thought, was where the expedition had begun.

She looked inside the box. Dust and chips of bone like small rocks. Flecks of other substance. Cloth? Do they burn you nude or clothed? She forgot to ask.

She overturned the box without ceremony—as she would an ash tray—then examined the inside. There was still some dust caught in the corners. She tapped every grain of it out over the water, kicked at what had dusted the rock she stood on, brushed off the tops of her shoes, and turned back for the car before the last of the gray pebbly film was lapped out by the tide.

She was imagining already the places in Maine she'd never seen, the places she'd never been allowed to go. There had been no place that wasn't painful for her mother. She'd always said she'd go to Bailey Island only when she was dead. Even when all those bodies, all the girls were washing up on shore, she refused to go. 'Only when I can be with your father,' she'd said.

Now, Mavis had a list. She knew this was what they'd do before they left. Henry was waiting in the car. Knowing it would be the end, he drove.

"Goodbye," Mavis said. Everywhere Henry took her, everything she looked at, even for the first time—"Goodbye."

EZRA

Ezra's son Charlie was tall and dark and had the muscular flabbiness and red face of hard work and still harder drinking. By the time he and Ezra had hit all their addresses the banquette was still only half full. Ezra squinted upward from under his sweatshirt hood, looped loosely about his chin, hiding all but his gray stubble. The brilliant fog had given way to a gray, constant light and the rain had turned cold and feathery.

"Want to do some drag hauling?" he asked.

Charlie said nothing.

Ezra lifted the mouthpiece to the radio. He rolled the volume knob in his fingers.

"Pop."

"Go."

"How about some dragging."

After a pause, "Where."

"Round Rock," Ezra said.

There was no answer for a time and Ezra hung the mouthpiece and looked into the banquette and shook his head.

"You know, Wanda's got to get down to the fish house on time to help Pop," he said to Charlie.

"She's got to get the kids off."

Ezra reached atop the console to align something that didn't need aligning. "Maybe you can help her get the kids off and then come down together," he said.

Clayt's voice finally came through the radio: "You feeling lucky, son?"

Ezra shrugged, as though Clayt could see him. He squinted out at the water. He lifted the mouthpiece. "I feel poor."

"Ten minutes."

Ezra didn't look at Charlie: "Set out the nets."

He slipped the boat into neutral then climbed up on the bow and shinnied up the tower toward the crow's nest at the top. The seas were three foot and better, the rain came in horizontal gusts, but he climbed as though flying up an orchard tree planted firmly in the ground on a sunny day while Charlie swayed below on the rolling deck, looking at the small gray face peering at him from far above. The tower's base was not merely unfixed but actually migratory, rearing as the water heaved.

Up top Ezra grabbed the duplicate controls, smaller levers and a miniature wheel, and swung the *Joanne B* into the white wash before him. Then a swell knelt and unravelled, taking the lee-side water with it, peeling back and baring a rocky spine. The ledges gleamed in the air briefly in the gray light then plummeted as the water gargled and spat all around them.

He saw Charlie straightening and looking into the water, then up at him.

"Tide's up now, Charlie," Ezra called. "That's all out at low water. Nothing but high tide ledges going straight across up to Cundy's Harbor."

Charlie nodded and waved but didn't look convinced, and when the boat jolted he grabbed for something upright but ended up just hugging himself, and he just shook his head, and Ezra let out a little laugh.

"We have twenty fathom straight down all along the other side of the ledges," he called down. "This in here, this part of the ledge, still here you got sure water. The top of that ledge there, that's Round Rock. That's probably as big as two of these boats. You make it over that and you got eighteen fathom of water there. You go on the east of it and there's eighteen there. You go to the west and you got ten, twelve fathom. And there's plenty of water all around it. Right here there's twenty feet of water and you can see how close you are. But tide's up now, see, there's plenty of water. When the tide is all the way down it's a solid mass of ledges just barely breaking the water the whole way to Ragged Island. You got to know in your head what's where because you can't see none of it."

Beside them, the fog darkened and congealed and parted around the nose of a trawler, hand lettered *Hattie B*. The tuna tower appeared, Clayt's hair like a white flame in the fog. The bow fell and Clayt brought the boat alongside. Behind the running board, Wanda had the nets in her hands. She was thick, flushed with drinking, mannish but for her breasts which swung free like sallow gourds in a loose t-shirt. She didn't look up. Clayt was looking down at her with his hands on his hips. Their mouths were set, neither said a thing, or raised their heads, as though they stood isolated and grim on the wrong side of an argument.

"Wanda, why don't you haul those across to Charlie," Ezra called over.

Wanda squinted into the boil. "You sure you want to get in that today? It's awful rough."

Ezra looked at Clayt. Wanda glanced at Charlie, who shrugged and took a cigarette from his mouth and handed it across. They stood smoking a minute. "He comes in here about once a year, maybe twice," Charlie told her. "He says it's no reason but I don't believe him."

"You shut up talking about it," Ezra bellowed. "Just pass 'em over."

Wanda looked over her shoulder at the water. "You're just going to lose the nets."

Clayt looked over at Ezra and it wasn't out of loyalty to the nets or even to the lobster they had or the lobster they didn't yet have, but to his son who'd set the task before them, and to his—Clayt's—willing collaboration. At risk was a generation of lobstering, already a ghost of what it was, and they already ghosts of their fathers, living out their dying lives. What stood below in the guise of son and daughter-in-law was something they couldn't name. But it meant the end of what they—Ezra and Clayt—had been, and they knew it. And Charlie and Wanda—humoring the two old men, humoring themselves, humoring each other—knew it but they had neither cause nor ambition to do anything about it.

"Just pass the goddamn nets over," Clayt said hoarsely.

Wanda and Charlie launched their cigarettes into the water and donned gloves. Ezra and Clayt brought the tandem closer to the ledges and then Ezra ordered them to drop, and Charlie and Wanda let out the nets, measuring the lines through their hands as the boats swung around as in a parade.

"We're going in for a quick shovel then pulling out," Ezra said.

The sucking and gurgling of the ledges, towing in closer, Charlie and Wanda throwing looks up and back at their pilots, down into the water and up and back and at each other. Finally Clayt looked at Ezra and nodded and Ezra called down, "Up!" and Charlie threw a lever. The boats leaned.

Wanda nodded. "Good haul," a smug grin she didn't keep to herself.

Charlie brought in the empty nets.

"One more time," Ezra said, looking at Clayt.

"Oh, come on," Wanda said.

"Down, Charlie," Ezra called, gesturing with his hand as though patting an imaginary dog, easy, easy, down.

Wanda threw the nets. Again the boats swung to and the four lines led into the water as though anchored there, as though the entire floor would be their load if they should catch it.

Again Ezra gave the sign and again Charlie threw the winch. The boats leaned, the water broke, cross-hatched, the nets hung dripping and mostly empty.

Wanda shook her head, hands on hips.

Ezra said nothing and Wanda threw up her arms and rushed her end of the nets. Ezra and Clayt grimly watched them descend then vanish.

"Up," Ezra called, monotonously, his head averted. As if this go wouldn't be the last.

This time the winches groaned, shuddering as though they did have the sea floor itself. The boats dipped more steeply still. Charlie and Wanda were leaning back against the deck just to keep their feet. Sheets of water spilled out of the banquettes over the deck.

"Christ," Charlie said, reaching for a handhold.

"Easy," Ezra said. "Easy."

"Goddamn it, Ezra, let it go, we're caught," Wanda called.

"There's give yet," Clayt said calmly.

"Give, shit," Wanda said. "Let her out, it's snagged—"

"Too damn close," Charlie called, backing up.

Then the boats jolted, as though kicked, and everyone snatched at something to hold and looked to the water. The ledges were gurgling, but not atop them. There was good water yet. The boats righted, the winches rolled easily and the nets were rising.

"Well, we lost something," Charlie said.

But Clayt and Ezra had set their mouths. They might have lost something yes. But there was another way this could go.

The nets surfaced. Charlie and Wanda stepped forward and peered into a writhing stew of weed and claw and viscous jellies. Charlie leaned in with his gaff and stopped. "What the hell—" He pulled back, brandishing the gaff as though out of self defense.

Ezra leaned off the tuna tower: set in the crawling muck, yellow and green galoshes, different sizes off different feet, adult, middling, child; metallic glints like coins in the mud; shouldering through the center, the peak of a boat's bow, a shard of planed wood fastened to a brass gimble that today held no flag.

"Oh jesus christ—" Wanda had her hand clamped over her mouth. Charlie leaned in. White sticks, charred firewood—splintered bone? femur, tibia?—a small stone, polished round, jaw unhinged, sockets plugged with sea grist. Through the weeds pale twigs like fingertips surfacing to the air.

Ezra looked at Clayt. He didn't have to wonder. But he watched his father stare and stare until his eyes narrowed, and he whirled, whirled again, looking over his shoulder, taking mental note of their position, measuring with his eyes the distances from here to various points of over there, back toward the Sisters, Ragged Island, Jacquish, ahead toward Orr's. As though looking for something he'd lost, or remembering something he'd forgot. Not a thing but a place. Clayt's eyes caught on his son. He and Ezra looked at each other, holding each other's gaze as in some match of wits or concentration. Neither said a thing.

The ledges had drifted closer. Ezra yelled down to Wanda, "Get that metal stuff out of there."

But Wanda wasn't moving. She froze where she stood, feet apart, legs pumping with the swells, sifting with her eyes.

"Goddamn it," Ezra barked. "Charlie, get them things out."

Charlie bent and reached and picked out what seemed hard and small. He reached for the stone ball.

"Let that go," Ezra called.

Charlie looked up.

"Just those other things."

"But we've got to clear the nets anyway," Charlie said.

"It's staying."

Wanda shook her head in little twitches, her eyes abstracted.

"We're putting it back down," Ezra said.

Charlie and Wanda looked up, surprised. Ezra could feel his father peering at him across the span of water. No one was moving.

"Now!" Ezra cried. "Cut it, cut those goddamn lines before they tangle us in."

Charlie looked down into the net as if trying to memorize what was there, then waved the gaff at his end of the line and the net fell away. Wanda swiped at hers and it fell away, and the middle plunged, the edges floating briefly, then disappeared without a flutter. For a few seconds the surface of the water blistered, then a swell passed and it was gone and dark. They bobbed in silence, looking at the blank water, the low fog passing between them, obscuring them from each other.

Entering Mackerel Cove, Ezra's eyes flicked right and left as though the fog were no impediment to seeing. He pushed the engine to full throttle. One last burst. The bow lifted to the water then dropped and they idled along. The tide had peaked, everything was flooded, the boats spun around their moorings.

The *Joanne B* idled up beside the raft with the big scale. A man appeared out of the fog in pressed slacks and rowing an awkward dory. He took the tin pails of lobster from Charlie and emptied them into a wooden crate and put the crate on the scale, and Charlie looked immediately less inept, very alert and smart while he watched the needle waver then stop and the man take a roll of cash from his pocket. Ezra Johnson looked away, suddenly looking a little shamed.

The scale man held out the cash before the needle stopped moving. "Not a bad day," he said, "But the price dropped last night."

"Price dropped, Charlie," Ezra said affectionately, even a little humbly. He reached for the twenty-dollar bills the man held out to him and peeled two off for Charlie. "But here's yours anyway."

Charlie didn't so much as tip his head before he stepped into the dory with the scale man.

"Charlie," Ezra called.

Charlie looked up.

"Nothing. Don't say nothing."

Charlie didn't answer. The scale man looked up. Ezra ignored him.

"You and Wanda. Nothing. To nobody. Not yet."

Charlie looked confused.

"I'll tell you later," Ezra said.

Then Charlie gave up and nodded and rowed off.

Ezra drove his pick-up quickly around the cove and up on the main road and off again, down a dirt track. His house lay at the end of a grass promontory, surrounded on three sides by water. Inside, he went directly for the phone. The TV was murmuring in the next room. Joanne wouldn't have expected him so soon. Ezra turned his back with the phone in one hand and two metal objects in the other, an algae-stained pocket watch, a pair of dainty binoculars, gold inlaid with silver brocade. Opera glasses. He dialed, then once more fingered the glasses over in his hand, and dug absentmindedly with his fingernail into the engraved initials, tracing the swirling letter L, then S—

"Arthur McAlister, please. Ezra Johnson ... Arthur? ... Yep, yep ... Look, Arthur, I think you better get down here."

At first there was no reply.

Finally, "How's tomorrow morning?"

"How's this afternoon."

Ezra could hear McAlister thinking, and remembering, probably looking around the office of the Rehoboth Falls Trust as Clayt had done atop the crow's nest, searching out under the desks and chairs, among the young foreign faces of the clerks and tellers. As if he could see obscured in the shadows, and in the unfamiliar expressions, something forty-four years gone.

"Two hours," McAlister said grimly, then hung up.

Ezra put down the phone and raised his head to the window. He followed the channel with his eyes out toward its mouth, where water and sky slipped away. The narrow channel was black and peaked. Ezra knew the water would get rougher before it calmed, the scale would lift and by this afternoon the fog would peel away. That by this afternoon, from the window, he'd see clear water again in every direction.

He'd never learned to swim. He'd never eaten what came from the water. He'd watched it and worked it, but he knew he didn't much like it. Today he liked it less.

He sat in his truck, facing the sea. The radio hissed, floating between stations. The windows were solid with twilight. Beyond the mouth of Mackerel Cove it was already night.

He took from his coat pocket the folded envelope and from that a yellowed letter, now quartered by frayed seams. He hadn't read it in thirty-two years. He read it, read it again, refolded it and returned it to its envelope and then his pocket. He looked up to the cove as though expecting the *Raven* to be with the other boats, shivering and rolling, braced against the rain like cows.

The cove seemed mostly empty, many of the moorings unsold, others torn out of the cove floor. It looked like itself at midday in decades past, but this was now Mackerel Cove in early evening, and all those boats that still worked the cove sat moored in their place. Half of what was once there.

He ran his fingers through his hair. He bared his teeth in the mirror and rubbed them with a finger. He picked a styrofoam cup off the floor and considered the puddle of day-cold sludge at the bottom then downed it.

The big car, an old Cadillac, pulled alongside, facing the same way. Ezra nodded to its driver, an old man who hadn't weathered his years well, hunched behind the wheel, breathing through teeth bared half in dread and half in determination.

They stood before their cars, shaking hands.

"Sorry to get you down here, Arthur," Ezra said.

"Where is it."

Arthur McAlister seemed to be smiling, but Ezra saw that he had merely braced himself.

Ezra grinned half-heartedly, as though at his own accumulated failures, and shook his head.

"Round Rock," McAlister said.

Ezra nodded.

"Who've you told?"

"You."

"Where's Charlie?"

"It's got nothing to do with him."

"Clayt?"

"Fucking around in the toolshed I imagine."

"He knows?"

"He knows."

Ezra walked behind McAlister as he struggled down the gangway.

"Easy," Ezra said.

McAlister was taking half-steps down, and Ezra scooted around him and held the dory steady against the raft as McAlister teetered. Ezra stood in the dory. He guided McAlister into the bow and undid the tether.

McAlister's chest was heaving, his breath hissing through his teeth.

"My lungs are for shit," he said, panting.

"It's that damn town," Ezra said. "All those sulfides and chlorine."

"Well, we didn't know then what we know now."

"It's always smelled like shit."

McAlister smiled weakly. "That smell's the smell of money."

"It's the smell of leukemia, Arthur. I read about those boys up there. Those six sons in one family all dead before they're twenty-five."

A weary look passed McAlister's eyes, fatigue and exasperation and a well-practiced determination to deny the face of truth. His hand—apologetic, defeated—passed through the air. "It's a lot better than it was."

Ezra saw McAlister's expression, shook his head and laughed.

"Okay, Arthur, whatever you say."

He turned his back to take the oars and shoved off, rowing choppily, quick pants rather than long breaths. They moved swiftly around the moorings and rafts. They passed the weighing raft.

Oars dripping, Ezra paused and they glided by, birds called to them from the trees onshore: "One thing that'll never leave me is all them women piled up on here with their eyes open. Stayed with me for years and years. I'd shut my eyes and they'd stare straight at me, like they were accusing me of something." He turned and looked at McAlister panting in his seat. "I still see them."

He took the envelope from his pocket and handed it back. "Take a look at that, Arthur."

He could hear the paper in McAlister's fingers, then he heard nothing as he rowed. He heard nothing for a long time. They were nearing his mooring when his right oar passed over two sheets of paper, spinning in the oily whirlpool, splitting off into eight identical patches of scrawl, just under a skin of water.

Ezra paused, then passed the oar through them, scattering them like leaves.

"You've seen that letter, Arthur?"

"No."

"Do you believe it?"

McAlister said nothing.

They reached the mooring, and Ezra hopped aboard the *Joanne B* and let down a ladder and hauled McAlister up by both arms. He held out an orange parka.

"Put that on."

McAlister held up his hand, refusing it.

"Put it on," shoving it into his arms. "It's cold out there."

The boat moved off beneath them. Evening was settling, a curtain of darkness swept across the open water like distant rain. The light at Halfway Rock winked off to the right. Pinlights wavered where there had been land. A solid constellation of red and green running lights held steady on the horizon.

Ezra nodded out there. "Russian factory ship," he said. "Big as three goddamn football fields. Russians and Japs all up and down here vacuuming up the floor. A few years time there'll be nothing left and I'll put up my feet and become a piece of furniture and stare at the water all day."

McAlister laughed. "I doubt that. You hate the water. You won't want to look at it."

Ezra nodded, looking down right and left for the shoals. "You may be right, Arthur. You may be right. Maybe I'll move up by you and go out on a good case of emphysema. Cancer better yet."

"I think that'd be fine," leaning against the console, looking backward, he saw the Xerxes plaque screwed into the side panel and laughed. "You old superstitious bastard."

Ezra slapped at it and laughed. "That aint superstition, Arthur, that's fact."

"That old Clayt's?"

"That's a copy. My father still has his screwed on tight."

McAlister shook his head. "He still goes out?"

"Every goddamn day."

"Sonofabitch."

"Yes sir."

Ezra brought them around Jacquish Island and out into open water and slowed. "He was out there dragging with me today. We brought it up together."

"You brought it up."

"I let most of it go."

McAlister nodded.

"Was it Varney?"

"I thought you'd ask me that," Ezra said.

"And I am."

"Do you really want to know?"

"I don't know. Do I?"

"Do your people up there want to know?" Ezra asked.

"There's still a memorial service every year, every June 29."

"But do they want to know."

"About Varney? I don't know."

"Do you?"

"Do you believe that letter?" McAlister said.

"I think I believed it didn't matter."

Gulls hung above them, following their speed, hovering like paper out of a fire.

"How long has Varney been gone now, Ezra?"

Ezra squinted toward the horizon, already bled into the night. "About twenty-five years, I guess. They never found him. Guess he ran off. That's what I would have done."

"Drowned himself, probably," McAlister said.

"No," Ezra said. He laughed. "You boys up there have this goddamn notion that a fisherman wants to die in the water and have his body slid under with a flag and taps and the whole nine yards. That's just bunk. A fisherman hates the idea of dying in the water. Scares the crap out of him. He knows how much it'd hurt."

Ezra clapped McAlister on the shoulder.

"But that was a long time ago. Feels like a lifetime, don't it?"

"But I guess it wasn't."

"No, I guess it wasn't. Not quite long enough." Ezra looked at him. "You know where I found that letter, don't you."

McAlister shook his head.

"That Historical Society you have up there."

McAlister said nothing.

"They got it from that writer, Leslie Everett Dove. Mean anything to you?"

"It's all a long time ago now," he said weakly.

"I found it about the same time Varney made it irrelevant," Ezra said. "You didn't know about that letter, did you, Arthur?"—less a question than a statement.

McAlister walked to the stern and back, dragging his finger along the running boards. "A long time."

Ezra cut the throttle. They bobbed quietly out of each other's reach. The tuna tower leaned above them, a flag every once in a while fluttering to life and dropping limp again.

"You know, we got a new rescue group now," Ezra said cheerfully, peering over the bow. "It's not like the past. One of these days we're going to bring one up alive." He laughed ruefully. He looked at McAlister. "Did you know you can put someone down in cold water for a half hour and still bring them back? They go into a deep sleep. Life is still there, heart's still beating, like a bear in hibernation. Some people struggle in the water. Some people black out. For some reason or another, the people who immediately pass out when they hit the water, the ones who stop breathing, those're the ones you're going to bring back. You got a half hour. They've developed machinery, sound machines, so that you can distinguish things on the bottom. So what we done, I hit a deer and took it and put him on the bottom, and christ you could see him plain as could be, it was just like a body. Over in open seas off Harpswell two years ago we got a call from the Coast Guard and they sent my father and me out there. They didn't want to go themselves. It was foul weather and they hate that sort of thing. So they ask me to go out. Christ, they weren't dead more than a half hour. Fifteen more minutes—if the Coast Guard'd just gone out themselves instead of taking the time to call me—these kids'd still be alive. They were Bowdoin students. A diving class. They just panicked under the water. And when they panicked—hell, it's just like in the woods, they throw everything away. Except the one thing they don't throw away is the lead belt. So there they are when we find them on the bottom, you can go right along usually and there'd be a line: the mask would be here, something else here, and here"—Johnson made a line with his two hands—"You keep going along that line and pretty quick you'll find them, and they'll just be sitting there, their arms just trying to float. And all they ever have to do is release that goddamn lead belt. But they don't do that. They panic, and in the process off comes the helmet, then the mask. And then there they are, just sitting there like they're waiting for you."

He shook his head. "Yes sir, one of these days we're going to bring up someone alive."

McAlister was looking at him with some kind of horror.

"I haven't forgotten those kids who went down on that boat," McAlister said, hugging himself.

"I told you it was cold," Ezra said.

"I don't know how you do it," McAlister shook his head. "Come out here every morning, in the winter."

"It's like anything, Arthur. You can get used to anything."

McAlister could hear the water breaking against the rocks. Ezra led him by the elbow to the starboard side. "Now right out there. What do you see?"

McAlister leaned far forward. Ezra readied his hands to snatch him.

"I don't see anything."

"Look again."

McAlister shook his head.

"Boats have been coming out here to this spot to lobster for as long as I been on the water and getting caught on something on their traps. See, there's sink holes all throughout these ledges. Eddies. Shit-holes, just like big sewers. That's where the big lobster like it, that's where you get the prize-winners."

"But where—" McAlister said, lifting his hand.

The mounds of water were unfolding out of the general sea and passing through them, pitching the boat.

"Tide's up now," Ezra said. "At low water, right where we're sitting, it's no fun. These ledges, you see. It was rougher than this, and to tell you the truth we got a little too close. I don't know, Arthur, I have to tell you, Pop and I haul seine in here a lot, a lot more than we should. I'm always over here when I shouldn't be, and half of me believes I always knew I'd find what I found today. Pop too. We never had a word about it. After a day hauling traps, we have no business in here, but we're always ending up here anyway."

Ezra opened McAlister's hand and put the opera glasses in. He went to the console and pulled a flashlight out of the banquette.

"Both of us had parts of her. Clayt had a big piece, a piece of the bow. I had a piece of the stern, the post with one of those gimbles that holds the flag."

"You sure it was the *Raven*."

Ezra turned on the flashlight and McAlister held out his hand. The pearl-inlaid opera glasses sat there in the yellow pool. McAlister turned them over, turned them over again, greened with algae and rust. He brought the cracked lenses to his eyes. He followed with his finger the engraved initials, *L.S.*

"We knew what it was," Ezra said.

"Lilah Sanders," McAlister said. "She was my secretary. I got her these. I sent her and her boyfriend in my place."

Ezra could feel the flutter of McAlister's head shaking in the dark. He reached in his pocket again and withdrew a wristwatch and laid it atop the opera glasses. McAlister put his finger on the circle of crystal.

"9:22," he said. "Morning or night?"

"Night, Arthur."

McAlister laid the watch on his wrist and looked at it there; as though contemplating its purchase; as though to see if it suited him.

"What else?" he didn't look up.

"We let it go. Clothes, mostly. Shoes. Pieces of her itself, like I said."

"Any bodies," McAlister said.

Ezra laid a hand on McAlister's shoulder. "Light was bad, kind of glary. Might've been, I suppose, but there was too much muck mixed in there and either way there wasn't going to be much left, much left that you'd want."

Ezra shut off the flashlight.

They considered each other in the dark.

After a while, McAlister said, "So it was Varncy."

Ezra peered out toward the ledges. A thin wash slipped over, baring the top of the crag in the moonlight, then tucked it under.

He cleared his throat. "Anyone who's made that trip knows Monhegan is a long, long way. Three, four hours. I don't know how fast that boat was, eight knots, ten maybe. And if it was choppy, which it was, they come by the Kennebec, Merrymeeting Bay, you know—by my figuring it's foggy and nasty and choppy and everything else, and they get most of the way then decide somewhere between Seguin and Monhegan to come back. I figure they pulled in at Damariscove and had some kind of picnic anyway. Floyd knew all these islands, and Damariscove's a nice spot even in the fog. We all used to go there on weekends sometimes, fish all day and night. There was a lighthouse station on it back then, but they wouldn't land at the lighthouse anyway. They'd land at the northeast end. There's a big beach, and a big island off the end of it, and you got a big sandbar, and a wooden catwalk. When the tide's up like this you got to walk across the catwalk, and walk across the northeast end of it. It's a beautiful beach. I had an idea, I don't know what, I just had an idea they landed there.

"And then they keep coming, see. Sometime before dark there's one or two lobster boats that seen them coming by Seguin Island, and they just go by the boat, you know, and don't say anything. They've got no reason to say anything, they see boats going by all the time, they're just fishermen, nothing in it for them. But there's no way of forgetting the *Raven*. It's the homeliest boat there was. And Christ, there's people all over the house, a lot of them on top. They seen it come by Seguin and then Floyd gets them to right about where we are now.

"Bell buoys for a fisherman at night. That's what he's going for. He's got to see with his ears. And there's a scale, what we call scale, in the night sometimes the fog just lifts then settles down. So he's going mostly by his sixth sense, feeling. A fisherman can sense when something is going to happen. We've spent our whole lives on the water, but I'll tell you something about fishermen you might already know. A lot of us can't swim. I can't. Floyd Johnson couldn't either. But we all know enough about the ocean to lash ourselves to something, a barrel or a keg, and lay on our backs to stay afloat. Christ, Floyd knew that. But he didn't do it that way. And there's the thing of it. When Floyd got in that water, he wanted to be found, but he never meant to be found alive."

McAlister lifted his face to the moon, and his face took on an unearthly glow, the two orbs set off against each other so that the source of the light and its reflection were not all that clear.

"And Varney?"

"You know he sent that telegram."

McAlister nodded not in acceptance but confirmation, as though the fact, lost long ago, lying like a splinter below the surface of good sense, had now risen; and it was no surprise.

"Poor Frances," he said. "She died just this year thinking Gordon had made good on his promise."

He looked at Ezra, then turned from him, facing the water.

"What are we going to do about this, Ezra," he said. It wasn't a question.

Ezra stepped back to the wheel and waited while Arthur McAlister lifted the opera glasses and watch above his head. Ezra had known, even as he handed them over, that Arthur McAlister would never want to keep them, that nobody would want to keep them, because there would be no way to keep them. In the end, they were just salvage. There was no way now, and never had been, to chase off the memory of this woman, the women—the way they lay on that raft, half-nude, thawing.

As well as he could, bound as he was in the heavy parka, McAlister heaved both into the water.

No sound intruded upon the calm hiss and roll as a wave passed. The water did not so much as dimple. They began to move.

And the light fell into the water, visible still, from just below the surface, from five feet, from ten feet, blurred and shattered into constellations by the cracked lenses. And the watch, keeping pace, marking the time of the fall, disappeared again into the murk. There a shoe. A snatch of hair. A slab of timber.

And they moved away from the hunched islands, toward the mainland massing in the dark, dim rows of windowlight flickering in the distance.

Near land the breakers surged, spraying against the rocks like fountains.

How long do twenty-one men and boys suspend in a forty degree ocean? A school of them just standing there, their arms just trying to float. A blurry forest of vertical men. How long until the cold water steals their shoes one at a time. And then their chains and their watches, the time, 9:42, having been and then passing, and then approaching, and been, and again passing, while here and there a shocked expression glints among them like a fishscale.

How many times do the bottoms of skiffs and lifeboats and the shadows of search-planes have to cross over their heads before they give up and sink?

And then rise.

Their gall bladders will rupture and inflate them with putrid air, and they'll lift—perhaps shoeless, eyeless, tongueless—a tuberous caricature of their former selves rolling solitary in the swells. They might float around a month or two like that, though they'll be even less of themselves each day. Something will get their ear, something else their other ear, then one nostril, then the other, and sooner or later those things will collapse like pricked balloons and flutter downward. For a while they will slow and hesitate and twirl with their unhinged arms flailing like a rag doll's in the undercurrents. But eventually they will drop, rocking back and forth like a leaf, or spinning as though being sucked down a drain. Twenty fathoms below the last light they will settle into a sinkhole, and the tides will stir them in with the other scraps. A bit of them here, a bit of them there. In with the abandoned traps and trap-lines and wreckage and chum and fish heads and fisherman shit and the femurs and spines of sailors swept off other decks in previous storms, their bones throwing up out of the silt and spinning in the undercurrents, burrowing back in some eddy, shifting to some other one, somewhere else every day, moving every day for more than forty years.

I would set before you a piece of a small tuna keg, a three-fathom length of rope, a braid of red hair, some pearl-inlaid opera glasses, maybe a bit of flesh from a finger or breast. And a crab. I would retrieve or gather all these things, though I might have to overtake a vessel and all its passengers to do so. If I were truly intent on making you see what happens, this is what I would do.

JUNE 29, 1941

THE RAVEN

Late morning Sunday, June 29, 1941, a group of employees of the Rehoboth Falls Trust Company and their spouses and friends gathered between the pillars outside the Trust on Congress Street. A blurry morning, a vaguely yellow morning beneath the gusts of fly ash from the paper mill, as clear a morning as you could have in Rehoboth. Many kept their handkerchiefs pressed over their noses and mouths: the Androscoggin River had flooded not two months before, and the silt still drifted through the streets, collecting against the storefronts and the portico of the bank like old gray snow.

Counting thirty-six heads including his own, Gordon Beauchamp distributed the crowd amongst the eleven sedans. It is clear now that neither Beauchamp nor anyone else knew the two boys sent to Earl Decker's car (they said they were brothers, the name was Mundt)—or how the two strangers talked their way into the expedition, or how old they might really have been—but one might imagine them—sixteen, nineteen, twenty-four—standing a little to the side of the bank's entrance, their handkerchiefs hiding all but their eyes, which never met anyone else's, never met anything above knee level.

Beauchamp took the wheel of the lead car, an old Essex—that is what they called it, *the Old Essex*—with his brother Alban beside him and his two sons in the back, and together the convoy began following the Androscoggin toward the coast.

By Peru the sun had begun to struggle. The river turned black. A thin mist leeched all color from the morning, turning it ash gray and the early sunlight sourceless. Further down the river the mist beheaded the dense forest on either side, stripping the trees to shadows of stubby branchless poles. The convoy slowed, the headlamps stabbed at the fog. The road itself became a kind of deranged river, the sideroads scattering crookedly into the woods like tributaries, the bends coming at last-moment watery places. The earliness, the rhythmic click of windshield wipers, the hiss of wet pavement—leaving the sun behind and mothers and daughters warm in their beds, the chatter diminished and the parade of merrymakers, hesitating, braking abruptly every few hundred yards, gave way to a huddled funeral procession snaking uncertainly toward the sea.

After Brunswick came the doorless and windowless room. The sunlight soaked the fog. The headlights could not make even a feeble scribble on the thick white smoke. Beauchamp leaned over the steering wheel as though the few extra inches would help, but drove neither faster nor more assuredly as the asphalt poured over the edge just within his sight. The convoy crept blindly on, toward the string of islands—Great Island, Orr's Island, Bailey—not really feeling the crossings, missing the squat bridges in the glare.

At the specter of the low white church, Harpswell Nazarene, its steeple erased, Beauchamp veered sharply left through a break in the trees, nearly knocking down the small hand-painted sign, Dyer's Cove Road. Some made the turn with him, others drifted by, stopping down the road. Eventually finding their way, the cars fell into line again. They parked. They cut their engines.

The horseshoe cove, its walls scoured deep as a basin's, closed off from the sea by the glare. Everyone stayed in the cars, giving the murk time to lift. It didn't, it wouldn't for three days, but with a calm determination—this annual expedition a year in the making, money had already changed hands—Gordon Beauchamp opened his door and shut it and padded down the gravel road. The other doors opened and shut behind him, and the thirty-five Rehoboth people followed with baskets and blankets and extra clothing across a plank of wood whose end they could not see.

At eleven in the morning there was some last-minute talk between the captain, Floyd Johnson, and his wife. Finally the rope was tossed to her. From the already half-vanished crowd there was a murmured and ambivalent hurrah as the boat drifted away from the jetty.

Though not before the puttering of a second motor from the

road. No doubt all on board heard it, but no one knows who on the boat did and who did not see the black truck actually emerge and drift past as though not intending to stop. Who saw the face in the window framed by the yellow fishing gear? The face that at the last instant did turn toward the water, toward Floyd Johnson, who, at the *Raven*'s wheel, glanced over his shoulder as though he had heard from the truck not Earl Varney's grunt but his subsequent nod, the half-blink, the a-okay. Johnson heard the truck but didn't actually see it. Sure it was Varney he had turned back to the matter at hand. Then there came the high, female cry off the jetty, and from the boat a reply from Johnson: "Beatrice!" But from the jetty there was nothing else. The passengers were momentarily concerned—had she slipped? had she fainted?—but the old salt Johnson had already begun to feel the *Raven*'s way out of the cove and across Cundy's Harbor, and Beatrice Johnson's cry was quickly forgotten.

At West Point Johnson pulled the *Raven* in at the General Store for potatoes and onions to thicken the chowder he was to assemble on board. Inside, the clerk glanced through the window at the young girl stumbling in her heels off Johnson's boat and up the gangway, around the stacks of lobster pots, flailing at her lost shawl. He murmured within Johnson's earshot about the fog and the good odds of a sudden squall and the number of people dangling their legs over the port side of the *Raven*'s house. (Later, the Weather Bureau log entry for Sunday, June 29, 1941 would say that electrical storms were hit-and-running the coast all day, but the keeper at the Seguin light would claim the seas around him were calm until 1:48 Monday morning.)

Calling out after the shawl, which was already drifting away on the tide, the young girl burst giggling into the store. The clerk shut up. He neither looked Johnson in the eye nor repeated himself to make clear the distinction between mere warning and threat. The girl asked to see the display of postcards. The clerk looked out of the tops of his glasses from Floyd Johnson to the girl and back to Johnson again, trying on the sly to get a whiff, suspecting he and she and the others were already soused. Even while the girl was handing him some coins the clerk kept his eyes on Johnson. But Johnson's gaze was out the door already, set on some distant point beyond the fog. "Here," the girl said, sliding toward the clerk a postcard that under normal circumstances would reach her mother in Rehoboth at least a day after she returned: *Feeling fine, not seasick, but there are still many miles to go.*

The white strands of hair wound around Floyd Johnson's legs and the fish house posts. They were winding around the *Raven* when he turned the motor over and pulled away from West Point. The wharf and the store collapsed into the obscurity, and all Floyd could see was rats, and that only because he could hear them plopping into the water off the wharf. Then just the laughter and shifting of his passengers and the gurgle of the *Raven*'s propeller, and the flap flap flap of the tail of his wool jacket against the base of the helm.

Earl had told him to stop at the store to pick up the potatoes to keep everything normal looking, keep it all innocent like. Now, instead of shooting through to the open bay, Floyd brought the *Raven* into the hiss of the eddying and shifting tides of the ledges. Earl had said, Just a little touch. But as he took the *Raven* nearer, Floyd thought about how well he knew what was passing below them, and how he could see down there better than he could up here. It wasn't only because of the fog: even on a clear day he knew it down there better than he knew it in the world he breathed in. Even now, if he looked—and he knew enough not bother—he wouldn't see past his hand. But he could always even now give a name to the peaks and canyons below, and call out numbers for the water between them like calling out the addresses of stores and the homes of friends he knew passing down the street: two fathom just a few yards over to the left. Sure water, ten or twelve fathom, below them this instant.

He pushed on the throttle, the bow lifted. Around him the laughter turned to shrieking and hooting. The air came harder and harder, and his breath shorter and shorter. It was a kind of darkness, Floyd thought, blinking at the fog. The reverse of it, darkness inside out maybe, but darkness just the same. You can't trust anything in the dark, not anyone's voice. If you were really smart you wouldn't trust your own. Then he blinked and he didn't know where he was, as though he'd fallen asleep in one place and woken in another. The words, "What am I doing out here," rose to his lips, but someone handed him a bottle and he raised it without questions. The liquor stung him, poured down his chin and then he knew where he was. He could hear Round Rock in front of him.

But between him and it was the *Raven*'s bow, where the boy stood facing outward with his hands behind his back like a captain keeping watch from the foredeck. And before that the top of the *Raven*'s house, where half the passengers lay sprawled in piles of three or four, their hair undone, their throats offered up to the glare. The clusters of cigarette cherries hovered above them like swarms of red fireflies. Arms waved through it half erased, already half gone—suddenly these were neither adults nor children but playactors, the men merely ripened boys straining the limits of their own stoicism, and the women nubile girls debuting their virgin puckers. The one boy at the bow, the true boy, the only boy up on deck, looked severe as the hands behind him passed the bottle among the wrapped bodies.

Floyd was surprised. He'd thought these churchly folk. He thought all highlanders churchly folk. He thought that's why they were highlanders. But anyway, good they're all bunched together, he thought, they'll keep each other afloat. He'll tell them to pair up, hug each other, to keep moving and stay together. And maybe the liquor will keep them warm and loose and they'll do what he says. Floyd practiced, envisioning himself on top of the house pointing in the water, crying out, Pair up, stay together! Then came Earl, out hauling traps, to save them all one by one. And then they would tie up at Dyer's Cove, and all those Rehoboth people would go on home just a little wet, and he and Earl would no longer be poor men, and Beatrice no longer just a wife among poor men.

Floyd felt his lips moving and his face making expressions—in his mind he'd been swimming, saving people two at a time, dragging them to Earl's boat—and stopped. He stopped completely, stopped thinking. He remembered he couldn't swim.

He cocked his head but heard nothing of Earl—only the water breaking up on the Sisters. He took a glance at his watch but his wrist was impossibly bare, plain bare skin. "Christ," he muttered, and saw his watch ticking safely at home on the dresser table. He'd never forgotten it, never. It was bad luck. "Christ, christ!" He turned toward a young woman just below him in the stern and glanced down at hers. It was not noon yet, five till. Earl was due at noon.

In the stern behind him sat the younger ones, the more subdued and self-conscious and those more content to merely drag their fingers through the water. There were two no one spoke to, two young men who stayed close together with their mouths shut and their legs crossed at the knees and their eyes on the water. And thin, the young men were thin, their faces gaunt not from tirelessness or drive but from worry. Floyd didn't like having that on his boat. No crazy people and no worriers. They were bad luck. But it was the boy up front he was concerned with now. He was pacing again, though there was no room to move. With his hands behind his back the boy paced in his place. Thinking, Floyd thought, not worrying. Thinking.

The leader Mr Beauchamp, arms linked with a woman in a long coat and knit hat, howled up the stairs from the stern.

"Mr Beauchamp," Floyd said, "Thought you said no children on this trip."

"What children?"

Floyd nodded toward the bow. "The boy."

"Who, Ivan? He's my boy," Beauchamp said, still laughing, "But he isn't a child. That boy's ten going on forty."

"You said no children."

"Captain Johnson, Captain Johnson," Beauchamp said, "Here now, he's a good boy. He's already better than the rest of us. He won't get in your hair."

"But can he swim?"

Beauchamp roared with laughter and slapped his knee. He put his arm around Johnson's shoulder and quietly asked: "Will he have to?"

Beauchamp's breath was hot and sweet. Already drunk, Floyd thought. "You said everyone would be able to swim."

"More or less, Pilot, more or less. Come now, we have Junior Carey here, state hero, champion in the Australian crawl. Surely he'll swim well enough for all of us. Onward!" Beauchamp roared, threatening the fog with his index finger, and stumbled off toward the bow. "Encore!" someone cried out, and Beauchamp skipped and whirled once around like a dancing bear and collapsed laughing where he was.

Floyd opened his mouth to laugh too but in his mind saw the waves licking at the rocks just ahead. He tapped his toe under the helm and heard the hollow thud of the keg. Then he looked behind him at those two keeping to themselves. He looked long and hard at them, at their hands lying quietly on their knees, their faces in repose practically bored, as though they were not beginning an afternoon's expedition on a boat but completing their daily commute on a bus, sitting in the aisle seat waiting for their stop, which they knew was coming, which came every day. They didn't return Floyd's gaze as much as recommence their long-standing observation of him from across the aisle. Then the young men exchanged wan looks and one leaned his ear toward the other. Floyd didn't like that on his boat either, no crazy people, no worriers and no secrets. Suddenly he thought of what Jesse and Clayt were talking about yesterday in the General Store, about German spies making getaways off the coast, and then about the U-boat they saw during that business with Lehman. Watching them whispering to each other, Floyd swore he heard something he couldn't understand, something foreign. He glanced furtively at the water, half expecting a periscope to be staring him in the face. But he couldn't see past the edge of the boat, so he was sure it was there, the periscope, and the rest of it passing beneath them, torpedoes and all. Again he looked back at the strangers. Only boys, he told himself, because he had to, though he didn't believe it. And he still didn't hear Earl's boat. He began to not believe that either. Earl had said this would be easy. Floyd whirled around to the deck and saw how easy: the flare of match heads, the glow of cigarettes arcing up and down, the bottles glinting, all those heads thrown back in laughter, the tangled thighs. And he could suddenly hear none of it, not even the water, just the tick-tick-tick of his watch lying safely at home in the middle of the lace doily on the nightstand, the leather band two humps like a camel's and the hands between them telling no one at all that it was noon. Noon, he thought. Noon. And there still stood the severe little boy at the bow, his back slightly stooped, his arms crossed, peering the length of the boat's house at Floyd as though over the treetops, over the writhing forest, over his own father wriggling against Mr Decker's crotch, Mr Decker's arm vanishing under his wife's blanket, his wife's shriek and kick; over Mr Wishart's head that is tilting and coming to rest for the first time between Miss Roach's breasts while she, pretending not to notice her own fingers combing Mr Wishart's hair, gazes off dreamily into the murk. The boy peered at Floyd Johnson above all this not as though asking him, What should we do with them? but daring him to go one up on what he already had in mind.

But Floyd knew nothing about this. He knew nothing about these people. You couldn't trust them, he thought. You can't trust anything in the fog, not even your own voice. But he could hear the buoy ringing off the back end of the Sisters now. He placed in his mind the buoy rocking side to side in the swells, and then he placed in his mind the ledges, just so. He opened his eyes. He was right: ahead, the dark jagged line shouldering through the glare. He could trust that. That would always be there waiting. And now the little explosions of water against the rock. He had two fathom beneath him at best, the height of a man beginning to kneel. Floyd whirled. The two German spies were leering at him, their arms and legs crossed, as though they had in their sights something they couldn't quite believe, some amusing notion. "Spies! Krauts!" Floyd cried out. The boat fell silent.

The two young men looked at each other, arched their eyebrows and began to laugh. Then the others threw back their heads and roared. "Krauts, subs, come what may, the Mundts are spies!" they cried, and howled into the fog like wolves. The two boys in the stern doubled over, hugging themselves, stamping their feet. Then a bubble rose from Floyd's gut to his throat and a bellow of chesty laughter exited. "Spies," he wheezed, rolling his head, going blue from lack of breath, "Ha ha. Ha ha." But the two young men had already recrossed their legs and arms and resumed their observation of Floyd as though they hadn't stopped.

Floyd was sweating. He did not remember starting to sweat, but his face was burning and hot perspiration was running down his neck. He jerked around. There lay the others on deck propped up on their elbows as though listening to a bedtime story, waiting for the Captain, waiting for the punch line from Pilot Johnson; and the boy at the bow, who seemed not to be waiting or watching him now as much as reconsidering him. Then Floyd stopped breathing. There behind the boy hovered the frothy swirl, the wreath of white wash riding the swells like water lilies. In the bull's eye of that ring, Floyd knew, just grazing the surface, making concentric circles no bigger than a raindrop would have, or a pebble tossed from shore, was the peak of Round Rock.

He tightened his grip on the throttle, then saw the pink flash in the corner of his eye. Flames, he thought, and whirled toward the stern. A girl in a pink dress had stood, hugging her bare arms, looking somewhere just over Floyd's shoulder with a smile caught halfway between subjection and curiosity. The fog had dampened the cloth of the dress and he saw that she was a girl on the edge of things.

His knuckles turned white on the throttle. Gordy Beauchamp rose behind the girl and replaced his sweater over her shoulders. "Anne," Gordy said, and pressed on the girl's shoulders to bring her back down with him. But she ignored him. She wanted to stand with her thin arms crossed.

That was it. Floyd threw back the throttle. The engine whined and the boat trembled with confusion. On the house arms shot out from under the blankets, heads snapped back, mouths spat out cigarettes and a liquor bottle rolled to the deck and dropped overboard. In the stern everyone, including the two young men, leapt to their feet around the girl in pink and grabbed for something upright to hold, the rail, the sides of the house, each other. Floyd gnashed his teeth and started shoving the throttle back against its casing. Then everyone looked up, and everyone, including Floyd, stopped for a moment: it wasn't the boat that moved back, it was the fog that slid forward, the earth that rotated. But only Floyd knew that the ledges had also retreated.

Around them now the gentle gurgle. Floyd slid the throttle to neutral and stood unbreathing, making sure he still heard nothing of Earl's boat. Anyway Earl hadn't done his part, he thought. All these people who couldn't swim, and that damned girl, and anyway Earl hadn't done his part. Where the hell was Earl? Before he started to breathe again he started to cackle, then bellow, then gasp for air, drowning in his own laughter. Again heads were thrown back, hands shaken, thighs were re-opened and pillows remade. Another bottle appeared on deck. The boy Ivan turned his back and faced out over the bow, half appeased, half disappointed. Anne Stisulis leaned into Gordy's arms.

Mr Beauchamp got to his feet and put an arm around Floyd's shoulders: "My friend, that was fun. This is fun. We are having fun. To a great sea captain. To a great day. Have a drink on us." Looking around him, searching for Earl one last time, Floyd said, "A drink," and, not thinking at all, not suffering, he grabbed the bottle and tilted it up into the fog.

Three hours later, passing to the south of Damariscove Island, they were still three hours from Monhegan. Only Floyd Johnson knew they'd gone anywhere at all, not that he cared. This water was clear and deep and he let the old bird drift slowly across it. For him this trip was not to be Monhegan but only the water, the miles and miles of it between him and Round Rock, and Earl Varney, and Bailey Island, and Beatrice.

They passed Seguin Island, and only in his mind could Floyd see the smothered lighthouse. But he heard it. Everyone heard it, the two-toned braying, ahead, then to their right, then behind them, then nothing at all but their own slow roll to and fro through the soggy wind. It was the miles and miles of water between them and Seguin that Floyd wanted, and he was piling them up. For the others, though, the drunk had worn off: they might have been lying hungover and blindfolded on a windy wharf, listening for three hours to the clatter of a boat idling in the cove. Unable to see anything, many were growing sick. The Mundts were pacing in the stern, searching the fog. And still they said little. Twice asked where they were from, one mumbled something about outside Lewiston. After that a small space was made for them in their corner of the stern. But Floyd paid them no more attention. Spies or no spies nothing would stop the fact of the water piling up behind them.

It was Mr Beauchamp who asked Floyd if there was somewhere else to land, somewhere close to where they were now to have their picnic. One place as good as another in the fog, he suggested. No offense intended: there was nothing to see.

Floyd knew Damariscove Island was above them, and he knew on the northeast end of it there was a place where you could cross a sand bar at low water and see everything on a clear day, the mainland, and Monhegan, and, if you walked down the beach a bit, Bailey Island behind you. But this was no clear day, and there was that catwalk before the sandbar, and then the sandbar itself to the island beach. No, he didn't want all these people working now, crossing that bridge still half drunk. He had them safe, out of the water, and he wanted to keep them that way, get them to a wide beach he could pull right up to, that everyone could toss their shoes to. And the gentlemen could help the ladies off the boat, and that young fellow could bring down that gal in the pink dress, and they all of them together could wade right on in with the baskets of food swinging from their arms. And they'd search the beach for driftwood and start up a bonfire, Floyd thought, then gather seaweed and pile it on the bonfire. And they'd hide the lobster under the seaweed and when the seaweed stopped writhing and flipping the lobsters would be dead. These were people who would certainly have had lobster in life, but that was before the lobster Floyd had in mind, the lobster he would have brought to surprise them, if this had been the picnic they had asked for.

It struck Floyd that their lives up till now were barren, lobsterless, empty of even the idea of lobster brought out of traps early that morning, just hours ago, and baked dark over a beach fire and the meat smoked bright white not in steam but in seaweed musk. And a tomalley not just sweet and green but a puddle of honey shivering on their tongues. Thirty-six wet chins and seventy-two hands webbed with the slime. And all that ocean to rinse in, and the girl standing up straight in the pink dress, damp again, her hair strung with seaweed. And all those miles of empty water behind her.

But there wasn't any but two or three lobster. Earl had told Floyd not to bother with more than that. Just a few plus potatoes and onions to keep up appearances. They weren't going to reach a beach, or need a bonfire.

At four o'clock Floyd started boiling up the dinner there in the stern. A thin chowder in a big black pot. The air smelled faintly of gasoline.

Both the Mundts stood. "We are not going to Monhegan," one of them said, "to have lobster?"

"No, boys," Mr Beauchamp said. "No use in it. The view here's just as good as it'll be there, and as it is we likely won't get back before dark. Today just isn't our day."

"Yes, it is," the one Mundt boy insisted, "It is our day."

"Boys, the Pilot knows this water," Beauchamp said, "and he thinks it's safer to have our picnic on the boat and turn around where we are. I'm sorry about that, but we're all disappointed."

The Mundts looked around them into the fog.

"Looking for something in particular out there?" Floyd said.

"The Island," the one Mundt said.

"Well, you keep on looking then," Floyd said.

The quiet Mundt whispered something to the other one, and they sat redfaced, recrossed their legs and said nothing more. Everyone but the Mundts forced down the chowder, swallowing hard at it. Before they finished, at five o'clock, Floyd got the *Raven* turned around.

There was an inch of chowder left. Gordy Beauchamp overturned the pot into the water. A white lumpy slick spread behind them. But before they'd gone very far Ivan, leaning over the stern, saw the chowdered water begin to boil, and the forked tails of serpents slashing at the surface. Then they were too far, and he could only hear the slurping and gnashing of the ocean.

Then it got dark. Not a dark which you could see through to yellow lights in distant windows and red lights blinking on top of hills and green running lights on the bows of sardine boats. This was the dark that strode right up to you. By eight the others had been quieted by the hours of it, dozing atop the house or squatting below in the stern. Floyd could see the lit cigarettes arcing up and down. One surged red at the bow, surged a good long time, idled then surged again then went out. Then a flame lit there, and the undersides of a man's face glowed orange then went dark, and the new cigarette burned slowly.

Twice Floyd heard the hum of a boat off to the left. He thought it might be Earl stalking them, seeing if Floyd had reconsidered, if he'd run them up Round Rock on the way back. Which would make more sense, Floyd thought, to run aground on the ledges at night. You could trust that more than you could trust running aground in the day, fog or no fog. But twice the motor died away, and it could have been anybody—it may as well have been—any lobsterman hauling traps in the fog. It was no one sardining, he thought, because it wasn't high water yet. But then he felt how deep the dark and thought the tide might be getting high. He felt for his watch. "Damn," he said, "Damn, damn."

"Captain Johnson?" It was the girl in the pink dress. She was standing beside him.

"What time you got, darling?" Floyd said.

"A little before ten o'clock. We lost, Captain Johnson?"

"Not lost. Just a little slow. It's thick out here. I'm going to get you home good and safe now. You can't see them islands and ledges in front of us but I can, and we're going in right behind them, slow and good and safe. I can see everything laid out in front of us like it's daylight."

"Good, because I'm cold," the girl said.

"I know you are. You get back there in the stern with your boyfriend and get out of this wind. It's still a little while."

Ten o'clock was almost high water, and going all the way around the ledges would make it ten thirty, and lower water. It was nothing for someone to shoot through at high water, depending on what you were hauling. And that was what was on Floyd's mind. His haul was people, a lot of them. But it was ten o'clock and plenty of water. And he'd run all kinds of weather through this same hole a hundred times, and so he went shooting through.

He listened for the buoy still swinging off the end of the Sisters and put it where he wanted in the dark. Keeping it to his left, going more slowly than slow, he swung around and made the first ledge, went around it, not seeing a thing, feeling the whole way. Then he went feeling for the next ledge and stayed to the right of that, aiming the bow, that glowing cigarette up there, at the white house he couldn't see. That would take him straight along Round Rock, then three or four hundred yards to Cundy's Harbor and deep water all the way, and then another four hundred to Dyer's Cove. Floyd started whistling. The open water had done him good, cleared his mind. He could face Earl now, make him understand why today was no good. The watch and all, he'd tell him. And the girl in the pink dress, and the crazy people and those two boys with the secrets. It was all bad luck. Today wasn't their day.

Floyd's whistling was like the first morning bird. Noise broke out all around him, whispering, humming. Cigarettes fired off the bow. The boat rolled a little now as people in the stern behind him started stepping this way and that, gathering up their things.

"You all be careful down there," Floyd said. "There aint no wharf next to us yet so don't go stepping off."

General laughter.

Then the boat jolted. "Hey now," Floyd said, "I said be seated now. We're still a good mile—"

The boat jolted again, then the sound of something cracking, like splintering wood. The wheel came up and stabbed Floyd in the gut. The water splashed, and Floyd looked up and saw only darkness at the bow, no flaming match, no burning cigarette. He could hear the people on the house scuffling and sliding. Then the stern rose behind him and the wheel stabbed him again and he felt a rib snap. The deck shuddered underfoot. Wood was splintering all around him, and now a loud pop and groan and Floyd knew the *Raven* was snapping its beams. He started counting to ten like he always did when there was something to face. But he couldn't really breathe. He started at one again, trying to breathe, but with each inhale a knife plunged into his chest. He'd cracked more than one rib. Maybe a whole side of them, he thought. At the end of ten seconds there was screaming and crying and water splashing all around him.

He found himself grinning and swallowing nervous laughter, thinking this couldn't be real, the plan couldn't actually have continued on without him, not after he'd stopped it. "Okay," he said calmly. He could see nothing. "Now what time is it?" he said, as though the right answer would mend the gash, fetch the people in the water and right the boat. But there was only the screaming and splashing. He reached to his right and grabbed a handful of shirt. "What time is it?" he said, more calmly, almost menacingly. He reached in his pocket and lit a match: a trembling wrist: nine o'clock. "No!" he cried, and threw the wrist aside. "That's the wrong goddamn time. What time is it!" He reached to his left and grabbed hold of what was there and held it still with one hand while searching for wrists with the other. He lit a match: nine o'clock. "You girl!" he bellowed, "You said it was ten, you girl! It's the wrong time! It's the wrong goddamn time!"

A high-pitched scream was followed by a loud splash, and then the whining and little splashes of someone struggling in the water.

Floyd had to speak in quick bursts. His ribs were ripping him through. "Okay," he said, weakly, "Now everybody sit down and count to ten. Have a drink." He made a funnel with his hands around his mouth and called feebly into the water: "Panic is the enemy. Now find someone and pair up, stick close together."

His voice trailed off. No one answered. Only cries and splashing. Then the boat reared up and Floyd clutched the helm. Someone was crying out: "Junior, Junior, Junior!"

Floyd struck a match but lit only a cocoon of swirling fog. He stripped off his shirt, dropped down to the stern and opened the tank of gasoline and soaked his shirt. Back up on the house he lit it and held it aloft: a black ragged ditch ran across the middle of the deck. The *Raven*, broken in two, sloped in opposite directions now like an opening drawbridge. The faded silhouette of a short, round man hung off the end of the bow, knee-deep in water, swinging his arm around, pointing randomly:

"My boy!" he cried, then tried another direction: "Ivan!"

The deck under Floyd dropped suddenly and slid back. The ditch widened and three bloodied hands shot out and clawed wildly at the splinters. The top of a head rose part way into the smokey torchlight, hair matted, strung through with seaweed, a pink shoulder. Then with the sound of rapid gunfire the remaining bolts exploded, the seams tore beneath. The stern slid and the ditch broadened and the hands clutched at shards of wood then vanished. Out rose the glistening crags of the ledge.

Gripping the wheel with one hand, holding the flaming shirt over his head with the other, Floyd could make out fingers and some whole arms waving in the water. Two or three bodies already rolled in the swells. The back of that pink dress swelling up around that girl's legs, and the boy swam arm over arm toward it, then dove and didn't come up. Didn't come up. At the bow, Mr Beauchamp called out: "Gordy, Gordy I'm coming!" The water beside the girl in pink erupted again, more bubbles then flat water. The girl bobbed dispassionately through it all.

Them that's struggling are already dead, Floyd thought. But some of the others would probably live. Those that're already blacked out, already they're not breathing, they hit the water and pass out but there's still life in them hearts, he assured himself, they're still beating, they're in that deep sleep like a bear into winter. Those're the ones that'll come back, he thought.

But then a wave closed over one and it did not reappear. And then another dropped. They started dropping all around him. The water cleared, and Floyd turned away.

"Okay now, everybody," he panted, "panic is our enemy. Everyone behind me, and over there on the bow, you all out of the water stay calm." He went on like that for some time, wincing to get the words out, ordering people to clutch together, to roll up in a ball when they got in the water like they were babies—until he felt no one left around him, only the gurgling pants and the now distant cries from out of the fog, and the creaks and yawns of Round Rock sawing through the *Raven*. And two boys' voices, guttural and foreign, calling to each other in regular intervals, drifting farther and farther apart; then just the one, unanswered, and then neither.

The bow was gone. No one called out from the water. The stern breathed up and settled down on the ledge.

Floyd could feel only above his knees now. He struck match after match and held them up to the ocean. The women rolled by, their undergarments swollen behind their legs, building up like balloons and dangling them, their heads just going with the rhythm of the swells, up and down, up and down, their hair spread out flat and pulsing.

The matches were gone. Them silks, Floyd thought in the darkness. Them undergarments'll make them a life preserver. He hadn't thought of that before. He didn't think anyone had ever thought of that before. He laughed. "Ha ha." His ribs ground together but he didn't cry out. Sucking at the air, he reached down into the water and felt for the rope under the helm. But he'd lost his fingers. He lifted them out of the water and worked them until they hurt again. Then he plunged them in and pulled up the keg, hugged it to his chest and turned to face the incoming tide. The deck shifted beneath him. He swallowed a mouthful of seawater. He'd last, he thought. But then he saw what he'd have to live with until morning, and then tomorrow night, and the next morning, and after: those men spinning down like rag dolls and then rising, and then dropping, all night criss-crossing below him; and all that silk bunching up behind the women and keeping them drifting and bumping against him; and the boat sliding under the ledge, already starting to rot. The British commander Clayt had mentioned, taking out boatful after boatful of men, losing them and asking for more; but that was war, and what was this? And then there would be Earl drinking hot coffee at the store, and Beatrice at home with Pearl, waiting, angry with him, waiting for him to explain. Explain, Floyd thought. Explain this.

It took him more than a minute to get his shoes off; it was like pulling bark off a tree. He slipped and fell in to his neck. Clutching the keg, leveraging himself against the helm, he got the shoes off, and the pants with them. He stood and lashed the keg fast to his chest. Then he thought: No. Don't want no accident. He undid the knot and fed out the keg the full length of its rope. Then he made one loop around his waist and knotted his knot again and grabbed hold of the helm. Without feeling his pain—he wouldn't need it—he pulled himself up the wheel shaft, out of the water. He didn't see anyone any more. He called no one's name. He balanced himself atop the wheel, the keg clutched under his arm. Then, looking down into the water, naked to the fog, he threw himself, outstretched, into the sea.

ACKNOWLEDGMENTS

Many thanks for their assistance in the research of this story to Warren Campbell, Bill Coughlin, Larry Hall, Rev. Jim Herrick Bernard Johnson, Joanne Johnson, Russell (Rocky) Lane, Edmund A. MacDonald, John MacKeith, Stuart Martin, Dave Sanborn, the Rumford Historical Society, and others in Rumford and Bailey Island, Maine, and elsewhere, who gave of themselves and know who they are.